PENGUIN BOOKS

921

AN AVENUE OF STONE

PAMELA HANSFORD JOHNSON

Pamela Hansford Johnson

AN AVENUE OF STONE

PENGUIN BOOKS
IN ASSOCIATION WITH
MICHAEL JOSEPH LTD

FIRST PUBLISHED MAY 1947
PUBLISHED IN PENGUIN BOOKS 1953

MADE AND PRINTED IN GREAT BRITAIN
FOR PENGUIN BOOKS LTD
HARMONDSWORTH, MIDDLESEX
BY WYMAN AND SONS LTD, FAKENHAM

To

ROBERT CHRIS

PART ONE

Chapter One

'As a class,' Helena said, 'we are doomed' – indicating consciousness of her absurdity only by a bright flash in my direction from her Tiberian eye.

'Oh, but Lady Archer –' Mrs Stillyer protested, elbows pointing suddenly and nose projecting into the tulips.

'When I was in Baxall's today,' Helena began, not loudly, but with that awful narrative authority that could silence the most persistent guest, 'in the Perfumery –'

Mrs Stillyer patiently relaxed, and her eyes glazed with vision. Helena had the most curious capacity for presenting, by the mere mention of having been in a certain place, a vivid and complete picture of herself in possession of it. I, at that moment, saw her moving over the soft deep carpets under the softness of the lamps and between the glitterings and jinglings of the women's counters, moving perhaps, not on feet but on small golden wheels, a processional goddess with mouth full of swords and stars. I was so fascinated by the picture that I did not hear the story she told, and was only brought back to the material, hostess Helena, by her peroration delivered with the fine submissive irony of an Irving – 'So I said to her, "Yes, I know. You are to be the masters now."' She paused.

'Oh, but –' Mrs Stillyer protested.

'No,' said Helena, raising her head a little so that the light poured on to her, and sharpened the waves of her hair like late sunlight falling upon a ridge of silken snow, 'I thought I should face the fact. So should she. That is how it is.'

I was tempted to expose this apocryphal encounter with the shop girl by asking what the girl replied, and would indeed have done so if old Mrs Sholto had not given the gentle preliminary moan by which she always requested a hearing. 'You know,' she remarked, 'although I think you are wonderful and most practically-minded, I'm afraid I should have been feudal enough to have called the manager and had the young woman rebuked: terrible of me, but there you are.'

'Who are we to rebuke?' demanded Helena, well away. 'For years they've suffered at our hands; now they're having their revenge.'

'I've never been rude to a butcher in my life,' Mrs Stillyer cried excitably, 'so why should my butcher be rude to me?'

'I am happy to say,' Mrs Sholto murmured, squinting slightly at the tip of her nose, 'that I have no complaint to make of any discourtesy from *any* shop assistant during the whole of the war. Perhaps it is how you treat them.'

Helena's brows shot up. Had she not been playing the fool she would have been really angry with the old lady. 'I can only say you've been most fortunate, then. Nobody is nicer to everybody than Charmian, for instance, but only the other day a bus conductor made a most disagreeable remark to her.'

'What remark?' asked Tom Leiper, a young man at the BBC who had married a cousin of Daniel's.

Everyone looked avidly at Helena, who simply frowned and said, 'No point in repeating these things. Claud was furious.'

This surprised me. Charmian had told me of the incident as a funny story, and I had retailed it as such to Helena. I wondered what was in Helena's mind now, in what light she had suddenly desired to present me. For five and a third years of war she had been married to Archer, and during that time had made herself into the pattern of a wife appropriate to his home, his career and his business knighthood. It had been – none knew it better than I – a tremendous strain on her, and to achieve it she had locked away nearly every trace of her old personality, admitting its existence not even, I fancy, to herself. I thought of her as she had been in my childhood, first as my father's mistress, in the house on the Dyver, in Bruges, and then as his wife. She had been a fine handsome termagant, hair dyed a fantastic yellow above her dark and burning face, tongue rough as pumice-stone and tart as a lemon; I detested her then. As my father's widow, and the mother of Charmian, I saw her mellowed to a crude good humour, a crude and practical wisdom; I had begun to like her, next to love her, and at last to need her. And then she had married Archer, bleached her hair white, bought dresses with little lace vests down the

8

front of them, and matched herself resolutely to her new responsibilities. I should have felt her lost to me had it not been for an evocative glance, now and then, or some vaguely off-colour remark made in an undertone for my ears alone. These things, at least, I felt she owed me; these cheeseparing hints of the past.

But now I was disturbed by her, feeling some current of mischief at work. In the old days I had seen her relieve the boredom of a social evening by the introduction of some fantasy, carefully contrived so that it should be recognized as such by no one but myself. I have heard her utter some despotic, random invention for no purpose save to spread covert unease among her listeners, well knowing that they could only sense (without being able to analyse it) this confrontation with the abnormal. I felt now that she was going to use me for her amusement by presenting me in some plausible but impossible light to persons who would guess (but not realize) that it was indeed an impossible one. I was all the more confirmed in this belief because she would not meet my eye. She sat monumental at the table's end, gaze downcast, lips pursed as if in guardianship of some distasteful memory.

'If we're doomed as a class,' said Daniel suddenly, with his Christmassy, sunless smile and mechanical twinkle through the gold and silver glitter of his spectacles, 'I give warning that I shall go down fighting.'

Only a constriction of one corner of Helena's mouth betrayed her annoyance, which, I believed, was not simply on account of Daniel's habit of picking up a conversation where someone had thrown it aside ten minutes ago. No. The reason was that she did not wish to be balked of the fun she proposed to have with me, fun for which the whole of this nonsense about the shop girl had been merely a preparation.

'And so will I,' said Cayley, Daniel's broker, 'and so will I.' He nodded his grey head, from which a few specks of dandruff fell like powder from a wig. A solemnity descended. 'Ah, ça ira, ça ira, ça ira,' cried Mrs Sholto, with a sudden sparkle and whoop.

'I'm non-political,' Tom Leiper proclaimed, 'the world takes me where it wants to. No odds to me.' He tried to look devil-may-care, but nobody noticed him.

Helena had an idea. Bowing in my direction, indicating me with so broad a gesture that she set a bowlful of rather pinched-looking narcissi jiggling on their stems, she said: 'And what do the army chiefs say?'

'I haven't been there long enough to know,' I replied. I had returned from Italy three months ago to take up my job as a major at the War Office. 'No use asking me.'

'No, no, no,' she cried, 'we want your views.'

'Pretty much like Leiper's,' I said, still hoping to avoid argument.

'Would you cheerfully hand over the reins to the bus conductor who insulted Charmian?'

I felt the awful, familiar constriction of laughter that Helena had meant to provoke, well knowing I could not give way to it.

'Mixing your metaphors, my dear,' said Archer jovially, 'you should have said, "Hand over the wheel." Days of the horse-bus are over, more's the pity. Had a quiet life, then.' He was feeling his years and his responsibilities so sorely these days that he could no longer speak the phrase 'quiet life' without a sickness of longing that seemed to make the lines spring out like streaks of grime in his face, the fat hang upon his bones. He, who had always looked like Santa Claus, now looked like a worn-out unemployable impersonating Santa Claus for one week only in a suburban draper's.

'Claud,' said Helena, determined, 'was furious. I had never seen him so angry. If the man had been there *then*, I think he would have killed him.'

The others looked bewildered, but impressed.

'To appreciate the situation,' Leiper said, recovering first, 'we should have to know what the conductor did say.'

'It was scrofulous,' said Helena, in a bass voice, dying away like Chaliapin's in the 'Volga Boatman', 'Claud was quite *white*.'

This being the kind of remark upon which no comment is possible, we were gripped by silence. Tom Leiper shot out his long monkey's hand from his white cuff and took a walnut from the dish, cracking it with a great noise. Helena gave a little replete sigh and I knew she was happy. I watched her warily.

Mrs Stillyer said at last, not confidently: 'Well, I feel sure I'd have felt the same,' and at the same moment Daniel said loudly to the broker, 'Do you think there's any future in Burma Oil?' Conversation broke out again, punctuated by Leiper's nut-cracking.

'I was thinking, Major Pickering,' Mrs Stillyer murmured to me, 'how much you resemble your mother.' She glanced at Helena and back to me. She was the wife of Daniel's most recent doctor, and did not know us well as yet.

I made the little speech long prepared to save people embarrassment. 'You know, people do say that, and I'm sure it must be true, probably the effect of propinquity. She's my stepmother, as a matter of fact. My father's second wife.'

This speech did not prevent the great Bacchic blush from bursting like a water-spout over Mrs Stillyer's features. 'I'm so sorry. I didn't realize. Do please –'

'But it's a most pardonable mistake. It's always being made.' Actually, it was a ridiculous one. I bore no more resemblance to Helena than a stick-insect to a bumble-bee.

'Once,' said Mrs Cayley, speaking, so far as I knew, for the first time that evening, 'I had the pleasure of meeting your father.' She spoke rapidly, softly, with the extreme clarity of the morbidly shy. 'I used to love his books. I always love really thrilling stories. I was browsing in a bookshop in Oxford when I saw a tall, very fair man talking to the shopkeeper about displaying Richard Pickering novels, and I heard the shopkeeper say, "Yes, certainly, Mr Pickering." So I guessed he was the author, and do you know, I dared to go up to him and ask him to sign his latest book for me! He was so kind about it, too. It was the most exciting day for me.'

I guessed it must also have been a most exciting day for my father, one of those writers who sell a steady six thousand copies of every book and never seem to attract the slightest attention. I can imagine how delighted he must have been by Mrs Cayley's request, how courteously, charmingly aloof must his response have been; and how he probably went straight off and bought himself a double whisky to celebrate the good time coming. I felt very warm towards Mrs Cayley for having given him so much pleasure. She was a pretty little woman with no sharp edges, no definite hair-line, nose-line, nor breast-line, and she was dressed in soft-coloured bits and pieces. 'You are *so* like him,' she said, 'only I don't think quite as tall – but just as fair, and thin, too. Slim, I mean,' she added in her clear rapid whisper. 'And your eyes are like his.' Her eyes met mine, hers blue and blurred and gentle, and I understood that they were thanking me for being my father's son. In a comfortable, quiet and probably happy life this small incident – the requesting of an autograph in an Oxford bookshop – had been an unforgettable disturbance, a thing upon which to pin all manner of consoling and ridiculous dreams.

'Charmian would be rather like him, too,' I replied, 'if she weren't so dark. Have you met Charmian?'

'Your half-sister?'

'Yes. Helena's daughter.'

'No,' said Mrs Cayley, and withdrew from the conversation by means of retreating so far back into her chair that she seemed about to appear on the other side of it.

At that moment Charmian came in, wearing uniform. She kissed Helena, patted Daniel, and came round the table to give a conventionally affectionate embrace to her mother-in-law, Mrs Sholto.

'I thought you wouldn't be back till tomorrow!' Helena exclaimed.

'I managed to get away tonight, as there wasn't much doing.'

The A.T.S. uniform was deplorably contrived, and most women soldiers looked as though they had been sewn into it for the winter. Charmian looked even worse than was necessary; indeed, it appeared quite talented for so pretty a young woman to make herself look so shoddy. Her cloudy dark hair, which she had refused to cut, was rolled up into a big bun and hitched well up on her head, to clear her collar. This collar was too large, the long slender neck rising out of it like a giraffe's from a float of leaves. Her tunic was creased, the brass indifferently polished. The advantage she might have secured by her singular smallness of hip and buttock was obscured by a bulging and seated skirt, on the back of which were three faint vertical stripes, as if she had been leaning against newly-painted railings.

She was introduced to Mrs Cayley and Mrs Stillyer, she

spoke to Cayley and Tom Leiper, told Daniel she had already dined, and came to sit quietly beside me.

'Hullo.'

I told her she looked a mess.

'One loses heart,' she replied cheerfully. 'How's everything?'

'Your mother's cut loose.' We were using the ventriloquial whisper successfully practised for years.

'How?'

'Making quiet fun.'

'Of whom?'

'Me.'

'Well, you can't blame her for that, Major P.,' said Charmian.

'Private P., ten days C.B.'

She made a vulgar gesture just below the table level. 'No, seriously. Is she –?'

'She's bored.'

'So am I.'

'You've only had five minutes of it.'

'What's the matter with Dan?'

'Matter?'

'He looks rotten.'

'Not more so than usual,' I said.

There was a sudden crash and roar that set the glass jingling and slewed the pictures on the walls.

Helena, Mrs Stillyer and Cayley rose to their feet. Old Mrs Sholto held her breath, exhaled it suddenly in a snort of air. Mrs Cayley said with quiet emphasis, '*Beastly* things.'

'Only a rocket,' said Helena majestically, and resumed her seat.

'But it was pretty close,' Mrs Stillyer protested, almost angrily.

'Quite four miles away,' Mrs Cayley corrected her, in her tiny, crystalline voice.

'Great thing about them,' I said, 'is that if you hear them you're O.K. If you don't, it really doesn't matter to you. I'd much rather have them than doodlebugs.'

Daniel spoke so roughly that they all turned to look at him. 'Damn it, Claud, don't be so damned callous. It's some poor devil's life, even if it isn't yours.' His face was as dark as bronze, and greenish, the sweat standing up viscous and grey on his forehead. He was obviously abandoned to sickening fear.

'Don't look at him,' Charmian murmured, 'one has to smooth it over.'

When we rose to go into the farther room, I held her back. 'Is he always like that?'

Though Daniel and Helena had stayed in the Pont Street flat throughout the war I had seen them only on my leaves, and for the past two years I had been out of England.

'Poor devil,' she replied, 'yes, I'm so sorry for him. It was wicked during the flying bombs – I didn't know how Mother could *bear* to keep him here, when he was absolutely crying out to go.'

I was staggered. I had always believed the heroism to lie with Helena, remaining at the side of a husband forced by his work to remain in a danger area.

'But could he have gone?'

'Of course he damned well could. But Mother is one of those appalling people who are actually incapable of certain kinds of fear. She simply could not see why bombs should make anyone afraid.'

'Did she ever see what they could do?'

'Oh, yes. She went out to see if she could help when Sloane Square Station was hit.'

'I didn't know that.'

'No,' Charmian said, 'you didn't. Well, she saw it. So did I. I can't think of it now without –' She swallowed, and wiped her face with a grimy khaki handkerchief. 'There was a naked girl dangling on the wires. And there was a man, he must have been a big man, compressed into about three foot square, blown into a sort of bloody parcel.' Charmian shook her head violently.

'And did Helena help?'

'Oh, yes. She was wonderful. I wasn't, I was sick. But you see, she wasn't in the least afraid. And she refused to let Daniel be scared in peace. I came home once on leave, last August. It was pitiful. We all went down to the basement shelter, only it doesn't really amount to much here, as you know. Daniel was lying on a camp bed, crying. There were people from the other flats, all a bit worked up, but talking, and smoking, and there was a little bridge playing – but Dan just lay on his side and cried, and the tears ran right down his cheek on to the pillow.'

'What did Helena do?'

'She played bridge. She didn't say a word to Daniel till about two a.m. Then she said: "I'm going upstairs to bed. If you're going to stay here you'd better get some sleep or you'll be worth nothing in the morning."'

'Claud!' Helena called, 'Charmian!'

We went in. By her sweet bland dominance she had reduced her husband and her guests to chicks beneath a great cosy wing. They were seated about the fire, the light mellow upon them. Above them, standing, her head reflected in the gilded O of glass, Helena threw her own white and golden light downwards to correlate and console. As I went to sit with Charmian on the slung and tasselled settee that was just a little too small to seat three persons, it struck me suddenly that despite the great disparity in our respective ages, only three of us in that room were young – Charmian, who was twenty-two; myself, thirty-six; and Helena, who was – the realization jolted me – sixty-seven. The rest of them had been old for ever. Daniel, certainly, had extraordinary business and social acuteness for his years – he was nearly eighty, and still in complete control of his firm; but it was impossible to imagine him as a young man, or even as a man of forty. Mrs Sholto, who could not have been more than sixty-two or three, wore old-lady colours, brooches and pieces of lace, and spoke in a small high voice, as if determined to forestall old age by giving it courteous and premature acceptance. Mrs Cayley and Mrs Stillyer were women who had no birthdays and in whom there was no light. Their hair, their eyes, their hands, admitted nothing. As for Tom Leiper, who was probably twenty-seven or eight, he had a dry and withered appearance, a saurian skin and a curious, old-man's habit of pretending to be a little deaf. When he teased Charmian it was with the gallantry of the octogenarian; self-consciously audacious, faintly scrofulous, and without the slightest promise or risk attached.

Upon this company Helena shed her extraordinary restless radiance and Charmian her cool and steady light. As for myself – the thought stopped me, making me wonder whether a stranger, thinking on the same lines as myself, would have classified me with Helena, or with Daniel and Mrs Stillyer. Had I been within sight of a mirror at that moment, I should have closed my eyes.

I made some remark or other to Charmian. Mrs Sholto said at once to Helena, with a beam, and with a thought, I am sure, of Augusta Leigh: 'Aren't those two inseparable? It always makes me smile.'

Helena ignored this completely; she detested Mrs Sholto both for her pretty, stinging decorum and because she was Charmian's mother-in-law.

'Tell me, darling,' Mrs Sholto said, swinging suddenly round and placing her pearly hand upon Charmian's knee, 'any news of Evan? I have to come to you for it now, you know.'

'Nothing since Wednesday. I did tell you he'd got to Bombay?'

I did not like Evan Sholto, a handsome, weak-eyed, oldish young man with a curious fetish of helplessness, a chronic stumbler and knocker-over of ornaments. Probably it was this quality that had appealed to Charmian, who had met and married him within six weeks, to the fury of his mother and Helena. I had searched my conscience carefully concerning my attitude to Evan, and had come to the conclusion that I disliked him for himself alone. I should have been perfectly happy had she married young Victor Tawney, once a gunner in my battery, who, upon inheriting an unexpected title, had telephoned Charmian twice, taken her to lunch once, written her a dozen letters and had been killed at Alamein. There had not been sufficient time for her to have fallen in love with him; nevertheless, when she heard of his death she grieved, and, I suspect, married Sholto to cheer herself up.

'You read me little bits of that letter,' said Mrs Sholto, nodding and dimpling, 'which was very sweet of you.'

'He's a very poor correspondent,' Charmian said apologetically.

'Not to you, it seems, and glad I am of it! It's the least he can do,' the old lady cried with a face of humorous fierceness, as if she would have slippered her son into duty to his wife, had he shown any signs of evading it.

Helena, impatient at this exchange, asked Charmian something or other about life in camp.

'Damn it, when are you going off to O.C.T.U.?' Leiper demanded. 'Absolute disgrace, you still being in the ranks. What's wrong with you?'

'I am such a very dirty soldier,' Charmian said pathetically, flicking a glance at me beneath her coal-black lashes, 'and I do everything so badly.'

'You are a dirty soldier,' I agreed. 'I never saw anything so awful. Why did you join up at all if you couldn't make a better job of it?'

'Don't speak to her like that, please, Claud,' said Helena tartly. After all these years she still could not tell whether I was teasing Charmian or being disagreeable to her.

'That's right,' Charmian said, brightening, 'call the dog off. Kennel up, Claud.'

'Seriously though,' Mrs Sholto intervened, 'you really should be commissioned, dear. Will it be proper for you to go out in uniform with Evan when he comes home?' Evan was a major in the Sappers.

'The war will be over by then,' Charmian replied comfortably. 'It will be over by the summer.'

'But surely something could be *done*. I know Lady — slightly, and if I spoke to her –?'

'Listen,' Charmian said, with great earnestness, 'if I were Montgomery's daughter they couldn't promote me. They simply could not do it. You see, I am no good.'

'God,' said Leiper, 'is that the Dunkirk spirit? Where's your ambition?'

'I try,' she replied, 'but I simply cannot improve myself. I enjoy it all no end, though.' Her face shone with simplicity and goodwill. Having seen Helena acting at the company for one-half of the evening and Charmian preparing to act at it for the other half, I thought I would go home, so I rose.

'No,' said Helena, bright and peremptory, 'you're not going yet, Claud. Sit down, Charmian's going to sing for us.'

Charmian had a small, pretty voice, less a contralto than a baritone; and she liked to use it.

Tonight she sang 'Ninon', Leiper playing for her. It was Helena's request.

> Moi, pour un peu d'amour
> Je donnerais mes jours . . .

The soft dark voice in the hush of lamplight had an easy pathos that caused Mrs Sholto to sniff, Daniel to wipe his glasses on a cushion, and Helena to lie back in her chair, close her eyes and breathe rather ostentatiously.

> Et je les donnerais pour rien . . .'

Charmian emphasized the word *rien*, cutting it off short as if a painful thought had wakened her suddenly from the pleasant hypnosis of being a performer –

> Sans les amours –
> Sans les amours.

I suddenly wondered if she were really in love with Evan Sholto, if she were unhappy, and whether she would tell me were this so.

'The old songs,' said Mrs Sholto.

'I wish I understood French,' Mrs Cayley whispered humbly in my ear, 'I think it is such a pretty language. I should know it, but I don't, though we were taught it at school.'

'Now something cheerful!' Mrs Sholto exclaimed, bouncing up out of her reverie with a pretty little clap of hands.

'All my songs are miseries,' said Charmian, 'I'm afraid.'

To emphasize this fact she sang 'Summertime on Bredon', which did not suit her at all.

After the guests had left and Daniel had gone to bed, I asked Helena flatly what had been the meaning of her nonsense about the bus conductor and my white rages.

She did not answer me at once. 'Ah,' she said, pouring herself a brandy, 'this is what I call the best part of a party, talking the guests over when they've gone. Why haven't you gone, Claud? You kept on saying you were going, but you never did.'

Charmian lay down on the big settee, unbuttoned her tunic, took off her tie, and put her feet up.

'I didn't go because Daniel kept offering me another drink, and I don't get black-market whisky every day. What does he pay for this?'

'I'm quite sure it isn't black market,' Helena replied with a show of indignation. 'Daniel is always straight.'

I asked her again about the diversion at dinner.

'Oh, I don't know,' she murmured, closing her eyes, 'it was so boring, and you looked so stuffy there with your crown on your shoulder and your little yellow moustache. I wanted to cheer things up.' Her eyes widened slowly, first a narrow black shine, then a dark and sombre ellipse, and finally the full unsmiling gaze. 'Well?' she challenged me.

'Bored?' I asked her.

'You'd be, too. Five years of it. Getting on for six.'

'But all this' – I waved towards the curtains, the china cabinet, the tray with glasses and decanters – 'should have been worth it.'

'Do you know how old I am?'

'I was thinking of it tonight.'

Charmian straightened a little. She had realized, as I had, that Helena was serious.

'I am sixty-seven,' Helena said, and with the words the years seemed to fall one by one like stones down a well. She added, after a time, 'and not dead yet. Damn it,' she said desperately, 'not dead yet!' For the moment, her flesh glowing, the fire of some inner conflict shining behind her eyes, she looked like a strong young woman amateurishly disguised as an old one, badly wigged, the wrinkles unexpertly drawn in with a lining pencil.

'Of course you're not,' Charmian said soothingly.

'You be quiet. You don't know. You don't know what it's been like. Dan's been good, but –' She stopped abruptly. Then she rose and set down her glass. 'I don't know what I'm talking about. I'm a bit tired.'

'Of course you are, darling,' said Charmian. It struck me that her attitude to Helena was no more filial than mine; that, like me, she had come to regard herself rather in the light of keeper to some engaging but unpredictable beast.

I told her to go to bed. She glanced from me to Helena, then shrugged and said she didn't mind. 'See you tomorrow, Claud?'

'Perhaps. I'll call in here before dinner.'

'Can't we go out to dinner?'

I told her I was sorry, I couldn't.

'New girl?' she asked me.

I told her no, the same one, and kissed her good night. When she had gone I turned to Helena.

'Now what's wrong?'

'Oh, what's the use of talking? I told you. Fed up. You wait, Claud, you wait' – she swung round on me almost vindictively – 'till you wake one morning and realize that you're *old*, and that you won't live more than a dozen years probably, and then you'll be in the grave you've often thought about but never believed in, only you don't *feel* old. You want more of life, much more of it, but if you took one foot out of the grave people would be disgusted because that's where they think one foot ought to be at your time of life.'

I tried to interrupt her but she swept on. 'The damned war's nearly over, and now I want to live again, as everyone wants to, but it's eaten up my last good years and now I've no years left. Now that I can wake up in the morning without being afraid –'

Surprised, I did manage to check her, and I told her the gist of what Charmian had said.

'Oh,' said Helena, 'I fooled them. I'm proud of that. Trouble is, they'll never believe, any of them, that I was scared. I used to go dead cold, and my stomach used to heave about and fold itself under like a mass of warm oil. I kept Dan under control, because I knew he could break me too, if I let him. He'd have dragged me down to gibber like he did. He's grateful to me for it, now.'

'That's where I'm sure you're wrong. You made it worse for him and for yourself. You'd both have felt better if you'd had a good gibber together. If he'd seen you were scared he'd have pulled himself together to comfort you.'

'Oh no,' she said, 'it wouldn't have stopped at gibbering.' She shuddered violently. 'Who are all these lunatics who are talking already about the "next war"? Do they think of all the bomb-shocked people who'd go mad if they heard a siren again? All the mothers who'd be trying to calm terrified children? Who are they, tell me that? It won't happen again, Claud, will it? You must know. You're at the War Office.' She came down with such a sudden rush from genuine anguish of feeling to self-conscious absurdity that an involuntary laugh at herself relaxed her whole body.

'Go to bed,' I said, 'it's going to be all right.'

'Do you really think so?' Her eyes searched mine, probing for miraculous consolation.

I patted her, and it struck me as pathetic that Helena these days should allow herself to be patted. In a second, however, she had slapped my hand down, and was grinning from ear to ear.

'Don't you patronize me! Next thing I know you'll be buying me a beastly little shawl and a pair of bed-socks.'

She almost pushed me from the room, waved Daniel's man aside and showed me out herself. 'See you tomorrow. I'll be back in irons by then. See if you can't find a nice young man for Charmian so she can divorce that appalling husband of hers. Isn't the old woman a devil? Little old lady passing by, the old battleaxe. Good night.'

She banged the door.

The night was very clear and starry, the streets empty. I felt elated, at first knowing no reason for my pleasure; then I realized that I had seen Helena again, the Helena of the world before the war, had seen my own youth in her. Because there was something left of the past I could not be entirely unhopeful of the future.

Chapter Two

WALKING home to my rooms at the Beaufort Street end of King's Road, I remembered something else about which I had meant to tease her. 'As a class we are doomed' . . . Helena, talking of class in a loud voice, relating herself to those others ranked by their money in the business of professional aristocracy, while triumphing inwardly at the thought that not one of them, not even Daniel, could challenge her right to do so. When I first knew Helena she was outside class, something apart from any social category; not a Juno at the Palace, or a Minerva at the High Table, or a Diana in the hunting field, but perhaps an Iris, a professional entertainer, in demand at all the best masques. There was so little of her that I knew, outside of my own experience. When my father first saw her she was booming contralto songs at a Belfast music-hall, a golden queen upon the stage and a Sally Slap-cabbage off it. In Bruges, where I had lived with them in boyhood, she had been remarkable and unclassifiable, always a size larger than life and a shade nearer to the animals. I remembered her fine hats and her foul tempers, white straw and peacock-blue ribbons towering over a face blackened with histrionic rage. No guardian for a small boy. What good could I have spoken of her then? That she loved my father greatly, that she could be generous when she liked, and that, in the right mood, she could be funnier than anyone on earth. There could have been less good to say later on when, as my father's widow, she had kept house for me at Battersea; but oddly enough I had liked her better then. During this period of her life she had been grabbing at all the lovers that came her way, the lodgers, the travelling men, the gallant partners of Masonic Ladies' Nights, grabbing at them with an awful haste as if time were too short and the park gates would close precisely at sundown.

When she married Archer, a freakish and magnificent match

for her, she seemed to have decided that I should know her no more. She presented a stranger to my view, like Texas Guinan offering a new star to the applause of patrons, and left her the stage. I had been completely deceived, had really believed that Helena in her sixties had become a better, a more boring, and a totally different human being. I was pleased to find myself wrong. Scratch a Lady Archer, I thought, and you find a Helena. I believed that had we been young and of an age I should have loved her, even as my father had loved her.

I have always recognized a tormenting emotion that lies between friendship and love; something stronger than the first and less demanding than the second, though it may well exceed it in endurance. It may exist between man and man, or between woman and woman, but, as it has some undefined sexual element, it exists more frequently between man and woman. It is a torment of understanding that can have no physical expression. For a lifetime it may remain unexpressed; if it seeks the normal expression of love it is ruined. It is, if one must give a name to it, the highest form of friendship, and is mysterious in origin. Two persons of complete diversity, socially, physically, intellectually, may feel it for each other. Each may be partnered in complete happiness by another person; but were he to lose the friend with whom he shares this third emotion his life would lose, irretrievably, a shade of colour, a degree of light. It is the very fret that keeps the emotion alive; as if both friends were seeking for an unnamed symbol lying between A and B, a vital force mysteriously unrecognized by science or by literature. Helena, but for five years, was twice my age. To say that I loved her would have been an embarrassing absurdity. To say that we were friends would have been a foolish understatement. Endearments, even of the slightest nature, never passed between us, unless you count the scrape of a kiss at partings or reunions; yet I felt that at my life's end I should know a sense of utter frustration that I had never been able to express in some physical fashion, or by some new form of words, the love I had for her. I am driven back even now on the terms 'friendship', 'love': on A and B. Neither will do.

The wind blowing off the river carried a perfume salty and rotten and sweet that gave me a swift and piercing vision of the quays and the canals of Bruges, of the dark green water deep with the sound of bells, the rayless houses doubled in the rayless flow. Her voice in my memory was sharp as a voice ringing out in the deserted streets through which I was walking. I would catch it when I got in. Claud! What the devil have you done with your brown shoes? Didn't I tell you you weren't to put them on till Sunday, you little swine?

I was so lost in this rowdy past, unappreciated when it was the present, that I did not remember letting myself into the house, walking up the two flights and unlocking the outer door of my rooms, and was recalled to the time, the day and the year only by a postcard lying on the floor. It was from Jane Elvorden, telling me she could not dine on the following night. All right, I thought, I'll take Charmian out; and felt rather relieved.

My own story is no part of this one, which is Helena's alone. I had loved Archer's daughter Cecil, who died of pneumonia during an American tour ten years ago. I had seen her perhaps half a dozen times in my life, and for her sake had made my wife Meg unhappy and angry, though it was not until several years after Cecil's death that we had agreed to part. I did not now, after so long a time, grieve for Cecil consciously, or even think about her very much; but I had not lost the habit of comparing other women with her and finding them lightless and stale. At present I was enjoying an agreeable and undemanding love affair with the sister of a subaltern who had been in my battery while I was in Kent. Ives Elvorden, as an individual, was a handsome nincompoop. As a soldier he was first rate. Jane, I felt, was very like him. She was beautiful, brilliant, efficient, effective and quite unpercipient. I was glad she would not dine with me, as I had a perpetual fear that one night, out of an impulse to self-destruction, I would ask her to marry me. And I knew what Helena would have to say about that.

It was a quarter to twelve, and I was tired. I went straight to bed, smoked my usual two cigarettes in the dark and closed my eyes. It seemed to me only a second before I opened them again in response to a knocking at the door, but I noticed that the light was slate grey around the edges of the curtains, that the bedside clock stood at a quarter to six. I got up and let

Charmian in. She was huddled into her uniform, overcoat rucked up to her ears, cap rammed down over hair that had been skewered up with a couple of hairpins, her face greyish-white.

'What's the matter?' I asked her, horrors sparkling through my mind like tracer bullets.

'Daniel was taken ill an hour ago.' She looked at me, telling me the rest with her eyes.

'He's dead,' I said.

She nodded and began to cry.

I gave her some whisky, which she said she couldn't drink at such an hour, and which she then drank at a great rate. Meanwhile, not asking her yet for details, I recited the usual words of sympathy and distress, hollow, but consoling. I was sorry for the shock she had had, though I know she had cared no more than I for Daniel himself.

'You know Mother sleeps like a pig,' she said at last. 'Well, I heard him moaning through the wall. I didn't know what it was at first – it woke me up. Then I thought I'd hear Mother getting up, but I didn't, and the noise went on. So I went into their room and he was lying on his face writhing all over the bed and his face was a ghastly colour. I spoke to him but he was past answering. I was afraid to wake Mother too suddenly – it would have given her such a horrible shock. I didn't know what to do. It was awful.'.

The room was cold. I switched on the fire and threw the eiderdown over her knees.

'So I crept out and got Hemmings,' she went on, 'and when we got back – I couldn't have been away two minutes – Dan was dead. He looked appalling.'

'Damn,' I said. 'I shouldn't have given you alcohol. I should have given you sweet tea.' There was no tea, so I found three lumps of sugar and made her eat them. She would have eaten a piece of sealing-wax had I put it into her mouth.

'Mother woke up then. She was all bewildered – didn't know where she was, or what we were all doing there. I put her dressing-gown round her and got her quickly into my room before she saw Dan, before she knew what had happened. Oh, my God,' Charmian cried out, 'I wish I hadn't gone for Hemmings! I wish I'd wakened her! But what could I do?'

'I think you did O.K. There was nothing else to be done.'

'We got Dr Stillyer. Mother knew Dan was dead then, and she'd pulled herself together marvellously. It was she who sent me for you. I was going to phone, but she said it would only be a shock to you –'

'Everyone saving everyone shocks.'

'And she said it would do me good to get out of the place even for a quarter of an hour. So I got out the car and came down here.'

'I'll get dressed,' I said. 'I bet I'll dress quicker than you and be less of a sight.'

She smiled at me weakly.

When I came back to her she was half asleep, the eiderdown round her like a cocoon. 'I'm so comfortable,' she murmured, 'and so tired I don't want to go back to it all.'

'Cheer up, I'm with you. And I'll drive, or there'll be more dead than poor old Dan.'

'How callous one is,' said Charmian in a feeble, self-reproaching voice, 'making jokes and wanting to go to sleep.'

'We'll both feel bad enough later on, when it's got time to sink in. Did he ever have attacks like this before?'

'Never, that I know of.'

We returned to Pont Street to find a scene of solemn upheaval. Helena, monumental and pallid in a dressing-gown of quilted cherry satin, was giving the doctor coffee. Hemmings was stationed outside Daniel's door, his back rigid against it as if he were expecting a raid by Burke and Hare, and Daniel's new chauffeur, whom I had not seen before and who had been summoned for no reason at all, so far as I could see, was walking ominously up and down the hall, taking care to tread on the carpet and not upon the parquet, lest he made a noise in the house of the dead.

I went to Helena and she offered her cheek for a kiss, this being an occasion to mark by some abnormal ceremony. I told her I was desperately sorry, that I would help her in any way I could.

'I haven't realized it yet,' she said. 'What worries me –' She paused.

'What?'

She looked down at her dressing-gown. When she raised her eyes I saw that they were thick with tears. 'I've only this to wear.'

'Go and get dressed, then.'

'Yes,' she answered, and stood irresolute. She moved a step or two towards the door. 'Yes.' She paused with her hand on the knob; then turned as if bewildered, as if she had no idea for what reason she had meant to leave us. 'Doctor! More coffee. You must. Dreadful for you to be called so early. Don't think I don't realize it.'

He looked at his watch. 'Thank you, Lady Archer, I think I'll be going now.' He came and spoke softly to her, urging her to lie down, to take some bromide. He bade Charmian and me farewell and then spoke to the chauffeur.

Helena shut the door on him and swung round. 'Charm! For God's sake go up and wash your face. You look frightful, and people will be coming. We've an awful day ahead. I –' She picked again at her dressing-gown. 'I must go and change it. It's dreadful. I don't know what the quack must have thought. Claud, do make Charmian make herself decent, it makes me ill to see her, and tell Hemmings to go and get us some breakfast. We shall all have to eat, shan't we?'

'I couldn't,' said Charmian in a strangled voice.

'I could,' I told Helena. 'You'd better, too.'

'I shall,' she said, with the air of an officer preparing to lead his platoon over the top, 'it's right that I should, however I may feel.' And she dived off into the hall where I heard her babbling excitedly of God knows what to the departing doctor.

It did seem to me a good idea to tidy Charmian up, so I made her give me her tunic and shoes while she went to do her hair, and I polished brass and leather for her in the kitchen while Hemmings cooked a meal.

At a quarter past seven we sat down to breakfast. There was bacon, sausages, and a dish of kidneys. Helena, who had sat down black-robed and calm, surprisingly burst into tears at the sight of the kidneys, lying puce-mahogany in their gilded gravy. 'Poor Dan,' she wept, 'he got those himself from a man he happened to know. He got them only yesterday.' She ate of these black-market meats with a sombre and tearful hunger. Only Charmian refused to eat, drinking cup after cup of tea.

After the meal Helena seemed to lose herself once more in a rag-bag dream, so I told her to lie down, telling her that I would do all the necessary telephoning. I could not begin this, however, till nine o'clock, when most people would be about, and in the meantime I sent Hemmings and the chauffeur off to their own breakfast and made Charmian play poker-dice with me. 'Such an extraordinary thing to be doing,' she kept saying, 'such an extraordinary thing. I expect to be struck dead.' But we had to do something.

Both of us were violently busy for the rest of the morning, as Helena did not wake till noon. When she did so she sent for me, and I sat down at her bedside.

'Do you know, Claud,' she said, 'I'm a widow!' She seemed aghast at the thought.

I said nothing.

'Poor old Dan.' She slid down into the bed, her bleached hair, once bright gold, now white as a cloud, spread out over the pillow, her eyes very dark and brilliant. 'I don't know how I feel. I can't be a hypocrite; I was bored stiff with him. But he was always kind to me, and he thought I was Helen of Troy. You can put up with most men if they really think that. I expect he's left pots. Poor old Dan, fancy sweating all his life like he did and keeping on after he should have retired to make pots for me, though he did say it was for his country, and what use is it to me anyway? All go to Charm, and she'll have a baby by that boiled owl of hers and it'll go to it. One thing, if you ever get short you'll know where to come. If only you'd married Cecil you could both have lived in style, wouldn't it have been wonderful? He adored Cec', you know, he was never the same again afterwards.' She looked at me sharply. 'Nor were you. You ought to get married, but don't go just marrying anyone. Did you spot Dan's new chauffeur? I call him Maud. His name is Snapely. Maud is not seventy, but he is tall and Snapely. He's sixty-eight, don't you think he's a fine figure of a man? Skin like a boy. That's because he had some skin trouble when he *was* a boy and the whole top layer came off and never grew again.'

She seemed to drowse, slack and stout, and was still roughly magnificent in the bedclothes she had dragged up around her. She asked for a cigarette. Mine had run out, and she told me to fetch Dan's. 'Now where –' She was silent. Then she said, 'There's a box of a hundred, but it's in his room.' Another pause. 'I don't think I do want to smoke.' Then, a little later and with fretful energy, 'I've got to have a cigarette.' She asked me with her eyes to go into the room where Daniel's body was.

'I'll go out,' I said, 'or pinch some off Hemmings.'

'He doesn't smoke.'

'All right, I'll go out.'

Not being a familiar customer at any tobacconist's in the vicinity, I had to hunt for twenty minutes before I could buy even ten cigarettes, and those of a disagreeable brand. When I returned to Helena's room she was smoking, silent and defiant, with the hundred box on the table at her side.

In the few days that preceded the funeral Helena showed a calmness and efficiency which had an element of the sullen. She refused to allow me to apply for leave from the War Office, and said all the donkey work could be done by Charmian. 'Not that it'll be a gay leave for her, poor pussycat,' Helena remarked in a sudden, rare moment of self-oblivion.

The morning of the funeral was mild and dry; a few buds were greening on the trees and the air had the pleasantness of promise. Helena appeared in a very smart black hat, but was inclined to tears. During the long crawl behind the hearse to the cemetery she did not utter a word, but powdered incessantly round her eyes till she had converted the tear-streaks into a kind of cement. Charmian whispered to me, 'I wish we could smoke.'

'So do I.'

'I wish I didn't vaguely like feeling important,' She peered out of the window at a man who had stood still in respect while we passed. 'I keep on wanting to bow from side to side.'

'Don't worry,' I assured her. 'At funerals we all do, unless we were very fond of the dead, and then we feel like hell.' I had noticed in Charmian recently this tendency to self-searching, and it worried me. That she gave expression to it in so naïve and trivial a fashion was significant, for in herself she was neither trivial nor naïve. I felt that the searchings in which she privately indulged were obscure and painful, that she was afraid of them becoming in some manner exposed, and hoped subconsciously by faked self-revelation to throw me off the scent. I was worried, too, by the extraordinary slackness of her appearance, which had a histrionic note. I knew perfectly well that if she turned up like this on parade she would have been in trouble, and that however badly she neglected herself in the army it could not be to the same extent as at home.

I saw Helena glaring at me.

'What's the matter?'

'Show a little respect,' she said, 'both of you. Grinning.'

I told her I was not grinning.

'Well, you were a moment ago. Like a Cheshire cat.'

We stopped at the cemetery gates, alighted from the carriages and followed the coffin on foot to the graveside. Helena walked weightily, looking straight ahead, the powder streaks sharply exposed in a sudden glitter of sun. Corder, Dan's solicitor, a man with a huge rumpled head of dark grey hair, walked at her side. Behind her followed Charmian and myself, then the Cayleys and Stillyers, Tom and Sue Leiper, Mrs Chavester in sables, Lady Esch in mink. A small but very distinguished burial.

As we grouped ourselves about the opened earth and the vicar began to read the service, I saw that from Lady Esch's hat, dangling on a thread of silk, was a long, elaborately upholstered emerald caterpillar. It swung with the breeze, rolled itself up and uncurled again, a happy insect with no more conception of Lady Esch's existence than an ant of a mountain's. A tug of laughter took me, and I struggled violently for the idea of some sobering grief. I tried to nip the caterpillar off the hat, but it swung deliriously out of reach, and as Leiper's glance had fallen upon me I dared not try again. Then, all at once, as the first handful of earth was thrown on to the coffin, I understood something: that Daniel had been Cecil's father, and that now there was nothing of her left to me, not even her image in his eyes. That it was she whom they were burying, her little, sharp lightness, her tiny peaked face, her heavy lids shadowed by the hyacinth curl of her dark red hair, terribly dark on the terrible green-whiteness of the flesh. My desire for her, dreamlike now, my memory of her, even now a little blunted, sprang up in anguish and, draining away, left me sickened and cold. I felt the clamp of conscience, a misery of regret that I had spoken and thought callously of Daniel's death and had urged Charmian on by a smile or even by the twitching of a muscle to do likewise. I looked across at her as she stood at Helena's side, and saw that she was crying.

The wind leaped up, sending a splutter of water drops down from the trees, and by causing Lady Esch to clutch at her hat, dislodged the caterpillar. The old desire to laugh returned to me, but this time freed of strain. It was all over; we began to move away down the narrow and winding path, away from Cecil, from Daniel, from the mirth and the horrible dread of death.

'Thank God for that,' Helena sighed, leaning back upon the cushions and folding her hands in her lap.

'Your powder's streaky all round your eyes,' said Charmian.

'Damn, and I haven't a mirror!'

'Here, you take mine.'

Helena peered at herself. 'My God, have I been like this long? Why didn't you tell me?' She spat on a handkerchief and dabbed at her face. She was full of energy. She wanted to start living again.

Chapter Three

AFTER lunch Charmian intimated by small gestures and side glances that she wanted to see me alone, but that no one else was to remark this. I rose and went out, across the hall into the spare bedroom. In a moment or so the door opened and she came in. 'Oh, here you are. I wondered where you'd gone to. Claud, I'm worried. I've got to tell someone, even at the eleventh hour.'

My mind flashed the pleasing sureness that she would tell me she couldn't stand Sholto any longer. 'Come on, then,' I said, 'and tell me quickly, because Corder's going to read the Will in a moment.'

'I know. That's why I had to get in first.'

I saw that she looked really apprehensive, very young, and exceedingly guilty, and was suddenly persuaded that my sub-conscious observation had noted this appearance before. I was about to ask her what the Will had to do with it, when she said quickly: 'Claud, Mother's not going to be nearly so well off as she thinks she is.'

Charmian walked across to the dressing-table and began fiddling with the things upon it. Her back was to me and her head bowed, that she might not see me in the mirror.

What's the matter?' I said.

'Dan settled eighty thousand on me six months ago. To dodge income tax. He made me swear not to tell Mother.'

I was so startled that for a moment I could think of nothing to say. In that moment her head came up and her eyes, in the glass, were full upon mine. They were coaly black and rayed about with a nervous light.

'He made me swear not to tell *anyone*,' she said. 'I don't know what mother will say. What she'll think of me. I was a fool to take the money, only he was so anxious. He liked me, you know,' she explained pathetically.

The necessity of regarding Charmian as a person capable of

any sort of concealment kept me silent for a moment or so longer. I was spellbound by this extraordinary discovery.

'But why,' I said at last, 'didn't you tell her anyway? And make her do the swearing not to tell?'

'I couldn't *do* that,' Charmian replied girl-scoutishly, 'I'd promised I wouldn't. He said he wouldn't settle the money on me unless I promised, but would give it all to Sue Leiper. And I did want it, not knowing what was going to happen when Evan got demobbed, because he hasn't really a *job*, you know, and he has to ask the old tigress for everything.'

'I can't stand this elaborate honesty,' I insisted, 'you could have told me. I'd have been like the grave about it. And I could somehow have managed to take the edge off the shock for Helena.'

'A promise is a promise.' She folded her lips tightly, stuck out her jaw.

'Oh, shut up!' I said. I gave her a cigarette which she lit mournfully.

'Mother will think I don't care about her. She'll think I've deceived her.'

'She'll think you're a snake,' I agreed. 'But is she really going to care about the money?' I did not know how much she would care, could not guess how much wealth in its degrees meant to her. She had married Daniel for money, of course, but would there be any real difference in her mind between an income of five, and an income of twenty, thousand a year? There was none in mine, certainly, as I had experience of neither: but in Helena's? 'What's Dan worth?'

Charmian shook her head. 'I'm vague. Evan thinks somewhere in the region of two hundred thousand.' I thought of this sum, and it meant nothing to me.

'You despise me,' said Charmian dramatically. Her eyes filled with tears.

'Not me,' I said, 'I'm fascinated. Come here.' She came and sat beside me, putting her arm through mine.

'What ought I to do?'

'What can you do?' I returned, and at that moment we heard Helena calling us.

The reading of the Will was a shock, not only to Helena but to Charmian and me. Daniel's fortune was surprisingly small, and what was left of it had been bequeathed in an extraordinary manner. To begin with, he had left about twenty thousand pounds to be distributed among some half-dozen women. One or two of the names I recognized, and I guessed that the gifts were tributes to former mistresses; Father Christmas, even after death, had opened the sack wide. I glanced at Helena, who was sitting like a ramrod and breathing down her nose, at Charmian, who looked bewildered and wretched. Then came a sizeable bequest to Tom and Sue Leiper, a few smaller ones to other relations and friends, a few remembrances to business acquaintances. To me he had left half a dozen paintings. He had collected water-colours in a hit-or-miss fashion for several years past. Three of these were valueless, but the others comprised an exquisite Bonington, a Girtin, and a particularly nasty Birket Foster. For this last I knew I could get between four or five hundred pounds, though I could not imagine why so many collectors should be willing to pay it.

At this point Helena interposed, in a thick and breathless voice, 'But what about Charmian?' – and Charmian, ignoring my signals, made her confession.

Helena stared at her. Charmian, on the verge of tears, stared back. Corder said something or other, but neither took any notice. Then Helena's dark face was irradiated, the brilliance shining through her skin as a lamp through parchment. 'Well,' she said, 'if you're not a puss!'

The sudden release of tension, the upsurge of good feeling, even of mirth, affected us all; even Corder ceased for a moment to look miserable. But the lid was clamped down again quickly enough at a cough from Sue Leiper, a light brittle sound of irritation and embarrassment. Charmian, as Corder hurried through the concluding paragraphs of the Will, looked from one to the other of the Leipers, looked at them questioningly, as if hoping nothing would happen to upset them. She felt, as I did, that Helena had excluded them entirely from her consciousness, had reduced them to the position of intruders from a world she had left hastily and to which she was never likely to return. Charmian, however, being soft-hearted, cared that a slight, however delicate, however unintentional, should be put upon them. I didn't care at all. This hour, alarming though it was, was entirely Helena's.

When Corder's apologetic voice had ceased she said sharply, 'Let me have it in easy words, please. What have I to depend on?'

He put down the Will, took off his glasses and looked at her, answering freshly and with a kind of admiration. 'When all duties are paid, you should be able to rely upon a clear income of sixteen hundred a year.'

'Oh,' said Helena, and looked down at her hands. The door opened and the cat walked in, a lion-faced tabby who had been discovered in the kitchen one morning and not permitted to leave. Daniel had been a cat lover. 'Tiggy, Tiggy, Tiggy,' she murmured, cracking her fingers. The cat strolled over to her, looked up in her face, miaowed, and sprang into her lap where it instantly fell asleep. 'No more salmon on points for you,' she babbled to it gently, 'not even a pilchard. Scraps from now on. Horse meat from the pussy-butcher. Bread and gravy. Bread and gra-a-a-vy,' she drawled, letting her voice fade away to a sigh.

After a long and awkward silence she added, 'And poor old Snapely, too. I expect he'll have to go. Hemmings has gone already.' She had not noticed that the Leipers were on their feet before her, full of valedictory politeness.

'Mother,' said Charmian, nudging, 'Mother, Tom amd Sue have to be going.'

Helena opened her eyes widely, as if in awakening. They were like black daisies. Then she rose, spilling the cat, and embraced Sue with an appearance of warmth.

'Look here,' said Leiper, 'anything we can do . . . all a frightful muddle at the moment, to my mind any old how. You give me a ring if I can help. We're all cousins.'

'That's right,' she agreed, jollying him a little towards the door, 'that's right,' she agreed, with the distrait acquiescence of a barmaid, 'all cousins.'

When they had gone and Corder also, Charmian and I said to her simultaneously, 'Well?' If there was to be an explosion we preferred to precipitate it.

'Well, now,' said Helena mildly, 'well now, well now.' She moved about the room, prodding inexpertly at the flowers, looking vaguely behind the window curtains. 'Anyone seen my cigarettes? Well now.' She smiled at Charmian, pinched her cheek. 'You might have told me, however much he made you promise.'

'That's what I said,' I agreed.

'But I'm glad you got it. That's fine. Fancy not telling me! Too good to live, you are. Not that he couldn't make people do what he wanted. I know that.' Her face seemed to swell and blacken. 'It's those damned women that upset me! Those damned women! I knew about them all. They were years ago. He used to talk about them – be proud as Punch.' I thought of my own mother, through whom Archer and I had first become acquainted, my mother who had died when I was thirteen. He had paid his tribute to her through me. The Birket Foster. 'To leave all that money to those … those … totties!' she brought out triumphantly and could not stop the laughter writhing up and through her rage.

'Poor old Snapely,' she mused then, 'poor old Maud. We were quite friends. And the flat – I shan't be able to go on living here, shall I, Claud?'

'What's the rent?'

'More than five hundred.'

'How much more?'

'Never you mind. But it's quite a bit over.'

'Then you can't. It would be too big for you, anyway.'

'I like big places. I shall stay here till the summer, anyhow.'

Charmian said, voicing my own thought, 'But why did Daniel do it? Mother, *why* did he do it? You always seemed happy together. I can't understand it.'

Helena stood arrested for a moment as in the children's game of living statues. Then she sat down and gathered the cat to her breast, smoothing her cheek against his fur. 'I suppose I don't, altogether; only I don't hope to. If you can't understand people before they die, you never will when they're dead. You've got to accept it that there are questions which can't be answered.'

I was impressed, but not convinced, by this philosophic flight. I said unkindly, to draw her, 'It makes rather a fool of you, Helena. It will flutter the Leiper and Sholto dovecots.'

She blazed at me, 'Don't I know that? If I had Dan here now I'd –' She stopped short, taken by superstitious awe at the dim vision of the shrouded bogey entering suddenly to accept a rowsting. 'No. This was how it is, I *think*. You see, he always knew I wasn't – that I hadn't been –' She tried again. 'He felt a big income was something he needed, but I didn't. I had to share it because I was his wife, but he knew damn well that sixteen hundred would have seemed a fortune to me *before* I married, and so I suppose he thought it would be quite enough to leave me with. . . .' She flung up her hands. 'I can't explain. I'm not angry with him except about those women; perhaps I'm not angry because I do somehow understand. You can't, Claud. Nor you, Charmian. But somehow I'm satisfied.'

'Charmian,' I said, 'has pinched eighty thousand from you. Are you satisfied about that?'

'She knows I'd give it her back the moment she wanted it,' Charmian cried fervently.

Helena patted her. 'Of course you would, don't I know you would? But that old money doesn't worry me. What's yours is mine, more or less, though I'd only take it if I was in the workhouse, and one doesn't go *there* on sixteen hundred, does one? No: it's only those women. And it makes me look a fool, too, as you so kindly suggested, Claud, thank you very much. Only I shan't mind that a lot, because thank God, being more or less poor – what *they* think is poor – I shall be able to cut free of that lot, make my own life, start afresh –'

The light was blazing in her again, making a mockery of her years; it was absurd, in the flush of the lamplight, that she should be more than forty-eight or nine. Charmian was so moved by her, so grateful for the ready forgiveness of virtue, that she went to Helena and embraced her.

'Now if only Claud gave me a good hug too,' said Helena grinning, 'which is unlikely, we should be the prettiest picture you ever saw.' She pushed Charmian away and went to the door. 'Outside, both of you. Go together or go separately, but go away. I'm dog-tired and I want to lie down with a nice meaty book.'

And certainly she was looking tired now, as if she had suddenly sickened of shocks and surprises and plans and heightened emotions. Before I left, she took from me my cigarettes and my copy of Vasari (she would not like it, I told her, but she said she only wanted something to take her off to sleep) and informed me that in exchange I might have Snapely to run me home. 'And you'd better take those old pictures Dan left you, while you're about it.' I protested that I had no right to touch them (I believed) until probate, but to my amazement she had them all ready wrapped for me in brown paper.

'When on earth,' I said, 'did you have time to do that?'

'Oh, a couple of days ago,' she replied, 'I always knew he meant you to have them and I had time on my hands. I had to do something.'

So I could do nothing but take the paintings, reflecting with a wondering pleasure where I should hang the Girtin and Bonington, and where I should hide the Birket Foster.

On the way home I asked Snapely to stop a moment, while I bought some cigarettes to replace those Helena had taken. 'I'll go for you,' he said. 'You won't be able to get any, not as late as this, but I know an old boy round the corner here who lets me have them. You wait, sir, I won't be a tick.'

I watched him go, a huge man with the carriage of a guardsman, ruddy-faced, the hairs still glistening blood-red at the nape of his neck. One could guess his age and know that he was young for it. He was gone some time. I was sitting in front with him, and to amuse myself picked up a novel he had left in the recess by the dashboard. It had a paper cover on it, showing a girl in a yellow chemise and black silk stockings and was called *Miss Bagshot in the Strand*. It started sensationally with the hero, who was the narrator, vomiting in a bar-room, and slapping a woman's face. Feeling I did not wish to read the rest with any real concentration I flicked through the pages rapidly in an attempt to get the gist of the story. As I did so a piece of paper slid out and fell to the floor of the car. Picking it up I saw that it was covered with Helena's writing and I automatically glanced over it. It was a dirty joke, rather a funny one. Snapely was coming back up the street. Hastily I put the paper back into *Miss Bagshot* and replaced the book where I had found it.

'Here you are, sir,' Snapely said, getting in beside me, 'twenty Player's. Tried to get you forty, but *no bon*. Had to talk him into those, even.'

I thanked him and he drove on.

'He's a funny old lad, give you anything when he feels like it, but when he doesn't feel like it he tries to fob you off with any old County Council Returns, even tries it on me.'

Snapely was airy, familiar, no offence in the world. Somehow I guessed his manner had been different towards Daniel. Fascinated by my recent discovery, I did not want to part from him until I had some light on it, so I asked him if he would mind taking me as far as Hammersmith Broadway.

'Yes, sir,' he said, 'pleased to.'

By devious routes – the war, soldier's songs, soldier's jokes – I led the talk round to the decline of humour. 'Even the Stock Exchange is silent. I haven't heard a good story for years.'

Diffidently, he told me a clean one. I laughed at this, and so encouraged him to tell me a second rather less clean and a third that was scabrous. Finally he told me Helena's. 'I like that one,' he said shaking his head, 'I like that one not a little, not ... a ... little.'

We had reached the Broadway. I thanked him, tipped him, and said good night.

When he had gone I went into the nearest bar for a drink and considered with interest this indication of how far Helena's foot had slipped. Poor Helena, so bored with Daniel the Business Knight and with his dismal friends, so bored with her own long and difficult role, feeling so much like an actress in a three years' run that threatens to achieve a fourth – yes, like an actress, grateful for the money, but sick to death of earning it. I knew how easily she must have slipped into this innocent, furtive comradeship of dirty stories with Dan's chauffeur, understood how unconsciously Snapely, knowing me to be her intimate, had offered me his manner to her rather than his manner to Dan.

I thought suddenly that the great drop of income would be a good thing for her could she but realize it, a release, a passport of re-entry into a more comfortable way of living. And I thought also that it would be a good thing for her to lose Snapely. Helena, I felt, was once more my care.

I was just leaving, when I saw John Field drinking beer alone in a draughty corner by the men's lavatory. It struck me as typical that he should choose such discomfort for himself, the thought occurring even before I was conscious of surprise at seeing him there. He had been a subaltern in my battery in Africa for three months, after which time he was sent away for medical reasons. He had interested me and I had liked him, though no one else had. His diffidence, self-conscious to the point of pose, his eagerness at all times to do the dullest job, accept the least comfortable quarters, take the stalest piece of bread from the basket, did nothing to endear him to men who took pride in doing as well for themselves as possible in the least hopeful circumstances. Irritating, too, was his curious habit of apology for his own intellectual interests. Finding him one day reading Kierkegaard I made some comment of casual interest. He answered at once, 'Oh, it's something to read. I don't suppose I really get the hang of it' – and later, when caught half-way through the final volume of Proust – 'I don't know why I go on with it really, probably because there aren't any chapters so you sort of can't stop.'

When I spoke to him now he jumped and flushed as though he were wanted by the police. His big black eyes grew comically in a series of widening expansions – a nervous habit even more pronounced than it had first seemed to me in Africa. He half rose, sat down again, jerked to his feet.

'Oh, hullo,' he said, 'fancy meeting you!' He looked at my shoulder. 'Major, now, by God! Cost sixpence to speak to you, or would if I wasn't out of it all. I can spit in a major's eye.' He gasped, and smiled nervously as if afraid he had said the wrong thing.

We sat down together. He rose immediately and left me, returned with more beer and bumped it down with such force that he slopped it all over the table. 'Look out,' he cried, 'it's going in your lap,' and rushed at me with a handkerchief.

'It's O.K. No harm done. You out of the army, then?'

He nodded. 'Couple of months ago. They found out my heart was funny.' He added hastily, 'Not *very* funny, you know; only that it wasn't good enough for me to sort of go leaping around. So here I am.'

'What are you doing, then?'

'Doing?' He gazed down into his glass as if he were looking for a mermaid. 'Just mucking around. They don't want me to do anything for a bit.' He changed the subject, told me various things that had happened since he saw me last, wanting to know what had happened to me, what it was like at the War Office and whether I had heard anything of so-and-so.

I noticed that he was looking thin, uncared for. 'Do your people live this way?' I asked him.

'Haven't got any people,' he replied, 'Only an aunt, and she's some sort of big pot in the Board of Trade. I never see anything of her nowadays. I'm living on my own.'

'Doing for yourself?'

'I've got a woman who comes in. I eat out.'

This forlorn picture touched me. Field was, I supposed, in the middle twenties, and I guessed that he was frightened to plan any sort of a future. On an impulse I said: 'Come and stay at my place for a week.'

He sat up with a jerk, the colour spreading oddly in two fan-shapes from the corners of his gentle, wide mouth to his rather prominent ears. 'I couldn't do that.'

'Why not?'

'One can't entertain people these days.'

'You won't get much entertainment. I'm at work all day. You can have your lunch out as usual and we'll scrape up an evening meal together.'

'I couldn't do it,' he repeated.

'Do you good. Anyway, I'd like to have you.'

After some argument, he acquiesced. 'Shall I turn up to-morrow?'

'You can come home with me tonight. Let's go and get your things.'

He took me back to a house in one of those streets which look like culs-de-sac under a perpetual twilight, and into his large, sad, grimy room. The bed was made and the place had been dusted, but the distemper and paint-work held the grime of years, and the carpet, pink and green, so far as I could judge, looked as though it would come up with the soles of the feet. There was a wardrobe, painted by some amateur of curious mentality with Louis Wain cats, a bamboo table piled with books, a tortured-looking piece of furniture half-desk, half-china cabinet, and a washstand with bright orange jug, basin and chamber pot. On the walls were many pictures. I noticed a reproduction, torn from some magazine and coloured by hand, of a picture depicting a fat child standing with arms out-spread on the bottom step of a flight; this was titled, *Tum and Tee Me Dump*. There were two stern photographs of, respectively, a very thin man with a bushy beard and a woman in a sunbonnet who looked much like my conception of Lizzie Borden. There was a coloured view of Llandudno and a piece of wood, for some reason carefully framed and glazed, on which was written in poker-work:

> Don't ask for Tick
> Or we shall be
> Sorry to lose
> Your Companee.

'Mrs Potter's old man used to keep a pub,' Field explained, seeing my gaze upon this exhibit, 'he made that up himself and Mrs Potter executed the whimsy.'

'Is Mrs Potter your landlady?' I asked him.

'Yes.'

'A comic music-hall type.'

'No,' said Field, sighing, 'no. No such luck.' He wandered about the room, vaguely packing a case, putting in pyjamas and throwing them out again. 'These are grubby. I've got a clean pair somewhere.' He went to the door and called, 'Mrs Potter!'

A mild-looking, rather pretty woman of fifty or so came up the stairs. 'Yes, Mr Field?'

'I'm so sorry to bother you, but did my pyjamas come back from the laundry?'

'The laundry didn't call today.'

'Oh, lord!' Field looked as if he would cry.

'They're so bad lately,' said Mrs Potter apologetically.

'You take the ones you've got and I'll get them washed up,' I said.

'I'll be away for a day or so,' he told the landlady. She said nothing, only peered about her as if expecting the laundry suddenly to materialize, glowing with phosphorescent light in the dark hallway. 'What shall I do about my milk?' He turned to me. 'You won't have enough milk. Oughtn't I to come and collect it every day?'

'You can get an emergency card for a week,' I reassured him, and he said, 'How clever you are.'

'You'll be away a whole week?' asked Mrs Potter.

'Yes; look, I'll pay you now, because I won't be here to-morrow.'

'You can let it wait over if you like.'

'Oh, I might spend it,' he said, counting out the money. She thanked him. 'Have a good time.'

She was lingering in the lower hall as we left. Field went out first and I was just following him, having stopped for a moment to adjust a mat I had kicked up, when Mrs Potter spoke to me earnestly, conspiratorially, in a whisper, 'It will do him good to be taken out of himself. I'm glad you're making him go. You see he gets something to eat for once!' Before I could reply she had gone, leaving behind her a whiff of some tired perfume.

When I joined Field in the street I was pleased to see his look of animation. 'Really, this is terribly good of you! God knows why you want to do it, but I don't mind telling you I get sick of that place sometimes. Not that Mrs Potter isn't kind ... but she's a bit depressing on occasion, like so many women who used to be pretty and have good times. She grieves for old Potter, too. She says he was so original. He used to paint all over any surface blank enough to be victimized. Don't I wish I'd shown you the bathroom! There's a big blue fish on the cistern. Honestly, Claud' – he was walking me along towards the Broadway at such a pace that he nearly forced me to run – 'it has its charms, but it's terrific to be getting out of it for a bit. I'm so grateful – you really can't imagine.'

To check this I asked him what he'd been reading lately, asked him what he thought of *Between the Acts*, *The Unquiet Grave*, various new periodicals. He answered, 'Oh, I don't really read, you know, only potter,' and in the same breath, 'The Woolf book's a Last Will and Testament. It made me want to read it standing up, as an act of respect. I'd trade her collected works – and what a bore she could be sometimes! – for that last chapter, with the play over and Isa and Giles ready for a get-together.' Then he looked startled, ashamed of himself, and all the way to Chelsea on the bus overwhelmed me with expressions of gratitude delicate and complicated as convolvulus.

Chapter Four

FIELD had been with me for three days when two things
happened. First, the War Office ordered me to Kent for a week
to attend to various matters at a depot there. Then, when Field
telephoned his landlady to tell her he was returning, he was
answered by her sister who said that Mrs Potter had been taken
to hospital with appendicitis, and would he please make his
own arrangements for a fortnight or so.

At this he seemed terrified, muttering vaguely that he could
easily go to an hotel, while at the same time, with an unconscious and betraying gesture, he fiddled with the money in his
pockets. I knew that even had he been able to afford an hotel it
was unlikely that he would find accommodation; as for lodg-
ings, they were unobtainable. Not wishing to leave him alone
in my rooms I told him, I hoped convincingly, that my stepmother would be delighted to look after him till I got back.
He was too relieved by this solution to make an effective protest – at any rate, not just then; by the time the arrangements
were made and Helena, after blackguarding me on the telephone, had agreed to make him as comfortable as she could,
he was protesting wildly that he would not go, that Lady
Archer didn't know him and wouldn't like him, that he could
fix up something quite easily, etcetera, etcetera. However,
I overcame all this and took him to Pont Street that evening.

I was glad Charmian was back with her unit, for it was just
possible that Field might have attracted her; he had a certain
vague but haunting resemblance to Tawney, without the
latter's exceeding good looks, and Tawney, I know, had a hold
upon her imagination that would never be quite loosed. Not
that I should have minded her falling in love with somebody,
had it given her release from Evan Sholto. But despite her tall
delicacy, her air of irresponsibility, her uncertain, often mis-
applied sense of fun, Charmian had a sturdy mind and purpose

44

and the capacity for decision. I wanted her to love someone who could match these qualities with his own.

Helena greeted Field with a bright courtesy that only too plainly covered a scowl. Irked by the intrusion, she had reverted to the social behaviour of the war years, when she had been Daniel's wife and the hostess of moneyed men. She was looking splendid in elaborate black, black and white cameo earrings flashing with the blacks and whites of her eyes. Field visibly shrank from her and his hand in hers lay limp as a kid glove.

'It's awfully nice of you to say you'll put up with me,' he said, 'you can't think how awful I feel about it, though, barging in on you like this. I tried to persuade Claud not to ask you, told him I could probably fix myself up somewhere –'

'Any help I can give to a friend of Claud's,' said Helena wrathfully, with a brilliant smile, 'I am pleased to give.' She made it sound like a line from Pinero. Ella, the maid, took Field and his suit-case off to the spare room, and when he had gone Helena said to me, 'My God, what a wet!'

'Always help the needy,' I told her, 'clothe the naked, dry the wet. Do you good to have something to occupy you.'

'I don't want to occupy myself with *that*, prancing and dancing round me, and getting up and down, and bowing me out to the lavatory and bowing me back, and apologizing ten to the dozen with every mouthful he eats. What am I going to do with him, tell me that?'

'So long as you feed him, you don't have to do anything else. He just reads all the time.'

'How jolly for me.'

'Don't be silly. You don't want him to entertain you, do you? You ought to enjoy feeding him up.'

'On what?'

'The tins Dan laid by for the invasion. You can't have opened a quarter of them. And you'll still have his black-market connexions to fall back on.'

'Dan got things by fair means only,' she protested grandly, not believing a word of it. 'And don't you be a prig. Everyone gets a bit on the side, anyway.'

'It's an odd thing,' I said, 'but when I was a child I was taught by my pastors and masters not to cheat, lie or take an

unfair advantage of my neighbour. I made a promise to myself at the beginning of this war that I wouldn't touch the
black market with a barge pole – wouldn't wangle petrol,
whisky, butter, or clothes coupons – and I haven't. And do my
pastors and masters admire me? Not a bit of it. I simply get
regarded as a harmless lunatic. My faith in common morality
has gone to pot.'

'If you were so moral,' she retorted triumphantly, 'you
wouldn't have stuffed yourself on Dan's food. You'd have
thrown down your napkin and said Faugh!'

'I never knew such rude words,' I told her. 'Besides, I was
often hungry.'

She snorted contempt, laughed, held up a hand for silence.
'Listen. Is that him coming back?'

'No.'

'Thought I heard him in the hall. Does he listen at doors?'

'No. He's a very good chap. You'll have to be nice to him
anyhow, because he's got a weak heart.'

She brushed this aside. 'So have you, probably. So have I.
Only we don't go running round to doctors making them listen to our chests.' Field came into the room. 'You'll be stopping to dinner?' she asked me in a loud, conversational voice,
making it perfectly plain that she had just changed the subject.

'I'd like to, but I can't. I've got to catch the eight-twenty.'

'We'll dine alone then, Mr Field,' she said, 'if you won't be
too dull.'

'I couldn't be,' he replied. He looked about the handsome
room, his gaze lingering upon the two pictures by Etty which
I had made Daniel buy. Both were of beautiful fat women,
with flesh like mother of pearl, bathing in bogus rushes under
a sky of burning turquoise. The hair of each was carefully
looped and braided in the decorous Victorian fashion, and
their nakedness was an enchanting incongruity.

'My husband's – and my stepson's – choice of paintings,'
said Helena, 'is not, I am afraid, mine. I am still old-fashioned
enough to dislike a picture if the subject of it is stout.' Sweep-
ing not only Etty, but Renoir, Rubens and Veronese away,
she drew Field's attention to a rather dull little Cox, which I
happened to know she detested.

I said good-bye to Field, leaving him to her bored dominance. When Helena was bored, she showed off; it was a palliation.

The accident that brought me back to live in Helena's flat was absurd enough. I had been three days in Kent when the owner of the house in which I lodged wrote to tell me that the ceiling in my room and in the passage had fallen – owing, apparently, to the vibration of a passing convoy which had proved the last straw to the ceiling's already broken back – and that he had not the slightest idea when he could get the floor fit again for occupation. I wrote, therefore, to tell Helena that she must take me as a lodger once more and to ask her if she would not also keep Field at my expense, till such time as he, too, could go home. Her reply was grudging.

Dear Claud, – I have to take you, I suppose, and I don't see how I can refuse to take that friend of yours, but don't you imagine I like it. I don't mean I mind you, I'm used to you by now, or ought to be, God help me, but I haven't got a word out of him yet and he goes around looking half-terrified. When people look terrified it always makes me want to give them something to be terrified of. Not that he isn't helpful around the place now we're short-handed, but he does it in a sort of lily-white-handed way and I keep thinking I ought to make him go and lie down. Oh, yes, and he plays the piano sometimes, but in a very furtive way and goes leaping up from the stool the moment I come in as if he's burned his bottom. Still, I told him your idea about him being your guest, and he kicked at that, and said he must at least pay what he was paying before to his Mrs Potter, which is three pounds a week with morning and evening meal. How she did it I don't know. Anyway, I agreed on that, and it seems fair to me. After all, times are hard and I have to look after myself. – Yours, Helena.

P.S.– Don't you talk him into letting you do the paying, because I don't know why you should.

The tone of this letter, with its insistence upon need and short-handedness, startled me, and my irritation at the arrangement Helena had made over my head with Field was allayed by amazement at the brand-new pose she appeared to have adopted. I was more amazed when I returned from Kent and, going to Pont Street, found Field alone in the flat meekly laying the table for dinner.

'Where on earth's Ella?' I asked him.

He smiled. 'Lady Archer's got rid of her. There's only a daily woman now, six days a week, and this is the day she doesn't come.'

When Helena came in he effaced himself at once, and I was able to ask her what was happening.

'You must remember,' she said, 'that I am no longer a wealthy woman.' She made this announcement as if it were the first sentence of a very long novel established in classical literature, and for a second I felt that spasm of awful boredom some people feel when they are about to have something read to them.

'Helena,' I said, 'a clear sixteen hundred a year doesn't seem starvation to me.'

'But I,' she told me in the voice of Dan's wife, 'have acquired certain standards during the past six years or so. And I have to face things.'

'But surely you didn't have to get rid of Ella and Snapely as quickly as all that?'

'Who said anything about Snapely?' Helena retorted with grandeur. 'I'm keeping him for a while. He's very useful. He can mend fuses.'

I protested that she could manage far more cheaply and quite as comfortably with taxis and an electrician, but she would not listen. As for Ella, she said, she ate too much. 'After all, I've spent the best part of my life looking after myself. And you. And your father. And Charmian. I shall manage perfectly with a daily help.'

A char and a chauffeur, I remarked, was a curious domestic staff.

'I like things that are out of the ordinary,' Helena beamed. 'One doesn't always want to do what the crowd does,' then rose in a decisive manner as if to conclude an audience.

I was interested, that evening, to watch her behaviour towards Field; it took me back to my own chivvied and bully-ragged youth. She could not, of course, be as violent to him as she had been to me. He was twenty-six, not thirteen; and she was not stepmother but hostess. All the same, I noticed that she had ceased to adopt before him the pose with which she had accepted him into her home. A tone in her voice, an abrupt movement, would recall the Helena of Bruges, the handsome rowdy with dyed hair, elbows like a Skelton ale-wife's and a love smothering as an eiderdown for one person only at a time. Myself not that person.

'If you don't eat your greens, Johnny,' she snapped at him, 'you'll get your blood out of order and then you'll have another of those boils.'

'I really don't like them,' he murmured, looking down at his plate, surreptitiously trying to hide some brussels sprouts under a potato. 'I think it's because I was forcibly fed with them as a child.'

'If more mothers were as firm nowadays,' said Helena sadistically, 'we'd hear less of children needing bottled orange juice and cod liver oil. Silly nonsense.'

Field grew very silent, but did not eat the greens.

Towards the end of the meal Helena became bluff. 'Well, boys!' she exclaimed, startling me. 'Not too bad a meal for war-time?'

She had reduced the flat in Pont Street, Archer's home, to a boarding-house of farce, with communal table, eccentric guests, and a Stranger in the third floor back.

'Indeed no,' said Field, in his pleasant gentle voice. 'I think you manage terrifically, Lady Archer, really I do.'

'If you mean that,' Helena retorted, 'you should show appreciation in the Chinese fashion.'

He blushed.

'Don't be coarse, Helena,' I said.

'Perhaps,' she suggested, icily, 'we aren't talking about the same thing.'

'There is no other thing. The Chinese eructate to indicate repletion.'

'No!' said Helena, leaning forward with a brilliant, amazed smile, and turning her gaze maliciously upon Field.

Later she made him dry up the dishes. 'Not you,' she said to me, 'you stay where you are. Warrior's repose. Johnny, you can wear Ella's apron and save your best suit.'

'That's all right,' he murmured, 'I'm very careful.'

She left him to complete the drying and returned to me. 'Get him back home as soon as you can, will you? You find out when that landlady's likely to be there again.'

'I'd have thought he'd be a help to you.'

'He gets on my nerves,' she said dryly. 'Anyway, I've got so much to think about that any stranger around the place interrupts my thoughts.'

'How long are you going to stay here?'

'In the flat? As long as I can.'

'What rent are you paying? Come on, now. It's about time you did confess it.'

'If I tell you,' said Helena slyly, 'you'll only begin to nag.'

'I can always ask Charmian.'

'She won't tell you. I'll tell her not to.'

'She doesn't tell you everything,' I said at random, and then was sorry; but Helena only shrugged her shoulders and said, 'Dan's money? Oh, that.'

'I can't understand her taking the promise so literally.'

'No,' said Helena, rather violently, 'for all that you make yourself out the hero who doesn't get it from under the counter, you still faint with surprise when you meet people who swear not to tell something and then really don't.'

'What I can't understand is why she made such a promise at all. Or why Dan made her make it.'

'Why?' she smiled, and blew out her lips. 'That was him all over. He never understood me. He could never get it into his head that so long as I was cosy and had my little comforts, I didn't care a damn about the extras. Of course I like money. But enough's as good as a feast. Not, mind you, that I thought he'd leave me quite so little as he did.'

'What had he against you?'

'Me?' Her eyes widened. 'Nothing. He adored me. Anyway, I suppose he reckoned that what was Charmian's was mine.'

'What are you paying for this flat?' I insisted, this time seriously.

'Six-fifty.' She looked proud.

'Well, you can't go on doing it. And you can't keep Snapely.'

'Snapely will pine,' said Helena with satisfaction.

The bell rang, and we heard Field go to answer it. In a moment he put his head round the door, muttering, 'Someone for you, Lady Archer – a Mrs Sholto,' and withdrew.

'*What* a fool!' Helena exclaimed, rising, hurrying to let the old lady in. 'You must forgive me. Claud's young friend has been doing a little buttling for me while Ella's out, and of course he doesn't know people.'

'He seemed a very nice young man,' Mrs Sholto said. 'How are you, Claud? Busy?'

I replied at the War Office not very, but that I had nearly completed another book.

'May I know the subject, or do you authors hate telling?'

She settled herself by the fire, holding out her frail and pretty hands, like skeleton leaves, to the grateful flame.

I told her it was a handbook on Picasso, commissioned for a series.

'Now listen,' she said, 'you really must tell me the truth. Being in the family. *Why* do you young people pretend to see anything in this modern art? How can you go and look at a Gainsborough one day, and then admire this stuff the next?'

I should like to have told her that I was not a young person, but a polite one approaching middle life; that the form of her question implied impoliteness to myself; that I would prefer not to waste my time giving her a reply to which she would not trouble to listen, the whole of her delight having lain in the query; and finally that if she fell down a hole in the road I should immediately take a shovel and fill it in. However, I said simply that it would be a very long explanation, and went into the kitchen to fetch Field, whom I found extended on his stomach before the gas stove, as before a tribal deity, poking beneath it for a dropped spoon.

He looked out of temper. When I asked him to come in and talk, he replied that he didn't want to natter to any old ladies, instantly countering this strange flash of spirit by adding: 'I didn't mean Lady Archer, of course.' However, he did return with me and was introduced to Mrs Sholto by Helena.

'This is Johnny Field, who is staying with us. Claud's friend. Johnny is very clever at knowing where everything is, and will bring us some sherry.'

Telling him to sit still, I went and fetched it myself. When I returned, the three of them were talking in an embarrassed and staccato fashion about the war.

'We have taken Düren tonight,' said Mrs Sholto, with an air of personal satisfaction which implied that this feat had been achieved by herself and the cook. 'Everything seems to be going well.'

'I must say I envy the soldiers who will enter Berlin,' Helena remarked, with a martial gleam.

'I'm afraid it will be the Russians,' Mrs Sholto murmured, frowning, smoothing the curve of thin grey plaits that ran like beading over the crown of her head. 'I don't feel we shall be able to celebrate the peace with entirely free minds.'

'Good luck to them,' said Field unexpectedly, 'if they get there first, which obviously they will.'

'Oh, but come,' Mrs Sholto whispered, playfully peeking to left and right over her shoulder in case spies were about, 'between ourselves.... Well, you mark my words. There's trouble to come one of these days.'

'I'm not fighting them,' he told her, 'I'm not fighting anyone. I don't see why I should. And I can't see why there need be any trouble if we don't go around looking for it.'

Mrs Sholto leaned forward, smiling. 'Mr Field,' she said, very precisely and clearly, as if it were a name both difficult and comical, 'you are young and how lucky you are to be so; but I *remember* a great deal more than you. That's why I have my misgivings.' After an effective pause, in which Field looked miserable and defiant and Helena stood the cat up on its hind legs and made it clap its paws, 'You understand me, don't you, Claud?'

'I understand, yes, but I'm afraid I don't agree.'

'Claud,' said Helena, 'is almost a Bolshevik. He will keep the Red Flag flying here. Pussy,' she murmured to the cat.

'That,' Mrs Sholto told me, 'is being young. What do they say? That if a man isn't a Socialist at twenty he is no good, and that if he is still one at forty he is a fool.'

'I'd better get you some more coal, Lady Archer,' Field said, rising. I watched the back of his head as he went out, and it appeared to pulsate.

'But what I came about,' Mrs Sholto said, 'was not to talk about politics, which are nasty, quarrelsome things, but to ask if you had heard anything from Charmian about Evan. I had a very exciting letter this morning.'

Helena and I expressed pleasure.

'Very exciting. It appears there is a chance for him of a job at home, and if it comes off he may be sailing within a month!'

'One of the lucky ones,' said Helena, trying to appear enthusiastic.

'I expect Charmian's heard too. Does she write to you often?'

'Not very. She gets home once in every three weeks now, and doesn't bother to write much in between whiles.'

'It's quite unusual for Evan to write to me, these days. Charmian has all the letters. But I expect to take a back seat; it's right and proper. I couldn't bear to feel he was one of these dreadful mother-ridden young men.'

'God forbid,' Helena agreed. Her eyes flickered. She hung the cat upside down by its back paws, and when it curled up to bite her, gave it a gentle smack and sent it spinning through space on to the settee. 'God forbid,' she repeated.

I went out to look for Field, whom I found in his bedroom reading, with apparent intensity, a Dream Book bought one day by Helena at a church bazaar.

'If I dream of pimentoes,' he told me, without turning his head, 'it means that I am going to lose a small sum of money in distressing circumstances. Did you ever meet anyone who dreamed of pimentoes?' He went straight on, as if he had not changed the subject: 'Saving your reverence and your friends, Claud, nothing infuriates me like these damned old warmongers. Let them go and try it. Let them have a cut at it. Where was *she* during the blitz? Not here, I bet my eyebrows.'

'Helena was.'

'She's different.' There was a shade in his voice of admiration, reluctant, but strong. 'No, I meant Mrs Whatsername.'

'Cumberland lakes.'

He threw the Dream Book down. 'I'm a swine, you know. That's where she should have been, obviously. Wouldn't have been any use for her to hang around the danger areas. Only what I meant was, she shouldn't talk about fresh wars when she's seen damn all of this one.'

I saw that the trouble with him was not so much anger but

fear; he was looking down with vertigo into his vision of the future. He was the type of human being who sees only the individual; his mind could not think in masses, or subdivide into social units. If he read of the degradation and torment of a mass of people in jail or concentration camp, he grew sick with the attempt to feel the suffering of each in himself; he could not accept the total sum of pain nor view it objectively. He was the kind of man to have served in war in a Friends Ambulance Unit, in peace as a polemicist for some ideal definite in outline but hopelessly nebulous in detail.

The Helenas of the world would be inclined for ever to treat him as my Helena treated her cat, and before them he would be helpless.

Throwing down the book, he went before me back towards the room where the two women sat. 'I don't know what's up with me,' he said, 'damn rude.'

For the rest of the evening, quite plainly, he was thrashing himself mentally for a discourtesy that no one but himself had so much as noticed.

One night a week later I returned to the flat to find him gone.

'Good riddance, I know,' said Helena, 'but you can't help being wild. He came in to lunch, all blushes, all shyness, and said he wouldn't have to trouble me any longer as he'd found a room in Redcliffe Gardens. He thanked me right and left, nearly cried at me, then snatched up his traps and bolted. I told him he'd better come back here to dinner anyhow and explain things to you, but no, he wouldn't take another meal from me – though I told him he was doing the paying and damn it, he did bits of shopping for me sometimes, too – and said he'd drop in for half an hour later on. God knows what he calls later on, because it's nearly nine now.'

He came at half-past, told me in embarrassment that he could not impose on Helena a moment longer, asked us both to dine out one evening with him, elaborately thanked us once again, and left within the hour.

It was a long while before we saw him again, for I was sent out of London and Helena flatly refused to have a meal paid for, she wrote, by any chap half in the pawnshop and the other half in the workhouse. 'Anyway,' she added, 'it will be years before I want to see that Billy Misery again. I like someone cheerful around the house, someone who can share a joke.'

Reminded of jokes, I wrote in reply telling her that Snapely must go, carried back as I did so by a waft of political reminiscence to 1938 and 1939. To this I received no answer, but when I returned found him gone.

To my insistence that she must move to a cheaper flat she protested, not without reason, that this would be impossible; there were no flats. 'I could keep on here,' she said, her smile stretching tight across her velvety and perfumed face, 'if Charmian weren't such a tight wad. I told her I thought she ought to help, and she said that though I could have the whole eighty thousand back if I asked her for it, she wasn't going to contribute to the rent of a place far too large for me and a damn sight too much like the lounge of a station hotel. Though why she should say that I don't know. Dan always had taste.'

I was lucky enough, however, to have offered me by a man at the War Office the last three years of the lease of a four-bedroom flat in Elm Park Gardens, at a rental of two hundred and fifty a year inclusive. She was delighted, dousing my suggestions that even this was too large. 'There's a room for me, and one for you – because you might just as well stay with me as not – and one for Charmian when she's on leave. The fourth will do for old Evan if he does get back. I'm not putting them in together, not under my roof.'

The move was a joy to her. She went ramping about the Pont Street flat, clearing and cleaning, sorting, rummaging, throwing to the daily woman things she would probably regret with fury a year hence. '"The old order changeth,"' she chanted, plunging the sofa covers into a dye bath, '"giving place to new,"' and afterwards I heard her singing, with a gusto that gave the illusion of youth renewed to her rough, warm voice, *Off to Philadelphia in the Morning*. She seemed to have lost the gloss, the opacity of the last few years, to have become sturdy, open and joyful again. On the day we went into the new flat she appeared defiantly at dinner-time in a bridge coat criss-crossed with rambler roses, a terrible garment which Daniel had long ago banished with a little, Christmassy, chilly jest.

She toasted me solemnly as we sat over a scratch meal in a kitchen still cluttered and swarmed with ware unpacked but as yet undistributed. 'To you,' she said, 'and to old times.' She peered down at a tiny fleck of cork floating in her glass and meditatively picked it out with a hairpin. When she looked up at me again her eyes were full of tears.

'You don't know what it's like when your body ages before you do! When your body's old and you still feel young. I feel about forty-five. I aged in myself till then, and then I stopped.' She paused abruptly as if there were no more to be said, then continued ramblingly, 'Not to be able to look at yourself too long in a mirror. You know those stories of how people look in a mirror and don't see themselves, and then they know they're dead. And I don't like to draw conclusions.' She added violently: 'Oh, I don't mean I see nothing! I see someone, I see a fat old girl with a lot of white hair and a jowl, and I can't think that's me. Do you think it's me, Claud?'

Knowing better than to encourage Helena when she was riding an emotional idea as she might ride a runaway horse, I was silent.

'Oh, all right, all right. Pretend you don't understand. There's nothing you don't understand, even as a small boy you had X-ray eyes, which was why I walloped you so often, I expect. You listen to me; I'll tell you what the future has in store for you. It's horrible. Wait till you look in the glass and you're not there, only an old man with a horse face, mopping and mowing –'

I began to laugh, and my laughter released hers. 'I'm damned if I'm going to mop and mow,' I said. 'I'll be one of those distinguished old men with a nasty tongue. I'll make the young ones hop. I'll play hell, and if anyone tries to answer back I'll blackmail him with my white hairs.'

I thought she would follow up the fancy, but she did not. She only said, in a much more moderate tone than she had used up till now, and in a manner very sad, 'I wish it wasn't all over, Claud. I wish I'd still got a life before me.'

'There's plenty of it left in you.'

'You know what I mean; don't make silly answers.' She rose and began to stack the dishes. 'You can dry up, I'll wash.'

'I'll wash,' I said.

'No, you don't. You're messy. You leave smears. I remember how you used to leave smears.'

We washed up the dishes together.

'What would Dan say?' she cried suddenly, turning round rosy with momentary pleasure. 'What would the Stillyers say, and Ma Sholto?'

'What would the Cayleys say –' I joined in, 'and Lady Esch?' – chiming with her speculations in an antiphony of speech which, owing to the wine, the weariness of the day and the oddity of our situation, seemed to me as charming as the chiming quartet in *As You Like It*.

'All the same,' she said insistently an hour later, as I was making ready to go round to Jane Elvorden's for an hour, 'it's miserable to get to a stage when you have to remember your age all the time in case you say something out of period.' I wished then that I had not to go out, for excitement had ebbed from her, leaving her chilly and at a loose end, to the futile contemplation of years and especially of hours.

Chapter Five

At the end of the following week Charmian came home on leave. Helena was spending a few days with the Leipers – not because she liked them but because, she said, they always had guinea fowl to eat, and this she was no longer able to afford – so my sister and I were alone. She took off her outdoor clothes before speaking, sat down before the small spring fire and smoothed back with fanning hands the hair that sprang, dark and fine and lustrous, from the parting that bisected a head dainty as a snake's. Her face was calm and unrevealing.

'I believe he really is on his way home,' she said at last.

Not knowing her thoughts I was not sure in what tone I should reply. 'That's terrific,' I said, hinting a query.

'He was supposed to have sailed a week ago today. When do you think he'll turn up?'

I told her that it varied. Perhaps three weeks, perhaps six.

'He ought to be here about the second week in April, I reckon.'

'Ought to be. We'll hope so.'

'He's very lucky, isn't he?'

'Very,' I agreed. I looked another question and she smiled; but the smile held no reply.

'How was Mother before she went?' she asked.

'Oh, all right. Why?'

'Only I thought she was looking rather under the weather last week-end. She isn't worrying about money, is she?'

'No reason why she should be, surely. You pay her. So do I. Good God, all this is wealth to me!'

'But she – Well, I mean, it's a drop from what was. Do you think . . .' She hesitated, 'Look here, Claud, do you think she feels bad about me? Because I'd give her everything if she did.' Again she paused, then continued rather quickly, 'But if she doesn't I'm glad I've got the money. We may need it. When the war's over and Evan's out of the army anything may happen.'

'What, for instance?'

'He was too young to have done anything before the war,' she said defensively, 'so it isn't as if he's anything to go to. He was only just down from Oxford when it began. If we can start with a little money –'

I laughed at this.

'All right, then, plenty of money – it will give him confidence, don't you see?'

'Does he need all that for his confidence?'

'You shut up,' said Charmian. She took a piece of gum from her pocket and began to chew it in the least tolerable fashion, lumping it from side to side of her jaw and even removing it in her fingers now and then to see how it was getting on. I protested at this, telling her also that her appearance would be a disgrace were it not for its comic aspect. Unexpectedly she retorted with the language of the barrack-room. It sounded extraordinary from her lips, less shocking than irritating in its absurdity.

I said nothing. She looked at me for a moment, flushed very slightly, then turned back to the fire. 'And that's that,' she said, braving it out.

'What on earth's the matter with you lately?' I asked her, as mildly as I could.

'Nothing's the matter. I just hate being picked on.'

'You deserve picking on. You're grubby and sluttish and untidy, and you use dirty language at me. I wouldn't mind if you used it with the right sort of verve, but you sound like a six-year-old spelling out "OXO" from a hoarding. What's the matter with you, for God's sake? Tell me, and I'll help you sort things out. Is it Evan?'

'What about Evan?'

'Are you worried about him in any way?'

She scowled at me, then rose and put her cap on. 'I'm going out.'

The cap, which she had adjusted blindly, was much askew, giving her a Napoleonic appearance; and I laughed. 'Come and look at yourself,' I said, taking hold of her and pushing her towards the mirror. She turned, speechless and tearful with rage, and fought me. Bewildered, I caught her arms down and held them. We stared at each other in silence, and I was wretched. There had been nothing like this before.

At last she released herself, smiling uncertainly. 'All right, all right, only you can be maddening.'

'So can you. What a revolting scene!'

'Well, you shouldn't laugh at me. I'm war-weary. I've no sense of humour.'

'I'll laugh at you as much as I like. You don't *want* to go out, do you?'

'Not particularly. Why?'

'I thought we might have an early meal and go to the pictures.'

'Could do,' Charmian said. Moving away from me, she threw up the window. 'It's stuffy in here.' We stood looking out into the delicate spring dusk. The dusk, the grime and the twilight of war lay over the street, and the shabby houses with their uncleaned windows seemed forlorn and amnesiac; but over the way a tree was greening over, clouding with uncertain jade the darkening blue of the air. I began to hope, then, for the unconceivable, for the return to the normality of summer evenings, the lamp burning high in the close, the notes of a piano through an open window, the lovers moving like heroes and heroines through the chorus of the crowds. I began to believe that the desolation of the crumbled streets would be some day like the memory of some vision in the silent and dusty rooms of nightmare, and that peace would be, not an ideal, not a privilege, not a temporary concession, but a thing simply accepted as *being*, as the sun is accepted, or the cycle of the darkness and the light. As I looked down I saw Helena coming along the street with Charmian a baby in her arms, even as I had seen her on a day over twenty years ago, when from another window I had watched her walking hugely on English soil, a vision from my ancient world, too big, too golden for the new. I fancied her looking up at the house numbers as if it were a matter of casual interest to her whether she found me again or whether she should fail, and so go striding on, diminishing ever in the dusky sunlight, the baby now no more than a flower at her breast or the knot of a shawl.

Then, suddenly, the vision was overcast by the reality, by

the real woman, strong and old; and it seemed to me in that moment that the gold of the spectre was blurred beyond her, like a bad lay of colour beyond the printed line.

Charmian saw her too. 'What's Mother doing back so soon?'

'We'll have to ask her,' I said.

'Do you think she mightn't be well?'

I detected in this an apprehension, a guilt: Charmian was like a child who, having caused some small offence to a parent, fears God will punish it by striking the parent dead.

'She looks all right.'

We waited, then, for Helena to come in.

She entered dramatically, stood stock-still like Clytemnestra in the doorway and said: 'I have struck.'

Beneath a genuine distress, and above all the distress that succeeds the taking of some difficult decision, she was enjoying herself. She was, beyond question, the star in whatever drama she had built around herself.

'What do you mean, you've struck?' I asked her, rather loudly. For years it had been my task to damp down Helena's emotions before they had had time to dampen her own sense of irony.

She did not reply, but instead made an outpushing gesture with her arms, as if the room were too small for her. 'I can't talk here. I can't breathe.'

'Where would you like to talk?' said Charmian, in a voice politely conciliatory.

'I don't know how you two can sit around in this stifling atmosphere,' Helena said, glowering. 'I must get out or choke. You can both come with me.'

She would not speak again until she had us walking on either side of her through the creeping twilight. The air was mild and the scent of ocean, far-borne, was in it. A few lamps were lighted, lime-gold in the dusk and the dust of the streets. We turned into Church Street, which was deserted save for a boy on a bicycle riding serpentine over the roadway with his hands in his pockets.

'I cannot,' said Helena, 'I will not endure these people any more. I sent myself a telegram, like that boy in *Crome Yellow*.'

'Did the Leipers swallow it? I bet they didn't. What did it say?'

'Be quiet,' Charmian rebuked me, 'first things first. I want to hear why she sent it.'

'Don't refer to me as She as if I was the cat,' said Helena, driven to absurdity by irritation at these interruptions. 'It said "New situation arisen. Need you urgently. Claud."'

I missed my footing and trod heavily into the gutter. 'What new situation?'

'Do try to walk properly, and not like a child. Any new situation. I thought it sounded convincing.'

'Did the Leipers?'

'But you didn't show it them?' Charmian cried.

'Of course I did,' Helena replied haughtily, 'or rather, I read it out.'

I asked her whether they were not mystified.

'I hope they were,' she answered. 'Give them something else to think about than little conundrums. You can't imagine what they're like to stay with! Tom's not so bad, but that slab-sided Sue and those sisters! And that dire little girl! They play ping-pong. And one of them has a comic matchbox that a snake comes out of when you open it. After dinner we sit round talking about who's on what committee, and whether Aunt So-and-so had any benefit from her infra-red treatment, and how the Council's put slum children in the house next door; and when that palls Tom brings out his wire-puzzle and Sue says she knows a very clever catch that you do with a tumbler, two half-pennies and a bull's-eye.'

'I don't know one with a bull's-eye,' I said, 'but there's a very fascinating one with a teaspoon.'

She turned on me in fury. 'What the devil does it matter what you do it with? It's the principle that counts. Oh, yes. And Rosemary, that's the elder sister, says do I know what it is that walks on four legs, sings on one note, and can't pay the rent, or something of the sort.'

'What *was* the answer?' Charmian inquired automatically.

'I don't know,' said Helena, 'and I don't care. I don't suppose I've even got it right. But that's how it was, *all* the time, and there was I sitting in the best chair saying: "No", "Really", "Was she indeed?" "How amusing" for hours on end and nobody making a move to go to bed, and the night before last I thought, why am I standing this? I don't have to stand it. I don't have to truckle to these people any more. I'm free now. I can choose my own friends. So I got up next morning and went for a walk and sent the wire.'

She smiled for the first time since her return and sighed deeply.

'Everyone will talk about you but you won't care,' Charmian said tenderly, putting her hand on Helena's arm.

'I won't care a damn.'

Charmian caught my eye and we were both silent with laughter.

'By the by,' Helena said briskly, as we came to the brighter lights and deeper dusk of King's Road, 'I met your friend Bill Swain just outside the Tube.'

'Swain?' I was interested. I had lost touch with him since the war. 'What's he been doing all this time?'

'I don't know. I didn't have time to ask. Not in the Army, I bet. He came bounding up shouting "Helena!" and panting like a sheepdog. He said he recognized me even with my white hair, and he'd like to paint me. I said: "Not you, I don't want an eye on my upper lip and six toes to a foot," but he didn't mind.'

'Swain's portraits are rather academic, as a matter of fact. Quite good, so far as they go, and they make him a bit of money.'

'He's coming over for a drink tomorrow night and bringing his wife. I asked him to.'

'When did he get married?'

'I don't know. Her name's Clemency.'

'Did you meet her?'

'No. He was by himself. Let's have a party tomorrow, Claud! You must know some people. I want to get the taste of the Leipers out of my mouth.'

She had quite forgotten her early role of decision and stress, and was lively with plans as a girl. She would not return to the flat for dinner, but insisted that we should all go to a snack bar in King's Road. Indeed, she was so happy, so full of hope for a new life that Charmian was moved to an aching remorse.

'Oh, Mother,' she said, jerking forward so suddenly that she splashed my coffee into the saucer, 'do let me give you that damned money! It's on my soul.'

Helena stared at her like a stranger in the district who is asked the way. 'I don't want your silly money, pet,' she said, 'I've no use for it, not now. What's yours is mine, more or less, anyhow, and if I ever get poor, which God knows why I should, you can support me and I'll be supported without a murmur. Can't you see,' she added rather feverishly, her eyes flashing, 'that it doesn't matter, *now*?'

Charmian murmured, 'So long as you know it's there when you want it,' and sat back again, looking happier than she had done since Dan's death.

'Any news of Evan?' Helena asked her.

'I meant to tell you. I think he's on his way home.'

'Funny things you girls forget.' Helena looked at her curiously. 'In my day, we'd have been nothing but blushes and half-sighs. Still, *tout passe, tout lasse, tout casse* – I can never remember the order.'

'You must admit yours was the biggest sensation,' Charmian said, laughing, 'coming in as you did. Claud and I imagined something atrocious.'

'All the Archer family, the friends and their relations, are atrocious. I always knew it, in my heart, but today I am sure of it. This,' she added, looking about her at the youngish people, mostly rather shabby, all eating hungrily, 'is the life. How did I ever get mixed up with another one, Claud?'

For the rest of the meal she netted us and herself in a web of reminiscence, embroidered with rich, gross jewels of the imagination.

When we returned home she insisted once more that we should have a party on the morrow. Charmian and I were ready enough to please her, but parties of the kind Helena contemplated were by no means easily come by. Since the war we had lost touch with so many friends; writing had been difficult, firstly because of addresses lost, and secondly because, owing to the cluttering of the mind with so many new things, it had ceased to be a pleasure and had become an effort. I telephoned Brickland and was answered by Muriel, who said: 'No, he's still in Italy, and I can't come because I'm expecting a baby tomorrow.' I did manage to get in touch with Crandell, who had given me my first opportunity for art criticism when he was editing *The Turnstile*. He was pleased to hear from me. No, he hadn't been in the forces. He'd been in the Ministry of Information. He was married and had two children. His wife's name was Nina. The children were called Adrian and Eliot. I rang several other numbers, but without result. 'I'll call Jane after ten,' I said, 'and I think that will have to do. What about you, Charmian? What about that friend of Evan's who came home recently?'

'I don't think he'd like it,' she said quickly.

'What does it matter if he likes it or not? We've got to have a party. Go on. You ring him.'

She shrugged. 'If you like. Give me the book.'

'I'll look it up for you. What's his name?'

'Tennant, Norman H. It'll be under his mother's name, Mrs Glendon Tennant.'

I found the number, and Charmian took the call. She spoke to him for several moments, amused, seemingly evasive. 'Yes, he might be back soon. . . . Oh, he seems cheerful. . . . No, nothing. I don't think he's had much social life lately. What I rang up about was, would you be free tomorrow night? Come round here for a drink? . . . No, not a party. Only my mother and brother, and one or two people. . . . Eightish, yes. Splendid. . . . Oh, I'm all right. Nothing wrong with me. . . . Yes. . . . No . . .' She laughed about something, but with cold eyes. 'Yes, I believe you. Well, look here, I'll look forward to seeing you. Good-bye, Norman.'

She hung up, swung round on the stool. 'There's another one for you, then. Don't say I don't try.' She spoke poker-faced as if she were holding her breath, but Helena noticed nothing. 'There's a good pet,' she said, and began to tick off our guests on her fingers.

'That's Swain and his wife, Crandell and his, and Charm's friend Tennant, and Claud's girl, Jane. One, two, three, four, five, six. Oh, I know who we've forgotten! Claud, you ring up Johnny Field.'

I stared at her. 'You want John?'

'Why not? It helps to make up a crowd.'

'But do you think he's the party type?'

'He can make himself useful,' she snapped, 'he can hand things.'

I told her I liked Field, and wouldn't have him used as a waiter.

'You ring him and do as you're told.'

'Not me.'

'Then I shall.' Helena grasped the phone as if it were a nettle and dialled the number Field had given her. 'That you, Johnny? Helena speaking, Helena Archer. . . . Yes, I'm well, thank you. Listen. I want you to come here tomorrow night. Just a small party, one or two people.' A long pause. 'Nonsense. Put him off. . . . Of course you can! Don't talk nonsense to me. You come. Be here at eight. . . . No, I insist. That's that. We'll be seeing you, then.' She hung up with a crash and beamed round at us.

'That's not inviting,' said Charmian, 'that's press-ganging.'

'Sloppy young idiot, I had to make up his mind for him,' Helena said. She might have been Alice with the serpent neck, talking down into the sea of leaves.

For the entire evening her good humour endured. As she stood before the mirror she said: 'I wish I'd never had my hair bleached; I could still have worn it gold, even now,' and when I told her she could not have, she took not the slightest notice of me but broke into one of the music-hall songs from her extraordinary repertoire, singing in the earnest bogus cockney of the provincial:

> Rowmeo, wot 'ave you done with Julier?
> Rowmeo, expline it if you can.
>   Ev'ryone's Peculier
>   To know wot you've done with Julier,
> Rowmeo, Rowmeo, you are a naughty man.

Charmian liked this, commented with interest on the use of the word 'peculiar' in such a context, and went to great pains to learn the song, being taken through it by Helena line by line.

I had expected Helena's rare spirits, the exaltation of this urge towards a new life, to have disappeared by breakfast-time; but it was not so. And she raced us through our Sunday-night supper, as she dressed herself and screwed into her ears two enormous flowers of salmon-pink glass, she sang about Rowmeo and Julier, told us ancient jokes and behaved altogether in a manner which Charmian found delightful and I found disturbing. Helena, I felt, was holding a pose too long. If she held it another day longer it would be an effort and a humiliation to abandon it; and I saw her for the rest of her life pegged to a nervous falsity, condemned metaphorically to a lie about her age and to an interminable third act upon which the curtain could never fall.

But she looked splendid, black, white, and pink in the varnished gold of the lamplight, her lashes peaked two by two with mascara, the rouge upon her cheeks more beautiful, because of its artificiality, its tint of azalea and pearl, than the natural rose of a child.

Bill and Clemency Swain were the first to arrive, he preserving still his look of an indigent Bulldog Drummond, she a tip-nosed, high-bosomed, smiling blonde girl, dressed with some vague resemblance to Rubens' portrait of Suzanne Fourment. When she walked she seemed to sail like a frigate, with clouds blowing about her head. Her hands, plump and white, she kept folded just above her stomach, as if to gather the folds of an immense skirt. When she spoke she said, in a careful, made voice like the chiming of little bells, 'It's epslutely wizard to meet you at long last.'

Norman Tennant came next, a dusty-looking man of thirty or so, with curious hair which was the dingy fawn-gold of a threepenny bit. He seemed never to smile, as if not smiling were his trade mark, his conscious fascination, and he had a trick of thrusting his tongue behind his upper teeth and withdrawing it with a smack before making any remark that expressed opinion. Helena whispered to me, 'Just what you'd expect Boiled Owl's friend to be like,' and watched him with some amusement as he went immediately to sit by Charmian, to look her slowly up and down, and then, after a smack of tongue and teeth, to say, 'Tremendous'. I was not surprised that she had been reluctant to invite him.

Field came next, whispered a greeting to Helena and acknowledged, in whispers, her introductions. He was very clean, very stiff in a new stiff suit. He had, he told us, got a production job with a small firm of publishers. 'The Nineveh Press,' he said anxiously, 'Have you ever heard of it?'

'Come on, Johnny Field,' Helena cried to him, 'no idling.

See what everyone wants, there's a good boy.' He rose meekly to obey her.

Jane Elvorden and the Crandells arrived together. Jane was beautiful as Helen on the Trojan walls. She had the great ease and spirit of the insensitive and Nina Crandell, who was little and plain as her husband, eyed her with wonderment and admiration. Women were not jealous of Jane; she was *hors concours*. Nina I liked at once, though I thought her manner of dressing, a thick tweed suit with no jumper beneath, hair flowing down to the small of her back, toeless shoes upon not too clean bare feet, very hideous indeed.

'Claud,' she said to me, 'I've read all your books and that's the truth. You can examine me on any one of them. I didn't like the one on the Eclectics, but then, I don't like the Eclectics anyway, so it wasn't your fault.' And to Jane Elvorden she said disconcertingly, 'Aren't you *lovely*?' She added to me in a murmur, a moment later, 'But I wouldn't want to paint her. I'd like a stab at Lady Archer, though.'

'Don't you let her paint you, Helena,' said Swain, 'you wait till you get to heaven and then ask Veronese if he'd have a shot at it.'

'Veronese?' I asked him, surprised.

'She's in the *Family of Darius before Alexander*, somewhere. Or if she isn't she ought to be. How do you find painting these days, Claud?'

I said I had precious little time to find it at all.

Swain mentioned Graham Sutherland, John Piper, Mervyn Peake, said he himself was better than anyone by miles. I replied that as he never did any work these days I wouldn't be prepared to back that. 'Work?' he retorted. 'Me work? I've only just emerged from camouflage. Was I brilliant! Anything I painted stood out five miles up.'

Helena bore down on us, shouting that she wasn't going to stand for any art talk tonight, and that it was her party, not mine.

'That's right,' said Jane, 'you stand up to him. If anything gets out of my depth I shall go home. Can't we play rude paper games? Very simple ones, of course.'

'This is my birthday,' said Helena untruthfully, 'so I shall choose what we'll do. We'll have an old-fashioned musical evening. Everyone does something.'

'None of the things I do is musical,' Crandell murmured. 'I should have to be Audience.'

'No one is going to be audience,' she insisted, 'not even Johnny Field here, are you Johnny?' She clutched at him as he passed with a tray, making him drop it. Luckily it had held only two glasses, both empty; but both smashed. 'There!' she scolded, 'isn't that just like you? Now you can go and get the dustpan – you know where it is – and sweep it up.'

He moved forward to the door, then stopped, and came back. 'It wasn't my fault,' he said, 'because you joggled me. If you got the dustpan and I swept it up, wouldn't that be fair?'

I was so astounded by this spark of courage, courage amounting almost to discourtesy, that I said Hooray, good for Field, and that to save controversy I would clean up the mess myself. I did not find the brush at once. By the time I returned I found Helena briskly organizing her concert and ignoring Field who, standing at her elbow, was trying to apologize.

It developed into that kind of party at which the guests are sharply divided into two categories: comfortable and uncomfortable. The smiling taciturn Clemency, Charmian, Jane, and Tennant – the last had promised with startling alacrity to recite *Kubla Khan* – were happy enough. Nina Crandell, perceptive, sensitive (I liked her, Helena said afterwards, because she admired my books, which is probably some of the truth but not all of it), was plainly uneasy, trying to mask this uncomprehended unease by a somewhat over-eager co-operation; Crandell looked embarrassed and kept glancing at the bookshelves as if he would do anything for a quiet read; Bill Swain murmured quietly to me, 'Doesn't old Helena get in a tear these days?' and Field went quietly out of the room.

The compulsion to achieve, on the spur of the moment, some kind of public performance can bring about an extraordinary revelation of character. People yield, under cover of farce, to hidden desires, look longingly backwards at withered ambitions. Clemency, a painting stepped down benevolently from the frame, sang *Only a Rose* with great enjoyment and a very flat and reedy voice, Charmian vamping the accompaniment. Tennant recited *Kubla Khan* without expression but with obvious appreciation, raising his voice in a surprised fashion on the last line as if there should be at least another stanza, if only he could remember it. Jane Elvorden sang *Water Boy* in an American accent so embarrassing that I felt I should be unable to meet her eyes for twenty-four hours or more. Crandell, sulking, rattled through Ogden Nash's poem about the Duck, but Nina sang, unaccompanied, a song from *Within the Gates*, and did it so charmingly that even Helena ceased to fidget and over-praise, saying simply, 'One night you must come along and sing me all the others you know, just for me alone.' I do not remember what was Charmian's contribution, nor Helena's; as for myself, I looked up the shortest of Dorothy Parker's stories and read it aloud. The concert took about three-quarters of an hour. The moment it was over Field reappeared.

'Ah, there you are!' Helena cried, looking thunderously upon him. 'Where have you been?'

'I'm sorry,' he murmured, 'I was feeling a bit off-colour. I went out for some air.'

'And now,' she said, 'you shall sing.'

'If you'll excuse me, Lady Archer –'

'Not a bit of it. None of us excuse you, do we?'

'I don't,' said Jane. 'I was forced to do my little piece and I think he should be, too.'

'You can read a little bit out of a book, as Claud did,' Nina suggested kindly to Field.

'I think we'll let him off,' Charmian said, speaking suddenly out of the depths of some apparently troubled conversation which she was holding with Tennant.

'Let him off,' Swain agreed.

'No, that's not fair,' said Clemency, 'he must suffer like the rest of us.'

'No one asked your opinion.' He slapped her cheek lightly with the back of his hand, gave her a kiss.

'I'll take a vote!' Helena gripped Field's arm firmly that he should not escape. 'Now then, all those for, hold up the right hand.'

He interrupted her. 'Even if the ayes have it, I'm afraid I'd still have to say no.' She glared at him. He stared back at her with the agonized determination of Casabianca.

'Mother's behaving badly,' Charmian whispered, as she brushed by me to get a drink, 'stop her.'

'Come on, Helena,' I said, 'be merciful. Field's coming out with me now, anyway, to make coffee.' I swept him away before she could protest, leaving her painted with a scowl which, for a second or so, she forgot to remove.

In the kitchen he said to me: 'I'm a lousy party man, I'm afraid. I've no sporting spirit. I do hope I haven't hurt Lady Archer's feelings, because she's been awfully good to me.'

I tried to reassure him by stating that if Helena's feelings were hurt occasionally it would be a good thing. He laughed rather ashamedly, repeating that he still wouldn't like to do it.

When we returned with coffee the party had sunk down like too bright a fire into a steady but not very warming glow. Nina was talking to Jane and Helena, Charmian and Tennant were listening to some arid and scholarly joke of Crandell's, and Bill Swain, in silence, was kissing Clemency's sweet and resilent cheek. By eleven o'clock all our guests were dispersed and Helena, saying she was tired, had gone to have her bath.

Though I was conscious myself of an uncommon tiredness, as if I had just passed through some period of stress, I did not feel like sleep. I sat reading over the fire for over two hours, and was just preparing to go to bed when Helena, in dressing-gown and feathered slippers, hair set in combs beneath a blue net, came quietly in and sat down opposite me. She groped about her for a cigarette and smoked for a while in silence.

'Can't sleep?' I asked her at last.

She countered, 'Did the party go off all right? Did you think it did, Claud?'

'I think everyone enjoyed it,' I replied cautiously.

'Why did that damned young Field get the needle? It was only fun.'

'He's no good at fun.'

'Well, he should be.' She sighed, and poked a pale spire of flame out of the falling coals. 'I don't like that man Tennant. Is he trying to cut Evan out?'

'Somehow I don't think so.'

'Charm doesn't seem to like him.'

'I thought not, certainly.'

'Your Jane made a horrible noise with her song. So did the porky girl in the picture frock. Crandell's wife is all right. I bet she was a professional once. She sang everyone else off their

heads, and she wasn't trying to do it; she was trying not to.'
Helena paused and for a moment brightened. 'Don't you love
talking people over? It makes them seem so much more interesting than they are.'

She talked on about them for several moments, then was
caught by a yawn. Her face softened into a sadder age, and was
coarsened by it. 'I'm all in.'

'You look it. Why don't you go to bed?'

'I'm too tired to move. Listen, Claud.' The youth returned
to her like life returning to the dead, blazing anguished and
purposeful in her coal-black eye, pouring along her hands and
moving them to expression.

'What is it?'

'I'm lonely here. Often you're not in till late. We've got a
room doing nothing and money's short.'

'Don't be silly. Of course it's not short.'

'I could do with more,' she insisted stubbornly. 'The loneliness is the worst, though. I must have people around me or
I shall rust out.' I knew something was coming, some new
fantasy, some plan hastily conceived and most desperately
held. I kept quiet, waiting for her to tell it me.

'Listen, Claud,' she said, 'I've got to have Johnny Field
back.'

PART TWO

Chapter One

ON VE-Day Charmian and I were both on leave and alone in the flat, as Helena had taken John Field down for a few days to the picturesque but insanitary cottage in Kent which, against the advice of us all, she had rented on a seven-year lease. They had gone down by hired car, carrying with them a great deal of junk that she supposed would look nice in rural surroundings, together with a box of tools, several cans of paint and a roll of linoleum.

'John will be busy,' said Charmian, as we walked slowly along the streets where flags hung limply beneath a thunderous sky. 'I wish she wouldn't fag him so. I suppose he enjoys it, but it embarrasses me. He must enjoy it or he wouldn't do it. It fills me with horror, I'm always expecting his heart to give out. However, he took all the trouble to go to the doctor and ask if a little lino-laying would hurt him, and the doctor said, "No, not in moderation." Helena was delighted.'

It was quiet where we were, all the celebrations, I supposed, being effected in the West End. I felt unaccountably depressed, my spirits at rock-bottom, and my head was heavy with a headache only partially repressed by too many aspirins. There was a quietude in the world, or so it seemed to me, more ominous than the noise of war. I wondered whether Helena was allowing Field to rise occasionally, in the intervals of tacking down linoleum, to drink to victory.

'Is he going to live here for ever?' Charmian said irritably. 'I don't mind indulging mother to an extent, but I am so tired of his damned politeness. He's the sort of man who's always apologizing for himself without meaning it.'

This surprised me. 'You think he doesn't mean it?'

'Oh, no.' She looked at me as if I were a child too foolish to grasp a simple lesson. 'He apologizes simply because he wants to be underrated. He feels life's easier that way.'

'Helena doesn't make it so easy for him.'

'Oh, he's the head cook and bottle washer, I admit; he works like a black. But I didn't mean that. I mean, he's so absorbed in himself that he doesn't want to be jerked out of it. He's a navel-contemplator,' she added, in a kind of giggling anger.

We passed down a side street where a children's tea-party was in progress, tables laid down the middle of the roadway. The children, in festive clothes, some of them wearing whole dresses of bunting, each with a patriotic emblem of some kind, were stuffing rather quietly through an enormous meal of sandwiches, cakes blanketed with soya-flour marzipan, jellies made of black-currant purée and lease-lend orange juice; the heads of the little girls, specially combed, looked meek and defenceless. Round about them the mothers crowded and beamed, their faces soft with love and with the joy that to-night, and all next week, there would be no bombs to frighten, to maim, or to destroy the girls and boys who had never before known peace. Each mother thought her own child the most clever and the most beautiful.

Charmian stood still, and was silent. She was neat in her dark green dress, her hair tidily done, her lips painted; but she looked tired and none too well, I did not speak to her. After a few moments she took my arm and drew me away. We turned back into King's Road. 'That gave me the only faint stirrings of victory emotion I've had today.'

'I haven't been so rorty myself,' I told her.

She began to speak again of Field, complaining about him and about her mother, asking why we should have to put up with a damned lodger anyway, and why he couldn't see that he wasn't wanted. She paused only because she was crying and could no longer speak steadily.

'What's the matter?' I asked her, refusing to pretend that I had not noticed her misery.

'Oh, don't take any notice of me!' She gasped, and smiled with all her teeth, the picture of distress. 'It's just one thing after the other. War-strain, I suppose. And then, Evan not coming home as I'd hoped. Being alone –' She stopped.

'Do you miss him all that much?'

Her glance flashed at me, a bright light instantly obscured. 'I don't really know.'

'But it's nasty being alone.'

'Nasty, yes. . . . Claud: you don't like neurotics.'

'No. No one who is one does.'

'You're not neurotic.'

'Doggedly not. Are you?'

'I try not to be. But lately – I'll tell you if you won't laugh.'

'I wouldn't laugh.'

'You might. You might laugh because you thought it would shake me up a bit and be good for me.'

We had come back to the flat. I opened the door and she went in before me, walked straight into the front room and sat down precisely in the middle of the big settee, as if it were the dock. I could see that she was losing control of herself, and that any sort of 'firm handling' would be the worst thing in the world for her just now. She wanted to talk, to be understood, to be allowed to cry.

'Tell me all about it,' I said.

'I'm frightened –' and for a moment her teeth actually chattered.

'What of?'

'Do you know how I've felt lately? As if I couldn't see outside myself any longer, only look *in* the whole time at my own thoughts. I always used to day-dream a lot. Now I can't stop it. It's been like that for a long time – nothing outside of me is real. I see you, and Mother, and Field, and everyone else, as though you're on the other side of a sheet of glass. Even when you speak to me your voices seem far away. I get into a state of panic that perhaps it will always be like this, that I shall always be locked up inside myself. It's horrible.'

I told her as gently as I could that this feeling arose, most probably, from some physical cause which a tonic would set right. 'After all, you've had a time of it. You never cared about army life, and I don't think you enjoyed the raids.'

'Did anyone?'

'No. But there was a minority of curious temperaments that were actually incapable of fear. You weren't one of them, and nor was I.' I had the persistent feeling that what she was trying to confess to me, beneath all these words, was a state of lovelessness. She had retreated into herself because she wanted to escape from Sholto.

'It's not war, I don't think, nor raids. I don't know what it is. But I look at you now, and you seem to me at the wrong end of a pair of opera glasses.' As she spoke she did stare at me intently, like a short-sighted person trying anxiously to focus sight upon an important detail, such as the number of an approaching bus or a name upon a programme.

'It'll pass,' I said.

'I hope to God it will,' she cried out passionately. 'I am so damned unhappy! . . . Now tell me lots of other people are unhappy too, that lots of people are starving, tell me how much worse off I'd have been in Belsen –'

'I won't tell you anything at all if you carry on like that, I won't try to help you.'

'No,' said Charmian, slumping suddenly from the sincere to the histrionic, 'no one will try to help me. No one can.'

I was relieved by this touch of the theatrical, for it showed me that she was at least vaguely conscious of an audience. I got up and brought her a glass of sherry, the last drink of any kind in the house.

Though she swallowed it down angrily it helped her to an extent, for she had a sudden desire to turn her violent emotion upon something other than herself. Rising suddenly she crossed the room to the bookshelf on which Cecil's photograph stood, and ran her hand across the glass. 'I loved Cecil! Don't you dare go and marry that fool of a Jane. I want you so much to be happy with someone, but *not* her.'

'I won't,' I said. 'That clinches it.'

She turned to me, her eyes expressionless with tears. 'What you must think of me, making all this shine about myself –'

'Look, I'm not feeling too good either. It's Victory that does it.'

'Victory,' she agreed docilely. Then she shuddered. 'How people can yell and scream! All I can think of is the horror and the waste of the past and the terrible business it will be building things up again. It makes me feel tired before I begin.'

'Before *you* begin,' I mocked at her, but she was still too upset for the mildest joke.

'You know what I mean!'

'All right, all right, I know.'

I looked out of the window – at peace, at the clouds hanging low, like the canopy of Collins' 'terribly strange bed,' in a sulphurous sky. I had been kept awake most of the night by the violent thunderstorm which had seemed to me, in the atavistic fevers of the small hours, symbolic. At the beginning of the war (so long ago!) surely there had been a storm too? In those small hours the emblem of the war to me had been the compound at Buchenwald. Not the heaps of bones; but the trotting, tottering, mindless living thing in the clown's suit of white and blue stripes, that survived over them. The air of this victory day was thick with the breath of the dead.

'. . . all those children . . .' Charmian's voice came to me, clear and of the present, intruding like a shaft of painful light into the subterranean horror in which (as the irritant sound made me realize) I was taking a degree of disgusting pleasure.

Under the window ran a child of eight or nine, a girl in a faded blue satin party-dress far too chilly for the day, her thin straw-coloured pigtails looped together with a strip torn from a Union Jack.

'. . . those children having their tea in the street,' Charmian went on, and I felt suddenly that fear of the future was dispersed and that, in the moment when it had obsessed me, I had been contemptible. It seemed to me that a high wind was blowing far off, rending the clouds to pieces and giving air into a million choked, barred and darkened rooms. If everyone, I thought, sat down and shivered on the rubble-heap, as I have been doing, then there damned well would be no hope for the children. Poor devils, so trusting, so calmly dependent upon the hopeless, the sick, and the suicidal!

'The hopeless, the sick, and the suicidal,' I said to Charmian, 'ought to be bloody-well ashamed of themselves.'

'I wasn't suicidal,' she protested indignantly.

'I didn't mean you. I meant all the people who were feeling as I felt a few minutes ago.'

She smiled at me. Her eyes were dry and there was in them a look of relief. 'Do you remember our *collage*?' she asked. 'Let's do some now.'

On one of my leaves, before she had joined the army, we had had a mania for cutting bits and pieces of photographs and advertisements from the newspapers and pasting them eclectically on to a sheet of cardboard, with results that were comic, or horrible, or so indelicate that Helena was outraged. I did not want to play this game again, because to pick up any abandoned activity seemed too much like spineless and futile groping for *le temps perdu*, but to please Charmian and to hold her attention away from her own unhappiness, I found scissors, paste, brown paper, and a bundle of old magazines stored for fire-lighting in the kitchen cupboard. We had just started to amuse ourselves when the telephone rang.

It was Helena, warring against a background of noise. 'That you, Claud? Happy VE-Day.'

'Thank you. Are you celebrating?'

'Am I what? Wait a minute, I can't hear you.' I heard her voice, diminished, shouting to someone else. 'Oh, do stop that hammering a minute! I can't hear myself speak!' The noise ceased. Then, to me: 'That's better. It was Johnny. He's nailing the carpet down for me. It has to be nailed or else it rucks the whole time. I've fallen over twice already. What was that you were saying?'

'I said, are you celebrating?'

'Well . . .' A pause. 'There seems so much to do still.' She added smugly, 'We're celebrating in our hearts.'

'Pooey,' I said.

'It may be to you, but not to me.' To Field, aside: 'Don't bring that thing in here. It belongs in the hall.' To me: 'How are you? How's Charm?'

'All right. She's here. Do you want to speak to her?'

Helena said yes. Charmian went to the telephone, spoke for a few moments, then hung up.

'What did Helena really want?' I asked her.

She pasted a female bust, advertising brassières, on to a vacuum cleaner, and admired the effect. 'Oh, nothing. Only congratulations.'

'One-and-eightpence for that!'

'Mother likes to celebrate,' said Charmian.

We played our game for a little while, and then she rose, saying she must dress. She was going out with Norman Tennant.

'Do you like that chap?'

She shrugged. 'He's all right. He's Evan's friend, so I have to be sociable.' I was surprised to see her flush brightly, and it occurred to me with a sense of shock that she might be in love with Tennant. All her life Charmian had been good-humoured and affectionate but never particularly communicative, and since her marriage the instinct for secrecy had grown more marked. I wondered why, growing up in the care of a fond and high-spirited Helena, a mother without the least tendency to prying or soul-raking, Charmian should have felt so great a need to keep her own counsel. Possibly, I thought, it was because when confronted with a mystery of any kind Helena leaped at once to an explanation and for ever after, no matter how false it might be, upheld it.

I was still bothered by Charmian's reticence over the money and over the cause of her evident unhappiness. The fact that I had drawn my own conclusions with regard to the latter made me still more eager that she should offer me a degree of confidence. With it, I could have helped her. Without it, I was powerless.

'Is he calling for you here?'

'No. I'm meeting him at the –' She mentioned an hotel.

'Will you get in?'

'Oh, yes. Apparently he booked a table for VE-night a couple of months ago. He's bringing his sister and her husband, so we shall have to royster and junket.' She sighed, and looked depressed.

'Why go, then?'

'I told you. He's Evan's friend. One has to do these things.'

She went to her bedroom and returned in a black hat and dress, looking very pretty indeed despite the slight touch of absurdity that formal clothes always gave her. She was rather too tall for the lightness of her build, and had the slight stoop of the overgrown schoolgirl ashamed at finding herself in a class of children half a head shorter than she.

At the door she turned. 'I oughtn't to have sprung this on you, ought I? Only I didn't really know about it till this afternoon. Would you like to come along? I'm sure Norman would like it.'

'Well, I wouldn't. Don't worry about me, I don't want to junket or royster. I've a lot to do.'

'Are you seeing Jane?'

'She's in the country.'

'Oh, well –' Charmian lingered. 'You're quite sure you'll be all right? I mean, it might be a bit morbid for you alone.' In the last strong light of the fading day her face looked washed-out and exhausted.

79

I told her firmly that I liked being alone, that I wasn't alone nearly enough, and that I was going to have a much better time than she was. This seemed to ease her conscience. She nodded to me and went out, running down the stairs at a speed that might have indicated either her eagerness to keep the appointment or to escape from memory of the afternoon's emotional upset.

I cleared up the *collage* mess, got out the manuscript on which I was working and made myself comfortable on the settee. I was not comfortable for long, however, as I remembered that sooner or later I should have to eat, and I thought I would rather disturb myself now than in an hour's time; so I went out into the kitchen and cut some sandwiches. What I had said to Charmian, that I was never alone enough, was true; but the strange thing was that when some arrangement of accidents did afford me solitude, I could never settle down sufficiently to enjoy it. Some demon would work to destroy my peace, urging me constantly to rise and perform some nonessential task, persuading me that it was necessary I should go out to buy some article or other, that I should make some telephone call or write some idiotic letter. By the time I had done all this Helena, or Charmian, or Field would have returned to the flat, or a visitor would have called, leaving me thoroughly irritable at the thought of my lost loneliness, so much desired, so gratuitously frittered away.

Even now, when I returned to my work, I felt a restlessness in the evening so distracting that after a while I got up and went to sit by the window, looking idly down into the quiet street. The sky was quite overcast now and the rain falling. A lorry-load of soldiers went by, the men all singing, but the song had a defiant sound as if the singers were the last living beings left upon earth. The silence in the flat was thick and watchful. I felt that I had only a yard's space of free air left between myself and the crush of invisible creatures so tightly packed that their arms were glued to their sides, their forward-thrusting heads held motionless by the terrible pressure.

I wished I had gone out with Charmian, had rammed myself into her invitation, or that I could recapture the mood of contempt which had filled me at consideration of my own pessimism. This, at least, was not a good day on which to be alone. To save myself from falling into the horror that had seized

Charmian, the introversion that makes a solitary cell of the body, I tried to peg my attention to the figure of a woman walking very slowly just over the way, as if she had all the solitude of the world at her disposal and did not care for the gift. As she passed into the range of the lamplight I saw her more clearly. She was middle-aged, so slender and sharp-angled that she would have given an impression of girlishness save for the low and swollen calves of her legs. In an attempt to conceal this defect, she wore her skirts a little longer than was the fashion. Her dress was brown and over it was a loose top-coat of some white woollen stuff. As she raised her head to look along the houses on my side of the street, I saw her face very clearly. It was a beautiful face, though haggard and without peace, the eyes set long and straight in the circular shadows of the sockets, the temples protuberant and shining as an infant's under the light hair, which was combed childishly backwards and allowed to fall in elastic curls upon the narrow, slightly hunched shoulders. The straight mouth moved as if in rehearsal of some vital speech. I thought she was most probably the kind of woman who, impelled by anxiety to rehearse the sentence with which she will enter a room, inevitably uses that sentence no matter how incongruous the mood or the conversation upon which she may intrude.

Suddenly she dashed across the road into the hood of the portico. Our bell rang.

When I opened the door to her I saw that her features, lovely through a veil of lamplight and twilight, were at close quarters too emphatic for beauty. The nose was so sharply chiselled as to give an impression of pain caused by incision; the lips were raised from the plane about them in the manner of bas-relief and had a deep natural redness less pleasing than the convention of paint. The eyes were bright and fine, but the brows above were untidy, thick, emphasized with some kind of dye that clung to the flesh beneath.

'You must forgive me troubling you on a day like this and send me away if it isn't convenient, but could I have a word with Major Pickering?'

I introduced myself, waited for her response.

'My name is Dilys Olney, Mrs Dilys Olney. I knew your stepfather, he often spoke about you. If I could have a word with you . . .' She shot glances about the hall, terrified yet bold glances, as if expecting rebuff but being determined to face it and beat it down. 'Perhaps now isn't the time.'

I told her I was alone and asked her in, stepping aside and indicating the front room. This appeared to throw her into a panic. She made a quick step forward in the direction of Field's bedroom, touched the handle, said, 'How silly of me,' then made a movement of vague retreat like the Blind Man in the game, bewildered from being spun about in the dark. I touched her arm and impelled her in the right direction, cleared a space for her on the settee and again waited.

'Could I smoke?' she asked me, plunging her hands into the big pockets of her coat and bringing them up again crusted with small articles – lipsticks, puffs, pencils, fobs, bits of jewellery, matches, bus tickets – like drowned creatures made coralline by weed and bubble and shell and the jewelled parasites of the sea. 'Oh, dear, I'm so untidy. I ought to carry a bag but I don't, and pockets seem so handy –' Finding with triumph a squashed and greyish-looking cigarette, she thrust the remainder of the mess back out of sight.

'That doesn't look very nice,' I said and offered my Player's.

'No,' she insisted, 'no, I can't smoke yours.'

She was a long time bending over it, using her flame-lit eyes at me in a manner half-bold, half-scared. She took my wrist and steadied it. 'Excuse me – so sorry. Shaking like a hag.' I was trying to guess her age, placing her between forty-five and fifty.

She drew on her horrible cigarette and seemed to relax. 'Well,' she said at last. Then she stared at a rather hideous fish of pink and amber glass that Helena had bought at the Paris Exhibition in 1937, and which she pretended to believe would bring her bad luck if not conspicuously displayed.

'How lovely,' said Mrs Olney, 'how very lovely! May I see it?' She rose and seized it, breathed upon it, turned it upside down, lost interest in it entirely and put it back in the wrong place. Then she sat back heavily upon the settee and said: 'I oughtn't to have come, I know it. But Daniel always said you were so nice, and I felt I could ask you.'

'Now look, Mrs Olney,' I said, 'will you tell me what it is? I'll help if I can.'

'One doesn't like to talk about money. Money's so *beastly*, don't you think? One can talk about sex and religion without feeling defiled, but money soils you.'

I said, to encourage her, that I thought money was rather nice, and that I was never embarrassed by it.

'Oh, I can't bear to talk of it! One has to have enough, I know, but so little's always done for me. It's only when even the *little* seems a bit short, if you understand me . . . ?'

I replied that I understood.

'You see, I . . .' Her gaze returned to the glass fish. She said feverishly, 'Yes, it is adorable. I always did go crazy over *tiny* things like that. I used to ask Daniel about collecting by the hour.' She removed her cigarette from her lips. 'Damn, it's gone out. Now why should it? I thought it was hard to draw. Oh, look! There's a tear in it, a little weeny three-cornered tear. Now isn't that a shame, when cigarettes are so short, selling ones with tears in them? . . . . Yes, thank you, I will accept yours. If I can't smoke I die.'

Then she stared at me and said: 'I heard Dan left some money to some of his friends. He was terribly generous. I thought if he'd remembered them he might just possibly have remembered me too, only when I didn't hear anything I suppose he couldn't have. Then I thought, sometimes the executors don't quite know where to find people, or perhaps in an estate like Daniel's things get overlooked.'

I said: 'I'm awfully sorry, Mrs Olney, you were not mentioned in the Will.'

'You're sure? Amalie Scowan was. I heard about it from someone.'

'I'm quite sure.'

She seemed to age with misery; it made an absurdity of the way she did her hair.

'I don't know what you must think of me, asking like that. Only' – she told me she had a son at a famous school – 'fees are awful. I wish everyone *had* to send their children to board schools, dukes and road-sweepers alike. Then people like me wouldn't have to be drained and drained.' She got up. 'That's that, then. I must make my apologies. You've been very patient.'

Pity for her, and a good deal of curiosity, made me say, 'You were a great friend of Dan's?'

'The last,' she said angrily, tears in her eyes, 'so far as I know. Yes. The last.' She went towards the door and I followed her. I thought she would go without another word said, but instead she began talking as if to herself. 'He bought a lampshade for Amalie from me. She sent him to my shop because she wanted to do me a good turn, but when he saw me he liked me more than her. She wasn't actually angry because she wanted to marry Scowan anyway, and it made things easier, only of course there's the jealousy there, she's no saint and you've always got the fundamental resentment, haven't you? We got on terrifically, Daniel and me, because he cared about artistic things and knew a tremendous lot about them, and of course they were absolutely my passion, though I hadn't any training. So you see I could learn from him, and you know how men do adore to teach women things.'

I saw them together, the haggard beauty with her intense looks listening, hands locked, knuckles like hardened milk, to the radiant fat man pouring forth his knowledge in the runaway joy that is dependent upon the absence of any person able to state that the half of it is nonsense.

'They *do* adore it, you know – let them teach you, let them tell you, let them lay down the law and they'll love you for ever. Or not for ever, because there was someone I had the idea of marrying. You see, there was Dennis to think of, with that damned school eating everything up, and after all, when you're no longer a girl you do realize passion isn't everything. But it didn't come off like Amalie's marriage, worse luck, and all it did was to scare off Daniel. He was terribly jealous, sickeningly so; people didn't realize that. They thought because he was a big man, and rich, and he'd got a title, he didn't have to be. But he was, and it always seemed to me so silly. I mean, not like a man being jealous of his *wife* . . .'

I took advantage of the trance into which she had fallen to say: 'He didn't leave so much as was expected.'

'Not so much to Lady Archer, I know – everyone knows that – Amalie looked it up at Somerset House, which was a rotten thing to do in my opinion. Lady Archer didn't get so much (I oughtn't to be talking like this to you) and everyone was surprised, but I wasn't so very.' All the time she spoke she was smoothing down her skirt, down and down from hip to thigh.

'My husband was a Commander in the Navy, not war-time, regular. I've been a widow for eleven years. Dennis is only fourteen. It all devolves on me. Boys need a father.'

She had lost the thread of what she had been saying before, and she looked at me rather wildly.

'Why weren't you so very surprised?' I asked her.

'Because he was jealous of her, too, horribly. Not men. I never heard anything like that (why do you let me talk? I oughtn't to be saying all this to you, but it's your fault), I never heard anything like that, but he used to say she was mad about you and Miss Pickering, that she'd never loved him and that she was always having secrets with you two that he couldn't share.' She looked at me furiously, as if this had been my doing. 'People didn't realize how Daniel *noticed* things, how half the time he was being jolly it was only on the surface.'

She stopped abruptly, staring down at herself, moving a leg forward to study it, then withdrawing it stealthily.

'I must go. I shouldn't have come.'

'I wish I could have helped you,' I said.

'It's not for myself. It's for Dennis. You know how people do forget how long things take, especially executors of a large estate, with all they've got to do. I only thought – if there had been anything it would have made such a difference.' She stared at me brightly, briskly. I felt sure she would burst into tears the moment she got outside. 'But there wasn't, so that's that, isn't it?' She shot out her hand. 'Thank you so much, then.'

Though I opened the door for her she made no move to go, raking over and over in her big pockets. At last she withdrew a rather grubby card, dog-eared, one corner missing, and pushed it into my hand with a modest air, as if she were giving me alms.

'In case you ever meet anyone who wants lampshades, I can do them to match any scheme. Old maps, you know, or views of London, or just futuristic sorts of pattern which people still go for, though you mightn't believe it – I hate doing this, pushing my wares, I mean, but business is business, isn't it? Thank you so much, Major. You've been terribly kind.'

Before I could make any remark, any pause, she had gone, leaving behind her a stain upon the air of some perfume which must have had a delayed action, since I had not noticed it during her visit.

Chapter Two

NATURALLY I said nothing to Helena, upon her return, of Mrs Olney, though I was perversely tempted to do so in order to witness what would surely have been an historic explosion of rage. Nor did I say anything to Charmian. Mrs Olney, I felt, was my own affair, my own curiosity; the pity, even the odd affection that had touched me, was quite unlikely to touch anyone else.

Helena looked well after her week in Kent and was full of fun. The fact that Field shrank from displays of exuberance certainly had not escaped her, for I could detect behind her public buffoonery a private grin. It pleased her to alarm him, to make him frightened of what she might say next. I felt that it was only laziness which kept him under our roof at all; it was comfortable there, the food was as good as it could be now that I had checked Helena's more open black-market activities (she could still find plausible explanations for some of the items which appeared upon our table), and his room was as pleasant as our efforts could make it. Nevertheless, beneath his almost Proustian politeness, his eagerness to oblige, I sensed an irritation so strong that I still wondered why it had not overcome indolence.

'I've had Johnny's nose to the grindstone,' Helena said with a loud laugh, 'and his knees to the lino. I've had the pants off him.'

'Well, I think we're pretty straight now,' he murmured, smiling diffidently. He was trying to read; he had been trying to read for the last half-hour, but Helena, though never actually addressing him, was doing her best to make this impossible.

'Now, now, now, don't you take all the credit to yourself! Who painted the kitchen cupboard and all the woodwork, when you said the smell made you sick?'

'I'd have done it but for that weakness,' Field said placatingly. 'I shouldn't have been much use to you if I had tried it.'

'Conquer yourself!' Helena flung up her hand and was the Statue of Liberty. 'Mind over matter!' She began to sing, 'Oh, dear, what can the matter be, Johnny's so sick if he paints.'

'Oh, let the poor chap read,' I said, 'he deserves a rest.'

'He can't be interested in that old muck.' Helena switched the books from his hands, flipped over the pages. 'Dickens! Nobody reads Dickens now, only poor kids in school. My father had a set and it smelled of Dickens, a sort of special smell, it smelled as the illustrations looked. Pooh!'

She put the book face downwards, open, on his head, where it sat for a second like a little roof. 'Love in a cottage,' said Helena, 'look at him, love in a cottage!'

'If you don't leave John alone,' Charmian murmured, glancing up from her mending, 'I shall retire in umbrage to the bedroom. I get enough high spirits in the army.'

He had removed the book from his head and was trying again to read it. Helena slapped his shoulders. 'He understands me. He knows my flighty little ways.' She moved rhythmically about the room, bouncing on the soles of her feet.

> '"I'm none of your flighty girls,
> Your hi-tiddley-itey girls,
> Since my old stick-in-the-mud . . ."'

Would anyone like some tea?

> ". . . took me for his wife. . . ."'

You would, I know, Johnny, you little soak. So would old stuffy Claud with his little moustache, looking like a wet week.' She went towards the kitchen, her voice diminishing as she passed from our view, like Chaliapin's in the 'Song of the Volga Boatman'.

> '"Fancy me a-smoking fags,
> Riding bikes and wearing bags. . . ."'

A moment's silence while she filled the kettle.

> '"And leaving off me bits of rags
> At my time of life."'

Charmian put down her mending. 'Don't let Mother tease you, John. I bet she fagged your life out at the cottage.'

'Oh, I rather like manual work. It does me good.' He shut the book and reached up to put it on the mantelshelf above his head. 'Back to work tomorrow.'

'How's the Nineveh Press?' I asked him.

'Oh, horrible. Mallion's decided that we ought to start a small fiction list, so he's going to kick off with a dreadful little novel by one of his friends. It's called *The Blood Bank*.'

'What's it about?'

'Oh, about some young lad in a field hospital awaiting an amputation. He dreams he turns into blood and they put him into a blood bank, and he finds it's a sort of totalitarian country where the red corpuscles are always oppressing the white corpuscles, and the worst of it is, he's a white one. Actually,' Field added, 'it's all an attack on Russia.'

Charmian laughed and said: 'He's original, anyway.'

'Not so very,' he replied mournfully, 'not in general conception, actually. Mallion reads a whole lot of them.' He glanced at the clock. 'I'm dog-tired. Do you think Helena would be very offended if I went off to bed early?'

'Whether she minds or not,' Charmian said, 'you go. Claud will bring your tea in to you and you can be really cosy and secluded.'

Though he looked wistfully at the beauty of this prospect he made no move to rise.

'Go on,' I urged him, 'escape while you can.'

'It's not a matter of escaping! Don't think that, please. It's only that I feel a bit under the weather tonight. It may be a cold coming on.'

But he would not move for all our persuasions and soon it was too late, for Helena had entered with the tea-tray and Jane Elvorden had come to pay us an hour's visit.

'Lady Archer, you've got second sight! You must have known I was coming. I was longing for some tea, actually longing.'

Helena looked at her without much favour; had the difference of age between them been less by even ten years, she would have regarded her as a rival. 'At your time of life,' she said, 'I preferred whisky. You know Johnny Field, don't you, Jane?'

'I do indeed. Hullo, Charmian, you're looking brilliant.'

'I'm not feeling it. My leave's up tomorrow.'

'I admire you stupendously. Claud, I've got a bone to pick with you.'

'What's that?' I did not feel strong enough for Jane tonight; even her beauty seemed too bright a light in too small a room.

'Oh, merely neglect. Simply neglect. Not a word from you through all the whoopsings.'

'You were in the country.'

'But not unphoneable! I gave you my number. I was pining for a friendly voice. I felt absolutely in another world, me being miles away from the tumult and shouting, stuck down with a cousin and dogs.' I knew from the very fact of her choosing this public occasion to make her facetious reproaches that she was hurt and annoyed.

'I'm sorry. I was feeling rather depressed right through the whole thing and I couldn't think of anything cheerful to say.'

'What an excuse! Mr Field, would you make your young woman an excuse like that?'

'However feeble it sounds,' he said, 'I think it's true. Claud said he felt bleak the whole time, and I can understand it.'

Helena sprang upon him. 'You can understand it! Are you telling me that you were miserable down in Kent?'

'I didn't mean ... I had a marvellous time actually, only there was that sort of feeling. Not conscious, really, but a kind of hangover –'

'Some people are easy to please,' said Helena triumphantly. 'I'm damned if I'd call lino-laying having a marvellous time!'

'It was your lino,' he murmured gracefully, and his ears reddened.

'There he was,' she cried, 'tick-tack-toe, tick-tack-toe, just like the carpenter in the song, crawling all over the floor for hours and hours with his little hammer, just putting up a hand to grab a bit of cheese off the table-edge, and then he says he was having a marvellous time!' Her face glowed with a dark radiance, a lantern for the flame of her pleasure. Standing over him, pushing the slopped cup between his hands, she was avid for dominance.

'We all have our own ideas,' Jane said, laughing, 'I must

say it's not mine.' She looked at me, inviting me to join in the joke.

'Helping you *is* a pleasure,' Field said quietly to Helena. 'I'd like you to believe that.'

She appealed to us all, arms flung wide. 'Why, if it hadn't been a pleasure he wouldn't have done it, would he?'

'No, of course not!' cried Jane.

'That'll do, Mother,' Charmian said softly.

'He knows he'd have done it. He wouldn't have dared not to!' Helena roared with fun. 'Old Johnny, nose to the nails, bottom in the air – '

She stopped and regarded him. He was looking down into his cup, his face expressionless.

'Lovely frock, Jane,' said Charmian.

This was successful. Jane's attention was diverted from Field to the thought of her own beauty, a thought which never failed to make that beauty more brilliant. 'Oh, do you think so? Do you know what it is? My dear, it's *half* my last year's second-best black, and half Aunt Sarah's bridge coat, all merged together by *me* – believe it or not' – I believed it; she was an accomplished needlewoman – 'at one of those Make-Do-and-Mend classes! I read about them and thought I'd try one, so I plucked up my courage and went along, and lo!'

'Low is right,' said Helena, poking a finger at the neck line.

'Lady Archer, you are a dreadful woman. I shall cut you when next we meet in the highways and byways.'

Charmian yawned.

'Don't let me keep you up, pet,' said Helena, 'will you? Or you, Johnny.'

This was less a rebuke to us than a hint to Jane. She stayed for ten minutes longer and then rose to go, saying that I must see her out. In the hall she kissed me, saying, 'When next?'

'Not this week. What about Monday night?'

She nodded.

'I'll call for you at seven.'

'Lovely. Do we go cheap or gorgeous?'

'I'll tell you when the time comes.'

'Am I going off, do you think?'

'Why should you be?'

90

'Neglect. Your neglect. It makes me so *unsure*.' She kissed my cheek. 'Claud?'

'Yes?'

'I could find other fish in the sea.'

I told her I was certain of that, and opened the door for her.

'Lady A's terrific tonight,' she said, lingering.

'That's so.'

'Why can't Charmian stand me? I may look flash, but I'm very gentle and domestic underneath.'

I would not answer this, but went with her downstairs and impelled her out into a night dazzling with stars. At the corner of the street she turned and blew me a kiss, with a gesture lovely as Ellen Terry's in the Guenevere photograph.

I returned to the flat, where I found Field and Charmian gone to their rooms and Helena sitting in the window, angrily rustling through the pages of Field's book.

'How can you people read this stuff?' she asked rapidly. 'It's so dated.' She pointed derisively to the drawing of the Lammles on the seashore. 'Look at these awful clothes, look at him with his silly hat and whiskers, and her with her tiddly little gamp. So depressing! Makes you feel all choked up.' She thrust it under my nose. 'You smell! Even this copy's got the Dickens smell, all fusty and damp and airless.'

I took it from her hand and replaced it on the shelf. 'Look here, Helena! Why are you behaving so damned badly to Field?'

She was the picture of innocence. 'Me? I haven't been doing anything. What have I done, anyway? You tell me.'

'You know he loathes having attention drawn to him. He hates being an Aunt Sally, just as anyone else does who isn't completely degraded. What's the matter with you? He was throughly upset. He loathes any woman being what he calls coarse, too, and you know it.'

'Now phwat,' said Helena, with the faintest trace of brogue, 'did I say coarse but "bottom"?' For a second she was enjoying herself, enjoyment transcending even her sense of guilt.

I did not reply to this.

'Anyway,' she went on, defensive again, 'he must learn to take a joke. It's absurd, at his age, behaving like a nicely-brought-up little girl. Let him learn our ways.'

'Helena, if you don't stop making a fool of him, I'll tell him to get out of here. I'll find him rooms easily enough, and I'll see to it he takes them.'

She glared at me. 'He doesn't want to go. He's happy here. He and I understand each other, whatever you may think.'

'I'm warning you.'

'You're warning me! Who do you think you are? I remember slapping your head, young Claud. I remember slapping it right in the market at Bruges, and you dashing off howling at such a rate you barged into a basket of eggs and smashed the lot. You warning *me*!'

I would not be cozened back to friendship by this sly invitation to reminiscence.

'You stop it, or I'll turn Field out of here. You might remember, too, that he's a friend of mine, and that by making an ass of him you're insulting me.' This touch of drama on my part impressed her.

She stared at me. 'You're serious?'

'You'll see.' I gathered up my own books. 'I'm going to bed. Good night.'

On warm nights, such as this, Field and I both slept with our windows and doors open. I had been lying in bed for about an hour, reading and smoking, when I heard a knocking next door, and Helena's voice.

'Johnny. Johnny, are you awake?'

The sound of a light switched up, and Field's inaudible reply.

'Can I come in? Don't look at me, I'm in my *déshabille*.'

I could picture Helena's *déshabille*, the cherry silk gown swathed with a safety-pin (she had lost the sash weeks since) over the elaborate nightdress, the thick, short plait of white hair pulled over one shoulder to bristle on the still-resplendent flesh.

'You weren't asleep, Johnny, were you?'

'No, I wasn't really. Just lying awake. Come in, won't you?'

A creak. I guessed that she had sat down on the end of the bed, overhanging him like a rock. The door was pushed to a little.

'Look here, Johnny, you've got to make allowances for old women.'

A murmur from Field, probably something gallant regarding her age.

'No, you don't; I can't be flattered. I'm over all that.' Helena made no attempt to lower her voice; if no hearer were visible, then to her it was impossible that hearers should exist.

I wondered if I should get up and close my own door, realized that if I did so Field would only be embarrassed by the knowledge that I had heard these exchanges. And I did not want to close it. I was too interested in knowing how Helena would make her amends. Her voice, disembodied, had a rough sweetness that might easily have been mistaken for youth. It was compounded of horse-hair and honey.

'I was rude to you tonight. I went too far. I'm always going too far and most people don't mind, but the trouble is I never realize it when some people do.'

A laugh from Field, and a few rapid words.

'Don't you laugh it off. I played the fool, I know. I was just in the mood. I didn't mean anything by it.'

A silence. Then Field's voice, quite clear. 'But it always is me, isn't it? You do use me for a bit of fun, Helena, don't you?'

Another pause. Then: 'Thank God he can answer back! I didn't think he had it in him. Yes, I suppose I do.'

'Why?'

'I don't know. You seem to ask for it. Claud used to ask for it when he was little, and then he used to catch it. Now that he's got tough as old boots I have to leave him alone.'

Field spoke again; I could not catch the words, but the sound of them was rather angry.

'Yes, I know. I know. What you say's true. All the same . . .'

'. . . not a child.'

Her voice rose. 'That's about what you are, to me. Just because I think of you in that way, you ought to know I don't mean to hurt you.'

He said diffidently, charmingly, in a tone quite alien to the one he had previously used, 'Anyhow it's perfectly all right. I assure you it is. I never did know how to take jokes, as Claud would tell you.'

'Don't you dare stop me apologizing!' said Helena. He laughed, but she did not.

The curtains of my room blew inward in a gust of wind, fluttering like wings in the quiet light of the bedside lamp and flicking a match-box from the dressing-chest to the floor.

Helena said: 'What's that?'

A long silence. Field replied at last, 'I don't know. The cat or something. It's pretty late, isn't it?'

'Don't you go going off to sleep. I can't rest before I've settled things with you. Listen, Johnny, I'm sorry about to-night.' Neither of them spoke for a second or two, then Helena said explosively, 'Good God, you ought to be honoured, me making an apology to you! It's the first I've ever made. Isn't it a good one, or has the cat got your tongue?'

'It's quite all right, Helena. It's really *quite* all right. I wish you'd believe me. But if you just wouldn't do it in future –'

Mentally, I applauded his firmness.

'I won't. Though it'll be hard. Why don't you stand up for yourself? I never tease people who do.'

I could catch only a few words of his reply: '. . . all your kindness . . . not the sort who . . . '

I heard the springs of the bed creak as she rose, heard her pacing to and fro. I imagined Field's large and wondering eyes turned upon her imperial progress, imagined him fascinated, excited by his own boldness yet uncertain how durable it would be if she stayed much longer. The blankets must have been for him a refuge warm and sweet as the womb.

She said abruptly, so loudly that I was afraid Charmian would wake in the room on the other side of Field's, 'Claud says if I don't behave better to you he'll find you another place. Would you go?'

'Sometimes I feel I ought, you know – all the trouble I must be, and the way you all put up with me.'

'I don't want any politeness. I said, Would you go? You wouldn't be pushed about from pillar to post by Claud, would you?'

He shushed her, murmured something.

'He's snoring by now. And if he isn't he ought to know listeners hear no good of themselves. You don't want to go away, do you? Not with all my funny ways?'

Whatever his answer was it satisfied her. 'Good. It's all right, then?'

'Of course it's all right,' Field said, with such warmth and colour in his voice that the vision of his face was instantly sharpened in my mind. 'You're grand to me. I'm stupendously grateful.'

'So you ought to be,' she told him triumphantly. 'Well, I'm losing you your beauty sleep. Good night. Sleep well.'

As she passed my door she looked in. 'Were you listening?'

'I couldn't very well help it.'

'If you'd got any decency you'd have coughed or something.' She crept to my bedside. 'He won't go, see? Not even if you bother and badger him. I told you we understood each other.' Relief inspiring her to one last manifestation of fun she switched off my light and flung the eiderdown over my head. I heard her creep away, laughing, and this time it resembled that laughter of age which, like a slow poison, agitates the body to a multitude of small pains while only a bubble of it rises beyond the throat.

Whether her attitude towards Field changed immediately, I do not know. For the next few days I was so busy that I did not leave the War Office until nine or ten at night, and by that time was too tired to sit around talking. However, whether instantly or by degrees, Helena's attitude had altered. She ceased to treat Field as, in my boyhood, she had treated me, behaving towards him now with something of the mild, uncritical affection she showed to Charmian.

On those warm summer evenings he sat on the balcony outside our windows reading, with a kind of sad contempt, manuscripts for the Nineveh Press. As Charmian's leave was over and Helena had conceived one of her sudden and disastrous passions for altering all her clothes, Field and I were much alone together.

One night, needing a confidant, I told him about Mrs Olney. He put down the manuscript eagerly, inserting a match-stick to mark the place, and turned to me with interest.

'She sounds awful,' he said. 'You didn't tell Helena, surely?'

'I did not.'

'Daniel Archer seems to have been rather a bloody old man, if I may say so.'

'Oh, he was. And the odd thing is, it took most of the people who knew him years to realize it.'

'You didn't like him yourself, though.'

'Couldn't stick him. But he gave Helena a pretty good time, and he did his best for Charmian, so naturally I never made myself nasty.'

Field looked at Daniel's photograph, at the shining face, spectacled, button-nosed, beaming through the glass at us as through a window. 'A sort of goatish Pickwick.'

'Yes. He had his points though. His home life was equably run. He always had the decency not to let his right hand know what his left was doing. His bar sinister,' I added, feeling this a fairly smart remark.

'Though it must have come as a worse shock to Helena in the end.'

'Not really; she always supposed that the women to whom he left money were old flames, well doused before he married her. That's why it would be a bad thing if she heard about Mrs Olney.'

'Did he know anything about pictures?' Field gazed around the walls. I noticed always that when he looked at any evidence of wealth his eyes were mournful; not covetous, but renunciatory.

'He knew all the names that fetched money, and he bought them. He had no taste. Once he'd acquired a picture he never looked at it again unless he was showing it off to somebody. Not that I should complain. He left a few to me.'

'He wasn't good enough for Helena,' said Field with conviction. 'I think she's terrific.'

This was his easy word, covering a dozen compliments of the heart to which his speech could not soar.

'Compared with Mrs Olney, she certainly is.'

'I wonder what her shop's like?' His interest in our family affairs was avid; he liked us enough to want to identify himself with us by common knowledge and experience. Already he was falling into the habit of using our family jokes, and knowing the same degree as myself of surprise when they brought blankness to the face of a stranger.

I looked at the clock; it was half-past eight. 'Let's go up and see. It's only at Notting Hill Gate.'

He rose at once. 'That's an idea.'

I called out, 'Helena!'

96

She came in, holding up against herself a black dress into which she had pinned sleeves of red and white satin cut from some abandoned curtains. 'Yes, what is it? – I say, do you think this is going to look smart, or is it a bit daring? I got the idea from Jane.'

'You couldn't wear it at Mrs Sholto's,' I said.

'I wasn't asking your opinion. You've got no taste. I was asking Johnny's.'

'What you really want with it is a straw hat and a banjo.'

'Oh, shut up, Claud! – Johnny?'

'You seem to have done it very well, but it does look a little bright.'

Helena gazed doubtfully down upon herself for a moment or so, then cried cheerfully: 'Hey, Massa Bones! Does your sistah like treacle pudding? I said, does your sister like treacle pudding? – All right. What you say goes.' She ripped out the sleeves and scrumpled them up. 'Do for iron-holders. Anyone want any sherry? I got a bottle today, and never you mind where, Claud, it was all above board.'

'We're just going out.'

'At this time of night?'

'It's not late. We want some air.'

'Very well, then. I shall drink up my sherry all by myself and cry into it. Have a good time. Oh, Claud! you know that old silk dressing-gown of yours, the blue and green one. You've done with it, haven't you? Could I have that to cut up?'

'No, you can't. I'm still wearing it.'

'Dog in the manger,' Helena grumbled, 'no one ever does anything to help me.' She went away, bearing the ruined dress with her, and Field and I left the flat.

We found Mrs Olney's shop situated in a narrow and depressing side-street a hundred yards or so from the Tube station, sandwiched between a hairdresser's and a herbalist's. The door and window-frames were painted a yellow that had once been bright, and on the hanging sign was written, in a curling script with a great banana tail to the 'y', DILYS. There was a street lamp opposite that shed its light on to the window. Peering in, we could see a dingy-looking display of lampshades, pyramidally arranged, with the smallest at the top. At the bottom of the window, pushed up against the glass, was a row of various objects prettified out of their original usefulness, a wooden match-box adorned with barbola work, a pincushion in the shape of a cat, a hat-stand dressed up as a pierrot doll; higher up, stuck near the sides of the pane, were illuminated horoscopes, daffodils for April, lilac for May, roses for June, and above them a notice inked in vaguely Chinese letters: 'What are you? What is your destiny? KNOW YOURSELF! One shilling only.'

Field, peering, pointed out a shade decorated with coloured photographs of Stalin, Roosevelt, and Winston Churchill, the parchment having been cut away behind them to give an effect of celestial illumination when the light was on. 'Now that's cunning,' he said appreciatively. 'I think your Mrs Olney has depths.'

I told him I preferred the one covered with the drawings and maxims of Billy Brown.

> 'So let's all move along, says Billy,
> To crowd the doorways would be silly,'

I read.

'Ah no, I can't cope with Billy,' he protested, 'I loathe the beastly cult of the little man. People never think they're little themselves, but they love to despise their neighbours. Who the hell wants to be mediocre?' He sighed. 'I don't. I want to be terrific.'

Mrs Olney slipped like a shadow between us, sprung from nowhere, conjured, to my fancy, out of the scraps in the gutter, the rags of silk at the back of the workshop, the coils of dry dead hair lying on the red velvet of the window next door. She greeted us. I felt as though I had been caught in some dishonourable mischief. 'I was passing this way when I spotted your shop. Let me introduce John Field. John, this is Mrs Olney.'

He bowed to her, staring.

'Come in and have a private view,' she pleaded, her voice hushed as if we were in church, 'please come in.'

'Well, as a matter of fact, we're on our way somewhere.'

'You've got time! Your friends will excuse you, I know they will. Just ten minutes.'

I looked at Field.

'Well, just a split second,' he agreed.

She whipped out a key, opened the door and pushed us into the lamp-shot gloom of the shop. 'I won't turn all the lights up; it spoils it if I do. Wait a minute.' She went scuffling a-round the skirting boards. In a moment a group of shades sprang up into pink and yellow and white. Another group followed, and another, till the whole pyramid glowed.

'Look quickly,' Mrs Olney gasped, 'I don't want the police fussing. We're not allowed to have displays lit up at night.'

We gazed for a second or so, and then the lights, cluster by cluster, went dark.

'Do you think they're original?' she asked us.

'The most original I've seen,' said Field carefully.

'I'm so glad. Do you know, when I came along (I was coming back from the pictures, I've got a room above the shop which is very handy and nice though a little squashy), when I came along I thought you were laughing.'

'I assure you,' I said.

'No, no, no, I know you wouldn't be. Only there's such a reaction against decoration these days, at least with some people, though others still adore it. Of course one doesn't want lots of patterns in a room, but say, quite plain walls and hangings, and some dark coloured carpet and *then* an elaborate shade. . . . It does give richness.'

She moved into the beam of the street lamp opposite and was at once so beautiful that I heard Field blow out his lips.

'So much a matter of taste,' I told her.

She turned to me. 'One hates to be a huckster – if it's a huckster I mean – I'm so bad at business, I only like the decorative side – but if you *do* know anyone, and would recommend me . . . ' She looked at us piteously. Field's gaze travelled over her. Seeing this, she edged scarcely perceptibly behind the pyramid, so that the lower part of her body was concealed.

'Of course I will,' I said, and wondered how we should escape from her.

'Should I be contravening any act if I bought one now?' Field asked, snatching at a more tolerable shade of white parchment painted with a scattering of small flowers.

'Oh, but you don't really want one, do you? I mean, you're only being nice –'

The pyramid collapsed. We all fell to our knees, scuffling and raking the shades together.

'Oh, just put them anywhere,' she begged us, 'I'll get the display fixed up again tomorrow. Please don't worry, Mr Field, it wasn't in the least your fault, because these things *will* happen.'

He rose, holding his choice, straining his eyes to see the price on the ticket.

A group of hooligans of the breed created by underfeeding, fathers in the army and the general anarchy of war, were pressing their faces to the window, banging on it, flattening fat pink tongues against the glass. One grabbed up a handful of muck from the gutter and threw it at the pane.

I went round to the side door, shouted at them and drove them, all yelling fantasies of insult, out of sight. When I returned Mrs Olney and Field were outside on the pavement. She was complaining bitterly, apologizing fervently, and begging Field who, in a moment of bizarre exhibitionism, had put the lampshade for safety on his head, not even to try to clear up the mess on the window with his pocket handkerchief. He assured her it was a pleasure, finished the job, and threw the handkerchief into the gutter. We returned to the shop. 'Now then, how much do I owe you?'

Mrs Olney protested. It was she who was in debt to him; she would love to make him a present of the shade, anyway it was only three and six.

'It says twelve and six here.'

'That's a mistake.'

'Split the difference at ten bob,' I said, giving her a note.

After a great pother she took it, and we insisted that we must go.

'Do come again,' she implored. 'Come again and have some tea. Please. I mean it.'

She followed us out into the street.

'I hate to think what you must think of me, Major Pickering, coming as I did the other day. But you know how one builds a hope –'

When we were rid of her I asked Field for five shillings.

'We'll share this horror and you shall give it to Helena in a few days' time. Why on earth did you buy it?'

He grinned. 'So you shouldn't go buying Churchill, Stalin, and Roosevelt, I expect. I knew we were for it.'

'I wouldn't have bought it. I wouldn't have bought anything.'

'I am so anti-Daniel,' he murmured, laughing, 'that I'd do anything to help a victim.'

'Even endure Helena. Look, it's been on my conscience: I heard that scene the other night, I couldn't help it. I'd got my door wide open and so had you.'

'Oh, I thought you'd heard,' he replied calmly. His eyes flashed in the light from a passing car. 'I told you Helena was terrific.'

I felt a twinge of emotion I could hardly define; something like, yet not as definite as, jealousy. All at once I wished he were gone, that our household were rid of him. Then he began to speak of the Rougon-Macquart novels, as a preliminary insisting that he had only read through them because there had been nothing else to read; and was so interesting upon this subject that I began to think I had perhaps been hard on him, that he was not such a bad fellow, that our household could do with a more cultural flavour and that, in fact, it was a pleasant night for walking.

Chapter Three

Towards the end of May a fine day's weather gave Helena the idea that she must go down to the cottage for the summer. What, she said, was the good of having a place in the country if you didn't go there when all the flowers were out? Besides, she added to me, for Sholto really was on his way home at last and was due to dock within the week, it would be nice for him and Charmian to have a proper honeymoon with the place to themselves. Even if he was a boiled owl.

But, I protested, they would not have it to themselves; if I went myself to an hotel for a week (which would be a self-conscious, ridiculous and expensive thing to do) Field would still be there.

'Oh,' said Helena, 'but I'm taking him with me. I can't run that barmy place all on my own.'

'Have you asked him? How do you think he's going to get away from his job for the entire summer? He needs what he earns, though it is a fly's eyebrow.'

She smiled upon me grandly, as if full of secrets, as if I were the only one not to know what the world knew. 'I'll take care of Johnny. He eats like a canary anyhow. He could leave his rotten old job without much harm being done; there'll be plenty of other things for him when he gets back. He doesn't have to worry.'

'But you can't go on keeping him.'

'I can do what I like with my own money, can't I? It's better than giving it to the Salvation Army.'

'But you weren't going to give it to the Salvation Army.'

'Oh, don't play chopsticks with me!' she cried, thinking perhaps of chop-logic or chop-and-change. She looked really angry.

'He won't let you anyhow.'

'He will if I put it to him reasonably.'

'He's not a ponce,' I said, and Helena told me not to be

coarse, my father had never been coarse, and my mother even less so from all she'd heard, if it were possible to be less so.

When Field came in that night she put her plan to him, baldly, no offence in the world. He was not offended, but he would not consider acceptance. 'It's grand of you,' he said, 'but I can't go chucking up jobs like that. Jobs are hard to get – anyway, the sort of jobs I can stand.'

'But you're due for a holiday, aren't you?'

'A fortnight. And that's handsome, all things considered.'

'Very well,' said Helena, 'then we'll go down for a fortnight. I'd only be bored if I had to spend all the summer hearing birds sing and cows moo. When can you get away?'

He told her he would let her know. When I had him alone I said: 'Don't you be driven into this. You need a real rest, not slaving away being handy-man to Helena.'

'Well, there's nowhere much else for me to go, and she can't run the place on her own.'

'Then she'll have to use it as a week-end place only, which was the original idea, after all.'

'Oh well, anyhow I'll see,' he said, and I knew she would have things as she wished.

He arranged to take as his holiday the last two weeks of June. June 16th was a Saturday, so Helena said I might as well come, see them settled in, and spend the week-end there. I was pleased enough to go, for Sholto had returned and he and Charmian, mutually polite and neither very conversational, seemed to use up all the air of the flat.

The thought of this holiday at the cottage seemed to have some great importance in Helena's mind, for she was in tearing spirits. For the hour's journey from Charing Cross she had bought (with my spare coupons and all Field's remaining ones) a new travelling outfit; costume of brown checked tweed and tan-coloured top coat, tan shoes, and a brown hat with a bright green cockade. She looked splendid and a little alarming. She was, I thought, contemplating her as she leaned her head from the carriage window, phenomenally young for her years. She might have been no more than fifty-three or four. She still walked well and briskly, her senses unimpaired save for a slight tendency to deafness in very crowded rooms. Her hair, white and springing, had a quality curiously unnatural; one might have sworn it was a wig worn out of freakishness. From the moment of the train's departure she was never still, never silent. She gazed upon the unrolling country with delight, digging us with her finger and pointing whenever she saw anything that seemed to her especially delightful. First it was the statue of a woman in a long gown, incongruously placed amid the washing lines and flowerless pergolas of a suburban garden. Then it was a hedge of rambler roses, then a gang of prisoners of war working in a field, then the tracery of white wool left by an aeroplane upon the sky, then a cottage with a duck pond, then a house roofed with tiles of brilliant blue. That morning Helena was the barker of the fairground of the world.

. Her spirits remained high until supper-time, when they began, unaccountably, to droop. Field went to bed early. The Kentish air had tired me also, and I would have followed him, but Helena did not want to go. 'It's early yet. Stay up for a bit and talk to me.'

Though the night was overcast, it promised warmth. The moths spun in from the garden to flutter their rags of white and gold against the globe of the oil lamp. The hedge had still, in the cloudlight, some quality of green. Beneath it something light-coloured ran swiftly – a kitten, a rat, or a rabbit.

'The country's so damned still,' Helena said, smacking viciously at a spinning-jenny which had flown into her face, 'it makes you think about yourself, and I hate thinking.' She turned her head, looked gravely at me. 'This is a flattering sort of light to you, Claud. It makes you look years younger, not more than twenty-five. How fair you are still! I used to tell Dicky his hair was girl's-colour, and it used to make him wild, but it never has looked girl's-colour on you. Your face is too bony for that, and then, your nose isn't too small, as his was.'

I saw her past in her silence, saw in her face the memory of an emotion almost as strong as the emotion itself had been; she had loved my father more than I had ever loved him, and I felt grateful to her because to him she had made up the short-weight of affection. She and I were sentimentally united in a mute sharing of experience.

I fancied her happy until she repeated fretfully, 'So damned still, so damned still. I never remember it till I get down here, and then I start wondering how I ever came to forget.'

She sighed deeply, the sound dying away in a sudden, troubled movement of the breeze.

'You don't know what it's like to grow old,' she said. 'I wish you'd never got to find out.'

I made some stupid remark about not wanting to die young simply to avoid the experience, but she ignored it.

'If only I could get over thinking of myself as a girl! No – not as a girl. In my mind I'm always about thirty-five. When I look at Mrs Sholto I think, "That old lady" . . . and then I realize she's two years, three years younger than I am, and it gives me the horrors; I think, does she call *me* "that old lady"? I don't feel old. I forget about age. Sometimes I start to run upstairs, or across a room, and then my body stops me: my legs are old as Adam, they're tied up, somehow, just as if there was a third leg and I was tied to it – like the three-legged races at school. It makes me feel such a fool!'

'You haven't even got rheumatism,' I told her, 'so you shouldn't grouse about your legs.'

'But they're slow. They slow me up. I feel as if I was always tugging my body along behind me. You know what I was thinking just now?'

She looked out on to the lawn, now live and mazing with leaf shadows cast by the risen moon.

'I was thinking that was a dance floor, and a waltz was playing and I was dancing out there.' She was silent for a long while. I lit a cigarette and gave it to her. 'Thanks. . . . It makes me miserable to think I shall never dance again. Not that I can't dance! I could dance Charm off her feet, even now. But if I danced these days I'd make a fool of myself. People would say, "Look at that old girl, mutton dressed up as lamb!"'

I tried to comfort her by saying that not many people danced nowadays, anyway, that it had gone out of fashion; but she was still following the progress of her waltzing vision, a ghost in the arms of another ghost, weaving and swinging and circling over a floor of glass, and leaves, and shadows like the shadows on the face of the moon. She was lost in love of this music, this universal movement of all things about the movement of the dancers.

She smacked her hand down on the ledge of the window

with such force that the vase at her side vibrated, giving forth the sweet and piercing note of a bell. The music stopped. The dancers vanished.

'Nothing more!' Helena cried. 'You think of that! Nothing to look forward to. All finished. I've got to live out the rest of my life on the things that happen to other people.' She shivered. 'Live in my children, as the saying goes. I never was the type to be satisfied with that. You wait till Charm gives me a grandchild. "What an interest for you!" they'll say. It won't be. I'm not that fond of Evan, as well you know. I'll like the bit of it that's Charmian's, but the strain of the Sholto family's so strong that it's bound to have boiled eyes and an Owen Nares chin, just like his. Aren't I awful? I'm unnatural. Claud. That's the trouble with me. I'm unnatural.'

She seemed to expect no response to this, so I made none. I fancied that in a minute or so she might have talked her way out of the *cafard*.

She continued: 'Then, of course, you're unnatural too, in your own sweet way. Funny ways of enjoying yourself. Messing around with that stupid Jane Elvorden, and bothering about politics, and what sort of government we'll have when the war's over, and whether we'll have to fight anyone else – it beats me. I suppose it makes you happy.'

'One hundred per cent introspection's the privilege of your generation,' I told her, 'not mine. We daren't let it be, or we might wake up some morning to find all sorts of nasty things had happened.'

'All right, Mr Smarty,' said Helena vaguely, 'that's enough of you. We've heard all about you.' She rose. 'I'm going to bed.' She stumbled, caught my arm to regain her balance. 'Drunk again.'

'Cheer up. You're still handsome.'

She did not smile. 'Yes, I am. That's not conceit, it's only what I see in the glass. If you didn't know me and you sat next to me in a bus, how old would you say I was?'

'I wouldn't even think about it. I'd only think, "Now, that's a fine piece!"'

She pinched my cheek. 'You're not a bad old Claud. Even when you were a little boy I used to tell people you'd turn out all right. Mind you lock up properly, will you? And don't forget the back door, as you did last time you were here, so the cats got in.'

She went on towards bed, humming a tune to herself. I felt happier. I could not endure that Helena should ever lie awake under the nag of thought. She was a woman created for sound sleeping.

I had been working over-hard recently, so was glad to follow her. I slept at once and woke, within a second it seemed, to find the room filled with sunlight ruddy enough to indicate a late hour. I lay on my back for a while looking up at the floating colours of light upon the ceiling and enjoying the sharp consciousness of being at rest. The sky was a full, soft blue with a quality of violet, the treetops gilded and coppered beneath a gauze of heat. The warm air was sweet-smelling, but with a sweetness less reminiscent of earth and grass than of clean closed rooms, where the ancient woodwork was newly scoured and the Venetian blinds, soft-coloured, through which the sun streamed in slats of watery gold, had lately been dusted with care, wood, canvas, string and all. It was one of those mornings that enclose the world in its walls of delightful heat and give the mind a sense of security, a feeling that heaven need never happen, nor hell, that the whole idea of a universe is a monstrous myth, and that *nothing is* save the sheltering world eternal, fixed in its globe of sky like a ship in a bottle.

I heard the voices of Field and Helena for some moments before I actually began to listen to them, to give them identity. I went to the window and looked out. They were walking across the far side of the lawn, the tall old woman, the young man a little shorter than she. Her arm was through his, and they were laughing together in an intimacy that suggested a secret, a surprise being planned, or a discovery just made. They stopped. Her hair was white as cotton wool against the hedge; I could see the aura of finer hairs about it.

I caught her words, 'You *are* a fool, you *are* a fool!' – and then she laughed again.

A cat ran between their legs. Field bent down and picked it up and they both loved it, rubbing their cheeks against its fur. 'Pussapussapussapussety-pop!' Helena cried. 'Was it a sweet, then, and did it love its auntie then?'

Field tired of the cat suddenly, lifted it up and then let it fall, watching to see if it would land on its feet.

They moved on, to and fro, entranced by the morning. They were strolling back now towards the house. I went to the window and called good morning down.

'Up at last?' Helena returned derisively. Her face, upturned, seemed large and flat, a plate of a face, a broad oval from cheek to cheek.

'"Go to the ant, thou sluggard,"' said Field, his eyes merry and dark. 'Do you know what the time is?'

'Guess,' Helena bade me, foolishly.

'I don't feel like it.'

'It's' – Field looked at his watch – 'it's seventeen minutes past eleven precisely.'

'Good God, it can't be!'

'Don't say it *can't* be,' Helena bullied, 'when Johnny says it is. Come on down and I'll make you some tea. You can't have any breakfast because we're having lunch at twelve, and I won't have you spoiling your appetite.'

'Why, what have you got?'

'You wait and see!'

By the time I had had my tea, bathed and dressed, it was noon. For lunch there was a chicken. I had noticed recently that our table was getting more and more luxurious. I did not so much mind this as long as Helena ate the luxuries for which she paid; but it occurred to me that Field could no longer be paying the half of his keep, and I did not like what appeared to be his growing dependence upon her.

He acknowledged it freely enough. 'Do you know,' he said, 'I'm having the time of my life?' He was in high spirits. 'I eat, eat, and eat. It's all like the sort of dream I used to have when I was a boy – you know – of stuffing and stuffing off gold plate on a gorgeous hot day and never getting full up. Helena, you make my dreams come true.'

She was pleased by this, but she would not make any show of accepting his gratitude. 'Not much gold plate about it. Utility china, my boy, and we're even short of that. I wasn't going to bring good stuff down here.'

'Why not?' I asked her.

'This is a holiday place. I'm not going to have people having to be careful of anything. Johnny, I've got a nice little bit of wing here.'

He shook his head. She persisted that he must have it: he talked a lot about eating, she said, but he never really did more than nibble.

'I'm overwhelmed by the luxury,' he protested, 'it inhibits me. At least, it inhibits me from the very last degree of gorging. I feel just like Aladdin. I only have to rub up the marvellous lamp –'

'Ah,' said Helena, so quick to check the compliment that she forgot to guard her secrets, 'you must go to our Dilys for marvellous lamps.' She began to laugh, then was silent. I looked at Field. He was cramming food into his mouth at a tremendous rate, and his shoulders were hunched up to his ears as if he expected the house to fall upon him. He flashed me one bright, terrified glance, then withdrew his gaze.

'I remember years and years ago, when I was a girl in Belfast,' said Helena, loudly and rapidly, 'having the most wonderful meal, and just at a time when I was down to my last shilling.'

I heard no more of this narrative, as I was absorbed in my discovery. I realized for the first time that Field and Helena were conspirators, that they talked most freely behind my back, and that he had for some extraordinary reason betrayed to her the very thing I had most wished to be hidden. However, I said nothing then, and managed for the rest of the meal to make ordinary conversation.

The three of us idled about the garden till two, and then I asked Field to come for a walk with me.

'Wait a tick,' said Helena, 'I'm coming as well.'

'No, you won't. We're going too far. You have a good rest and we'll be back about four-thirty.'

'I don't want to rest. Why should I rest? Only old ladies rest.'

'No, don't be silly. We're going for a long, quick march. You'll be worn out.'

Field was just about to protest that he, also, would be worn out, when I caught his eye. He said hastily to Helena, 'Claud's right. You be nice and comfortable here, and then we can all go for a nice lazy walk this evening, when it's cooler.'

We set out down the lane, between hedges powdered with

white dust and shimmering with sun, crossed a stile and started uphill. The top of the field was rounded on the vapour-
rusted sky, brown-gold against brown-blue. Field had not
spoken since we left the cottage. He walked rapidly, hands in
his pockets, cigarette sticking up like a pipe stem from the
centre of his mouth. The light made his sallow skin seem ruddy, brought out a reddish quality in his hair, and in his long,
feminine lashes. But for the bonyness of shoulder, the narrow-
ness of hip, he would have looked a little like a woman dressed
as a boy. I thought of him in the mess, so conscientious, so
courteous, so eager to please, and always so much a source of
irritation to the others.

I had liked him because he read a great deal and would,
when encouraged out of his shyness, talk with perception and
originality of what he had read. He was the son of a suburban
solicitor who had, I gathered, been fretted all his life by fruit-
less literary ambitions and had hoped to find in his son the
genius he had once so passionately sought in himself. John
Field, however, had no creative talent of any sort; but he
could perceive and analyse the talent or the genius of others.
He had, I believe, a sense of shame that so far from fulfilling
his father's hopes, he had no skill to be anything but a com-
mentator, and so it was hard at first acquaintance to make him
display what gift he had. In the mess, of course, it was the last
gift likely to cut any ice. The cultural level had been low, and
Field's bookishness had been regarded irrationally (but in this
case accurately) as an indication of ineptitude in all practical
matters. At this moment, watching him walk a little ahead of
me as if with some thought of escape in his mind, I was taken
by a surge of hostility so strong that it made the feeling of
warmth I had once had towards him seem disgusting to me.

'Why the hell did you tell Helena about Mrs Olney?'

He stopped dead and faced me, clenching his hands like a
schoolboy caught in some desperate mischief from which even
the wiliest lie will not save him. 'I was afraid you'd have
noticed.'

'No one could help noticing. Why did you do it?'

'I'm sorry.' His eyes sought, as if in longing, the round
brow of the hill. 'It was one of those things. Bloody weakness
on my part, I suppose you'd say.'

'What right had you to tell Helena? I only told you in confidence, as you damn well know.'

'She didn't mind. I thought she would, but she didn't.'

'Never mind whether she minded. Why did you tell her?'

'She made me.'

My attention wandered from him for a moment, caught by the curious colour of our shadows, lying giant-like across the furrows. I had an extraordinary desire to drop the business about Helena and instead, to ask him of what that colour was composed: how much violet he thought there was, how much blue, how much orange.

'It was hard to refuse,' Field said.

I saw him again. 'Let's walk on.'

We moved upwards.

'When did it happen?'

'The day after we went to the shop. I was home in the afternoon. She wanted to know where we'd been on our walk. I said nowhere in particular, but she seemed to know I was hiding something. She talked and urged me, and made jokes, and said I owed her a secret for all she'd done for me. Somehow she got it out of me. I'm sorry.'

'Good God, couldn't you have told her a good lie to keep her happy?'

'She'd have known,' said Field. He added rapidly, 'I made light of it. I only told her that a woman who'd known Archer had come to see you and wanted to know if any money had been left to her. I said Mrs Olney kept a shop, and we'd had a sort of urge to go and have a look at it. I didn't tell Helena we'd seen her there.' He looked at me hopefully, as if this last reservation was a condoning virtue.

'Once you'd gone so far you might have told her the rest.' I was baffled. I simply could not understand this extraordinary and weakling breach of faith.

'But she didn't mind! I can assure you of that. She just laughed. She joked about Aladdin. The only thing she said about you keeping it from her was, "Poor old Claud, he does think I mind some funny things.'

I wished him out of our house, wished to be rid of his intrusion into our family matters. It was as if he were growing about the structure of our life like some delicate-seeming but ineradicable vine.

We had reached the crest of the hill. Before us was the rich downfalling of the hopfields, so bountiful that they made the spirit restless. Not so far from here was the village where I had been in training in the summer of 1942. I thought of the men I had known – Lilley, who had got into trouble and been dismissed the service; Tom Glaiden, who gave up the bottle when he got promotion; Menhenheott, the troop sergeant, who had won the Military Medal at Cassino; Philip Strutt, now a lieutenant-colonel in the Far East and Cassilis, dead; Tawney, dead.

'I think I'd better clear out,' Field said.

'Clear out?'

'Of the flat. I'll go back to my own. I've hung around you all too long, as it is.'

I made no comment.

'I'll tell Helena tonight.'

We went down in silence, and came to a village. It was deserted, save for a few children in Sunday dresses playing around a duck pond. We rested on some chains slung between wooden posts. One of the children came up to Field and asked him for sweets. He seemed distressed not to have any, but gave her a penny. He was still raking his pockets as she ran away. She was almost out of earshot when he shouted to her. She came running back. Field, looking happy, gave her a screw of paper in which there were two pieces of chewing-gum. She looked at it. 'I don't like gum.' 'That's a pity. Don't any of your friends?' She called, 'Ernie! Dorrie! Maureen!' They came around her, clustering, staring at Field. All three of them, unlike their companion, did like gum, but there were only two pieces. Field took out his penknife and meticulously divided the gum into three portions, distributing it. The children ran away.

'I don't suppose Helena would let you go,' I said, 'but for God's sake don't go telling her anything else. I'm damned if I shall give you a chance to.'

'No, I shall leave.'

He did not speak of the matter again till we were nearly home. 'I'm terrifically sorry. It was an incredible thing to do.'

'Oh, let it alone now,' I said. 'There doesn't seem to be much harm done.'

Helena was waiting for us on the lawn, lying back serene in a deck chair, hands in lap, fine legs tidily crossed at the ankle. She had smartened herself for our coming by putting a big orange rose in her lapel.

Field walked straight across to her. 'I'm no end sorry, Helena, but I'll be moving out of your flat as soon as we get back. Claud knows I told you about Mrs Olney and he's furious. Quite rightly, of course. Still, he is angry.'

I was taken utterly aback by this move, through which he had thrown himself upon Helena's sympathy and so made her his ally against me. He stood there, apparently unconscious of double-dealing, his eyes gentle and suppliant. Mutely he asked pardon of us both, not caring a damn whether he had mine and knowing that she would consider him without a fault for which to answer.

Helena looked from one to the other of us. 'How did Claud know you'd told me?'

'He heard you mention her at lunch-time.'

'And what's he being angry about? It doesn't matter one way or the other. I thought it was funny. Don't stand there looking stuffed, Claud! I got the story out of Johnny; it was my fault if there's any fault in it; and there's no need for you to start bullyragging. Of course he's not going to go. There's a housing shortage.'

'Honestly, Helena,' Field said, 'I mean it. I ought to be off on my own, anyhow. You all make things too easy for me, and I tend to drift.'

'You work like a slave for that silly firm of yours. You deserve a little peace when you get home of a night.' She had not moved from the position in which she had been seated on our return. She was intensely conscious of herself, of her capacity to simulate the ease of youth. Now, however, she got up, laying her hand upon Field's arm as an aid to rising. 'I'm going to get tea. And when I bring it out we'll talk of sensible things.'

She went indoors. Feeling I could not trust myself, at that moment, to speak to Field, I followed her.

He made several attempts that evening to reopen the subject of his going, but each time she laughed at him. I did not see her alone again till the next morning when, rising at six in order to catch my train, I found her in the kitchen getting my breakfast. 'I thought you'd oversleep or something, and then not get there, and then they'd cashier you. We can't have that sort of thing in our family.'

I thanked her, told her that there had been no need to disturb herself, but that I was glad of company just the same.

'A real egg,' said Helena, putting it down scrambled in front of me.

'I thought we hadn't any.'

'We hadn't yesterday. Do you know what I did when you were out? I was sitting in the garden when I saw a hen trotting along by the hedge, one of Mrs Wignall's up the road. Oh! – I thought, so I stalked it, hoping it would drop an egg. Out it went into the ditch, and I stalked it along there, but it didn't drop one. God knows what I must have looked like. Then I heard a cough, and I looked up, and there was Mrs Wignall giving me the most peculiar look, so I said, "Oh, Mrs Wignall, I found your bird in my garden, and was just bringing it back." Of course she had to thank me, and I got talking about how the hens were laying, and how few eggs they seemed to lay. So she couldn't very well do anything but go in and fetch me a couple. The other one's for Johnny.' She paused. 'I expect she thought my way of returning the hen a bit queer. Still, she couldn't say I wasn't bringing it back, could she?' Helena widened her eyes, delighting in her own clowning.

'Whatever she thought, you got the reward. Listen, Helena, I've been wanting to talk to you.'

'If it's about Johnny, you can save your breath to cool your egg. It wasn't his fault. I badgered him. You know how I hate mysteries, and you two went out that evening looking as if you were going to crack a safe.'

'Never mind that. He had no right to tell you.'

'And I say it didn't matter a damn. Don't you dare appoint yourself my guardian, Claud. At my age I shall hear what I want to hear.'

'I think he ought to go.'

'Well, he's not going,' Helena said quietly, brightness fading from her eyes, 'he'll stop. I say so. It's my flat. He'll stop. And I don't care how many atmospheres you choose to make.'

She looked at the clock. 'Better hurry up, or you'll never catch your train.'

'Speed the parting guest.'

'I'm not sorry to speed you. You're interfering.'

'Good job someone does.'

'You're stuffy and boring. You're jealous of Johnny because he's got brains.'

This was so absurd that I did not reply.

'Sulk, sulk, sulk,' she said. She did not speak again till I was ready to go. Then she walked with me to the gate, her red gown draggling the wet gravel and catching in the dewy shrubs. 'I'm going to give a party when I get back.'

'Who to?'

'Charmian and Evan. There ought to be a celebration. We'll have the Stillyers, and the Leipers and the Esches – it doesn't do to get quite out of touch.'

'But you've cut away from them, haven't you? You said you had.'

'Don't pick me up on what I said or didn't say. Sometimes I feel like one thing, sometimes like another.' She paused. 'Claud, is Charmian happy with Evan?'

'I don't think so.'

'That's what I wonder. He seems happy enough, doesn't he?'

'It's always hard to tell what he's feeling. He's so damned "korekt".'

'She looks miserable to me,' said Helena, looking miserable herself. 'Couldn't we do something to help? If he makes her sick she ought to be able to get rid of him. Can't we fix it somehow?'

'I wish we could.'

'You *think*,' she urged, 'you think. You often have ideas. Get along now. I want to go back to bed.'

Until I reached the corner she waved to me, a fantastic figure of white and crimson leaning over the gate like Punch over the box, the high bushes spattering her with dew as she disturbed them by gesticulations. All the way back to town I was troubled and confused by worries about Helena, about Field, about Charmian. I half expected the colours of the morning to fade, but it remained fair.

Chapter Four

SWAIN had painted a new picture. It was called *Roadmending*, and showed a group of labourers drilling up a main street. There were trees along the pavement, parrot green against a thunderous red-black sky. The men were very hot; their faces glistened as though they had been oiled. It was a triangular composition, the men forming a central pyramid, enclosed within a larger inverted one marked by three spots of red – the red flag indicating work in progress, the red of a striped sunblind, and the red flash of a bus in the distance. It had the restless, exasperated vigour of hard work in extreme heat, the effect of labour emphasized by two complementary groups of idle onlookers, one in the foreground, one in the middle distance. I liked it very much and asked how much he wanted for it, but he said that his prices were beyond me these days, and that I was lucky to have the two *plage* pictures I had bought when he was unknown. 'All the same,' he added, 'if I don't sell it for a really huge sum within a couple of months, I might knock it down a bit for you. In fact – you get married again and I'll even give it to you.' I said that it was the most serious inducement to marry which had yet been offered to me, but that I didn't think it was good enough.

'However,' he said, 'I didn't come to show it to you. I came to show it to Helena. It was her idea, that I should paint the chaps digging the road up.'

We were talking in the hall of the flat. 'I don't think you'd better show her now,' I said, 'she's got a dinner-party. All Archer's old friends.'

'Oh, has she?' said Swain. 'Well, then, she'll want cheering up. Is the meal over?'

'Nearly. But you wouldn't like the company.'

'Are you suggesting,' he said, with a fine assumption of umbrage, 'that I am not good enough for your swell friends?'

'No. I'm suggesting that you won't like Helena tonight. She's Lady Archer again.'

'Ah, I'd like to see that.'

'You come again tomorrow.'

'Certainly not,' he said, 'you go and announce me.'

He was not quite sober, and Swain, in this condition, was apt to realize his position as an Artist and to demand its recognition. Really, he was the most modest of men, interested only in his work and, secondarily, in the money it made him; he had no other source of income, so was unable to enjoy the affectation of disinterest on this score. The smallest amount of drink, however, seemed to awaken in him the idea that by his very modesty he was missing one of the fruits of his labours: the public acknowledgement of his prestige. Even while he insisted that he should be presented to Helena's guests he was laughing at himself, conscious that he was playing a game upon himself, upon me, and upon Helena.

I knew him quite well enough to make him go away and call another time, and would have done so had not Charmian come out into the hall.

'Hullo, Bill! I was wondering who it was.'

'Claud's trying to tell me I'm not good enough for her friends. What a bloody old Claud, now, isn't he?'

She glanced at me. 'I expect he's got his reasons.'

'Phoh!' said Swain, 'p-h-o-h!'

It was not that I cared whether or not the Stillyers and the Esches would want to see the painting. It was simply that I did not wish him to see Helena while Helena was acting. He would think she was funny. I resented the sharing by any outsider of my amusement. I laughed with her: he might laugh at her, and share the joke with Clemency.

'Don't you like me, kind Charmian?' he persisted. 'Don't you want to introduce me to your husband with blushes and eyes downcast? When I remember how I used to dandle you on my knee – '

'Oh, come on,' she said, smiling at him. She opened the dining-room door. 'Bill Swain, Mother.'

They were sitting at coffee, Helena presiding with the satisfied grandeur of an Italian Madonna at a concourse of saints. The folds of her dress were sculptural about her, scooped and smoothed and pleated in tones of sapphire and indigo by the lights behind her head. Beside her the others looked smaller than they were, almost unnaturally small, like the portraits of donors in the side panels of a devotional painting. Mrs Stillyer, in pale green, old Mrs Sholto, in grey, were rendered ghostly by Helena's dominant radiance. Even Lady Esch was subdued by it, humbled, made to look not a personage with an account at half a dozen department shops, but an uncertain old woman trying to hide the myriad worries that were on her mind by putting too much paint upon her face.

'How very pleasant!' said Helena. 'How are you? Evan, dear, please put a chair for Mr Swain. Will you have some coffee?'

'No, thank you. I've just had some beer.' Swain looked cheerfully about him, waiting to be introduced. 'I've heard all about you,' he said when Charmian presented Sholto, and he said it in a way which indicated that whatever he had heard about her husband was unprintable. He spoke nicely to everyone else, looked down the neck of Sue Leiper's dress, which was too low, and then sat down on the extreme edge of the chair brought for him, hugging his picture to his chest.

'How is dear little Clemency?' Helena asked him.

This was absurd, for Clemency was not less than five foot nine, and generously fleshed. Swain stared at her, recovered himself and replied, 'Itsy-bitsy as usual, thank you, Helena. Look, you remember the road drills? I've painted them. I've brought you the picture to see.'

'Mr Swain is a famous painter,' Helena told the company. Her smile enfolded him in its golden patronage. 'Claud will tell you that. You'll believe his word, I know.'

'That sounds very exciting,' said Mrs Stillyer, with an uncertain air.

'I don't think one has to have Claud's word for it,' Evan Sholto said unexpectedly, 'everybody knows it.' He turned to Swain. 'We had one of your pictures in the mess. Reproduction thing.'

'Which one?'

'Bulldozers clearing a beach.'

'Ah, that was me reconciling the old with the new. I used to paint only beaches. War brought the bulldozers. Did the mess like it?'

'It was no end popular,' Sholto replied.

'How do you like this one?' Pushing back Helena's cup and the cup of Mrs Stillyer, who was on his right, Swain planked the picture down on the cloth and pulled off the wrapping paper.

'But how charming!' Mrs Stillyer exclaimed, too soon.

Helena looked at it. 'It looks all right to me,' she said, forgetting her role. She added quickly: 'Oh, that really is splendid, Bill dear! They *do* look hot, poor fellows.'

'I like it,' said Sholto, 'but not so much as the bulldozers. It always takes me ages to get used to anything new.'

Charmian leaned over his shoulder. The big bun of hair, below which the tone of her small neck was golden, gave her the look of an adult fairy in a Rackham drawing. 'I like that better than anything I've seen of yours, Bill. You weren't meaning to give it to me as a wedding present, were you?'

'I'll say I wasn't.'

Old Mrs Sholto said in a voice like a little bell, 'I'm terribly silly; I just *cannot* understand modern art.'

'Why, what's funny about this?' Swain asked her indignantly. 'No women-terrified *au-bord-de-la-mer* about this. It's plain sailing.'

'Women doing *what*?' she asked, delicately frowning.

'Give it to me.' Helena rose, took the picture, and carried it to the far end of the room, where she propped it up against a lamp. She stepped back, regarded it, backed cat-like once again, and stood in silence.

'Here, here,' Swain said, 'you can go nearer than that. It's not the Delphic Sibyl. Take a good look and then make me an offer.'

'You must name your price,' Helena demanded resolutely, 'I shall pay it.'

'Gertcher!' said Swain.

Charmian laughed explosively.

'My dear Lady Archer,' cried Mrs Sholto, 'how decisive of you! – Just like that.'

Helena returned to the table, leaving the painting where she had placed it. 'Shall we go into the next room?' Chairs scraped and squeaked. The Stillyers and Lady Esch followed Charmian into the hall. The Leipers and Mrs Sholto came to look at the picture.

'I shall give a party for it,' Helena said affectionately. 'I inspired it, so it shall be my special household god.'

'It's not a dirty-clothes-basket,' Swain murmured to me. 'What on earth's the matter with her? I want a hundred and twenty-five for that picture, and that's special terms.'

'You can positively feel the chap sweating,' said Tom Leiper, putting his nose to the canvas, 'it makes you go hot all over.'

'My dear Tom,' Mrs Sholto cried, all cherry-ripe dimples, 'you really will rouse Mr Swain's wrath if you talk like that! That's the sort of thing we used to say in the days when every picture told a story. Those were *my* days, I'm afraid. Nowadays you have to say, "What wonderful patine!"'

'No you don't,' said Swain rudely. 'He's quite right; he said what I wanted to hear. I wouldn't have taken all that trouble to make the blokes look hot if I hadn't wanted people to see they were hot.'

'Well, well,' Tom Leiper murmured, 'hooray for me! I'm the expert, Sue.'

'Darling, we all know,' said Sue Leiper, paying no attention to him. As usual, she was looking far-away and worried. She and Tom had a daughter of six, a child of perfect manners and irreproachable behaviour who was always in and out of the hands of psychiatrists. 'Of course you are.'

'And are you going to buy this, Lady Archer?' Mrs Sholto inquired. 'Suppose he asks five thousand pounds?' She laughed at her own fancy.

'If I want a thing I do my best to get it,' Helena replied.

'Hunnan twenny-five,' said Swain fiercely.

Helena flinched, but bowed.

He looked at her. She met his eyes courageously. 'Now come along, we're all going into the other room. I want you to see a little picture of Daniel's that Claud unearthed.'

'I think I'll be going now. I told Clemency I wouldn't be half an hour.' He took out the wrapping paper he had crumpled into his pocket, picked up the painting and made for the door.

'Now, Bill!' Helena protested merrily. 'Stop, thief!'

'We'll discuss things tomorrow,' he said, 'fix up all the sordid part.' She did not stop him. Charmian and I went with

120

him to the outer door. Charmian was shaking with a kind of sorrowful laughter.

'Nuts, nuts, nuts,' Swain mumbled, 'mad, mad! *Wahn, wahn!*'

'I told you not to burst in on Helena tonight,' I said.

'She won't really buy it, will she?'

'Not unless you come down to twenty quid.'

'Well, I shan't. The labourer is worthy of his hire.'

'I *am* sorry, Bill!' said Charmian, still laughing.

'I'll give you thirty for it,' I said.

'Hunnan twenny-five's what I'm getting. I'll cut off the five for a friend.'

'You go home,' I said.

When the door had closed behind him Charmian leaned against it and dabbed her eyes. 'Oh dear! And the frightful part of it is that not one of them, with the conceivable exception of Lady Esch, believed for one minute that she meant it. They *know*. I do wish Mother realized how much people know!'

'Your *belle-mère* will take a prod at Helena later, just to take her down a peg. You'll see.'

'I don't doubt it,' Charmian said wearily. Sholto came out to us, tripped over the edge of the carpet and kicked it irritably into place. 'Shush now,' she whispered, narrowing her eyes at me.

'Come on, darling, you're wanted,' he said. 'Has he gone?'

'Yes.'

'He was a little tight, wasn't he?'

'A very little,' I replied.

'Must be nice to have his job. Paint a picture, collect, and have the rest of your time to yourself. I'm going to be an artist in my next incarnation,' said Sholto.

We rejoined Helena's party, which was now in the lowered stage of looking at objects shown to it. Helena was exhibiting an eighteenth-century miniature which I had found in the pocket of Daniel's overcoat, and a pair of bed-slippers she had bought at the St Dunstan's shop in Tottenham Court Road.

'Oh, Charmian, dear! Do show Lady Esch that bag you had made by those saddlers in Leamington. It's perfectly beautiful – wonderful leather and such workmanship.'

'I could do with a bag,' said Lady Esch, ruminantly, 'I could do with a bag. Mine has pepper in it.'

I saw that Charmian, still feeling the strain of Swain's visit, was on the point of a painful outbreak of mirth. I told her to do as Helena had told her.

'They put it in a spill and I had no shopping basket. Then it burst all over everything, and however much I scrub the lining I still sneeze sometimes. It's war-time,' Lady Esch added fretfully, 'it's all the result of the war.'

Mrs Sholto was examining the miniature. 'What a charming face! One feels a sadness, somehow. He reminds me of some-one. Look, Evan dear. Does that remind you of anybody?"

He shrugged. Sometimes he made me think of Tony Lumpkin.

'Now let me rack my brains . . . I know! Lady Archer, it's exactly like that young man of yours!'

'Young man?' said Helena, arching her brows. It would have been better had she simply said, 'Field?'

'Your young man, Whatsisname, the one who stays with you. Claud, you support me! Isn't this just like him?'

'I can't see it,' I said. I could not. There was no resemblance whatsoever, save that both faces were dark.

'Oh, but it is! Like – wait a minute – Mr Field. Where *is* Mr Field, by the way? One grows so used to seeing him about.'

'He's dining with a friend,' I said. Field, not wishing to meet Helena's guests, had gone out with the owner of the Nineveh Press.

'What a pity! He has the most charming manners, and most young men – I do except you, Claud, and Mr Leiper, and oc-casionally Evan' – (Mrs Sholto was arch, a playful tiny queen cat teasing her great big tom of a son) – 'have none whatso-ever.' She sprang. 'I envy you your *sigisbee*, Lady Archer.'

'I beg your pardon?' said Helena.

'Your *cavaliere servente*. Your knight *sans peur et sans re-proche*. What a lot of foreign words I know! Mr Leiper, you must get me a job in the Foreign Office.'

'If I were in the Foreign Office,' Leiper replied gallantly, 'I certainly would.'

'Johnny's not a knight,' said Helena, annoyance defeating her pose, 'he's a lodger.'

Mrs Sholto threw back her pretty head and laughed till the sinews of her neck were hard as the roots of trees. 'Oh, oh, oh?'

'I hear he's sweet,' Sue Leiper said, a vague consciousness of time and place entering into her roving, distracted eyes.

'He was down in the country with you, wasn't he?' Mrs Sholto persisted.

'He was luckier than I was,' I said. 'I wanted to go, but couldn't get leave. He and Helena had all the weather.'

'If I were younger I should envy you, Lady Archer.'

'And now we're both too old to be envied by anyone,' Helena said mildly, musingly, blazing with temper, 'isn't that sad?'

Charmian returned with the bag. The women admired it, wanted to know the saddler's address, compared the price of it with others they had seen in shop windows. As she went to return it to her bedroom I followed her out. She turned on me. 'Was that devil *belle-mère* hinting that Mother was improper to go away with Johnny? At Mother's time of life?'

'She was. It's your fault for marrying into the damned family.'

'Oh, shut up!'

We went into Charmian's room.

'Field must go,' she said.

'Why?'

'Why?' She echoed me. 'I thought that was your idea, too.'

'It is. I only wondered – what made you say it just then? I thought you quite liked Field these days.'

'I like him all right. But I'm beginning to wonder if he's making Mother look silly.' She made a gesture of distaste. 'Making such a friend of a boy like that!'

'He's older than you.'

'What's that to do with it? Tell him he's got to go.'

'I have.'

'When?'

'Down at the cottage.'

'What brought it up?'

I could not answer this without telling her about Mrs Olney.

'Nothing, really. Just a fit of my own.'

'Well then, get him out.' She paused. 'Evan and I are going, anyway. We're getting a flat of our own, It seems pretty certain that he'll be staying at the War Office, so we may as well have some sort of a home. Besides –'

'Besides what?'

Her face tightened. 'It's not comfortable here. It's perfectly obvious that you and Mother don't like Evan.'

'Do you?' I asked.

She looked at me furiously, then turned her head as if she were going to cry. Without answering me she went out of the room and back to the party.

When the guests had gone and we had settled over late tea to the pleasures of talking them over, Helena did not, as I had expected, start by attacking Mrs Sholto. She could have done so, for Evan was seeing his mother home and Charmian felt, in my opinion justifiably, that she owed the old lady no loyalty. Helena, however, was full of an idea of her own.

'You remember how I told them our class was doomed, Claud, and you laughed at me? They don't think it funny. One way and another, the war's about done for them.' She was herself again now, so much so that the gown of blue velvet looked like a stage costume. 'Lady Esch, now. She's always got her income from property owning. Look at what's happened! More than half her houses have been blitzed, and she's either drawing no rent from them at all or about a fifth of the pre-war figure. The local council have taken over four of her houses in a square that used to be swell, all filled up with carriages in its heyday, and put in bombed-out people from the East End. She said she was only living for the time when they'd put them out again, but I told her she'd never get her houses back, and that they'd be bashed to pieces even if she did.'

'Very malicious of you, Mother,' Charmian said.

'Well, it's true, isn't it? And old Stillyer's sure the Socialists will get in when there's another election –'

'The Churchill prestige is too strong,' I interrupted her.

'Well, Stillyer doesn't think so. And he says when Labour's in power the stock markets will drop to bits. As for Ma Sholto –' Helena's eyes flashed; she seemed to swell and glisten with joy.

'What's going to happen to her?' Charmian asked.

'Nothing, if you go on keeping her on Dan's money – which you will, if it ever comes to that. And she had money in house property, too, and I gather things aren't so rosy. What worries her, though, is people being rude. She says, "London's so dirty, and the tradesmen are so impolite, and I can't see the least hope of any improvement."' Helena paused. 'I'd give my' – she thought what she would give, searching for a fair exchange – 'I'd give my toenails to see a bus conductor slap her on the behind. Serve her right.'

'Why, is that what they've been doing?' Charmian inquired, smiling.

'I expect so. She'd mean that sort of thing, though. Bus conductors telling her not to be all day about it, butchers asking her if she knows there's a war on (because they don't know there isn't yet), and greengrocers telling her she can't have any oranges because the kids want them. Hooray, I say!'

She paused to pour herself a fresh cup of tea. 'Did you hear her making nasty remarks about poor old Johnny? Horrible-minded old woman!'

Charmian and I were both silent.

'"Sigisbee,"' said Helena, glowering, 'I bet she thought I didn't know what it meant, and I would have, if it hadn't been in a crossword. I've caught her at it before, trying to catch me out.' She brightened. 'Didn't I behave nicely tonight? Old hand hadn't lost its cunning.'

'Swain thought you were crazy,' I remarked.

'Well, he shouldn't have come breaking in like that. Couldn't you keep him out?'

'He wouldn't be kept.'

'I like that picture of his.'

'So do I.'

Helena considered. 'He didn't mean it about a hundred and twenty-five, did he? It was my idea, anyway. I told him what he ought to paint. Wouldn't he let me have it for fifty?'

'No,' I replied.

'Well, I think it's very ungenerous. I'll have to see what I can do with him. I'd like old Mrs S. to see that I'm not in rags yet.' She looked thoughtfully at the table on which the painting had stood, as if the ghost of it glowed there still. 'You wait till I see him again. Won't I let him know what I think of him, walking off with it like that, as if my money wasn't good enough!'

Charmian started to laugh, and could not stop. She laughed at first because of Helena's absurdity, and afterwards as a disguise for a new thought in her mind.

'Stop it,' I said, 'you're hysterical.'

'I'm not, I'm not. I can't stop, Oh God – I can't stop. – Mother! – Poor mother, your money wasn't good enough. What a pity! How distrustful of Swain!' Her laughter ceased suddenly.

'Well,' said Helena, nodding, 'I hope you've had a very good giggle at my expense.'

Sholto came in. 'Ah, tea! Any left for me?'

'Wet and warm. Fetch yourself another cup.'

He returned with a Crown Derby cup in a Utility saucer.

'What do you call that?' Helena asked indignantly.

'First that came to hand.' He stretched himself at length in his chair, beautifully creased.

'Dear, dear,' he said to me, 'back to the battle shack tomorrow. What a life.' His blue eyes were pale and clear, slightly myopic. He reached over and took his tea from the tray. 'Thank you, Madame Helena.' This was his own designation for her, and it annoyed her very much indeed. 'Phew! It's stuffy out.'

'*Belle-mère* get home all right?' Charmian asked him, not caring for an answer.

'All right, all right.' He frowned down at his polished toe. All conversation was halted. Charmian picked up a magazine and began to read. Helena peered at the ghost of Swain's picture. The telephone rang, and I answered it. It was Jane, affectionate, apologetic, vindictive. She wanted me to hear the news first. She didn't imagine I'd have any hard feelings, but she thought I'd better know right away. She had just become engaged. I asked to whom, made a few appropriate inquiries, and wished her luck. She said anxiously, 'We are friends, aren't we?' 'Of course' 'You're not just saying that?' 'No, no, of course not. Bring him round some time.' She was silent: 'I feel rather a low type, Claud. I've got a guilt complex.' 'No need for it.' 'I know there isn't. We hadn't any *understanding*' – she exaggerated the word – 'had we?' 'No. You've nothing to

feel guilty about.' 'Nothing whatsoever.' She paused. 'But
. . . oh well, I'm glad you're O.K. about it. I think you'll like
him.' After a few more exchanges, she said good-bye and rang
off.

I felt chilled and rather jealous. It was not that I had wanted
to marry Jane; I was, in fact, grateful that my long association
with her had been brought to an end; but I regretted, meanly,
small-mindedly, that I should no longer have the pleasure of
entering a restaurant in her company and seeing heads turn to
admire her rigid fair beauty. Losing Jane was like losing a
decoration of which one had been proud.

'Jane's got herself engaged,' I said.

'Good,' said Charmian briskly.

'Who to?' Helena asked.

I told her.

'Never heard of him.'

'She's a terrific bit of Gorgeous,' Evan said. 'You ought to
have snapped her up, Claud.'

'It wasn't worth it,' I replied, 'I should have lived hence-
forward in her shadow.'

He rose. 'Going bed-o. Come along, Charmian, I'm tired.'
She put her magazine away, just caught his cup and saucer before they slid to the floor. 'Our lodger not in yet? What an
old stop-out.'

'Evan,' said Helena, 'I wish you wouldn't talk about Johnny in that sneering way. You might remember he's a friend of
Claud's.'

He looked at her, surprised. 'Sorry, Madame H.'

'Johnny's a very nice boy,' she persisted, 'and I don't like
the way some people criticize him.'

I looked at the clock. 'He'll be in in a moment, so I don't
think we ought to start a debate.'

'I didn't mean anything,' Evan said.

But she was squared for battle, ominously gentle, the memory of Mrs Sholto's remark irking her like a blistered heel. 'I
am telling you that I don't like it. I know your mother meant
to be amusing, but I was not very amused.'

'*We* were not,' I said, simply intending a reference to Queen
Victoria; but Evan mistook it for an announcement that I was
on Helena's side and meant to fight with her.

'Really, I don't know what on earth this is all about. My mother made some joke or other. That's all there is to it.'

Helena was monolithically still.

'I assure you –' Evan said, in the face of this immobility.

'I think it would be better manners if your mother made less jokes.'

He flushed, the colour looking like paint on his cheeks. 'I can't accept that. No one has ever suggested that my mother lacked manners.'

'Now look,' said Charmian tiredly, 'this is silly. Let's all go to bed and stop being stupid.'

'I don't suppose I can expect any support from you,' Helena shot at her.

Charmian was exasperated. 'Mother, please!'

'I must defend myself.'

Evan sat down. 'Madame Helena, please believe that no conceivable offence was intended. And I'm sure you didn't mean to suggest that my mother was bad-mannered.'

'That's what I suggested,' said Helena, her hands trembling, 'and I know what she suggested.'

'But it's ridiculous. You –'

She got up and rested her arm along the mantelshelf. She looked very tall, very brilliant, and, strangely, very old. I had for her a spasm of love and pity, a desire to support her in any nonsensical idea or venture, to make her feel that she had always been, and ever would be, right.

'Don't talk to me, any of you! What right have you to try and make me miserable? At my age I can do what I like. I can make what friends I like. I won't be criticized and scolded and suggested at. What is there left for me, anyway? What fun is there for me to have? I've lost nearly all my money – which you've got' – she said unfairly to Charmian who, however, only smiled, knowing this to be no more than a peroration – 'and now I'm even denied the right to my own friends.'

Hearing Field's key in the lock I signalled to her to stop, but she swept violently on.

'You shan't turn Johnny out of here! He's lonely, and his heart's bad, and he needs looking after. And I like looking after him, and I won't have him driven away by suggestions or hints, or anything else you –'

Field came in, sensed a crisis at once and halted. Helena turned to him, her face flaming, her eyes as shining and black as tar. 'Johnny! You're not going to leave me, are you? You tell them you're not going to. This is my house and I say you shall stay! You won't leave me?'

He moved towards her, looking curiously shy and tender. 'Of course I won't, Helena, if you don't want me to. What's the matter? Has anything happened?'

'I think we'd better all go to bed,' I said. 'Go on, Charmian. Take Evan with you.'

'We can't keep putting things off,' she replied slowly, not budging.

'Does someone want me to go?' Field said, addressing Helena, 'because I've often thought it would be better if I did. Claud thinks so, too.'

Helena held his gaze with hers. 'Never mind what Claud thinks. It's what I think.' She was quieter now, the years that had been added by rage falling away from her. 'I want you to stay here, Johnny, because I like having you. You're home more than the others, and you help me. If you pay any attention to them I shall think you're ungrateful. I've looked after you, haven't I?'

For a moment, a shade that was something like anger passed across his face. I was certain that he would make some quiet, courteous answer with which to terminate the scene and his association with us all. Then the shadow passed. He smiled, and said simply, 'I'm very grateful, Helena. So long as you want me here I'll stay, unless Claud and Charmian really want me to go.'

She slid down into her chair and began to cry. It was pitiful, the more so that it was not quite sincere.

Charmian said, 'This is a storm in a teacup, John. Mother's upset. I hope no one's going to upset her any more.' She put her hand on Evan's arm. 'Come on.' They went out together, and I followed them.

'He stays,' she said, smiling oddly, 'obviously. Mother is set on it.'

Evan shivered. 'Did I precipitate all this? I hope not. I hate scenes.'

'Frankly,' I told him, 'your mother was tactless.'

'No,' he said, 'it was a joke. Tactlessness implies that you say by accident something you really think but didn't intend to come out with. She didn't mean anything disagreeable.'

'Anyway, you and Charmian will both be out of the scenes and uproars.'

'I think we'd better set up on our own now,' he agreed, 'better all round for everybody.' He smiled. 'Good night.'

I went back to where Helena and Field were sitting in silence before the fireless grate now screened by a sort of fan very badly worked by Helena in *petit point*. They turned when I came in and smiled at me, but I felt that they were within a magical hexagon into which I could not set my foot. Loneliness for Jane, wounded pride, merged with loneliness for Helena. A small personal grief can open the mind to the fret of a whole world. For the first time in many weeks I had a sense of defeat, the years behind me lying in dust, the years ahead of me stretching lifeless and without colour. Because of my personal fret I was aware of the wastes of the world, the starving present, the infernal memories of the past, the daunting labours and dangers of the future. I said to myself, Tomorrow I shall recover again, see straight: and I knew that this would be so, that I should again see straightly. Nevertheless, at the moment I forgot that men in every century had known the terror of believing that history had come to a stop and that it would never again be possible to wake in the morning without the fear of desolation.

'You look washed-out,' said Helena, as if nothing had happened. 'Haven't caught a chill, have you?' She pulled up a chair for me, desiring to establish the harmony without which she was ever filled with guilt and anger. I sat with them, but the rim of the hexagon was still between us.

I told her I didn't think I'd caught a chill, but that I felt low.

'Have a drink,' she said, 'and Johnny, you go to bed. Off with you.'

He obeyed her, casting a backward glance at us, half-ashamed, half-apprehensive of what we might say when he had gone.

For a while, however, we said nothing. Helena, solicitous, motherly, poured me a whisky and lit my cigarette. She wound the clock, and went about the room putting tidy this or that. At last she spoke. 'Sorry about the to-do, Claud, but I couldn't stop myself. Anyway, the air wanted clearing.'

'We won't start that again. You've cleared the air away so thoroughly that it's difficult to breathe.'

'Don't *you* start,' she threatened me, 'don't you start.'

She came to stand before me, looking down from her sloping height. Her voice was quiet, but full of an urgency that worried me. For the first time that night she was utterly sincere.

'You've got to understand this, Claud. This ... young Johnny ...' She stopped. A muddle in the stitching of the firescreen arrested her attention. Bending down she scraped energetically with her finger-nail as if hoping to obliterate it. 'This is the last important thing that will ever happen to me. The last.'

She straightened herself slowly, drawing my gaze up with hers.

'All right,' I said, 'all right.'

She patted my arm and went towards the door, turning for a second to say, in a tone the more appealing because she scarcely understood her own words, 'The last thing.'

Chapter Five

ONE afternoon in June, as I had little work to do, I left the War Office at three o'clock and strolled down into St James's Park. It was a close grey day, promising rain and possibly thunder. The air was electric, insinuating into the mind the impression that something exciting was about to happen, something splendid, something to alter an entire life. To douse the flicker of this marsh light I sat down under the trees facing the Mall to read my paper, but found I could not concentrate. For some reason I thought of Nina Crandell, little, plain, badly dressed, who had been so pleasant and sung so charmingly, and to my surprise was taken with desire for her. It was, in fact, a bad day to be alone.

For the past few weeks, increasing my restlessness, my household had been disturbed. Helena was cross-grained, agreeable to no one but Field, with whom she now had all manner of private jokes. He, always cheerful when she was by, was ill at ease when alone with me, feeling himself an intruder and, I think, half longing to leave the flat, but having no strength to resist Helena's tidal will. He was sucked back and forth by it, dragged and driven, abandoned to the curious pleasure of being helpless. Of Charmian I saw little. She and Evan had taken a service flat at Regent's Park and she complained that the Army overworked him. Like myself, he had a War Office job, but it was with the Welfare and Education Department in Eaton Place.

Charmian, now posted to a Surrey unit, managed to get home for week-ends. 'It's long enough,' she said, rather bitterly. 'I gather he gets home at all hours during the week, so it wouldn't be much use if I were out of the Army. Even last Saturday he wasn't in till nearly midnight, and I was kicking my heels all the evening.' She spoke of him nowadays with a degree of resentment, and always as if she wished to add something that she wanted me to guess but dared not tell me. My conviction that she was no longer in love had become very strong. Her complaint of seeing so little of him I put down to the fear that any prolonged absence from him would force her to admit lovelessness even to herself; and once such an admission is made consciously, a marriage is dead.

I had attended Jane Elvorden's wedding the previous week and had been depressed ever since, not because I had any desire for her (the placing of the ring on her finger had, in fact, given me a sensation of joy and security), but because I felt left behind, like someone in a dull country district who has just seen a friend off on the nine-fifteen to town.

All in all, the interest of life seemed suddenly to have run dry, and I could not imagine from what new source it might spring again. It was not, indeed, a good world for renewals, was like a patient awakening sickly from a major operation, still leaden with the anaesthetic. Outside the slow-waking world of England (here a finger moves, here a leg twitches, an eye slews round in a paralysed face) was the universe of chaos, of hunger, of displaced persons, of the great crocodile of the dispossessed moving from nowhere in particular to nowhere that bore a name, but always moving, moving. And inside England government was halted, awaiting the word from the polls. Nothing would happen for the time being; nothing could; the millions that sensed this stoppage subconsciously, knew by instinct that most of the problems of private life, also, would find no solution for the duration of the calm.

As I watched the crowds which seemed to move in slow motion beneath the canopy of dust that underhung the sky, I vaguely noted two women strolling together, one wearing a piratical black hat that was like Helena's. Had the hat not arrested my attention I should not have looked closely enough to realize that it was indeed Helena, and that her companion was Dilys Olney.

They were walking animatedly, intimately, like friends. Helena made some remark and Mrs Olney flung back her head in a jerk of laughter, exposing her splendid white teeth and a strip of gum. She was hatless, her hair taking lustre from the sombre light of the day. She wore her white coat over a mustard-coloured dress that hung to the middle of her great calves, and she carried on her arm a purple handbag nearly large enough for a valise, through the strap of which was thrust a rolled umbrella. They stopped within three feet of me, waiting to cross the road to the Duke of York's Steps. I heard Helena say, 'That's all you know, then! Dan could always arrange things if he liked.'

I got up and went to speak to them. Helena started when she saw me, blushed, then looked defiant. Mrs Olney simply smiled, bowed and stepped back a little, as if any business I might have was unlikely to be with her.

'Hullo, Helena, what are you doing here? Good afternoon, Mrs Olney.'

'You didn't know we knew each other, did you?' Helena said. 'We're quite old friends.'

'Well, more or less,' Mrs Olney chimed in, coming forward again to stand at Helena's elbow. 'How are you these days, Major?'

'Why aren't you at work?' Helena demanded. 'I thought you were in Whitehall, polishing off the Japanese.'

'We're slack this afternoon.'

'We were just going to have some tea,' said Mrs Olney feverishly, 'we've been shopping.'

The two of them were like schoolchildren caught in mischief. They even nudged each other.

'Will you join us?' Helena asked me. 'We're going along to Simpson's. It's nice and quiet there.'

'No, thank you, I must be getting back to work now. How's business, Mrs Olney?'

'Oh, it might be worse really, considering people don't want to spend, and anyway they feel guilty buying luxuries.'

'Have you someone to leave in charge of the shop?'

'No, but this is early-closing day. I always do my own shopping in the West End on Thursdays.'

An elderly Polish officer passing by was attracted by Mrs Olney's dulled beauty. He gave her a half smile. Unsmiling she glanced back at him, betraying only by the scarcely perceptible twitch of her mouth her interest and acknowledgement. Then she concentrated her attention once more upon me.

'You're looking terribly well. How do you manage to look so well when there's so little to eat, or are you one of those fortunate people with a tiny appetite? I know I feel half-starved all the time. Must you really go back to work?'

I said I must, spoke to them a moment or so longer, and left them.

When I got back to the flat that evening Helena was still out. Field was lying on his bed trying to write clerihews for a *New Statesmen* competition; directly he saw me he began to read them out in a rather depressed voice. 'Are any of these any good?' he asked, when he had finished. 'I shouldn't think they were.'

I told him which I liked best and was just going to question him about Mrs Olney when he said, 'Nineveh Press is going bust. I got slung out today.'

'Bust? Were you expecting it?'

'Sort of. Mallion's been worried for some time, and filthily snappy. His production costs were always too high, anyway, and there weren't enough millionaires to buy what he produced. I think it's quite clever to fail as a publisher in wartime.' Field grinned joylessly, then said, 'I suppose I'll get something else. There ought to be simple jobs lying around for people like me. Basket-making, or something of the kind.'

He thought of a new clerihew, wrote it down rapidly, read it through, then scribbled it out again. 'I'll probably have to leave here soon, Claud, any old how. I shan't be able to pay the rent. You won't be sorry, will you?'

'Oh, it won't come to that,' I said weakly. I had made so many attempts to edge Field out of our household that now a real hope had arisen of this coming about, I had no heart to press the matter. 'Listen: how long has Helena known Mrs Olney?'

He sat up like a jack-in-a-box. 'It wasn't my doing! I swear it wasn't. You know Helena – she's unstoppable.'

'I didn't say it was your doing. What do you know about it, though?'

'You'll think I've been hiding things. I would have told you, only I hoped it would simply stop, that Helena would get fed up with it, and then there'd be no harm done.'

'She doesn't get fed up with things easily. Go on, tell me the story.'

'It was about three weeks ago. She asked me where Mrs Olney lived exactly, and when I told her she said, "I'm going to meet her." I said you'd be furious, but there was no holding her back. Off she went, and when she got home she was tremendously pleased with herself. Apparently they'd made friends.' He was silent, looking dismally down at his feet.

'What do you think her idea is?'

'God knows.'

'Why didn't you tell me, for God's sake? – However long you imagined it would last.'

He looked at me, his eyes clear. 'I suppose I thought it was Helena's business, really. I didn't want to interfere.'

I tried to explain to him, as delicately as I could, that Helena was not fitted to have business of her own. That in her own interests she needed supervision.

'Oh, I don't know,' Field said, 'I think she'd work things out all right for herself if she was left alone.'

Recognizing this as one of Helena's ideas forcibly implanted into his belief, I made no remark. He was hers now, working for her always towards whatever ends she meant to pursue, entirely disregarding his lack of knowledge of her background, and Charmian's, and mine. It was enraging, and yet there was no help for it. He really did see her as a victim, myself as a tyrant. He misunderstood every word that passed between Helena and me, misunderstood the character of the acid exchanges, the rough jokes, which had grown little by little out of the very fabric of our personal history.

Guessing that I would want to talk to her, Field went out after dinner, saying he would not be back until ten or so. When I tackled Helena about Mrs Olney she opened her eyes wide. 'Can't I do what I want to? Have I always got to come to you for a yes or no? I like Dilys. She's a poor creature, but she amuses me. I'm sorry Dan didn't leave her anything. Why should the other bitches have had it and not she?'

'She's the last person I'd have imagined you wanted to be friends with.'

'Why?' Helena snapped. 'Am I so small-minded? What's past is past. If Daniel got any fun out of her, good luck to him. Why should I care? Besides, she needs help.'

'What help?' I asked suspiciously. 'Is she hard up?'

'What do you expect her to be, selling nasty little lamp-shades?'

'I expect her to be hard up. You haven't been giving her money?'

'She's the proud type,' said Helena with noble confidence. 'There's no question of that.' She thought of her friend for a little while, and her eyes softened in reminiscence. 'Do you know, she was on the stage for a bit too?'

'I shouldn't be surprised.'

'Her first husband was a comic. She was only nineteen then. She was his feed. She used to start singing a song – you know the sort of thing – and then he'd come butting in like a drunk and say, "I beg your pardon, madam, but is this the Wandsworth Cemetery?" and then she'd tick him off and start singing again and he'd come wandering back and say, "Somehow I was certain this was the Wandsworth Cemetery." . . . It's an old gag, but it always makes me laugh.'

I told her it didn't amuse me in the least, and that I wasn't amused by Mrs Olney. 'For God's sake! She was Dan's mistress, and she's a prize cadger. And she's quite an experienced cadger, because she doesn't ask for anything the first few times.'

'What a beastly mind you've got!' Helena said scorchingly. 'I should be *ashamed*. She was so nice about you, too.'

'I bet she was. Oh yes – and another thing. You asked Field not to tell me you were meeting Mrs Olney, didn't you?'

'Yes, I did. I didn't want you chewing over everything I chose to do.' She had that look of cunning, fighting childishness so piteous in the old, and I had a flash of love for her.

'I'm fed up with Field's damned interference,' I said.

Helena reared herself like Farinata from his tomb in the place of heretics, as if she had Hell in great despite. 'I won't stand it, oh I *won't* stand it! Pick, pick, pick at Johnny all the time, ever since he's been here! It's only because I'm fond of him that you do it. You think you can hurt me like that. If you can't stop sneering at him you can go and find somewhere else to live. I will be happy! I won't be upset by your pickings and spites! I mean it. I don't mind if you go. I don't care if you do.' She left the room, slamming the door behind her with such a great jar that the pink glass fish admired by Mrs Olney fell down and was smashed to bits on the hearth.

I was depressed, not because I took seriously Helena's attempts to turn me out, but because her attachment to Field was strong enough to drive her to such furies. Too troubled to settle to work or reading, I spent half an hour writing boring letters to people with whom I did not in the least wish to correspond. I had just stamped them and was going to take them out when Helena came in, all good humour, asked me if I wanted any socks darned and promised me my bacon ration with a shell egg for tomorrow's breakfast. I gave her some mending, talked scandal with her for ten minutes or so until I had tacitly convinced her that I was no more upset by her recent outburst than by any of the thousand outbursts of the past, and went out for some air.

By the time I reached Oakley Street the promised rain began to fall heavily, so I turned down a side road and went into the saloon bar of a small public-house I had not visited before.

It was one of those houses that have a tiny private bar, not much larger than a cupboard, adjoining the saloon, and separated from it only by a low partition of glass and wood. I had just ordered a drink when I heard Field's voice. I was sitting in a corner by this partition, and the voice appeared to come from a spot directly behind my head. Looking through a transparent star set in the frosted glass, I saw him sitting with a girl in trousers, whose fat, experienced face was surrounded by a Queen Anne-ish tumble of curls. They were alone in the bar and he did not lower his voice. I was wondering whether I should join them, though I had no particular wish to do so, when the name 'Helena' caught my attention.

Field was speaking in a tone unfamiliar to me, the tone of a man confident of a particular woman and assured of her admiration. The girl replied to him softly, ironically, inaudibly, but with a note of intimacy that was unmistakable.

'It's terrifically embarrassing,' he said, 'but there it is. I am loved for myself alone.' She made some comment and he laughed. For a moment there was silence. Then he said, 'No, I assure you it's pure! She's a pet. But I simply happen to enthral her. It's absolutely no credit to me.' All this was uttered in a manner of humorous self-depreciation, which implied that the speaker was offering only a grain of truth in a bushel of nonsense. 'She's been enormously kind; God knows what I'd have done without her, but –' Here the girl again interrupted. 'That's right,' said Field, 'a *thing* about me. It cheers me terrifically, because nobody's ever had a *thing* before.' Her reply was audible this time. 'How do you know I haven't?' 'I'm quite sure you haven't. You haven't the right sort of look in the eye.'

Unable to stand any more of this, I got up. He had risen at the same moment to have their glasses refilled, and we looked at each other. 'Hullo,' he said uncertainly. He had gone white.

'I want to talk to you.'

He said very softly, 'Oh, Christ,' and looked at the floor. The girl stared from one to the other of us, raised her eyebrows and made a round mouth.

'I'll wait for you outside,' I told him.

I walked down to the corner of the street and stood beneath a lamp. In a moment or so he came out of the public-house with the girl and spoke to her briefly. She shrugged, patted his cheek, and went off with big, strained strides in the opposite direction.

When he came up to me I said, 'You're a bloody sort of swine, aren't you?' I was so giddy with anger that the houses and trees seemed to slant at the nightmare angles of the old German films.

'You heard, of course.'

'I couldn't help it. You were shouting your damned head off.'

'I know I was. I always do.' He shivered violently, the movement running over his body like wind over a pond. 'Let's walk.'

We turned towards home. I could not speak to him.

'I'd give my ears to put the clock back an hour,' he said. 'I'd give my eyes. I don't know what I can say.'

'You're going tomorrow.'

'Yes. Of course. Claud. let me try and say something for myself.'

'Go ahead.' I could not bear the feel of him at my side, could not bear to see even his shadow walking with mine. When his coat sleeve brushed against my own I put a few more inches between us.

'It's only talk. I've never got on easily with women; I have to try to impress them. That girl used to live over Hammersmith way when I was there. She was engaged to a chap I know, only it's all bust up. I've had a drink with her here once or twice.'

Halted by a taxi at the corner of Cheyne Row, we had to wait till it had gone. Field looked at me, and he was like a man in physical agony.

He went on: 'I love Helena; I think she's one of the most terrific women I've ever met. I don't know why I had to sell her to that damned girl. I don't know why I talked as I did: but I always do! I'd be lying in my teeth if I said it was the first time. I can't help it. Something starts me off, and I can't stop. I've done it time and time again, selling people I care about, getting so sick with myself that I want to cut my throat. You wouldn't understand it – you're so damned self-confident. I envy you. You haven't got to show off.' There was a note of attack in his voice now, which was stronger and more like his voice of every day. 'If you hadn't heard me, there'd have been no harm done, would there?'

'I did hear you.'

'I'm going all right. Don't imagine I'm trying to excuse myself. It's only that if you could see my side of it at all, you'd be able to feel, some day, that I wasn't entirely lacking in gratitude to Helena and to you.'

'If you mention Helena again, I think I'll kick you into the gutter.' Rage, and humiliation on Helena's behalf, had given me a violent headache. I should not have spoken to him in this way if I had not suffered a spasm of violent pain caused by a stub of the tow at an uneven paving-stone.

'I'll get my things now, tonight,' Field muttered. 'I'll clear out right away. I can get in somewhere.'

We came out of Church Street into King's Road. Again we had to pause, while the crowd coming out of the cinema drifted past us. Two girls with flowing hair were singing in high, flat harmony, arms and voices flowerily entwined. Because we stood in their path they separated, clutched us, swung round us as round a lamp-post, came together again like two streams meeting, and passed on.

'Didn't you ever say anything just to show off, just to make yourself look a hell of a fellow?' Field cried out. His eyes were closed, the lashes stuck and shone. Then he opened them, shuddered, and crossed the road at my side.

I could not answer this. All I could think of was Helena humiliated, presented in a farcical, obscene role to a strange girl who would never discover its falsity; Helen made to play an absurd part in support of Field's hero. She could, as I knew, be ridiculous and wicked, but it was an outrage to me that she should be made the subject of a bar-room giggle by two people who could never in a lifetime comprehend a single part of her total splendour. Had Field talked in this night's fashion to Swain or to Crandell, I should not have cared so much; in their company, because of their knowledge, the joke would have fallen to flabbiness. It is more painful to hear one's friends denigrated to strangers than to their enemies.

The rain was heavy again, the roads like black satin. Field lifted his face to it as if grateful for any sort of discomfort, however slight, that might serve as punishment. He looked very young, his ears prominent, his eyes heroically desperate. I had seen him like this in the mess once, after some baiting from an elderly captain whose wit had been toughened by failure.

Just as we were crossing Church Street an army car swung out of a side turning, skidded on the wet roads and came at us. I managed to get clear, but the mudguard caught Field and knocked him down. The car stopped fifty yards or so up the road and the driver, a sergeant, got out. As he reached us Field had just risen to his feet. He was trembling violently and his teeth chattered. The sergeant, himself thoroughly shaken, wanted to know if we were all right, blamed the roads, his brakes.

'I'm O.K.' said Field, smudging ineffectually at his trousers, which were stained with mud, 'no harm done. Not your fault. Wasn't anybody's.'

'Are you quite sure you're oke?' the sergeant persisted. 'Try and see. Walk a bit.'

'There's nothing wrong with me. You just sort of tipped me over, that's all.'

'Christ, I thought I'd killed you! You are quite sure . . .?'

Field replied impatiently that he was unhurt.

'Look, hadn't you better take my name? If anything did come up –'

'He's all right, sergeant,' I said, 'he's only a bit shaken up. He'll be fine, soon.'

Leaving the driver only half satisfied, we went on. I asked Field if he was sure he hadn't bruised or cut himself, and could hardly force the inquiries from my mouth. I remembered how sick with fury I had always been when as a child, hating Helena, I had been forced by her cold, her headache, her influenza, to pretend a sympathy I could not feel. Illness or bereavement rig out people we dislike in disguises that embarrass and enrage us. We hate them for being set apart from us (and in some curious way becoming superior to us) by some external thing outside their own control. I detested Field now for the incident that gave him momentary shelter.

We went up the steps of the house and into the hall. The filament of the electric lamp had broken on the previous night and had not been replaced, so we had to feel our way upstairs. Once, in the dark, Field stumbled and caught my arm, and would have fallen backwards had I not held him.

We came into the room where Helena was sitting. She had both the top lights on and to me, coming suddenly from blackness, the glare was painful. She said something or other that I did not hear, and then, 'Johnny! What's the matter?'

I looked at him. His face was green-white and seemed perfectly smooth, as if even the smallest line had been ironed out of it. His eyes flickered and expanded, flickered and expanded, giving him an appearance of dumbfounded amazement, and on his forehead the sweat was like a band of cellophane. He took two steps forward, put out his hand towards Helena, and fainted.

She was entirely helpless. She knelt beside him, calling to him in a panicked voice, and when I brought some water to bring him round, impeded me by trying to snatch the glass. I had to lift her up and make her sit still, telling her briefly of the car in Church Street.

'The swine!' she said passionately. 'Johnny might have been killed. The shock might have killed him. Careless damned devil, why couldn't he watch what he was doing?'

Though I told her the accident was no fault of the driver's

Helena went on abusing him automatically, her mind concentrated upon Field's blank face. Now, however, she did not interfere with me but sat in a corner of the settee, quite still.

He opened his eyes and said feebly, smiling, 'How damn silly.' I helped him up. 'Damn silly,' he repeated. 'Thanks, Claud.' Then he remembered, or pretended to remember. He looked away.

'Better lie down on the sofa,' I said.

As Helena came to bustle about him, enfolding him in her anxious love, he drooped slightly towards her. The two of them, she with her arms around his waist, he leaning forward against her, looked like marathon dancers at the end of the first twelve hours. 'Not the sofa – we'll get you straight on to the bed, Johnny, we'll have you comfortable right away. Go and turn the bed down for him, Claud.'

She made me help him undress, made me assure myself that he had no injury upon his body. When he was between the sheets she came to sit beside him, holding his hands and chafing them, smoothing his brow, looking into his eyes as if she expected to see in them the date of his death. He seemed content to lie there in her warm shadow, but now and then he looked at me half-shy, half-sly, and I wondered for a second of which I was ashamed, how strategic his faint had been. That he had been shaken, I knew; and I believed that the preliminary stage of fainting – the sudden fading of colours, the melting of all solid things – had indeed attacked him. What I was not sure about, however, was how far he had abandoned himself voluntarily to it, and whether he could, by an effort of will, have recovered himself. I was fairly certain he had regained consciousness some moments before he opened his eyes.

'You leave us now,' Helena whispered to me urgently, 'I'll look after him. He wants to be quiet with me. He doesn't want people hanging about.' I did as she asked me.

There was silence in his room for a long time save for her occasional whispers; I think she was trying to make him sleep. Later, however, I heard her cry out to him, as if she were comforting a child, 'We'll look after you, Helena will always look after you. She'll make you well!'

In a little while she came out to me. She had been crying.

'My poor little Johnny! Oh, Claud, my poor little Johnny Field! We'll take care of him together, won't we? We'll have the doctor tomorrow, our doctor, not one of those silly idiots he's been going to. We're going to get him well, see? We'll do it together. Claud, I'm so fond of Johnny, so fond of my poor little ill Johnny!'

'Oh, we'll get him right,' I said. I knew now that he would not leave us, in the camera of my mind saw him lying there in the room beyond, a smile behind his closed eyes. I was overwhelmed by the sickness of secrecy, by the shady knowledge which, so far as I could see, I should have to carry within me till its urgency was faded and all the persons concerned with it had become insubstantial as my shadow on the wall.

PART THREE

Chapter One

By the first week in July I had found living with Field and Helena intolerable and had returned to my old rooms, which were now repaired. This decision to move, a decision taken suddenly in a fit of that irritation which must either provoke action or fester into a nervous crisis, followed an artificial elevation of my spirits. I have often noticed that when one's personal affairs seem the worst entangled, some series of accidents will bring about a feeling that, after all, everything is well and the weather sunny. Shortly after Field's fainting fit I had met Jane Elvorden, Jane Crossman, as she now was, in the street, had been invited to dinner at her house, and had there met a cousin of hers, a lively girl with dark, pointed face and eyes like a Siamese cat's, who was sailing for South Africa in a month's time. She did not fall in love with me nor I with her, but we had great pleasure in pretending that love was between us, thereby enjoying all its graces without its obligations. We danced, went to theatres and cinemas, and spent a week-end or so in the country. It was all so much like a love affair of the cinema that I was for the time being perfectly happy, and persuaded that I should never be out of humour again. The freaks of Helena, the modest, adhesive presence of Field seemed to me of no importance; I could not understand how I had ever let either of them worry me.

Then, on a black and rainy morning, the pathetic fallacy at full blast, I saw Jane's cousin off on the boat-train, and returning to the flat was seized immediately by all the jilted furies which I had left behind there. Awaiting me also, relevantly, was a letter from my landlady telling me that the ceiling of my rooms had been repaired, my walls repainted, and that I was welcome to return if I wished.

Field was pottering about the place in a self-effacing fashion, that seemed to annoy Helena, who accused him of going on tiptoe. 'Why can't you make a noise like other people? If you make me jump like that again, I'll tie a bell round your neck.'

'I thought I was making a terrific noise,' he said. 'I'm sorry.'

Helena's doctor had seen him on the day after his faint, and had said that though there was no need for him to lie about all day, he had better go slow. So Field was going slow, moving like a slow-motion film, seeming even to smile more slowly and to consider carefully whether it might not be dangerous for him to laugh. Helena lapped him in her love, that flowed like a sweet, slow river about him. Even her bursts of rage were demonstrably playful, affectionate assurances that he was not really an invalid and was strong enough to share the setbacks of normal men.

I do not think I should have been so quick to leave the flat had not Helena, after dinner, requested Field to tune the piano. This, it appeared, was one of his accomplishments; he had always had a remarkable ear and as a boy had picked up the rudiments of the craft from a tuner who had come regularly to his father's house.

So he sat at the piano, tapping and listening, ping, ping, ping in the treble, bong, bong, bong in the base, his head cocked, the attentive ear seeming to spring like a gladiolus, pink and stiff, from the stretched cord of his throat, while Helena from her easy chair beamed at him over the spectacles she had recently taken to wearing. The cat lay sleeping on her knees beneath a great mass of botched and disregarded knitting.

It was dusk and the lamps were not lit. Out of the heavy air the infuriating notes fell, always on the same spot of my nerves, and I thought of the torture in which drops of water were allowed to fall, one by one, on to the victim's brow. They were like water, and they were like voices – incessant voices that babble behind a wall when one is trying to go to sleep. Occasionally Field played a bar or so of a tune, and I longed for him to complete it; but he always stopped, and the voices began again.

This had been going on for an hour and ten minutes when I showed Helena my landlady's letter and told her how I should answer it.

She looked at me mildly. 'I should, dear,' she said, nodding

her head, seeming to adopt, out of some freak, the manner-
isms of a very old lady. 'I think it would be very wise. You'd
have more peace for your work.' I had recently finished my
book, and she knew it. 'I do feel authors need to be quiet.'

Field was less happy about my move than she, and when
we were alone hinted his wish for reassurance that he was not
the cause of it. I took no notice of the hints, and moved my
clothes and books out on the following evening.

For a while it seemed that I had done the right thing. I did
enjoy being alone again, and when I went back to the flat for a
drink once or twice a week, found Field and Helena so cheerful, so much a *ménage*, that I began to wonder if I had not, indeed, been behaving badly to them both.

Helena was in splendid spirits. All manner of visitors had
called – 'It really does make you feel the war's over,' she said,
'when the door bell rings after nine' – and on her birthday
Swain had walked in and made her a present of *Roadmending*.
I heard the story of this from Charmian, who had been present.

'You might as well have it,' Swain had said, 'you worked
hard enough to get it' – and had given her a grin of love, of
admiration, and of contempt.

Roused by this, Helena suggested that he was giving it
away simply because he had been unable to find a buyer.

'Right,' said Swain, snatched up the picture and walked
out of the flat with it. Helena raced after him (Charmian assured me that she really *had* raced) and caught up with him on
the pavement outside the house. 'Come on, come on,' she insisted, 'you've given it to me and it's mine.'

'You don't get it,' Swain told her, ''till you say Sorry. Go
on, say Sorry.' He treated Helena always as if she were a girl,
and she loved it.

She roared at him that she was not apologizing to pip-
squeaks, and snatched at the painting. Swain hung on to it and
they had a serio-comic tussle back and forth across the pavement.

'Look,' he said, 'we're getting an audience. We're stopping
the traffic.'

'All right, take your picture!' She sought for an insult, considered (Charmian was certain) what I might have said had I

wished to scarify. 'You go and give it to the Royal Academy! That's all it's good for.'

She let go her hold suddenly. Swain staggered backwards, tripped over the kerb and fell into the gutter, where he sat silent, the painting held tightly to his chest.

'It was wonderful,' Charmian told me, 'it must have been like the old days in Bruges. A Canadian soldier and a girl were watching, two old ladies and a grocer's boy. I've never seen Swain look so surprised. He got up, dusted himself down, then took Mother firmly by the arm and led her back into the house. Then he told her she was a horrible old woman, gave her a kiss and the picture, and went away. She was tickled to death.'

Helena hung the painting in the star position on the wall of the front room, in the full light just over Daniel's desk. She really loved it and never tired of pointing out to me new beauties she had only that minute perceived.

One night I looked in at the flat, round about ten o'clock, to bring back a pair of shoes my landlady's son had re-soled for her. I thought Helena looked rather embarrassed when she saw me, though her greeting was cheerful enough.

'Those my shoes? Oh, your man is a lamb! Do you know, old Drabble round the corner wouldn't promise anything for a month?' She paused. 'Come on in. Dilys is here.'

I found Mrs Olney sitting in the window, looking through the contents of Helena's ragbag. Her lap was full of shreds of cotton and silk, and she wore a pair of green-rimmed glasses on the point of her handsome nose.

'You know Claud,' said Helena, rather loudly.

Mrs Olney said it was lovely to see me again, asked me how I did and told me she had not thought I looked well upon the occasion of our last meeting. She seemed much at home, and I had the impression that this was not a rare visit. 'Are you a connoisseur?' she asked me. 'But of course you are. Do you like this bit?' She held up a strip of flame-coloured silk dotted with cream. 'You don't get that sort of quality these days. . . . Do you, Johnny?'

'I shouldn't think so,' Field said, rising, and coming to take the silk in his hand. 'This is heavy stuff.'

'Johnny's had the most wonderful idea!' Mrs Olney insisted to me. 'Helena always said he had a business head, and she's perfectly correct.'

Helena glanced at me covertly, to see how I was taking this liberal use of christian names.

'You remember my little shop?'

I replied that I did, very well indeed.

'Well, I should be a hypocrite if I pretended that we were doing too wonderful business, shouldn't I?'

This was rhetorical.

'Johnny says what I want to do is to advertise that I'll make lampshades out of customers' own materials – what do you think of that? You know, to match their rooms. To match coverings, or curtains, or even walls if there was a patterned paper, only you don't often see patterned papers.'

'Which I think is a pity,' Field interpolated, in an assured tone. 'Wall-papers can be quite smashing, if they're well designed. I'm getting as sick of our creams and off-whites as people got of the beiges and oatmeals of the twenties.'

I had never before heard him express any interest in interior decorating and was interested. This was the first time I had ever known him speak of a subject as if he had some positive intention connected with it.

Mrs Olney leaned forward, bringing her face near to mine. Her fawn hair swung across her cheeks, framing a great and luminous earnestness. 'But what do you think of the *idea*, Major Pickering? You're an art expert. Do you think people would like it?'

Some vague unease, some sense of a lack that I could not define, prevented me for a moment from answering her. Helena took this hesitation for ill-humour, and said rather snappishly, 'No good asking Claud. His advice costs a guinea a yard and he doesn't give it free.'

'No, no,' I said, 'I was thinking about it. Yes, I suppose it might be a good thing. Anyway, worth trying.'

At that moment I discovered what had been worrying me. *Roadmending* had gone.

'Helena! Where's Swain's picture?'

She stared at me, insisting with her eyes that I was to be quiet, that I was not to ask questions now. 'Being cleaned,' she said at random.

'Cleaned? But good lord, you only had it the other day.'

'It needed cleaning.' She did not flicker an eyelash, but concentrated her gaze as if trying to hypnotize me.

Mrs Olney asked me some question or other, and the subject of the painting was dropped.

But later that night, when Mrs Olney had left and Field had gone to his own room, I asked Helena again where *Roadmending* was.

'I sold it.'

I was dumbfounded. As if she had said her last word she turned her back on me and began to bundle the silks back into the ragbag.

'Why?' I demanded.

'It was mine, wasn't it? He wasn't lying when he said what it was worth. I got a hundred and twenty-five pounds.'

'Who from?'

She named a picture-dealer, one whom Daniel had often patronized.

I did not, for a moment, know how to speak to her. It was a beautiful little painting, Swain at his best; and I believed that despite the reputations of various other men, there was no better painter in the country. His personality was mature, and his philosophy complete. He was profoundly interested in men and women, in the work they did and the worlds in which they moved; he painted them not as the components of a design, but as thinking and breathing beings, their fears and anxieties dark as night behind their eyes, and their hopes brilliant as day.

'Why did you do it?'

'I wanted some money,' Helena told me briskly, her face defiant with shame and rage. 'That's why.'

'But you couldn't have wanted a hundred and twenty-five quid that badly! If you had, I could have lent it to you, but you know damn well you didn't.'

'It's my business.'

'I'd have bought it myself rather than let it out of the family!'

'You couldn't have afforded it. Anyway, I didn't want a lot of questions and arguments.'

As she would say no more than that and as she was obviously much distressed, I was forced to let the matter drop, beyond a comment that I couldn't imagine what Swain would have to say if he knew.

Helena made no answer to this, but she looked as if she were about to cry.

On my way home I wondered if it would be possible for me to get the painting back from the dealer, but realized that the price he would ask me would be so much in advance of the price he had paid that *Roadmending* was now well beyond my reach.

Once, as an excitable boy, making the discovery that Helena, my father's widow, had not spent in celibacy the years that followed his death, I had struck her. I had often looked back with regret on the incident; now, I simply felt that it justified the old and the new.

Charmian, when I told her about the sale of the painting, was horrified; but not for more than ten minutes. Other matters were occupying her interest and she had much to tell me. This was the week-end following the General Election results, and she had dined the night before with Mrs Sholto and some friends of hers, who were also acquaintances of Helena's.

'The *belle-mère* was taking things badly.' Charmian smiled, and for a moment looked less weary. As usual these days she was carelessly dressed, an old red woollen cardigan, none too clean, worn over a summer frock that had faded from several years of washing. I interrupted her to ask why she didn't buy something new.

'No coupons.'

'Have you used up Evan's?'

'I think he wants them himself. Anyway, he doesn't seem to have any. Oh, leave me alone – I'm comfortable. I was telling you about the old lady. She was really upset; I believe she expected the mob to break in at any moment and hang her on a lamp-post. She took me aside and said, in a trembly voice, "*This is worse than losing the war*."'

I made an abusive comment.

'Oh yes, yes,' Charmian agreed, 'but from her point of view it's logical. If Hitler had ever got here she'd have collaborated like fun. You know, my hairdresser told me that during the worst of the invasion scares one of his customers came in for a perm. She said, "If the Germans do come, I think it's up to us all to look our best."'

I jeered at this as apocryphal, but Charmian assured me it was true.

'Well, Helena once told Mrs Sholto and the Leipers that they were doomed as a class. Perhaps they're beginning to believe it.'

'Do you think they are?' Charmian grinned savagely, her eyes bright with vision. 'I'd love to see the *belle-mère* as a lavatory attendant.'

'They'll be sunk eventually. But I still think they'll have quite a run for their money first. I suppose it was a gloomy evening?'

'It was a hushed one,' she replied. 'I found myself looking over my shoulder and giving little starts. However, we did have one diversion from the General Election, and it worried me a bit. Evan wasn't there, you know, or he'd have stopped it somehow; but the talk turned on Mother.'

She told me, half-laughing, half-uneasy, that there had been a good deal of covert criticism of Helena and Field. It began with some delicate, malicious little joke of Mrs Sholto's relating to squires and *sigisbees*, and with the help of the Rothners (people who had known Daniel and his household for some years) had developed into a censure motion. 'It was so well done, Claud, so repulsively good-natured! There was nothing you could catch hold of. The only way I could defend Helena was by making little jokes of my own, and I'm not a patch on the *belle-mère* at that sort of thing. Obviously they didn't think it "nice" that Mother should be living alone with a young man, and they tried to blame you – I can't tell you how subtly they handled it! – for leaving them together in the flat. I could hardly believe my ears at first. I said, "I think Mother should be able to take care of herself at sixty-eight," and tried to giggle it off; but the old lady patted my hand and said, "Your mother is still an extremely attractive woman," whereupon' – Charmian paused, to give this literary word effect – '*whereupon* they all overwhelmed me with compliments and told me how much I looked like Mother, especially when I did my hair in a certain way. I tell you, I had a rush of blood to the head.'

'But they weren't serious?' I asked her, not because I thought they weren't, but because I wanted to lighten the matter for Charmian.

'Of course they were serious. There really is gossip, and the *belle-mère* started it. I suppose we might have guessed she would. Isn't it fantastic? It makes me feel rather sick.' Charmian rose, went to the mirror and took down her hair, filling her mouth with hairpins. She knotted the big bun up again, no more tidily than before, and began to skewer it into place. A couple of thick black pins, protruding from the corners of her lips, gave her the appearance of a walrus, and I told her so.

'Oh, do take things seriously,' she pleaded. 'What can we do to stop this nonsense? It'll be all round the Leiper family next, if it isn't already. I wish the mob would string the old devil to a lamp-post. I'd kick the chair away with pleasure.'

She appeared very young and lanky, had as yet no married look. 'Let them talk,' I said, 'real nonsense always wears itself out.'

'You see,' Charmian explained to me, wrinkling her brow, 'they really can't stand Mother, any of them, never could – and so they can't stand me. I gather from the *belle-mère* that Mother's telegram trick went the rounds of all the friends and relations. The Leipers dine out on it.'

I had a turn of pity for Helena, naïve enough to imagine that she had deceived them. 'Well, let them. Indirectly, she's done them a good turn. She'd given them a topic on which they might manage to be faintly entertaining for once. We oughtn't to regret our good works.'

'That's one way of looking at it,' Charmian agreed, smiling spontaneously.

'And anyhow, I don't suppose she'll be seeing much more of any of them. If she spends at her present rate, she won't be able to keep up with them at all.'

'Is she spending?' Charmian was alert.

'She must be. Why did she want that ready cash?'

'I don't see any signs of extravagance. She hasn't bought any clothes recently. She had that costume earlier on, but nothing since. Where do you think it goes to?'

Until that moment I had had no idea. Now, however, one flashed into my mind, but since it was pure conjecture, I did not tell it to Charmian. 'Lord knows. I feel rotten about that picture, though.'

She said quickly, 'You needn't. I'll go down in the morning and buy it myself.'

I had forgotten that she was now a woman of considerable means. 'Will you honestly?'

'Of course I will. I'll give it to you.'

This I would not have. 'No. But you can lend it me, if you like.'

'Why can't I make you a present?'

'You'll pay as much for my presents as I can pay for yours. That is, nothing over five quid. I'm proud.'

'You're an ass,' said Charmian. 'All right. I'll buy it to lend you, indefinitely. Which means that it's just the same as a present, so you're simply being hypocritical.'

I replied that in this case hypocrisy soothed me, and made her promise that if the painting were already sold, she would try to find out the purchaser and make a further offer.

'I'm not doing this for you at all, really,' she told me gravely, 'I'm doing it for Bill Swain's sake. His feelings would be terribly hurt.'

Then, prompted by the thought of hurt feelings, she began to speak again of the gossip that had sprung up concerning Helena and Field, and I found it hard to ease her mind.

'I'd hate it to come to Field's ears,' she said. 'I don't think a tremendous lot of him, as you know, but he is a decent sort of lad in a weak way. I can't imagine him doing anything sneaking or' – she laughed – 'in bad taste. Sometimes I think a little really *bad* taste would improve him tremendously. You don't like him as much as you did, do you?'

I told her briefly of Mrs Olney, of Field's revelations in this matter to Helena, and of the curious friendship that seemed to have grown up between the three of them.

Charmian stared at me, bewildered. 'Why didn't you tell me all this before?'

'It might have bothered you, or annoyed you.'

'That's stupid! Why should it?'

'I suppose I still think of you as nine years old. It all seems a little sordid.'

'Not so much sordid as crazy,' Charmian said slowly.

'Mother was furious about Dan's other women. Why take up with this one? Unless, of course . . .' She hesitated. 'Unless she gets a kick out of discussing him with someone as intimate with him as she was. I can imagine that.'

This struck me disagreeably, as if it were indeed the precocity of a child. 'What a mind you have!'

'I can understand how it would be,' she said rather doggedly, 'how it would seem a sort of renewal . . .' and I felt that perhaps, in some ways, she knew Helena better that I.

Later that evening I asked about Evan, how he was getting on.

'He'll be out of the Army next month. I'll be glad, I can tell you. He's never home. We'll both be out about the same time.'

'What will you do then? Any ideas about a job?'

To my surprise she coloured and looked angry. 'Why have people always got to be hustled into jobs? He's going to have a rest, of course, which he deserves. I don't see why he's got to be badgered into working right away.'

I protested that I had meant nothing beyond a casual inquiry.

Charmian, subdued, a little ashamed, asked when I was due myself for release.

'I'm voluntarily deferring myself for a bit.'

'I believe you like the army,' she said curiously.

'It's extraordinary, but I really think I do, in a way. Not that I could make it a career, even if they'd let me.'

'Wouldn't they let you?'

'Of course not. I'm too old.'

She laughed.

'It's true. You know, this war has hurried on old age. Before it, one could be quite young at thirty-six. Now, one becomes useless on the thirtieth birthday. I never thought of myself as old before the army told me all the things I was too old for.'

Norman Tennant called. It was a quarter to eleven, but he walked in as though he meant to stay a long time. He was in civilian clothes, and the dull, threepenny-piece colouring of his face and hair was more noticeable than ever.

He said to Charmian, 'Evan not back yet? Good God,

what an old stop-out. What's your influence at the War House, Pickering? Can't you get them to let the fellow go home at a more reasonable time? Charmian's getting tired to death of my company, though I do try to keep a smile on her lips.' Tennant's jokes had an awkward sound; he made them in a tone that seemed to disclaim responsibility for them.

'Don't go,' she said to me, 'it's really not late.'

'I think I'd better. I've got some work to clear up.'

'No,' she insisted, 'no. Half an hour more won't hurt you.' She looked at Tennant oddly, as if she disliked him and were praying that he would go; but when she spoke to him her voice was intimate and warm. I could not understand the relations between them: all I understood was that she really wished me to stay, that she was most eager that I should not leave her alone with him. I stayed till midnight, when Evan Sholto came in, tired, but full of good humour.

"They'll wear me out, lamb,' he said to Charmian, kissing her, 'they'll wear me to skin and bone. Anything left to drink?'

I fancied he had been drinking already, though he was quite sober.

When she had fetched him some whisky, he and Tennant talked army shop into which I refused to be drawn, as I thought Charmian looked exhausted and fit for nothing but sleep. But nothing, it seemed, would bring the evening to an end. When I left the men were still talking and Charmian was lying on the settee, her eyes closed, a cigarette drooping from her mouth and spilling its ash all over her breast.

The next time I saw Helena I told her I was troubled about Charmian and Sholto. Field was out; his aunt had asked him to dine with her at the private hotel in Kensington where she lived.

'He went out looking quite beautiful,' Helena said fondly, 'I saw to that. I pressed his suit for him and found him a tie of Dan's. Johnny hadn't got one that wasn't a string. . . . . Why, what's happening at Regent's Park?'

When I had told her my various impressions she said shrewdly, 'He's not really working all those hours of the night. What does he get up to? And where does this Tennant come in?'

She urged me to try to keep an eye on Sholto. 'If that boiled owl's making Charm unhappy, I'll murder him.'

'All I imagine she wants is to be rid of him.'

'Not to marry Tennant?' Helena looked alarmed.

'I don't think so. I don't understand the set-up there, but I feel sure that's not it.'

'Well, then, she *must* get rid of Evan! It was a stupid marriage in the first place, much too hasty and starry-eyed. I told her it was, and what's more, I told her at the time that it was only infatuation.' Helena's expression took on a wise sternness, as if the young girl were at that moment before her, hands in pockets, toes turned in.

'What did she say?'

'Oh, she laughed at me and said did I really think Evan was the type one became infatuated with? I got angry and said I could only suppose it was love after all, and Charmian said, "Naturally." You watch him, Claud. You see what you can find out.'

I told her I could not imagine a nastier or more degrading job than spying on Sholto.

'What does degradation matter,' cried Helena, tossing her head, 'where Charmian's happiness is concerned?'

But I would make her no promise.

A few days later, going into the Roebuck for a drink on my way home early from work, I found Field there, a basket of groceries he had fetched for Helena on the bench at his side. He greeted me with an open and cheerful look, either as if he had forgotten the trouble between us or for some reason considered it resolved. I must have a drink with him, he insisted, tell him about things; he had not seen me for ages. He had been to dinner with his aunt – an Event, he assured me, a tremendous event occurring as rarely as an eclipse of the sun observable from Hampstead Heath.

'It isn't that she doesn't like me – she does, quite a lot, in her way – but she dreads what she calls "encumbrances". She doesn't tell me I'm an encumbrance, of course, but that's what she means. She's a lone wolverine. She's very handsome, too, only of the small-boned type. Not like Helena.'

That reminded him, he said, of a piece of luck that might come his way; his aunt had promised to look for work for him.

She had nothing specific in mind and would make no promises, but the very fact of her having mentioned a job was good enough angury in itself. 'You see,' Field said, 'it's really time I found something again. I'm getting more and more in Helena's debt and it simply won't do.'

Earnestly he took out a small red note-book and showed the contents to me. Tabulated in it was every penny of the rent he had been unable to pay Helena, the approximate value of every meal he had eaten at her expense. The writing was clerkly, the pages beautifully ruled in red ink and the dates written in the most delicate of figures. He appeared extremely proud of this record and eager that I should give it my whole attention. 'I don't forget,' he said, 'and I hope she realizes that I don't.'

He looked so young, so sincere, that I began to think I should take at its face value his explanation of the outburst to the girl in the public-house. After all, had I never said anything of one person to impress another, knowing that it was completely untrue, simply to satisfy some abstract and irresistible desire to behave badly? Petty wrongdoing for the sake of nothing at all could, I felt, be so great a pleasure that only the strong-minded were able to resist it completely.

Finding no comment to make on Field's note-book I asked him some question as to how his aunt had felt about the General Election.

'Oh,' he replied, 'she's pretty red, in her respectable way. Anyhow, she thinks the Labour people will simply do efficiently what the Tories would have done inefficiently. According to her, any government would have to put through mines and steel nationalization to keep the country running at all. She had an argument with her secretary, who was rather dewy about the whole thing and really thought the Red Dawn had come.' Field paused, and looked down his nose. Then he said casually, 'Talking about secretaries, they seem an absolutely new type these days.' I felt that this was the matter of significance to which the comments on his aunt's political views had been simply a preamble.

'One upon a time secretaries just looked clever and mousy and wore navy blue costumes with shirt blouses. Now you'd think some of them were glamour girls from the Windmill Theatre. My aunt's secretary's terrific, really fair hair – natural

– and dark eyelashes. She had a suit on, but not at all office-ish. A bright green one.'

Enthusiasm gave him a resolute look, seemed to add a stone to his weight. 'What's her name?' I asked him.

'A very good one. Naomi. Naomi Reed. My aunt bully-rags her tremendously, but it hasn't the least effect. They seem to get on wonderfully.'

Field rose, altered the position of a cauliflower and some potatoes in the basket and heaved it up. Now he had achieved the satisfaction of speaking the name of a girl who had attracted him, he was ready to go. 'Shall we see you tonight?'

I told him no, asked him to give my love to Helena. I felt now that our positions were reversed; that he was the member of the family, myself the privileged visitor.

'I will.' We walked to the corner of the street together. 'I do hope something comes of this job,' he said. 'Even if it doesn't I've something else in the wind – anyway, something that might conceivably work. However, that's only an idea as yet.'

As I left him he called after me, 'I *am* going to pay my dues. You can be sure of that.'

Chapter Two

Helena in a bad temper was no longer formidable. Once her rages had seemed to me as awful and unanswerable as lightning over the sea; she had expressed anger with every muscle of her body, every hair of her head, every lash of her eye, anger working out through the activity of every corpuscle. As a boy I had dreaded these black moods and hidden from them, had believed that somehow or other Helena had sufficient influence with the elements to bring the whole sky crashing down on my head. Now, however, only a part of her mind participated in these outbreaks of wrath. The rest of it was aloof, watchful, without confidence.

Her fury, upon this occasion, was directed at Swain, who had called unexpectedly, found his painting gone and demanded to know exactly what had happened. On discovering that she had sold it to meet some unexplained commitment – 'He went for me as if I were a pickpocket,' Helena stormed, raising her arms with a gesture that would not have appeared petty in Mrs Siddons, 'he challenged my right to do as I liked with my own property, he bullyragged me, he shouted till I could see right down his throat. I ordered him out of the house but he wouldn't go. He just stood and raved until he could think of nothing more to say, then went into the kitchen, drank half Johnny's milk and charged out of the place.'

'Why on earth milk?' I asked, surprised.

'Because he likes it,' Helena snapped at me, 'and what's milk got to do with it? You can tell your friend Swain, when you see him, that he'd better not show his nose in here again.'

'If the Cayleys and Leipers heard you,' I told her, 'your name would be mud.'

'Oh, be quiet, Claud! I'm serious about this. I want you to tell Swain –'

'Never mind. I've got the picture myself.'

Helena's rage abated suddenly. 'You've got it? How?'

'Charmian bought it back; she got it for a hundred and fifty. She wanted to give it to me, but just as I was weakening, and going to accept, I heard from Curtis Brown in America that they'd sold my book about Utrillo over there. The advance worked out at a little less than the price of the picture, so I added a bit of my own and bought it off Charmian. A hundred and fifty quid up my shirt because of your tom-foolery.'

'Claud,' said Helena, sitting down and speaking gravely, 'you have no right to talk to me like that. After all, you must remember that I am a great deal older than you.' She sighed, closed her eyes as if resigned to insult despite any protest she might make. Then she asked me sharply: 'What are you going to do with it? Are you going to bring it back here?'

'No, I'm not,' I told her, 'it's going to be safe from now on.'

She rose and looked about her. 'Where is it?' We were in my rooms; she had made a special visit to tell me of Swain's behaviour.

'At the framer's. I didn't like the thing Swain had got on it.'

Helena threw up the window and looked out upon the dust and flash and greenery of King's Road. 'Aren't you noisy up here? I couldn't stand it. ... There's Johnny!'

I joined her. We saw Field walking with a tall girl dressed in yellow, whose fair hair threw off the sun with a flash of whiteness.

'That's Naomi,' said Helena, 'that's his young woman. He brought her along last week.' She sounded amused, a little tender.

'I heard about her. Is it serious?'

'How can it be? He's as poor as a church mouse. Besides, she's not the right type for him. She's one of these brisk girls. I suppose he's bringing her along to see me now, so I'd better get back.'

'Why's he bringing her?'

'Oh, his aunt gave them theatre tickets for tonight. He was going to take her to dinner in town, but I said they might as well dine with me first. It'll save him money.'

Her face clouded. She began absently to stroke the nap of her suède handbag back and forth, turning it first to dark grey, and then to deep and silken black. Field and the girl were lost from view in the crowds, and her eyes did not strain to follow them.

'What's the matter?' I asked her.

She did not reply at once, and when she did so her voice was lost in the surge of the traffic as the lights changed. Going behind her, I shut the window. Helena blinked at me forlornly and came to sit on the couch.

'What did you say? I didn't hear you.'

'Probably a good thing you didn't,' said Helena.

I urged her to confide in me.

'Never speak ill of the dead.' She was glum.

'What ill did you speak of them?'

'I said I thought Dan had behaved pretty badly, when one came to think of it.'

'The Will?'

'I have all I can do to get along,' she told me, not meeting my eyes, 'he shouldn't have left me like that. It was a rotten thing to do. I always made him happy.'

I said I thought it had taken her a good long time to find out just how rotten Daniel had been, but that I still saw no reason why she should be hard up.

'Perhaps I shouldn't be,' said Helena fiercely, 'if I lived on rice and lentils. Perhaps I shouldn't be if I wore other people's second-hand clothes. Perhaps I shouldn't be if I never spent money on anything that interested me, but just kept it to buy a crust and a covering.' Receiving no answer to this she looked slyly towards me in search of my laughter, and when she perceived it, laughed silently herself.

'Oh no, no,' she protested, as if I had spoken, 'I have got a right to Extras!'

'What extras?'

'Well . . . to spend my money as I want. Risk it, if I want to.'

'How are you risking your money?'

But I spoke too sharply, for Helena at that point told me to mind my own business, and took her leave.

I went that evening to see Charmian, and told her about Helena's financial worries. At the mention of them Charmian's guilty conscience, some time dormant, stirred again and she spoke of settling a sum upon her mother immediately. I advised her against this, however; advised her at least to do nothing of the kind until we had some idea of how it would be spent. I was uneasy.

To my surprise, she made no attempt to argue with me, but said I was probably right. She began to talk, then, of her husband, how tired he was, how kind he was, what a really remarkable brain he had when one got to know him. She insisted that beneath his slowness he was subtle; that underlying his slow, considered speech was a rarity of wit. I could not understand the point of this advocacy, unless it were meant to strengthen failing affection by the strengthening of pride. The less we love people we passionately desire to love, the more we recite to ourselves the tale of their virtues. Only the strongest love can endure, once its object in any way falls into despite. We desire to be loved in return: and what sort of feather can we stick in our cap if the opinions of our lover are not respected by outsiders?

'When we're together again things will be better.'

'What's wrong with them now?' I asked her, pouncing.

Charmian gave me a weak smile. 'Oh, nothing more than you'd expect, when two married people only manage to see each other for a few hours a week and have to spend three-quarters of them asleep.' She came behind my chair, crossed her hands over my chest and rocked me to and fro. 'Don't you worry about me. I look a well-preserved fifty, I know, but as soon as things straighten out I shall be young again. Do you remember the stories I used to write?'

In her early teens, inspired by the row of my father's books, she had been ambitious to become a writer of thrillers, and had indeed produced several tales of quite precocious liveliness.

'I remember the one about the schoolmaster who sat down on a poisoned drawing-pin and died in terrible agony.'

'That was a good idea, wasn't it? There were twenty-five little boys in the class, and all of them suspects.'

'Only I told you at the time that a child must never be the murderer in a crime story. No publisher would put up with that.'

'Well, anyway, I want to start writing again. Do you think I could?'

'I don't know. Try, and see.'

163

'I should like to have some outside interest,' said Charmian, rather wanly.

'Outside of Evan?'

Releasing me suddenly, she walked away. 'Don't be silly. I meant outside kitchen, church, and children.'

'Children?'

'Oh, we'll have some, I suppose. I hope so. Evan isn't keen, but I expect he would be if he actually had some of his own.' Her voice was dreary. 'Would you have liked them, Claud?'

I thought of my wife Meg, who either could not, or would not, have children. I had never spoken to Charmian of this. 'One wants all the routine experiences of life. Yes, I rather looked forward to being a father.'

'A woman has to have children,' Charmian said fervently, 'it's one of the things she's for. I hate to admit it, but it's probably the most important.' She paused. 'Or it isn't. I don't know. I suppose it would be better to say that having children is what women *and* men are for.' She spoke rapidly, with a kind of fretful excitement. 'You talking about the routine experiences of life – that's what I feel about it. I'd be so disappointed on my death-bed if I felt I'd missed anything. *Anything.*'

'Some things are better missed,' I told her, thinking of Evan.

'No, no, no; you know what I mean. If I'd missed the things I was born for . . .' She giggled. 'Fulfilling my biological functions.' The phrase pleased her. 'My biological functions,' she repeated.

'And Evan doesn't want you to.'

'It isn't that. It's just that everything's so unsettled.' She tightened her lips in a way I knew well; it meant that she intended to put a stop to the conversation. I said nothing. In a moment or so she threw her tunic and button-stick on to my knees and asked me to polish the brass for her. 'I'll give them a shock tomorrow by turning up looking soldierly.'

As I rubbed up the buttons I drew her attention to a picture that hung askew on the opposite wall, and which had been irritating me for an hour past. 'Do you like it like that?'

Charmian turned her head, regarded the picture with indifference. 'Oh, that? It's a bit skew-whiff.'

'Doesn't it get on your nerves?'

'It doesn't seem to matter,' she said, and turned away again.

The flat, a furnished one, was tasteful enough, light, airy, pleasantly decorated. It held only one abomination, which was a small shelf of dummy books let into the wall above the fireplace, an idea, Evan had told me, of the previous tenant. I asked Charmian whether this never drove her mad, and she replied, 'No. I never seem to notice it.'

Some women can make a home, not only of an hotel room but of a railway carriage, if the journey is more than an hour's duration. At eighteen Charmian had been like this; able to express her own personality by the importing of a book, a picture, or a vase, or by making some slight alteration in the position of the furniture, the drape of a curtain. To this flat, however, she had given nothing of herself. If it hinted at a character at all, it was at the character of the last occupant who had, I felt, been a difficult type of man. It was impossible to realize that this was indeed Charmian's home, that she had ever slept there, taken a bath there, filled its cupboards with her belongings. She seemed to have the indifference that comes from being too long in one of the transitional stages of life, and I was worried about her; yet I dared not ask any more questions.

I gave her back the tunic. 'Here you are. They'll probably give you a stripe tomorrow.'

'Not me.'

'You'll be glad to be out of it.'

'Yes, I shall now. Once I didn't care one way or the other. I get on all right with the other girls, but I have no real consciousness of a high mission.'

'Do you mean to tell me all the rest of them have?'

'Look,' said Charmian earnestly, leaning forward and pointing her finger at me, 'to be a female soldier you've either got to have the consciousness of a high mission or the consciousness of a high old time. Without either, you're sunk.' She looked at the clock and dismissed me abruptly. 'You can clear off now. I'm dog-tired and I'm not going to wait up for Evan. Try to find out why Mother's hard-up, will you?'

I said I would try. I had two things to find out about: Helena and Sholto.

A day or so later, Helena asked me to dinner to meet Field's young woman. 'We're going to have a little party,' she said.

'Who's coming?'

'Only Bill and Clemency.'

'Why, have you made it up with Swain? What did you tell him?'

'The truth,' said Helena proudly.

'And what did he have to say about it?'

'He said the joke was on you, but that it ought to have been on me. He said we were both mad, but that it didn't matter to him either way. Either way he'd get no money out of it. By the way, Clemency's expecting.'

'Just six of us, then.'

'Seven.'

'Who's the seventh?'

'Only Dilys,' Helena replied blandly. 'Poor old Dilys, she doesn't have much fun.'

'I'm not coming if that woman comes.'

She told me not to be stuffy, insisted that her friends were no business of mine, grew very angry, then reminded me that it was her birthday. 'So you'll have to be pleasant, won't you? I'd put Dilys off if I could, but it would only be awkward. Besides, she ought to have a celebration, too. The shop's been doing quite well since she tried Johnny's idea of making up customers' materials.'

I did, of course, agree at last to attend Helena's little party and was amazed, when I got there, to find an eighth guest: Mrs Sholto, smiling and old, pretty as a picture: Helena, managing to draw me aside under some pretext, told me with pride that this had been a brilliant afterthought. 'I've never got over her hints that night. I thought if she came here and saw Johnny's girl it would put a stop to her.' She gave me a bright look, squeezed my arm, and returned to the others.

I was fascinated to see how she would behave; her manners towards Swain and towards Mrs Sholto were entirely different, and impossible to reconcile. She did not reconcile them. That evening she was Lady Archer, and Swain was bored stiff.

Naomi Reed I liked very much, though there was in her a trace of the sporting schoolgirl, the Girl Guide, which chilled the ordinary gallantries of conversation. I imagined her greeting a proposal of marriage with a fresh, level glance, a friendly smile, and 'That's awfully nice of you, but why? Do tell me why you want to marry me. I'm honestly interested to know.' She had a charming fair face of the long type; bright blue eyes and a delightful mouth, full and curved, rather deeply indented at the corners as if it were perpetually hard for her to repress amusement.

Field seemed proud of her, but prompted her conversation less with the air of a lover than of a father whose daughter has just honoured him by winning a scholarship. 'Do tell Claud about that extraordinary woman in the office.' 'Helena, Naomi was telling me the most fascinating thing the other day about a man who works with her who used to live in Bruges.' 'Naomi, do tell them about the letter that got lost, and the rumpus there was about it.' The girl, thus urged, would smile at him rather reproachfully and obey him, but tell her story as briefly as possible. I admired her good manners, found her deference towards Helena and Mrs Sholto doubly pleasing because of a delicate implication that it was a tribute rather to their superior experience than to their years.

'You young business women,' Mrs Sholto said, 'leave me breathless. How you manage to be so efficient and so feminine at the same time amazes me. We had clever business women in my day, too, but they always thought it necessary to wear special clothes to be clever in.'

'Little straw hats,' said Clemency, nodding like a portrait out of the frame, 'and collars and ties. And bloomers.'

'No, no,' Helena protested, 'no woman of my generation ever went to business in bloomers.'

'Well, it seemed like it,' Clemency beamed, smiling round upon us all as if she had uttered a witticism.

Swain was gazing with interest at Mrs Olney, who seemed glum that evening. 'What do you think?' he asked her.

She shook her head so that the light hair rustled and swung. 'I'm afraid I can't help.' She gave him a look drably arch. 'Just a little before my time, Mr Swain.'

'Foot in it again,' he said, his eyes admiring the sharp angles of her cheek and jaw.

Mrs Sholto was regarding her also, obviously wondering what she did in Helena's galley. 'Lady Archer tells me you have a little shop. I always feel it must be very exciting to own one.'

'Sometimes it is. Mostly it's a worry.'

'Oh come, Dilys,' said Field, 'surely not lately!'

She looked at him holding his glance rather a long time. 'Bless you,' she said slowly, dwelling on the sibilant.

'Johnny had some excellent ideas,' Helena explained to everyone.

'About lampshades?' Mrs Sholto's eyes became more blue, more sweet. 'Are you one of those clever young men who know how to decorate?'

Clemency grinned like a cat. I saw Swain nudge her.

'Lord, I don't know anything,' said Field.

'You've something better than knowledge,' Mrs Olney told him intently, 'you have instinct.'

'Johnny is remarkable for instinct,' Helena said broadly, claiming him as her own. 'Even Claud admits it, and there are *times*' – she was roguish – 'when Claud feels no one but himself has any real taste.'

Naomi Reed, taking this for delightful family teasing, raised her eyebrows at me, and the corners of her mouth deepened.

'So in this case,' Helena continued, 'Claud is the authority.' To Naomi she said, 'I do think some men have a sense of dress, and of furnishing, and all that, superior to any woman's.'

The girl agreed. 'Just as most men can't cook at all, but the best cooks are men.'

'Oh, but I deny that they're the best dressmakers,' Mrs Olney cried. She looked slightly flushed, slightly rumpled, as if she had been drinking. 'I love Schiaparelli best of all.'

'Lucky you,' said Mrs Sholto, with an affectionate glance at the speaker's undistinguished and rather shabby brown dress, 'to be able to patronize her. You make me very envious.'

'Oh,' Mrs Olney replied quickly, 'this isn't one of hers. This is a very old thing.'

'It's an unusual shade of brown,' Naomi remarked, 'it's awfully attractive. I always wish I could wear brown, but I can't.'

'It was a colour my husband disliked,' Mrs Sholto said, in a voice implying that for this reason it should never be seen upon decent people.

The conversation ran dry suddenly. Bill Swain ostentatiously stifled a yawn; it amused him, sometimes, to appear boorish.

'You're looking tired tonight, Bill,' said Helena with poisonous solicitude.

Field and Naomi began some discussion of their own, Mrs Sholto occasionally contributing a remark of the greatest authority and irrelevance. Helena nagged quietly at Swain, and Clemency sat in contented silence enjoying her food. I looked across at Mrs Olney. She was staring frustratedly at Field, as if the breadth of table separating them was the Hellespont and he a Leander who, for some reason, did not feel like a swim that night.

I felt the warmth of the room, the pressure of emotion that made it seem crowded and small. Around the table was a tightening belt of silence into which the minutes glittered and slid away like drops of gold. The faces of Helena's guests seemed to me unnaturally clear, unnaturally sharp in colour. Field's black eyes flashed and widened, narrowed, widened again; there was a tinge of pink on his cheekbones, the lobes of his ears, the tip of his delicate, rather long nose. Helena's large eyelids darkened to brown, and there were brown shadows, like thumb-marks, beneath the sockets. She looked half asleep, though active in her drowsiness like a dog which, in slumber, mimics the action of running. Mrs Sholto, I observed for the first time, had a curiously strong jaw, scarcely noticeable in profile because of the way the skin had slackened about it; it gave to the rest of her features, the little mouth, little nose, little sweet eyes, a kind of pathos, as if the good nature implicit in them would never stand a chance against the jaw's threat of wrath. This, however, was a face clothed with caution, and with awareness of itself: Mrs Olney's face was naked. It was ridiculous in its candour, ridiculous and sad. The hungry eyes, with the brows straining to meet above them, the lips parted, the nose peaked and whitish, revealed the truth: that Mrs Olney loved Field not as Helena did, concealing incomprehension under some vague verbal ideas – 'mother', 'son', 'protection' – but actively and consciously, without circumlocution of thought.

Few men can understand what women see in other men.

They are apt to envy the tall, the extraverted, the conventionally handsome, are unable to grasp the fact that whereas beauty of face and body is profoundly important in a woman, it is not by these things that women (I am not speaking of the adolescent or the screenstruck) choose men. I was prepared to accept the fact that the charm Field had for Helena and for Mrs Olney would never be appreciated by me. To my eyes he was a decent-looking, rather weak-faced boy whose diffidence was in itself repellent. It was a diffidence for which he found expression in over-modesty, embarrassed silence, self-denigration, and not infrequently in actual, physical wriggling. I had liked him because (I supposed) he had been the only one in a small and closed community to share my tastes. There could be no such kind of attraction where the two women were concerned.

He turned his head suddenly. 'Claud, do show Naomi the photographs for your book!'

There were a dozen reproductions, illustrating the various periods in Picasso's development.

'Would you be interested?' I asked her.

'I should, very. I don't know a lot about painting, but I do like it and I'm trying to learn about it.' She smiled. 'Only I won't make any remarks while I'm looking at them, because amateurs always say the wrong things.'

Dinner was over. We left the table and went into the larger room. I showed Naomi the photographs concerning which, as she promised, she made no comment. 'You tell me things, please, and I'll remember. Then I'll tell them all to somebody else, and get a huge undeserved reputation.'

Field teased her a little about this, which made her look pleased and stimulated. She was having a very happy evening.

Swain was not. At half-past nine he said he must go.

'Oh, not yet!' Helena urged him, at the same time rising to show him out. 'It's so early.'

'I had a bad night last night. Clemmy, go and get your coat.'

Clemency rose up in the middle of a sentence she had been addressing to Mrs Sholto and went with such cheerful obedience from the room that Swain might have been a Frankenstein who had succeeded at last in getting some beautiful monster under complete control. She went, indeed, with such celerity that Helena had to hasten abruptly to catch up with her.

'Well, well!' Mrs Sholto exclaimed to nobody. She leaned forward to speak to Mrs Olney, who was sitting quite motionless and withdrawn, as if posing for a life-class. 'You come and talk to me, my dear. You look most restful.' It was Mrs Sholto's habit to treat women no more than fifteen years her junior as if they were mere girls.

Mrs Olney turned to the old lady, raised her eyes and waited for a topic to be broached. 'Isn't this a charming little flat?' Mrs Sholto said at last, defeated.

When Swain and his wife had gone, Naomi said that she, too, must not be out late. 'I've got to be up at seven.'

'I'll see you home.' Field got up.

She protested. 'No, please don't. It's only a step.'

'Of course I shall.'

'I don't want to take you away –'

'He shall see us *both* home,' said Mrs Olney with decision, a mirthless smile stretching across her face, 'and make himself really useful. You said you lived at Earl's Court, didn't you, Miss Reed? Your way's my way.'

Field said he would be pleased to escort them both.

'I'll see you Sunday, Dilys,' Helena reminded her.

'Of course you will. You're coming to me.'

They kissed.

'Johnny,' Helena domineered, 'don't be late back. The doctor said you needed long nights, and I'm sure Naomi will see you obey him.' Her mouth twitched, as if she were seeking through what she had said for some vague salacity.

I went with the four of them into the hall.

'Thank you very much for such a very nice evening,' Naomi said to her, 'you can't think how much I've enjoyed myself.'

'My dear,' Helena exclaimed, 'I'm afraid there hasn't been very much to enjoy! Not very exciting for you.'

Naomi was wearing a small green hat rather formless in contour, reminding me of the bowls I used to make as a boy by melting old gramophone records over the fire. In it she looked brisk and young and guileless. 'The moment I come into your flat,' she said, 'I feel as if something exciting's going to happen,' She smiled fondly at Helena.

'And it never does.'

'Just being here is exciting. Thank you so much.'

When the door had closed behind Field and the two women Helena said, 'I don't wonder that young thing's good at her job. She says the right thing so well that she shakes my nerve.'

'Don't you like her?' I asked.

She looked at me as if I were mad. 'Like her? Of course I do. Though she always looks as if she was going to bully-off, or whatever girls do. Come on, let's rub her into the old lady.'

But Mrs Sholto did not appear interested in Field and Naomi. 'Mrs Olney is a curious type,' she said, 'almost Nefertiti, only of course she's fair and not very young. She must have been most striking. Have you known her long?'

'Oh, ages and ages,' Helena replied. 'Don't you think Naomi Reed's a little like Evan to look at? As handsome in her way as he is in his.'

'Is she clever?'

'Very, I believe. She's secretary to Johnny's aunt, who's a very important person, so I'm told.'

Mrs Sholto ts-tsed herself and was prettily confused. 'No, no! I meant Mrs Olney. I am stupid. Is Mrs Olney clever?'

'She's artistic,' said Helena stoutly.

'Oh, I feel sure of that. She has an artistic face. Is she a great friend of Mr Field's?'

My nerves tightened in anticipation of wickedness.

Helena looked bewildered, 'I suppose so. I introduced them. He's been giving her ideas for her business.'

'Oh,' Mrs Sholto breathed, with a small, mysterious smile. 'I see. I thought perhaps they were old acquaintances.' She looked at the clock. 'I, too, must be making my way.'

'It's a little slow,' said Helena apologetically. She was lying.

The moment Mrs Sholto had gone she said, 'Now what's she up to? Good God, canst thou not minister to a mind diseased, etcetera etcetera, the woman's mad! Is she accusing Johnny of carrying on with poor Dilys now?'

'I wouldn't bother a lot, if I were you.'

Helena sat down, rested her chin in her hands and thought for a while. Her face cleared. 'I know what it is. She's furious about being done out of a scandal where Johnny and I are concerned, so she's revenging herself by inventing a new one. I expect she was furious to find he had a girl.'

'How fond is he of Naomi?' I asked her.

She shrugged and smiled. 'Lord knows. It's all very boy-and-girl, I think.'

'One can never be sure. He's quite capable of deciding to get married.'

'He can't. I told you he couldn't. He hasn't any money.'

Though I felt the presence of danger like a third invisible presence in the room, I could not stop myself. 'Supposing it were possible. Would you like it?'

She looked up at me, panicked. 'But it isn't! Why talk about things being possible when you know they aren't?' She hesitated. 'It would be mad for Johnny to marry. He's not well enough. He needs care. Claud!' Her gaze was round and full.

'What?'

'You wouldn't suggest it to him? You wouldn't give him the idea, would you?'

'Of course not. It's none of my business.'

'But you might well make some joke or give some hint. Promise me you won't.'

'I won't,' I said.

She leaned back, closing her eyes. She looked tired and sad. 'Because,' she said, speaking very quietly, 'it would be cruel of you. He's not fit to marry yet because he's ill. One day he'll be better, and then no one will be more pleased than I shall. Only now . . . In a minute you'll start thinking as *she* does, as old Sholto does. It must almost sound like that, mustn't it? I'm fond of Johnny. I feel he's in my charge. I love looking after him – that's all.'

'That's all,' I said, wanting to soothe her, to comfort her, to assure her of my understanding. But she could not believe that I might, indeed, understand.

Now she spoke very slowly and carefully. 'You see, Claud, it's only reasonable. If it wouldn't be right for him to marry yet awhile, and if it makes me happy to have him here with me – as if he were mine, mine and Dicky's, if you like . . .'

She paused, the reference to my father, only half-voluntary, pushing back the years for her. Then she recovered herself.

'If it's good for him and it makes me happy, it would be cruel of you to try to alter things, wouldn't it?'

I saw, and was bitterly sorry for it, that she was tormented by a fixed idea: which was, that there was nothing I would not do to take Field away from her. It had had some substance once; not now.

'I shan't do it, Helena,' I said.

'Oh,' she cried passionately, 'how fed up you must be with me! Years and years of me – all my fits and cranks. I don't know how you've stood it. God knows how you have.'

'All right, all right, you needn't worry. I've enjoyed it.'

'I expect I had my funny side when I was young. When you're young you can be cranky. But a cranky old woman makes everyone sick.'

'Poor old woman,' I said, 'I shall buy you an ear-trumpet and a wooden leg. Why aren't you dead yet? Listen, you can't be pathetic; you're too tall. . . . Pathos is for little people.'

She rallied somewhat at this, telling me the wish was probably father to the thought, and that though I might *think* I should care when she died, I should actually breathe a sigh of relief when the event took place. When I left her she was assured of my intentions regarding Field (which were, to do nothing at all) and had recovered her spirits.

'Don't hope too hard,' she said at the door, 'I'll outlast you yet. My father lived to ninety-one and my great-grandfather to ninety-eight, so don't you go counting your funerals before they're hatched.'

The lifting of her depression, however, only deepened mine. I could think of nothing now save the hunger of Mrs Olney and this one new and saddening discovery – that Helena was no longer able to see everything that lay beneath her nose. For the first time she was defenceless.

Chapter Three

I AM forced here into indirect narration, filling in a good deal of dialogue, arbitrarily, out of my knowledge of the persons concerned. The whole story was told me by Helena on the day following her quarrel with Field; whether she was in a fit state then to record what was said and what was done with any degree of finality, I do not know, but at any rate her record was fundamentally correct. Between her and the event lay a sleepless night, during which I dare say she had suppressed the words of others, embroidered upon her own; anger is the greatest of all temptations to lying. However, at least she had gained her point for the moment and on that account must have calmed down to a certain degree. When she described the affair to me she was sufficiently soothed to find a trace of fun here and there in a phrase, or a gesture, but all the same, she was far from achieving any real objectivity.

At the beginning of August Mrs Olney suddenly asked for more money. For some time now, Helena had been putting money into the shop, convinced that it might some day become – she used the phrase to me – 'a little gold mine'. Dilys Olney's rather wretched beauty and what seemed to be her courage in hanging on to a business venture that did nothing but pile up a load of debt, appealed to Helena. This, she felt, was spirit.

Once, as a woman in her thirties, she had bitterly regretted the passing of girlhood, the adolescent frenzies, the gimcrack symbols (the note, the photograph, the pressed flower) of early sexual experience. In her forties she had regretted the passing of her summer; how fine it had been to be beyond mistakes, confident and secure, yet still young enough to invite the glance of a young man in a bus or a teashop! In her fifties and sixties she raged at the stupidity of her forties; looking back at them she saw how young she had been in reality, and how much of that last youth she had wasted in believing herself to be middle-aged. Now, on the edge of her seventies, she glorified the memory of her life with Archer, giving to it in retrospect a radiance it had never really held. So, perversely, she clung to Dilys Olney as a sharer of that life. That Mrs Olney was a sharer, she had not known at the time; but this seemed unimportant now. As widows in a harem might exchange nostalgic reminiscences of the Bashaw – all competitive instincts now faded, all jealousy in dust, all passion spent – so these two women grew close in spirit because both had been part of the intimate world which was Archer's.

From friendship to business. Mrs Olney said frankly that for her, success was a mere matter of capital. She had ideas, she had skill, she had drive; but nothing in the bank. In fact, there were debts – small ones, but they niggled. 'I hate debt,' said Mrs Olney, 'all our family have had a positive dread of debt. If my mother forgot to pay the milkman for a single day it was an illness to her.'

'Look here,' said Helena, friendship swarming up from her heart like a great blush, 'there's no need for you to worry while I'm about. I'd like to help you. For Dan's sake.'

(This is verbatim reporting; she was proud of these words of hers and had repeated them precisely to me. She seemed to have no conception of their staggering absurdity.)

Mrs Olney bowed her head, pressed her lips together. She might have been praying. 'It's like you to say that. You're wonderful. Only ... I wonder what you must think of me? You must think I've been trying to' – she sat up straight again, staring gallantly, dry-eyed, before her – 'trying to ... I won't shirk it: to cadge. You didn't think I was fishing, did you, Helena? I couldn't bear that. And anyway, I'd die rather than accept your offer.' Pause. 'Your tremendous offer, It just means an enormous lot to me to know you could make it. As if I had strength to go on now.'

For this nonsense Helena fell completely. She found herself pleading to be allowed to give Mrs Olney money. Wouldn't some sort of business investment be possible? 'After all,' Helena urged, 'I've got the right at my time of life to a little gamble. I could spend my money on horses, couldn't I? – and lose the lot. So shouldn't I be safer investing it in you?'

But Mrs Olney, being wise, was adamant; for the time being. She would not take a penny. Independent she had lived, independent she would die. Her mother's ghost would never forgive her. Hang on a bit longer: that was the thing. Things would get better. Young people would be coming out of the forces to set up homes, and they would all need lampshades. It was all a matter of *grit*.

Then, one night, Field had his casual idea. It had pleased Helena to see how well he and her friend got on together. He seemed to like Mrs Olney very much, and yet to keep a degree of confidence from her. He talked to her freely, without diffidence, embarrassment or self-depreciation; but it was towards Helena that his glance swerved when he needed an assurance of any kind, a confirmation. He understood Mrs. Olney, but did not make the fatal mistake of understanding her better than Helena did. He and Helena could, in fact, 'share' the friendship; they were as one in their offerings of advice, hospitality, oil and wine.

Mrs Olney, for her part, seemed to miss Johnny Field if he were not there when she called. 'Where's our Johnny? I like that boy, he's got such nice manners and such a sense of humour. My Dennis would like him, and Dennis doesn't like everybody – he's quite a difficult young man in his way, I'm afraid, but wouldn't that just be a phase? I want our boys – yes, I always think of Johnny as *your* boy – to meet each other. They ought to be friends.'

('You see,' Helena panted to me, 'she was preparing the ground. Wanting Johnny to meet her son! I know.')

On this particular night, however, Field was home. After dinner, discussion turned as usual to Mrs Olney's shop and to possible ways of making it a success.

'I wish that shade of yours was red, like the cushions,' he said idly to Helena, 'it would look terrific in that corner.'

'The pattern of that silk is delightful,' Mrs Olney murmured, studying the colour and texture, 'you don't see material of that sort these days.'

'If Helena had a shade covered with it, it would look rather out of the way, don't you think so?' Field suggested. 'You ought to cover them with the customer's own material, Dilys. It might be a go.'

She stared at him. 'Johnny! What perfect genius! Do you think one could?'

Here I imagine Helena made some loving gibe at Field's expense, telling him that he should go in for the thing professionally. Mrs Olney's enthusiasm, however, was not to be diverted. She praised, she admired, she planned. An advertisement would be put in the papers next week. She would display a sample shade or two in the window.

'I've got a piece of bright green silk upstairs,' said Helena, excited, 'with a queer sort of satin stripe embroidered in yellow. You might make something of that and pretend it's an order. In fact, it's going to be an order. I'm going to start the ball rolling myself!'

('When I think of how I tried to help her, Claud, how all my thought was for her!')

Mrs Olney did put in her advertisement, and it had a promising initial response. 'Really,' she said to Helena, 'I can't help feeling the tide's going to turn. If only I could *branch* out a little bit . . . but then, we must work and pray, and hope all that will come later.'

Then Helena broached her idea of the partnership. 'Why not, Dilys? I'm not a fool. I don't make investments that won't pay dividends.' She assured her friends that in this proposition there was no friendship: it was business, business, purely business, business all the way.

Field was called in to the consultation.

'Johnny, tell Dilys it's a marvellous idea. Tell her I know what I'm doing, that I always had a business head.'

Mrs Olney turned slowly towards Field, her face dim and beautiful as if blurred by a gauze. They looked at each other. 'The truth, now,' she said in a sad voice, a tone lower in the register than usual. 'Should I let her, Johnny? You tell us.'

He protested that it was not his affair, that he was not qualified to advise, that any opinion he gave would be worthless. Helena began to badger him, nagging at him to speak on her behalf. Mrs Olney said nothing. One would have thought that the matter was no more a concern of hers than of Field's. Only when Helena began to lose her temper did she speak. 'I'd like to hear what you've got to say, Johnny. Please.'

('You know, Claud, I had a vague thought at the time that they were saying something to each other without actually speaking, only I didn't exactly take it out and look at it, if you know what I mean.')

Field said, 'If Helena wants to help the shop along I think it would be an interest for her, as well as manna to you.'

After a long verbal minuet, graceful advance, modest retreat, a bow and a curtsy, Mrs Olney yielded. No partnership arrangement, however, was ever made. Helena simply gave her some money and then, in a week or so, a little more. Certainly business in the shop appeared to be looking up. 'You must look smart if you're going to attract the right sort of people,' Helena insisted, and bought her friend a coat and skirt the price of which was twenty-seven pounds ten. Dennis' school fees fell due and his mother was very depressed; so Helena paid half of them. Passing an antique shop one day, Mrs Olney was violently attracted to a curious lamp standard of baroque design. 'I'd adore to show my shades on that!' she cried. 'Let's ask how much it is,' Helena suggested. But her friend was brave. 'Well, you can't *have* it,' she said sternly to herself, slapping her own hand smartly. She explained: 'When I was young and very poor, I had a little trick to stop myself wanting pretty things. If I saw a hat or a frock in a shop window and simply started lusting over it, I'd give myself a big shake and say, "Well, you can't have it!" Sometimes I forgot and said it aloud, and passers-by thought I was perfectly mad!'

('What a damned fool!' Helena commented vindictively to me.)

Mrs Olney refused to inquire the price, walked resolutely away and refused to mention the subject again, though she was rather wistful during the rest of the day. Next morning Helena went out and bought the standard for her.

Mrs Olney came to protest less and less, and very soon ceased to protest at all. In fact, in the first week of August she asked frankly for more money. If Helena could just tide her over, she would be able to drag the business on to a really profitable footing. She made the request with charming boldness, her head a little in the air, her big legs straddled. 'If you were one tiny bit less generous, if you'd made me feel the least little bit beholden to you, I'd never have dared to come to you like this. I'm being honest as a tribute to your absolutely splendid generosity. I'll repay you for it, I promise. With interest, my dear, handsome interest, bless you!'

Now this attitude annoyed Helena very much indeed. Like most liberal-handed people who genuinely detest thanks and are profoundly embarrassed by it, she was inevitably shocked into disgust when her liberality was suddenly demanded as a right. The demand took from her the one reward she had for giving; pride in being able to bestow pleasure.

She temporized, tried to turn the request into a joke. Mrs Olney became a little tearful, then a little hard. She was in need. What was the use of a friend to whom you could not declare your need?

'It's all right to declare it,' Helena said, 'but whether I can do anything about it is another thing. I'm not so well-off that I can do all I like, Dilys.'

Mrs Olney was silent for a moment. Then her shoulders drooped. 'All right,' she said, sounding as if, Helena told me, her mouth was full of wool, 'I understand. I've been crude. I've been unpardonable. Forgive me. I shall get along somehow.'

At the door she kissed Helena warmly and patted her shoulder. It was an infuriating, forgiving pat. 'Don't you worry about poor old Dilly-dally. She'll dree her own weird.'

Helena, still furious with hurt and disappointment, was determined that Mrs Olney should dree what she liked. She determined also that Field's eyes should be opened, and waited with impatience for his homecoming. He went out every day, in a desultory manner, to answer various advertisements relating to jobs obviously unsuited to him.

When he came in, she denounced Mrs Olney with heat and force; Field listened silently, and when she had done, made a surprising attempt to change the subject. Helena, so confident of his championship, his sharing of her own emotion, was chilled with foreboding. 'It was like talking to somebody else,' she said to me, still in a tone of utter bewilderment. She had known the shock that dates from childhood when a friend of our parents (as we think) passes us in the street, and we run to him, speak to him, and find he is a total stranger. As children, our identification of persons is unsure. Grown up, we are shocked by our failures to identify the heart.

So Helena refused to follow Field on to a new track of talk, but instead demanded his attention and denounced Mrs Olney all over again. 'Would you have believed it? That she could be such a bloodsucker?'

He replied uneasily that the whole affair should not be taken too seriously, that people were often bad at expressing themselves, that Mrs Olney, up till now, had shown no sign of the cloven hoof.

Helena charged him with taking the side of the enemy. Probably she had ceased to care by now what were the rights and wrongs of Mrs Olney's demand; all she knew was that Field was trying to betray her. It was a dreadful knowledge. Before this, their thoughts had been so close that they had spindled together into a single thought. He had understood a question before she had asked it. In the smallest thing he knew her mind; knew, in time to join her, whether she would laugh at the angle of a hat on the head of a stranger, knew the depression that would seize her at a certain turn of the weather, knew to what extent a chance word or glance would flick her into fury. At this moment he knew no less than he had always known; but he disregarded the knowledge.

('He knew how wild I was,' Helena insisted, 'and he simply didn't care. He was sticking up for her, all the way along.')

She could not bear this polite, affectionate, implacable hostility, so she forced an opinion from him.

'Well,' he said, 'I do think you're taking all this frightfully seriously, as I said. The fact that Dilys did ask you for money only proves that she trusts you. She told you as much, only you didn't believe it.'

'A lot of damned nonsense!' Helena cried.

'Oh, I don't know. It's queer how we always do disbelieve anything anybody says about himself. We think he's just putting up a front. Yet how on earth are we going to get to know people? The only person who knows anything about one is oneself. I think Dilys was telling you the literal truth.'

'And I think she was sponging.'

Field stretched his legs and sighed deeply. Then he sprang up, came to Helena and took her by the wrists. It was the first time he had ever touched her in any kind of intimacy.

('He clung on to me and bobbed down to look at my face,

181

and behaved all winningly, just like a five-year-old. He thought he could smooth me over, but he was wrong.')

He told her it was a wonderful evening, just the evening for walking. They would go out for a little walk, and then she would stop brooding over a lot of rubbish and be happy again. He hated her to upset herself over nothing at all. A little walk would be just the thing.

Helena, however, did not feel like walking. She made him sit down again, and for the third time started to explain the wrongdoing of Mrs Olney.

After a while he stopped her. 'Look here,' he said, 'I've got something to tell you. I meant it to wait, to be a sort of surprise, but it had better come now.'

Though his manner was cheerful, his voice warm. Helena's bowels turned and she wanted, she told me, to be sick.

He began his revelation cautiously. 'You know how awkward I've been for a long time about living here. Claud doesn't like it, and even apart from that, it makes me feel a worm myself. If I went I could see you just as often as I do now –'

'How could you?' she interjected, frightened.

'– or nearly, and everything would be so much smoother and easier. This is my idea, and I'm sure you'll think it's a pretty good one when you've thought it over.' His idea was (and Dilys's, he said) that he and Mrs Olney should go into partnership. She believed that he had ideas, and he was beginning to think so himself. They had talked it over.

('The snakes!' Helena exclaimed to me at this point. She was desperate. She was sincere. Her comic sense had deserted her.)

The prospective partners had agreed that Field should furnish ideas, try out new ways of improving the business, keep the accounts and help occasionally in the shop. He would receive, for the time being, one-third of the profits and occupy the big front room over the hairdresser's shop next door. Mrs Olney had made inquiries about the latter and had arranged for him to rent it at fifteen shillings a week. 'I could afford that for a bit,' he told Helena enthusiastically, 'and things would get easier as the business got better. I should be able to feel I was completely independent, which would be good for me. What do you think?'

'Think? Think?' Helena cried, breast heaving, eyes flashing wrath like golden fire. 'I think it's appalling! I think it's mad! I think you're both crazy!'

He replied good-humouredly that naturally it sounded strange at first, but would improve upon rumination. He could never be sufficiently grateful to Helena for all she had done for him, but she must see that he had a duty to himself – if that didn't sound terrifically pompous.

('It did sound pompous, Claud, and it sounded like black lying.')

She must see that he couldn't go on for ever doing nothing. Doing nothing made him take a poor view of himself. Even if his health was a bit C3, there was no reason why he shouldn't do something useful in the world.

'You call that useful?'

'Oh, it's a good thing to make the world a bit prettier,' he said, smiling. 'Dilys has been failing because her taste is awful. If I can correct that, she ought to get on like a house afire. She's had six orders this week for shades made out of the customers' materials. I've got another idea, too; I want us to do ordinary electrical repairs, as well. We could afford to get in one of these young chaps who know all about fiddling about with things.'

'So that's what you and Dilys have been discussing behind my back,' Helena said bitterly, disregarding the electrician.

Not behind her back, he pleaded, or only chancily so. Actually it had all come up the other night, when Helena was at the theatre and Mrs Olney had called. It was more or less of an inspiration.

Helena could think of nothing to say. She sat in silence, rage, misery, and disgust rolling over her like the tides over a sunken ship.

('It was as though I'd been struck dumb. My brain wouldn't work. My tongue wouldn't work. When I looked at Johnny I seemed to be seeing him from miles away.')

At last, thinking to attract him with the one weapon against which he had no defence, she burst into tears. She could not really, she told me, help herself. It was as if someone had pressed a button.

She could not have anticipated the result. Field got up, said,

'Oh, for Christ's sake!' and kicked a leather pouffe from one side of the room to the other.

Helena's tears ceased. She stared at him.

He was conquered, not by her action, but by his own.

('He looked so surprised at himself,' she said, with the faint, sour shadow of a grin, 'that it was almost funny. As if he'd found himself with three legs or a tail.')

He apologized fervently, his eyes startled, his whole body alive with regret. He didn't know what had come over him. Whatever she must be thinking of him, he was all that, and worse. 'I suppose I was so bowled over to see you crying; it was so awful. I didn't know what to do. I just felt I couldn't bear it.'

According to Helena, he became sensible then. He sat down quietly at her side, blaming himself, justifying himself, telling her that he wouldn't upset her for the world if he could help it, and that she must tell him what he must do to avoid such a catastrophe.

Wily, she would not tell him. I imagine she knew she would gain her point now only by refusing to refer to it. Instead, she said that he could please her by not worrying any more about the whole silly scene. She had not been well. All that day she had felt a headache coming on, she had felt sick, she had even wondered whether it could be some slight food poisoning.

Into this fiction Field entered with gusto. What had she been eating? One had to be terrifically careful these days. One had to be specially careful with fish, the way it got hung up at the ports. Had Helena been eating any fish?

No, she replied, or none that he had not shared. Did he, by any chance, feel under the weather? No? Then they must think of something else.

In a beautiful, padded calm, like the quiet emergence of sunlight after the hailstorm, they analysed every detail of Helena's diet for the past forty-eight hours. Field, playing up to her with spirit, urged her to see the doctor. 'I really think you should, just for safety's sake.' But Helena would not, and he did not press the matter.

Like a good son he fussed about her, made her lie down, asked her if she would like anything to drink, lit her cigarette, brought her a magazine from his room.

('I really was feeling queer, Claud. It might have been poisoning for all I know.')

They had a quiet meal together – Field prepared and served it – and no further mention was made at that time of Mrs Olney.

At half-past nine Swain looked in for a few minutes. 'I just thought I'd drop up, as I was passing. I felt so depressed I had to have human society, and I can't have Clemmy's as she's in the country with her mother for a few days. I suppose you heard the news?'

They told him they had not.

'I didn't hear the six o'clock myself, but I heard it just now.' It seemed, he said, that the Americans had dropped a new sort of bomb on Japan. It wasn't much bigger than a biscuit tin, but it had probably killed a quarter of a million people.

Helena said it sounded horrible, but it ought to bring the Japanese war to an end, oughtn't it?

'Is it official?' Field asked.

Swain replied savagely that it was official, yes, and he thought it stank. How we were going on shouting about the brutality of German bombing when we did that kind of thing quite cheerfully ourselves, God alone knew.

('He kept on and on about this bomb, and it did sound frightful, but somehow I couldn't take it in. I was so worried about Johnny.')

Swain sat for an hour raging, prophesying, apostrophizing, but I gather neither Field nor Helena gave him much encouragement. Field simply sat nodding his head and dolefully agreeing. When the guest had gone he said to Helena, 'Everything seems to get bloodier and bloodier. I suppose we'd better listen to the late news ourselves and find out what this is all about.'

They did not listen, however. ('We couldn't,' Helena said to me, 'we were both too upset. People like Swain always do come in at the wrong time – they have a genius for it. I just felt that a visit from him, all Jeremiahring, was the last straw.')

She and Field had said good night and were going to their rooms when he told her suddenly that he had changed his mind: he would not be going into the business with Mrs Olney.

Helena, perversely, demanded why he should not. Because, he told her, it obviously made her unhappy.

She replied that her happiness was nothing, his was all; and she began to urge him to do as he had planned, to let nothing stand in the way.

('I couldn't bear him making sacrifices for me. I felt as though I'd been selfish, that I'd behaved rottenly to him.')

No, Field said, he had made up his mind and he would tell Mrs Olney tomorrow that the plan was cancelled.

I fancy, from what she told me, that he must have forced Helena to plead for the thing she so little desired before he would consent to reopen the discussion.

It was late, by then, past midnight, and the flat was full of a tiredness that had the smell and heaviness of stale air.

'You were right the first time, Johnny,' Helena said breathlessly, 'you were right and I was wrong. You do need your independence. It's no life for you dancing attendance on an old woman.'

He told her, like a courtier, that she was not old, that she would never be old. He said, 'Why, you're my Best Friend!'

(She repeated this to me several times, the words like honey in her mouth. 'Yes, he said I was his Best Friend – you know, as if it had capital letters, *that* kind of best friend.')

She protested, however, that old she was, whether she liked it or not, and that he had his years before him. If Mrs Olney could offer him a real interest in life, if she could make him feel that he was doing a job of work, good luck to her. She, Helena, was not going to be a dog-in-the-manger.

But Field was obdurate. Faithful-looking, his voice gentle, he protested that he would not leave her on any account. The room over the hairdresser's had just been an idea, scarcely debated. In all probability the man wouldn't have let for fifteen shillings when it came to the point, not with the housing shortage as it was. Also, Field doubted very much whether he could have afforded to live alone, with food to pay for, and light and heat, on his small capital. The sensible thing was for him to stay with Helena for the time being, and go on searching through the Situations Vacant. Something would turn up.

So it was all settled, wasn't it? And everything was happy?

I imagined him lingering by the door, his bright gaze meeting her own, his face foxlike in eagerness, lingering in the hope that she would not really accept this as an exit line.

It was not until a quarter past one that Helena, exhausted, had managed to make him agree that he would spend at least a few hours a week helping Mrs Olney in the shop.

'He really was wonderful, Claud! I was still angry, but I had to admire him. There I was, thinking he'd been conspiring with her, really believing he wanted to push me out of the way so that he could go and be with her – and then, when it came to the point, it was as much as I could do to make him have anything to do with her wretched shop at all! It just shows how little we know people.' She added musingly, 'Johnny's finer than you think. There's a real vein of iron in him.' She elaborated with satisfaction, 'Something deep down. I tell you, he'll get on one of these days; I know it. Then I'll be able to crow over you all.'

I reminded her of Mrs Olney's demand for money. How was she feeling about that?

'Oh,' replied Helena, 'I'm still furious with her. It was *so* ungracious. But I dare say that there was something in what she said – if I hadn't been so nice about giving her the first lot, she wouldn't have dared ask for any more. One has to be charitable. Not, mind you, that I couldn't wring her neck.'

When I tried to tell her just how I myself regarded her friend, she checked me with an episcopal gesture. 'We have to give people the benefit of the doubt.'

'Or enough rope to hang themselves.'

'Oh be quiet,' she said dimly. She thought of Field, and her face softened and glowed. 'You know, I can't help feeling that, somehow, last night was a turning point in my life.'

So, now that she was comforted a little, I left her. She would be angry again in an hour from now, but Field, I felt, could bear the brunt of that. He deserved it.

Chapter Four

'I've found a new friend for you,' Helena said, with the air of one bestowing a royal favour. We had met by chance in King's Road, a few days after VJ-Day. She was looking splendid in dark violet, some furs Daniel had given her as auxiliary to her bright face as the florist's baize to his flowers. She wore a remarkable hat that swerved up from her left temple, swooped down below her right ear, a hat with Stuart influences, needing only a cascade of ostrich feathers.

'What shall we do together,' I suggested, 'bowl hoops?'

She rebuked me. This was serious, this was important. She had met Mrs Cayley that morning in the Army and Navy Stores, and with her had been a young nephew just returned from the Middle East who was now working in the Army Welfare Department in Eaton Place. 'I told him you were in Whitehall and said I was sure you'd like to know each other. I've asked him to dine out tomorrow night – not in, because this isn't Johnny's affair – and you've got to come, too. We'll meet at the Good Intent, seven-thirty. You remember Mrs Cayley,' she ran on, 'the bitty one, all nervous? His name isn't Cayley, it's Benedict. He's rather fat, but he's quite good-looking.'

I asked her what particular interest I might have for Benedict or he for me.

'Oh, you are obtuse!' she scolded. 'He works at the same place as Evan, and you might get on to something. By the way, I think it would be a good idea if I didn't turn up. You meet him instead, introduce yourself, and make my excuses. You'll know him because he's fat and has a big gingery moustache.'

When I asked her why she would not come she replied earnestly, 'Because men never talk properly when women are there. They daren't, in case the women found out what they were really like.' Derisory, temporarily feminist, she gave a little frowning jerk of the head in my direction, as if to include me in her strictures. In that nod were the disillusions of a life-time, in infidelities discovered, the shams broken down. Helena, like so many women interested intensely in men, held most of them in contempt.

We walked slowly along together. 'The whole war's over now, thank God,' she said, 'so we can really start looking after ourselves again. That's why I bought this hat and costume. . . . Because the war's over,' she laboriously explained. 'I haven't such a bad conscience about buying things now. I wanted to celebrate.'

She gave me instructions as to how I was to pump Benedict.

'I don't like pumping,' I said.

'Never mind what you like. This is for Charmian's sake, not yours. Pretend you're a spy behind the enemy lines. Perhaps a lot of them didn't like it, but they had to do it.'

But Evan, I protested, was not a proven enemy.

'He will be,' she assured me, her eye threatening judgement, 'so it all comes to the same thing.'

I did care enough about Charmian's unhappiness to fall in, to an extent, with Helena's plan. Benedict seemed a pleasant fellow of the torpid variety, though a little puzzled by the forced circumstances of our acquaintanceship and a little put out by Helena's absence. He sensed, I think, some positive factor underlying her eagerness that we should meet, but was too lazy to bother much about it. For so big a man he ate with almost ludicrous frugality, putting very tiny portions of food in his mouth and chewing them in a very precise and minikin fashion. During the meal we talked army shop, and I did not broach the subject of Evan. Afterwards, however, we went down to the King's Head for a drink and in a while were beered into greater ease and intimacy.

'I know a man who works in Eaton Place,' I said. 'Have you come across anyone called Sholto?'

'Bunny Sholto? He works in the room next to mine.'

It came as a shock that Evan, in circles into which his family could not intrude, displayed the type of personality to warrant such a nickname.

'Do you know him well?' Benedict inquired casually, but his eyes showed an anxiety to ascertain how far he might go in his comment.

'Oh, so-so. Not particularly.'

'Conscientious chap. Really enjoys Bumph, which I bloody well don't. Funny, the Bumph-mind. It's something you're born with.'

'I gather he works hard enough.' I had lost my sense of self-disgust at the pumping process and was able to feel a degree of pleasure in its subtleties. 'So far as I can make out, he never gets home before eleven or twelve.'

Benedict stared rather wistfully at a girl with long fair hair and very long legs. 'There's a nice bit of crumpet,' he murmured. He returned his attention to me. 'Well, I don't know where he gets to, then. He usually leaves round about six, same as I do. . . . I say, what do you think that girl does for a living? Not an actress, I shouldn't think, but she might be a photographer's model. . . . Oh no, old Bunny doesn't do much overtime, though he sweats like a fiend all day. Chap I know who actually works with him says he has to sweat because he's not too bright, but I wouldn't know about that.'

Two young men came bursting through the doors in a great gust of dust and wind, and claimed the fair girl, whose somewhat morose expression instantly changed to one of high vivacity. Benedict began to hum beneath his breath:

I'm gonna buy a paper doll that I can call my own,
A doll that other fellows cannot steal.

'Pickering,' he said abruptly, checking his song, 'drink up. The hour grows late, and we have work to do: liquor to drink.'

We sat for half an hour longer above our own ash and beer-slops, until the bar was cleared at ten.

'Well,' he said, 'I'd better be getting along. Many thanks for the meal, I've had a good evening. Give my regards to Lady Archer and say how sorry I was she couldn't come.'

I walked with him to Albert Bridge, where he hoped to find a taxi, and managed to introduce Sholto's name once again.

'I tell you,' said Benedict, 'I don't know anything about old Bunny. You want to meet Finucane, who shares a room with him. You'd like Finucane – he knows a lot about painting. Lady Archer said you wrote books about it, but I had to tell her I was the complete Philistine. I used to like *Derby Day*, but old Fin says it stinks.'

I expressed an interest in Finucane. 'I like talking art,' I said, 'there's nothing like it for showing off.'

'Well, come and have a drink with us both then, one night,' Benedict suggested. 'What about the Café Royal?' Facetiously democratically, he pronounced it 'caff'.

I agreed to this, and an appointment was made. 'I ought to tell you,' I said, 'that I'm Sholto's brother-in-law. Not exactly by my choosing.'

Benedict looked alarmed. 'God help us! I'll bet I've said all I shouldn't.'

I reassured him. It was true, I said, that despite this relationship. I knew Sholto very slightly. We had never found each other particularly interesting, and besides, he had only been home for six months at the most of his married life, and that much in two instalments.

It seemed to me dubious whether or not I should get any information out of Finucane who, by the time we met, would certainly have been told in what relationship I stood to Sholto. I got none. When I did tentatively introduce the subject he said, 'Oh, Bunny's a good chap. The solid virtues, more or less,' and shut up like an oyster. For the rest of the evening we talked of painting, and Benedict was bored into a series of yawns and little tunes sung beneath the breath, the one alternating with the other.

At first, when I told Helena the results of my disagreeable activities, she shrugged her shoulders and said, 'Much good as a sick headache'; but a few minutes afterwards she exclaimed, 'We know one thing, anyhow, and that's that he doesn't spend from six till midnight at the office.'

'I never really thought he did.'

'Well,' said Helena briskly, 'when one door closes we must open another. You think hard, and perhaps you'll get a fresh idea. If Boiled Owl is misbehaving himself we can get Charmian out of it. I bet she'd give her ears for evidence.'

I thought so, too, and we agreed to harry our brains for a new line of action.

At this time this business of Sholto was the only thing, outside of John Field, which had any place in Helena's mind. Since the scene that followed his proposal to leave the flat, a serenity seemed to have descended upon her. She looked hand-some, confident, in excellent health. As yet she felt none of the post-war psychological reaction that was to overtake her in a year's time. The war was over, Hitler was dead, there were no more bombs, and one could be gay without remembering to be grim. As for the future, it could take care of itself; Helena knew nothing of it, and if she had known, could have done nothing about it. She had, in fact, precisely the same sense of licensed cheerfulness that she had experienced (so I gathered from her reminiscing) in 1918. Field, to my mind, had also taken on a certain light-heartedness. It was as though he had suddenly given up tormenting himself about the state of the world, and had boxed his looking forward and backward into a span ranging from the day before yesterday to the day after tomorrow. He was Helena's little boy, gentle as a lamb, always ready to pay her some comforting small compliment or to make the jokes that would please her. Three afternoons a week he spent at Mrs Olney's shop; on three others he went out after futile jobs, and every night returned to Helena's robust cherish-ing. Mrs Olney still visited the flat, but not quite so often. On her visits they played three-handed whist. Field, Helena told me, was starting to take up his music seriously, putting in an hour's practice before breakfast each morning. He was learn-ing, she whispered with an air of pride, Grieg's *Butterflies*.

I asked him once to play to me, but he refused. 'I play like hell. I love it, but I'm no good.'

'Helena says you can tackle *Butterflies*.'

'Not by my choice,' he said hastily, 'believe me. But Helena insists. She likes it.'

He did, however, play for Charmian one evening, when she called unexpectedly and found her mother out.

'He's not good,' she told me afterwards, 'but he touches you somehow. He plays everything as if he were far from his homeland and trying to remember it.'

I said it sounded bogus to me.

'Probably it is,' Charmian agreed, 'but it still makes you ashamed that you're not more simple-hearted. . . . Mind you, I don't think *he* is. But one feels one has to be dewy towards him.'

She sighed deeply and began, in a sisterly, ineffectual manner, to move to an empty shelf some books I had stacked on the floor.

'Here, don't do that. They're throw-outs. I'm going to sell them.'

'All right, do your own work. I was only trying to help.' She was on a week's leave. Sholto's leave could not be made to coincide with hers, and she was at a loose end. 'Isn't there anything I can do? You're in a dreadful mess.'

'My rooms may be, but not my person,' I retorted, looking at her.

'I simply can't be bothered,' Charmian said lightly, but she glanced automatically at the mirror. 'Don't nag me. I am as I am.'

'I often wish you were as you were.'

'Alas!' said Charmian, with mock pomposity, 'we grow old. We change.' Her voice slid into music. '"Flow over me with your waves and with your waters, Mananaan, Mananaan McLir." I must read *Ulysses* again.'

'I don't think your mother-in-law would consider it nice reading for a young girl, would she?'

'Nonsense. We're all married, and the children are in bed. ... Do you know she's been nagging me about that? Why don't I have some children?'

'Tell her to mind her own damned business. All the same, why don't you?'

'You can mind your own.'

'I'm privileged.'

'Well,' she said, stretching her arms above her head so that her body was tensed and strengthened, 'I simply don't want to. Not at present. And the more the *belle-mère* hints, the more I determine to wait till she's dead before I start.'

'In fact, you just can't stand her.'

'Is there anything good about her?'

'I feel there should be somewhere. People aren't all black or all white.'

'Oh, aren't they?' said Charmian rather vindictively. 'If you'd heard her about Mother recently, you wouldn't be so generous-hearted.'

I was seized by a fury I did not wish Charmian to suspect. 'Why? Has she said anything more?'

'Not to me. She daren't. She knows I'm ripe to bite.' Charmian, when really angry, had the sincere and ridiculous savagery of a baby bear, without the bear's capacity to nip. She was the kind of woman whose desire to be hard, to be pugnacious, to intimidate an enemy, would always run far ahead of her psychological ability to achieve any such thing, the kind of woman who, when attempting to tongue-lash a man who had annoyed her, would ever be infuriated to see flood into his eyes the same ravished, amused indulgence which is extended to a belligerent toddler. '*But*,' she went on, 'I ran into Alice Storford.' This was a distant cousin of Sholto's with whom Charmian had been very friendly, and who had visited the Pont Street flat on one or two occasions. 'I gathered from Alice that the *belle-mère* had suggested Mother and John were living in sin.'

'I think Alice wouldn't be above a little exaggeration.'

'Not on this occasion. Of course I just laughed, but I felt so sick and so furious I could hardly hear what she was saying after that.'

I told my sister that such drivel was beneath her contempt, that Alice Storford was a thundering liar anyhow, and that there were far more important things in the world than the fanciful pruriencies of old ladies. I took her out to the cinema and she let the whole matter slide back into the detritus of her mind. She justified my suspicion that, for all her rage, she would take it more lightly than I.

Next day, a Sunday, I called in the afternoon at Mrs Sholto's flat. The old lady rose from her chair in the wide window, from which she had been watching the lovers strolling in Kensington Gardens, the children running on the grass, the last traditional nursemaids rustling in their starchlike sheets of tissue paper. By her alacrity she managed to suggest that it was I of whom she had been thinking only a minute before, I for whom she had longed as a harbour wife longs for the return of the sailor. I told her at once that I had come on a disagreeable matter, but this she seemed unable to grasp. The furniture was upholstered in dove grey, the violet curtains were patterned with white and blue. In a vase that stood upon the sill, a sheaf of garden flags, silk and velvet, gave off their lemony, remembering perfume. Into this room no disagreeable thing could intrude; she was so convinced of this that she turned a deaf ear to any such attempt at entry.

She spoke to me of Charmian and of Evan, inquired after Helena, told me she thought I looked a little tired, and asked me whether I did not agree with her that the garden flag, were it rare, would be more prized than the orchid, being more beautiful.

I tried once or twice to approach the purpose of my call, but she succeeded in stopping me. I could not help but admire her; most people, however much they dreaded the introduction of matters mysterious and disagreeable, would have found their distaste conquered by curiosity, but Mrs Sholto seemed to be above this emotion. Making me sit in the window seat, she drew my attention to this and that in the street below; her observation was lively, her sense of irony sharp as a young woman's. I thought what importance she must have attached all her life to femininity; she emphasized it so strongly in her dress, in the way she did her hair, that it had some oblique effect of caricature. The front of her blouse was ruffled and flowers were pinned at her breast. Her skirt was fuller than the fashion, her slippers were decorated with little paste buckles. Her hair, which had the dull shine of pewter, was intricately braided over her head, and fluffed out here and there to give softness to her brow. I felt that this insistence upon her sex was a disguise for a hard and mannish mind; more than probably she handled all her own investments and despised her broker.

She spoke suddenly, startling me out of my thoughts. 'And now, Claud, you want to be disagreeable. I can hardly believe it, but I mustn't put any obstacle in your way. What is the terrible trouble?' She smiled at me confidingly, as if we were both about to share some wonderful joke.

As briefly as I could, I told her of Charmian's meeting with Alice Storford and of the gossip the latter had attributed to Mrs Sholto.

'Oh,' the old lady said, fingering one of the rings with which she emphasized the spawn-like transparency of her hands, 'oh!' There was a silence. I believed her disconcerted.

Then she rose briskly and rang for the maid. 'Lucy, will you bring us some tea, please? I'd like some of the Romary biscuits, if there are any left. – My one real greediness,' she told me, tapping her own wrist in playful self-rebuke. When we were alone again she said, 'Yes. Now about all these dreadful things you've been saying. . . . Not that you put them dreadfully, Claud dear; I will say for you and Charmian that you *are* most tactful. It's a gift, of course; one can't acquire it. Yes. Poor Alice's naughty little tongue.' Her face became prim, satisfied, quietly cruel. 'She's a bad little tattler, that girl. She was just the same as a child, only her mother never checked her. She should have done as my mother did when I began telling her some schoolgirlish scandal; she made me put out my tongue and gave it a tiny nick with her embroidery scissors. It didn't hurt very much, but oh, how ashamed I was! Of course, nowadays those old-fashioned methods aren't approved – I believe you call them "sadistic", or something of the sort, which seems to me quite absurd when I think how Mother worshipped us all. Let me tell you, though, that she was quite scientific in her way. I remember her dipping the scissors in Condy's fluid first.'

This horrid detail took me so by surprise that for a moment I could find nothing to say. Mrs Sholto looked at me with a sweet and secret longing, thinking (I shouldn't be surprised) how much she would like to serve me in her mother's fashion, but without Condy's fluid, and with garden shears.

She came out of her reverie suddenly, like a fish swimming up from the river bed to the surface. 'Well, now, Claud: you're a man of the world, and I think we should be able to talk sensibly. "Get down" to things,' she added, proud of her slang. 'To begin with, Alice is quite unreliable, and I'm really surprised at you taking all she says at its face value.'

'Did you suggest,' I said, 'even in fun, that Helena's relations with Field were in any sense dubious?'

'No,' said Mrs Sholto promptly, folding her upper lip over the lower as if she were closing a purse.

The maid came in with the tray.

'We'll have it on this little table,' the old lady cried, all animation, 'and you, Claud, shall sit here in the low chair. It's very comfortable, and you can put your cup on the arm.' She settled me, dismissed Lucy. Lifting up the lid of the biscuit jar she peered inside it, and her face fell. '*No* Romarys! Oh dear, why did we have to have an awful war to make everything so miserable? Never mind, we must all be grateful for what we can get.'

I had a vague idea that I should refuse to eat her salt, a more positive one that I should only make a fool of myself by so doing.

'Now then,' she said when she had poured the tea, 'let's go back to all this disagreeableness. I did not suggest anything of the sort – I mean, anything of the kind Alice inferred, and I am just a little surprised that you should have taken her seriously. You're usually so level-headed, Claud.'

'Something must have been said. . . . I'm sorry, Mrs Sholto, I don't enjoy doing this, but it isn't the first time I've heard gossip.'

'Very well.' She looked towards the window, seemed to take a decision. 'In that case I must try to remember exactly what I did say to Alice.' She broke off. 'Claud, you are one of the few people khaki really suits, and I never imagined it would. . . . Yes. What I said to Alice. She asked me what news I had of Lady Archer. I replied that she was well, and mentioned that she now had a young man, a friend of yours staying permanently in the flat. Alice made some silly little smart remark, and I said "Evil be to them who evil think" – making a joke of it. I should have been cross with her, I know, but she really is an engaging child, for all her nonsense. Her mother and I were very attached.'

This appeared to be her last word. She was so slippery an adversary that I had no idea how to take her. I could not, despite my conviction of her mischief-making, give her the lie direct. We sat in silence, Mrs Sholto gazing with serene appreciation at the Florentine blue of the sky beyond the window, the rounded and ruddy shadows cast by the flags upon the wall.

Then she said, 'But my dear Claud, as one grown-up person to another, don't you think we should admit that such gossip is only to be expected? Your stepmother is a remarkably vigorous and youthful woman for her age, and unconventional – very often – in her way of expressing things. I know perfectly well that Mr Field is a child to her, and that she looks at him in that light: but people are so uncharitable, and so eager to make a moment's amusement at the expense of somebody's reputation. If you want me to be frank' – she raised her head, bestowed upon me the full-sweet beam of her eyes that were faded by years and short-sightedness to the colour of violas – 'I *have* heard talk. I've heard it myself.'

I was so angry that I could have kicked over the tea-table. 'Who from?'

'Now, Claud, one doesn't tell tales.'

'The Leipers?'

'You really must not pump me. I don't like scandal,' she said with rapt effrontery, 'and I certainly shan't contribute to it in any way.'

As I said nothing, she decided that I was convinced of her innocence and ashamed of myself. She assumed the awful brightness of the person who loves forgiving others. 'Now let's forget all about this storm in a teacup and fill our own teacups again. I think it's very fine of you to stand up for your step-mother, even though you *were* misinformed, and very brave. Few young men of your age have the honesty to be so direct. Tell me, now, is the book out? How you manage to write when you've been at an office all day I can't imagine.'

I said, 'If any more malicious talk about Helena and Field comes to my ears I shall see Helena sues for slander.'

Mrs Sholto stared at me, arrested in the act of pouring hot water on to the tea-leaves. A dark colour swept up from her throat into her face, staining it like cochineal. 'Claud! Are you *threatening* me? Because if you are, I don't like it at all.'

'I'm not threatening. I'm telling you what I shall have to do. Apart from anything else, Helena is Charmian's mother, and you're harming Charmian.'

'I,' repeated Mrs Sholto, speaking in a tone of incredulous obedience as if she were learning some fantastic lesson under threat of flogging, 'am harming Charmian.'

Her arm jerked, and hot water flooded over the tray. She rang the bell. 'Lucy, bring a cloth, please.'

We had to wait while the maid mopped up the water and brought a clean tray-cloth. When we were alone again I told the old lady I must go. I had said all there was to be said, and wished for both our sakes that the matter had been a more pleasant one.

'*I* am harming Charmian,' she repeated. 'I must ask her if

she thinks so, and if necessary beg her pardon. I would rather apologize for something of which I am innocent than cause my son's wife any distress.'

I noticed that Mrs Sholto was now 'talking like a book', taking pleasure in the dramatic fluency of her sentences.

'If you'd just use your influence to stop any further dirty-mindedness,' I said, 'it would help more. And please don't say anything to Charmian. This is your affair and mine.'

She rose, and stood with her head bowed. She said nothing, so I walked towards the door. I should have left, I am sure, without another word from her had not a sudden and violent incident occurred. The maid ran into the room, her face twitching and as white as chalk, rushed up to Mrs Sholto and cried, 'Oh, madam, oh, madam, the kitten!'

The old lady startled, and trembled. 'What's the matter, Lucy? What's happened?'

'Oh, come quickly, do come quickly! He jumped on the stove and upset the kettle, and it's awful!'

Seizing her mistress by the hand, she pulled her towards the door. I followed, and the three of us went into the kitchen where, in silence, a little cat mad with pain was circling the room, leaping half up the walls, dashing itself at the corners.

'My lovely, my lovely,' the maid cried, 'don't do it, oh, don't do it! Come to Lucy, my lovey-dear!'

Mrs Sholto stood quite still, as if holding her breath. She put out her hand and touched me. 'You help, Claud, you help.' It was not a human voice; it might have been produced by some mechanical means, some arrangement of engines.

I grabbed at the cat as it came round and held it tightly, while it scratched and clawed at me. Its eyes were like a child's. Lucy had turned to the wall as if she could not bear to look on. When I had quietened the kitten to some degree I examined its burns. The boiling water had splashed only over the feet, but these were swollen up like the paws of a bulldog.

I asked Lucy if there were any tannic jelly in the flat. She tried to answer me but could not speak. The cat struggled between my hands, arched its body in a spasm of pain, and urinated.

Mrs Sholto went out of the room. She returned in a moment with a tube of Tannafax and a roll of bandages which she gave to me. The tears were running down her face.

The two women watched me while I gave first aid and tried to make the kitten drink some milk into which I had crushed an aspirin. Lucy was still half-hysterical. Mrs Sholto, to soothe her, put an arm about her shoulders.

I went to telephone the veterinary surgeon, and when I had done so found Mrs Sholto waiting for me in the hall, tremulous, but very controlled.

'Do you think he's in very much pain now?'

'I think he's a bit easier. The vet'll be able to help him, and he should be right over it in a day or so.'

'You must think we are two silly women, Lucy and I,' the old lady said quietly, 'but we love our little cat very much. He is very important to us both.'

I said good-bye.

'I shall not say anything to Charmian,' she told me, her voice rather stiff. This was her way of thanking me for my treatment of the kitten. 'We won't refer to it again, Claud.'

We shook hands solemnly. I fancied she performed her part of the ceremony with a ritual air, like a defeated boxer who wants to maintain his reputation for sportsmanship.

On my way home I considered Charmian's remarks about blacks and whites, and my own feeling that practically all people were merely grey. It struck me now that most of them, certainly the Mrs Sholtos of the world, flashed for ever from extreme to extreme, black on one occasion, white on the next. They were grey only in the sense that we should receive an effect of greyness if we watched a strip of paper barred vertically with white and black drawn rapidly through one of those little machines through which children pull strips of cinema film. Refraining with some effort from becoming sentimental about Mrs Sholto's love for the kitten and her comradeship with Lucy in the sharing of this love, I told myself it was a pity that the old lady should be an angel to a cat and a devil to Helena. The two sides of her nature – complete devotion to an animal, motiveless malice towards another woman – were not factors that could be combined to ensure a tolerant judgement. I also told myself that I should have been less moved by the incident in the kitchen had I been a passionate dog-lover.

Nevertheless, illogically or not, I felt rather less sure of myself and my rightness than I had felt when making my empty threat of a slander-suit. The threat was, of course, entirely empty. No amount of damages won in such a suit would be able to cleanse Helena of the inevitable ridicule attendant upon bringing it.

I had not been home ten minutes before I had a visit from Swain. He was curiously attired for summer in white duck trousers and tweed sports coat; under the coat he wore a peach-coloured shirt of peculiar texture and cut.

'Don't look at my blouse,' he said, 'it's the jacket of my only silk pyjamas. All my cool shirts were in the wash, so I thought this was a good idea.'

I offered him a drink. 'There isn't much left. I get a ration from the off-licence of a bottle a month, and I'm not due for any more till next week, but you're welcome to what there is.'

'I can do without it.'

He said this so significantly that my attention was diverted from his surprising clothes to his face.

'What's up?'

'God, I've had a shock today. You'll have one too when I tell you. You remember Nina Crandell?'

'Yes, of course. Very nice girl, too nice for him.'

'Well, she's done herself in. Silly damn fool!' he added, in a voice of rage and regret.

The shock he had promised me jerked her picture on to the screen of my mind. I saw her small, humorous, rather mouse-like face, her toeless sandals, the grotesque cascade of hair that hung down like a child's almost to the small of her back. 'How? Why?'

'She left a note. She couldn't face the "Atomic Age", she said. What rats people are!' Swain burst out. He would have killed her a second time could he have reached her. 'I always thought she was so sound, a real, good, sensible girl! Couldn't she see how she was letting the side down?'

'Crandell must feel like hell,' I said.

'What bloody right had she to *make* him feel like hell? Where should we be if we all lay down and moaned and whimpered and stuck our heads in the gas-oven? ... That was what she did. The little beast,' said Swain, working himself, in sorrow, to a passion of fury, 'Who told her she could do it? There's only one test of what's right and what's wrong.

A thing's right if it's right for everyone, and wrong if it's only right for one's self. Did she think she was God Almighty, to have the privilege of cutting loose when life got a bit tricky?'

'I nearly fell in love with Nina,' I said, 'after a couple of hours' acquaintance.'

'Oh, everyone got a "thing" about her. I would've, if it hadn't been for Clemmy. Nina looked like nothing on earth, but people fell for her like ninepins. Any respect I had for her, however, has gone to pot. I tell you what – if anyone's worth even twopence halfpenny they don't do themselves in, because they never stop believing in the good time coming.'

I noticed that his voice had blurred a little; there had been no more than two double whiskies in the bottle, and I had poured myself one of them. I saw now that he had been drinking before he came to tell me his news, and that my whisky had been just enough to tip him over the edge of sobriety.

'The belief in a good time coming,' said Swain portentously, 'is philosophically correct, even when it is obvious that there is no more hope of the good time actually materializing than a snowball in hell, that is' – he corrected himself – 'no more hope *than for* a snowball to continue to exist in hell. Put it down, Claud, put it down, you'll need it for my biography when you write it. Not less than a hundred thousand words, please, and forty full-page illustrations.'

Rising, he flexed his knees. 'Bah! Sickly suiciding. Why put yourself out before your time when even a lifetime isn't long enough to see five per cent of all the pictures or smoke point O one per cent of all the cigarettes? I haven't seen the Bouts *Last Judgement* at Lille or the Piero *Resurrection* at where-ever-it-is in Italy. Even that thought would be enough to make me careful of my own skin.' He paused. 'Inquest on Tuesday, but it's all cut-and-dried. Unsound mind. And quite right too: the only people who commit suicide while sane are the financial millionaires who get caught out. Better a million years in hell than fourteen in Dartmoor. Chalk that up, too. You can have an Aphorisms Section at the end.'

When he had gone, I tried to throw off my depression at Nina Crandell's suicide by thinking of Helena. She, at least, would believe to the last in the good time coming, regarded good times, in fact, as the natural order of things and bad ones as lunatic phenomena. She was one of those people to whom all world crises, depressions, panics, wars, come as great surprises. The reason for Nina's death would be past her comprehension. It would be impossible for atomic, or any worse kind of warfare, to destroy Helena, whose birthday was always next week, and whose party was already arranged. I wondered for a moment what she would do if Field did leave her, comforted myself by the thought that her fancy was still young enough to stick itself, like a burr, upon something new.

Yet I could not be sure of this. Those who live their lives quietly, unmoved either by great sorrow or great joy, are often, in their final years, granted the dispensation of Discovery. Now, for the first time, they find out the secondary roads of the imagination, the side-streets, the alley-ways, the low doors each with a key in the lock. They have leisure now to study (academically, at least) the books with fiery letters that they never had time to read, contemplate the paintings they had stored in the lumber-room, out of the way.

But those who have lived richly, exhaustively, staring into every face, attentive to every voice, are only too often pursued by the spinster Furies, and are driven at the end down avenues of stone where the walls reach to the sky, and the doors are sealed, and the pavements are rubbered against all sound but the beat of the hurrying heart.

Well – Helena would say – And even if I understood all that . . . and believed it . . . wasn't it worth it?

Chapter Five

HELENA was more upset than I had expected by the news
of Nina Crandell's death, at first taking much the same attitude
as Swain – that the whole thing had been an outrageous im-
pertinence, an intolerable arrogation of right – and then behaving as if it were an insult to herself, an abuse of hospitality.
The fact that she had met Nina perhaps three times and enter-
tained her once was of no importance. A person who had eaten
Helena's salt was unmannerly to deny life in any fashion. The
truth of her emotion was, however, simpler than all this. She
was beginning to look upon death as a reality, to fear it, to regard the mere fact of being alive as the most precious of all
things, and she could not bear to think of anyone throwing
this gift away. She was somewhat consoled by the later information, which I had from Swain, who had it from Crandell
himself, that Nina had killed herself less out of fear of the
Atomic Age, or any other such public matter, than because of
a cumulation of private miseries, including her distress at her
husband's infidelity. 'He's getting his punishment now,'
Swain had said, 'he's as eaten by remorse as a corpse with
worms. Serve him right.'

'Well,' Helena said to me, 'let the dead bury their dead.'
She was not sure of the meaning of these words, but she liked
them because they had a conclusive sound, were proper syllables with which to round off a thoroughly disagreeable affair.

I was standing at the door of Field's bedroom, watching her
dust his dressing-table. She had asked me to dine there that
night, and because work was slack I had arrived early. Helena,
dusting for Field, had an appearance of devotion that was almost sculptural. She might have posed for the figure of Charity
tending the sick, Martha performing the solemn tasks of the
household. Her face was grave, absorbed, as smooth as wax.

The room was beautifully tidy, everything in its place.
Pyjamas were neatly folded on the swathe of the sheet, water-

bottle and glass, ashtray and matches, were arranged in two groupings upon the bedside table, the distance from each to the edge of the tabletop being the same as the distance between the two of them. On the glass top of the dressing-table were brush and comb, a tray for oddments, writing-pad and fountain-pen, and a row of books. On the window-sill was a cyclamen plant, the flowers thick and white as kid leather. On a chair at the foot of the bed was folded a dressing-gown with slippers placed on top of it.

I complimented Helena upon this pleasing order.

'Oh, it looks all right now; but you see it an hour after he's got up tomorrow and it'll look as though a cow had kicked it.' She spoke with the ruefulness that conceals pride; everything about Field was precious to her, including his incurable untidiness.

The book standing nearest to the cyclamens was a bright yellow, and attracted my eye; the whiteness and matt texture of the flowers, the colour and glossiness of the volume, were complementary to each other, and the arrangement seemed to me, for the moment, a miracle of fortuity. I went into the room to look at it more closely, and then was diverted by the book itself and the others in the row. Two or three I had seen on the dressing-table before, but half a dozen were new. I stood there taking up one after another and looking through the pages. 'He's been splashing it lately,' I said. 'I wanted this Edmund Wilson myself.'

'New, are they?' Helena was looking out some laundry from the linen basket. 'I wouldn't notice.' She held out a pair of socks at arm's length. 'What disgusting brutes you men are! — Full of holes, and filthy dirty. I tell him, he's only got to let me have his darning *right* away and I'll see it gets done.'

I remarked idly, most of my mind on what I was reading, that I couldn't think where Field got the money to buy half a dozen books, at present prices.

Helena rose, put back the lid of the basket and bundled the washing in a tottering pile on the top of it. Then she came and looked over my shoulder. 'Why, what does that one cost, the one you're reading?'

I looked in the flap of the jacket. 'Eighteen bob.'

She looked rapidly inside the other jackets, her lips doing a silent sum. Then she said, 'Three pounds fourteen.' She gave the books a push that sent them toppling. 'Yes, where does he get it?'

I looked at her, saw that she was excited. 'God knows. Why shouldn't he buy books, anyhow? It's his business.'

'Oh, is it?' muttered Helena, 'oh, is it?' and returned furiously to listing the laundry.

'Now look here,' I said, 'don't you go bothering him about his own affairs.'

She did not reply and soon began to talk of other things, but I felt the heaviness of her thought.

At half-past six Field came in, Mrs Olney with him. In the strong sunset light I noticed about her something that had never struck me before: that she was none too clean. Her face powder looked as if it were the last of several layers, her lipstick a re-coating of an earlier smear. There was a faint line of grease and powder around the neck of her pale blue dress, and the upturned collar of her blue coat was faintly reddened where it had brushed against her cheeks. Her shoes had not been cleaned, her stockings had black marks at the ankles. With all this she retained a pervasive attraction, a persistent promise. She was like some ageing beauty of the screen sinking steadily down in the B films, yet still able to command a certain faithful following.

Helena was surprised to see her, and said so.

'I met Dilys on the way,' Field said. 'She's been shopping. She's exhausted.'

'Not shopping exactly,' Mrs Olney explained, pushing her hat to the back of her head so that it had a rodeo look. 'I was told of a man round here who makes a special sort of frame for lampshades, so I shut up shop early and came along, but of course he'd gone away in the blitz, and then someone told me he'd moved to Battersea, and I even went along there, but nobody had ever heard of him. How cool you look, Helena! I'm sure I look like the boy on the burning deck.'

'I told her a drink would set her up again.' Field seemed impervious to Helena's palpable displeasure. 'Have we got any?'

'I'm in the way,' said Mrs Olney, 'you're expecting somebody. I'll go forth into the night, shall I?'

'Oh no, no.' Helena was ungracious. 'May as well stay now you're here.'

'Let me put my poor tired tootsies up for just three minutes, and then I'll fly.'

She passed with a swaying gait, expressive of exhaustion, into the front room and sank down with a long, deflating sigh on to the settee.

Field went to see what drink there was left, and Helena went out to the kitchen.

'Major Pickering,' Mrs Olney said, 'do tell me if I'm interrupting. Helena would never tell me – she's too kind-hearted. Is there truly no one coming?'

I told her I didn't really know.

'I simply felt that I couldn't go another step. Do you know that feeling of nightmare one gets sometimes when one's walked too far, as if it's a mile to the next lamp-post?'

Field came in again. 'A very small gin and the last of the vermouth. Yours, Dilys. . . . There's a drop of sherry if you'd rather, Claud. Dilys can't bear it.'

'One should be able to bear it, because it's such a well-bred sort of drink,' she chattered, 'but I simply can't, and when I let Dennis try just a sip, on his last holidays, he was ferociously sick. But with ferocity,' she added, her syntax Gallic, her mind far away in contemplation of vomit.

She lay back and closed her eyes. 'Ah, heaven! . . . Just to rest, and be at peace with the world.'

'Poor old Dilys,' said Field affectionately, 'the fates do dog you.'

'Oh, they do,' she replied, 'they do, Johnny. Double, double, boil and trouble. Or toil and trouble, whichever it is. . . . When I got to Battersea and found that man wasn't there I could have died on my feet. Yes, you're right. Dog is the word. Fate dogs me.'

She opened her eyes and smiled upon him, like a princess awakening after a hundred years. 'Tell me when I must go, Johnny, and then carry me out. You'll have to carry me, because I'm sure I'll never be able to walk. My feet hurt quite appallingly.'

'Take your shoes off for a moment,' he suggested.

It was, of course, the worst thing she could have done, for

having taken them off she could not get them on again. When Helena came in to announce dinner, she found Mrs Olney hobbling about the room uttering little oohs and ahs of pain, her toes inside the shoes, but her heels projecting a good half-inch over the breaking backs.

'You'd better stop and have something with us,' Helena said, because there was nothing else she could say.

'No, no. I wouldn't for the world. I wasn't expected, and I never push myself in. I'll be able to go forth in a minute. Just give me a second.'

'I can't give you a second,' Helena told her brusquely, 'because the fish will spoil. Come along, Dilys, and don't be foolish.'

So we sat down to dinner, Helena, Field, myself, and Mrs Olney shoeless. Helena seemed to have recovered from her bad temper, and she and her friend fell into the kind of cryptic banter common with women who have been much in each other's confidence.

'How wonderfully you do cook!' Mrs Olney exclaimed, finishing her sweet with appreciative slowness. 'Really, Helena, I simply don't know where you get all your talents.'

'My cooking's only so-so,' Helena replied, 'as Claud will tell you. I'm quite good at making it look nice, though, and that's half the battle.'

This was true. Her cooking, beneath the elaborations in which she took so much pleasure, was indifferent. Nothing had very much flavour, or was quite hot, or quite cold.

'Claud would not be so ungallant,' Mrs Olney replied severely. She gave me a little smile. 'Major Pickering, I should say.'

I didn't offer her the use of my first name.

'You don't know Claud,' said Helena. 'Johnny, give Dilys a cigarette.' He did so. 'Now me. Don't forget me. The matches are behind you, Claud, if you look.'

I searched for them unsuccessfully.

'Don't worry.' Field took out a lighter, which flamed instantly, and lit our cigarettes with the panache of a head waiter.

'Fancy having one that goes at once,' Helena said. 'Usually you snip and snap at them for hours. Let's look at it.' He handed it to her. I bent over her to examine it. It was a minute thing, no bigger than the joint of my fourth finger, and was covered with red leather.

Helena looked up. 'When did you get this? Is it new?'

'Brand new,' said Field. 'Oh, I just bought it.'

Memory shot through her eyes. 'I think you're a millionaire in disguise. What with that and other things.'

'What other things?'

They seemed to me like actors playing a scene in duologue, Mrs Olney and myself no more than paintings on a backcloth.

'Three pounds fourteen-worth of books.'

He stiffened and looked angry, but when he spoke his voice was mild. 'I have to buy myself a little treat sometimes, Helena. It gives me the illusion of wealth.'

She held up the lighter accusingly. 'What did they make you pay for this?'

'That's my small secret,' said Field.

Then Mrs Olney smiled swiftly, fleetingly, and Helena saw her.

'Did you give it to him?'

Mrs Olney emerged from the backcloth, became one of the actors. 'That's *his* secret,' she said, the smile returning.

'Helena,' Field said, 'I made the frightful mistake of letting Dilys know my birthday.'

'Which was last Thursday,' said Mrs Olney, looking like the Mona Lisa scoring over a next-door neighbour.

'Which was last Thursday. Before I could stop her she'd rushed off and bought me this. I didn't show you, Helena, because I thought you'd only go buying me a birthday present, too, and I felt you'd been kind enough already.'

For a moment I believed that she would accept this explanation. She looked at him piercingly, as if she would read the script behind his brow, and her face was anxious and sad. We all sat in silence. Hearing and feeling a slight scuffle below table level I looked down, and saw Mrs Olney fumbling with her toes for the discarded shoes, saw her stealthily retrieve them and slide her feet, which had now shrunk as they had cooled, down into them.

Then Helena asked, 'Did she give you those books, too?'

'No,' said Field. He looked like a wine bottle, narrow, all neck, shoulders sloping down into darkness. I felt that in another moment she would seize, shake and break him, and that it was incumbent upon me to intervene somehow or other; but there was a tightness between the two of them that seemed to exclude me utterly.

'Then how did you get them? Who gave them to you if she didn't?'

'Nobody gave them to me. Please, Helena, this can't be much fun for Claud and Dilys.'

I saw then that such scenes were not new to them, that they had been played many times, always in disgust and in fury, ending always in a reconciliation more sickening than the quarrel itself. But this was the first time such a scene had been played in public.

Helena cried, 'She bought them for you, didn't she? She bought them for you out of my money!'

'That'll do,' I said.

Twisting round in her chair she gave me the full, blank insult of her glance. 'Be quiet, Claud! How dare you interfere? This is between me and Johnny.'

'And two other people, don't forget.'

'Damn the two other people! Be quiet.' She turned to Field again. 'Didn't she? Didn't she buy them with my money?'

'No,' he said. His hands had gone white from fingertips to knuckles. 'It's gone cold all of a sudden,' he murmured distractedly, 'I'm absolutely freezing. We ought to have the fire on.' Ducking away from the table, he fumbled by the skirting board for the switch.

Helena rose, came round from her seat like lightning, and kicked the switch up with her toe. For some reason we all watched the electric heater as it turned from dull to sparkling red. Then we turned to Helena.

'Dilys,' she said, quite levelly, 'you've been giving him my money, haven't you?' She was quite sure that this was the truth. So was I.

Mrs Olney got up, staggered a little in the agonizing shoes, and righted herself. She disregarded Helena. Instead she touched Field's shoulder, and he rose from his knees as if the pressure of her fingers were magnetic. 'Johnny, you know what we said. If you can't stand it you needn't. We can work together and I can get the room for you.'

He looked at her pathetically, Andromeda wondering if Perseus might not be more dangerous than the sea beast.

'You'd go and live on her?' Helena cried brutally.

This seemed, surprisingly, to soothe him. He said, 'No more than I'm living on you. Rather less, because I should be earning my keep. . . . I don't seem a very fine type, do I?'

'Earning your keep! There isn't twopence halfpenny in that shop, and there never will be.'

'If you'll excuse me, Helena,' Mrs Olney interposed, with an air of dignity that intruded very oddly, 'there you are wrong. The business has shown a very good profit for some weeks.'

Helena said, 'Johnny. You wouldn't go into her hare-brained schemes, would you?'

He seemed unable to reply. Instead, he looked at me as if only I could help him.

'Johnny. Just tell me whether she's been giving you my money. It doesn't matter about the money itself. I only want to know if she's been cheating me.' Helena spoke very softly, as if Mrs Olney and I were shut away behind a thin partition and would not be able to hear her if she whispered.

Field said firmly, 'I'll come in with you, Dilys, for a bit, anyway. It's all I can do.'

'You won't!' Helena was beside herself.

'I must. I can't stay here now, can I?'

'Don't be a fool! You can't be serious about that tinpot business, not after what you've seen of it. You know why she wants you to go in, Johnny!'

'You're offensive, Helena,' said Mrs Olney.

'All this is offensive,' I put in, 'and I think it had better stop.'

Field looked at me and coloured deeply. He jerked up his hands as if making them ready to emphasize some words he would speak. Then he let them drop, turned his back on us and walked out of the room.

For a few moments we had nothing to say.

Then Helena smiled frightfully at Mrs Olney. 'You ought to be ashamed of yourself.'

Had Mrs Olney retorted in kind it would have been in keeping with the sadness, the scruffiness, the shoddy fantasy of the whole scene; but she only said, 'I must talk to Johnny.'

'He doesn't want to talk to you. He's upset enough already. If you had the least consideration for him,' Helena told her hotly, 'you wouldn't want to bedevil him like this.'

'I didn't start it,' Mrs Olney said steadily. 'And I didn't insult him.'

Helena cried, 'You're not a young girl!'

'We're neither of us young girls. He wants to come in with me because of his self-respect.'

Helena gave a bark of irony.

'Perhaps it seems all right to you,' Mrs Olney muttered, trembling, 'to keep him from earning a living. But it doesn't seem right to him. I know, because he told me. We've had many a talk.'

The thought of these secret conversations, these soul-barings, brought to Helena's face and to her whole body a look of terror, of shrinking.

'You can't mother him for ever,' Mrs Olney continued, 'he's too old. He's not a boy, he's a man. And he's proud.'

It struck me that her restraint was remarkable. Helena had made ugly suggestions to her, and she could have thrown them back; but she did not. Perhaps this unexpected manifestation of decency had its effect upon Helena, for she did not cry out that Field's pride was a matter for debate. Instead, she sat down in her place at table and stared desolately at the soiled plates, the empty glasses.

'I think we'd better be going home,' I said to Mrs Olney. 'It isn't going to do very much good if there's a lot more talk.'

'Perhaps you're right,' she said, and glared at Helena's still head with a kind of keyed-up contempt that gave her the appearance of slight drunkenness.

Before we could move, however, Field came back into the dining-room. He was very pale and looked as if he had been crying. 'I want to say something, and I'd like you to listen.'

'Look here,' I said, 'Mrs Olney and I are going now.'

'Stop a minute. I want you to hear.'

He sat down facing Helena at the far end of the table. Between them was the litter of the meal and a long space of white light. He spread out his hands upon the cloth, broad hands, short-fingered like the pads of a mole, and contemplated them in silence.

'If you've anything to say,' Helena shot at him, 'say it. Then you can make your plans.'

He looked up at her. His eyes were tender, beseeching, pleading for her concentrated understanding. 'You must have known I'd have to go, Helena. I tried to go before, but you wouldn't let me. I'll have to go now, though, and I think you'll be glad later on. You've been so terrific to me, and I've treated you vilely.'

At this she protested, warmth returning to her suddenly and making her seem doubly handsome.

'I have. Claud will tell you. I don't know why, Helena, but since I got out of the army I've lost my grip. I never was a strong character, and now I don't seem able to check myself.'

His voice, which had at first been low and feeble, was gathering strength. In it was an eagerness for confession that suggested delight. He was like a man who has longed all his life to be able to present himself dramatically in a certain aspect and has at last found an attentive and sympathetic audience. He was speaking now without emphasis, as if there were no need to force our belief.

'I betrayed you stone-cold, Helena. I boasted about you devoting yourself to me, I boasted about it in a pub one night to some twopenny-ha'penny girl who laughed like fun. Claud overheard me, and he could have cut my throat. So you see, you're having a pretty good loss, aren't you? I can't help showing off once I find somebody innocent enough to believe me, and that's what I was doing that night in the pub.' He seemed about to weep; nevertheless, he was having the time of his life. The agony of confession was acute, torturing him like a spiral of physical pain, yet it pierced him with pleasure. He sank lower in his chair, making himself smaller, less responsible for his own errors, more like a child who has made the shocking discovery of the difference between wrong and right.

Mrs Olney was looking at him in utter bewilderment. Automatically she pulled a puff from her bag and began to pass it in slow, heedless circles over her face.

'You expect too much of me,' Field said fretfully, his tone changing, 'you always did, Helena. Dilys doesn't expect anything. She'll let me get on with a job and leave me to it. You can't leave people alone.'

'What do you mean?' Helena exclaimed. 'Haven't I considered you always? Didn't I try to have your room as you wanted it? What else could I have done?'

'People can't read when they're with you,' he told her, with a quick wrench of his body, 'you wouldn't understand what I mean, because you can read a bit, then look up and ask a question or make a remark, and go right back to where you were. But you always talk when I'm reading, and even when you don't I can't concentrate, because I always think you're going to start.'

Helena looked devastated. Her gaze travelled from his face to mine, from mine to Mrs Olney's. She was struck by his cruelty as by lightning. I would have intervened, but things had gone too far. It was necessary now for a conclusion to be reached.

'But Johnny –' she cried out, only herself and Field in the world.

'There!' he said excitedly, 'that's how I am. That's the kind of thing I simply have to say, when I'm so grateful really, so grateful. . . .' He attacked her again. 'You do too much for me. It's too much for me to *thank*. I behave like a swine because I don't know how to behave well *enough*. I wouldn't have to thank Dilys, because she'd be helping me in return for something.' He broke off. 'My God, Claud, I bet you regret that day you brought me home!'

'Yes,' I replied, 'I do.'

'Well, then, make Helena see I must go! Make her see it's a good thing.'

'I don't care if you do talk about me to a lot of silly girls,' she murmured. 'Why should I care? It doesn't matter to me. And I don't want thanking. I've always hated being thanked.'

He came round to where she sat, put his hand emotionally upon her shoulder. 'Oh, Helena, if only I could get it into your head that I think you're the most terrifically kind person in the world!'

She would not look at him.

They stood there like figures in a living tableau, sentimentally posed and lit.

Mrs Olney said sharply, 'Oh, get your clothes, Johnny. They'll put you up next door to me, and I'll see if I can't fix the room for you tomorrow.'

He did not move. 'Helena,' he urged, 'you'll try to understand, won't you?'

Rising abruptly, she pushed him aside. She seemed now not merely an inch taller than he, but a giantess who could sweep him up into the palm of her hand. She was a fine old woman fit to launch a battleship or ride to hounds, a woman rightly and splendidly offended, and ripe to crush the offender.

'*I'll* get his clothes,' said Helena.

When she had left us, Field went to the front room, and automatically we followed him. It was a relief to be free of the settings of drama, to stand in untroubled air. He smiled wearily at me. He was like an actor exhausted after the play, dazed by the fall from the one life into the other. 'All right, all right,' he said, 'it's been a disgusting exhibition, hasn't it? Couldn't have been worse. I'd apologize if I could, but it seems beyond that.'

In the bitter cold of the calm, the exhibition that was past seemed to me less disgusting than ridiculous; I could scarcely believe it had happened.

'Yes, I think it's beyond apologies.'

'I make this sort of mess everywhere I go. It's always the same. Dilys makes muck-ups of things, too, so probably we shall get along.'

Mrs Olney said fiercely, 'He only wants peace. At least I'll see he gets that.'

It seemed an age till Helena's return; there was nothing left to say. Mrs Olney sat down and eased her feet up and down in her shoes. Field stood stiffly at the window, his back to us. There was something timid about the back of his neck, as if he expected some sudden attack from behind. It was nearly dark. We had forgotten to turn on the lights, and were now enveloped in a dusk that thickened the darker colours and gave a curious luminosity to hands and faces. The dark roses in the mantelshelf bowl were almost blue.

Helena came in, lugging a big suit-case. 'Clothes, books, oddments. The lot, I think. If I've forgotten anything you can send for it.' She pushed the case at him.

'Good-bye,' she said.

He looked at her, not speaking.

Helena went out of the room and banged the door.

'I think you'd both better go,' I said, 'as quickly as possible.'

'But I can't, not before I've talked to Helena,' Field protested.

'She's nothing more to say to you.'

'I must confess,' Mrs Olney cried, in a high, aggrieved voice 'that I don't see why all this should have been so horrible! It could have been done in a perfectly decent way. Helena is *not* being reasonable, and she can be most understanding when she likes.'

'Please, Mrs Olney,' I said, 'I think there's not much point in talking any more.'

I opened the door. As she passed me she stiffened her arms closely in to her sides, as if to touch me would be a contamination. Field followed her, suit-case in hand. They looked, proceeding singly across the hall, like a couple of sacked employees, a pilfering lady's maid, a tippling valet. When they had gone I turned up the lights.

Helena came out of her bedroom, bright-eyed, full of energy, and she said what I had expected her to say.

'Well, good riddance to bad rubbish.'

I waited.

She put her arm through mine.

'Well? Now tell me I've made a fool of myself. Crow over me. Go on. Claud, tell me you knew it all along.'

'I knew it all along,' I said, smiling at her. I was very anxious.

She led me out of the hall. 'What was all that about the girl in the public-house? You ought to have told me. I do wish you wouldn't keep things from me.'

To satisfy the curiosity with which she was easing her hurt, I gave her a watered version of the incident.

'Well,' said Helena shrugging, 'it doesn't matter much.' Her eye flashed. 'That Dilys business won't last long! It's mad!'

'What happens if it doesn't? Are you going to have him back here?'

She stared at me. 'After tonight? You're mad, too. Your poor mind's unhinged.' She began to croon to herself. Never again, never again. 'You know, I think that boy will end in jail.' She followed him, in her mind's eye, through successive disasters to final catastrophe. 'Yes,' she mused, 'you ought to crow over me. You enjoy that kind of thing.'

She glanced at the clock with a gesture too broad to be spontaneous. 'Did you know it was as late as that? I'm going to have an early night. I won't clear, because Gladys comes in at eight tomorrow. Really, I'd have a girl to live in again, if I could get one, only I can't afford it.' She added sharply, 'Did you know she was giving him my money?'

'We don't know that she is.'

'Of course we know. I saw it in her face.'

'I don't think it was actually money. Presents, perhaps.'

'What a devil to take them!' she exclaimed, raging suddenly.

'No. But as weak as water. He'd think it was nice of her, though a bit tactless, and he wouldn't like to hurt her by refusing.'

'Don't you defend the little pig,' said Helena. She stretched her arms theatrically. '"Alone at last," as they say. I think I shall enjoy it. I believe I've been wanting him to go, *sotto voce*.' Helena liked to amuse me by pretended malapropisms, hoping I would take them seriously.

'Subconsciously.'

'Subconsciously, then, or whatever it is. I believe I've been pining for it. I believe I'm going to be happy.' She forced an expression of extreme, astonished happiness. 'It may be lonely at first. What about you moving back here?'

But this I would not do. I had settled comfortably in my rooms, and I did not want to be involved again, at close quarters, in Helena's affairs. Besides, Field had been right about the reading.

I left her (knowing myself cowardly) before the anodyne of wishful thinking had drained away from her. At the moment it was working strongly, giving her warmth, and strength to endure at least the early hours of the night. I was encouraged somewhat by the belief that pride would save her from the fall into utter misery.

She would lie awake detesting the girl to whom Field had made his confidences, would create in her mind a wax image into which she could stick pins. And hatred would be a saviour which, in time, might subdue the longing for Field that would take her with the first light.

PART FOUR

Chapter One

I WENT up to Scotland for a fortnight at the beginning of September to report on conditions at a camp there. I sent Helena a letter and a postcard, but she replied to neither. When I got back I went the same night to see her, and at the corner of Elm Park Gardens met Naomi Reed, who stopped and spoke to me, asking if I remembered her. I asked her, in return, what she was doing in my part of the world and she replied, 'I've just been seeing Lady Archer.'

It appeared that she and Helena, while I was away, had become great friends. 'She's so stimulating,' Naomi said enthusiastically, 'she seems to wake all my ideas up. I do think she really is the most wonderful person' – accentuating, in her sincerity, the words 'do', 'is', and 'wonderful'. It seemed that Helena had also made the acquaintance of Miss Norrish, who was Naomi's employer and (though for the moment I forgot it) Field's aunt. Naomi told me of a delightful dinner-party at which, I gathered, Helena had been a host and a guest in herself, and of several intimate evenings. 'She tells me the most exciting things, all about Ireland in Queen Victoria's day, and then about how she lived in Belgium, and then about Cecil Archer, who I do wish I'd seen. People say there was no one like her.'

'There never was,' I said, touched more to love for Cecil and pity for myself by this casual tribute than by a score of luxuriously mournful reminiscings with Charmian.

'I've got several of her records,' Naomi told me, and hummed a tune.

Out of curiosity, I asked her for news of Field.

She smiled tenderly, as if preparing to discuss an infant son and his prowess at the kindergarten. 'He seems happy,' she said. 'I don't really imagine that shop will ever become a multiple concern, but it does give him something to do.'

How, I inquired, was Mrs Olney?

'She is *good*, you know. She's managed to find him a very decent room and she rushes round him seeing he gets enough to eat and goes to bed early. She's one of those selfless people.'

I decided Naomi was stupid.

'Only I do hope he doesn't let her smother him.' She spoke with an elaborate, anxious detachment. 'I find her a little intense, as a matter of fact, though I know it's ungrateful of me to say so.'

Perhaps Naomi was not stupid after all. I saw in her face something watchful, acute.

'I think she's frightful, myself,' I said, 'though I dare say she has Field's welfare at heart.'

She said nothing for a moment but stood irresolute, as if uncertain whether to go or stay. 'I say,' she said at last, 'he was under you in the army, wasn't he?'

'He was in my battery for a bit.'

'I shouldn't think he was much of a soldier.' Naomi pushed back from her forehead the thick and polished golden hair. She was looking tired, and there were vertical lines between her eyes as if she had spent the day poring over figures in a bad light. 'Never mind, he'll do well when he finds something that really suits him. The army's not everything, is it?'

I replied that indeed it was not, and after a few moments' further talk she went away.

I found Helena looking determinedly lively and well. When I told her of my encounter she said smoothly, 'Yes, dear little Naomi. I'm getting quite fond of that girl. She has manners.'

When I wanted to know how it was that this friendship had so suddenly developed, she opened her eyes very wide and replied that it had grown out of nothing, simply nothing at all. She had telephoned Naomi one day to ask for assistance with a certain clue in a crossword puzzle. 'But why on earth Naomi in particular?' I asked her. 'Because,' said Helena very gently, as if in response to an idiot child, 'it was a clue about the Board of Trade. I thought she'd be the one to know.'

This was effrontery, even from Helena, designed to let me know that if I asked silly questions I must expect silly replies.

'I asked her to look in and see me one night, and she did, and once she brought her aunt.' Helena stared at me, minatory.

I said nothing.

After a moment or so she smiled, and relaxed. Sitting down by the small fire she took out her glasses and spread upon her knee a piece of canvas which she was embroidering horribly with green and orange wool. I had so strong a sense of *déjà vu* that I half-expected to hear the notes of a piano being tuned, to see Field crouched over the keyboard, his cocked ear seeming twice as large as a normal ear and having an inner illumination of its own.

'The older I get,' said Helena cosily, as one who means to talk for a very long time, 'the more I like the company of young people.' Her tone, the expression of her face, were old-ladyfied. 'Naomi Reed is a very nice girl. Her aunt is a pleasant woman, too, but rather talkative. When she went I had quite a headache.' Her phrasing, the very words she used, were so unnatural that I knew she was trying to conceal something, and that what she was trying to conceal was her reason for encouraging the visits of Naomi Reed.

On the wall to the left of the fireplace was a long mirror that had once hung in the hall at Pont Street. It had only recently been placed there; up till now, the space had been occupied by a very doubtful Constable bought by Daniel against everyone's advice. Because I had not expected to see a mirror in that part of the room, the shock of meeting my reflection and Helena's gave me a momentary sense of complete detachment. I saw her and myself with a stranger's eye, without the distortions of preconceived ideas accumulated by the past like layers of gauze. In the arm-chair was a tall old woman with hair white as lamb's wool above her stern and swarthy face. The lips were stretched and hard as if in defiance, the rather protuberant lids were lowered so that the lashes just touched cheeks which had begun to mottle faintly, like the leaves of old books. In a chair upon her right, facing the glass, was a thin, very fair man of medium height, wearing khaki. He had a long face, narrow shoulders, long bony hands that drooped over his knees. He looked weary and exasperated. Had I not caught this glimpse of him I should not have realized how tired I was, how long the journey had been; how resentful I had at last become of my guardianship of Helena.

And yet, she had never demanded that I should burden myself with her; she would have passed doggedly enough through her own distorted joys and sorrows, torments and delights, without me to stand as arbiter between herself and the event. The very fact that I understood her perhaps as thoroughly as one living being can understand another had made me vain, and my vanity had urged me to accept in her life the official position I no longer desired to hold. I had forced her confidence, given her a sense of security in my willingness to pass judgement. Now, looking at her, at myself, I knew I had no right to resentment. She was my responsibility, by my own choosing, until the day she died.

The shock of seeing the truth in the mirror was only momentary. In a second beauty had come upon her again, the beauty I remembered so strongly that I had never realized its passing. She turned her head. Her reflected gaze met mine.

'Well,' she said sharply, 'admiring yourself?'

'Not so much as I did,' I replied.

Helena bit off a tail of wool. 'That's one good thing.' She paused. 'Naomi's not the kind of girl you like?'

'Oh, I like her all right.'

'I didn't mean that. You wouldn't fancy her for yourself? She'd make a man a good wife,' Helena added sententiously. She grinned at herself, was grave again.

'She's Field's girl, isn't she?'

Helena threw up her hands affectedly, with the gesture that is accompanied in the comedies of the eighteenth century by La, or Fie, 'Boy and girl nonsense.'

'Is he still seeing her?'

'She saw him in that attic of his once, I believe.' Helena pushed her embroidery at me. 'Does that strike you as bright enough already, or shall I put in some blue?'

I advised her not to complete the work at all.

'You don't know anything about it,' she said, snatching back the canvas. For a little while she worked in silence. Then, without preamble, she demanded that I should return and live with her. 'It's so lonely here all day! I get queer ideas. Last week I was scared stiff because I thought I heard someone creeping about, and it was only the water-tank. And yesterday I suddenly had the fancy that if I went into the bedroom I'd find myself sitting on the bed. It was all I could do not to go and see.'

'Why didn't you go?'

'I'd have looked such a fool.'

'Who to?'

She grew thoughtful. 'Oh, I don't know. Ay, there's the rub, as Dicky used to say. I did look later on.'

'And were you sitting on the bed?'

'No. But I couldn't get away from the idea that I *had* been, just before I opened the door.'

'I'm not coming back,' I told her. 'I've just settled myself nicely and got all my stuff in order. I'm only just around the corner, anyway. I drop in and out of here all the time, don't I?'

'I suppose so, but it's not the same.' Her features took on a weakness unfamiliar to them. Lips and eyelids drooped. With anyone else but me, she would have given way to tears. Helena was beginning to crave for all things to be easy.

Because I was kept late at Whitehall I did not see her again for some days. Then Charmian and Sholto, both of them demobilized now, called at my rooms.

'Mother's ill,' said Charmian. She spoke not with an anxious but with a puzzled air. 'Do go round and see her.'

I asked her what the matter was.

She and Sholto exchanged a glance, half-humorous, half-exasperated. 'She phoned me up. We both went to the flat and found her in bed. Ella's back for the time being, looking after her.'

'What does she say is wrong? Has she seen the doctor?' I disbelieved at once in Helena's illness. Had it been genuine she would have telephoned me before Charmian; as things were, it looked as if she wanted an idea put into my mind before I saw her.

'She won't see the doctor,' Sholto replied, peering at himself in my glass to see if he could discover a piece of grit in his eye. 'Damn it, it hurts like sin. Charmian, do come over to the window and see what you can see.' He ducked down, so that she could dig gently with her handkerchief at the rims of his eyes.

'That better?'

'No,' he said, 'it's still in there, whatever it is. Do look *properly*.'

'I am looking properly.'

'You must be blind. It feels like a rock.'

'Well, there aren't any rocks,' Charmian snapped at him.

'Oh, all right, leave it alone.' Pushing her aside he returned to the mirror and continued to dab at himself, grimace, pull down his lower lid. Remembering me, he said, 'She refuses point-blank to see a doctor. Says she only wants rest and a low diet. She looks perfectly well.'

'I wouldn't have said perfectly,' Charmian retorted in a voice exceedingly quiet and restrained. She gave him an angry look.

'Blooming with health,' said Sholto, jerking up his chin.

I asked of what Helena actually complained.

'Pains round her heart,' Charmian replied, 'palpitation, and giddiness. She says she's all right if she just keeps still.' Her glance flashed in Sholto's direction, was swiftly withdrawn. 'You will go round?'

'Tomorrow afternoon, if I can get away.'

Sholto grew tired of his eye and left it to water. With the idea of paying him for his bad temper towards Charmian I asked him what he proposed to do, now that he was out of the army.

'Give me a chance,' he answered rather hotly. 'I've only been back in civvy street a fortnight. I haven't had time to look around.'

'We've all sorts of plans,' Charmian told me, smiling at him.

'Plans and plans and plans,' said Sholto, 'enough to rebuild Greater London and two-thirds of Manchester.' He looked at her. 'Do you know you've got ink on your arm?'

This began a long, quiet bicker, obliquely, even politely conducted, but none the less unpleasant to hear. It was the bickering of two people who normally despise any public display of discord as degrading and bad-mannered, but who are driven by nervous tension to break their own rules. Once or twice each of them made an attempt to check it. Charmian made some small joke, ventured some warning intimacy; Sholto touched her cheek, or put his arm round the back of her chair; but always one or the other was driven, as by a private demon, to some remark, some implication that made the atmosphere electric again. Once I glanced at Charmian to see her staring at Sholto with a look of utter desperation, and I was furious that he should ever have dared to give her cause for such an emotion. She seemed, in comparison with him, so young, so unformed, so vulnerable. Even her body had the air of an overgrown child's, the arms scarcely rounded out, the collar bones so prominent, the breast so delicate and shallow. Her courage was like Helena's and her tongue, upon occasion, could be as rough; but she had the tender weakness that was my father's, his incapacity to hurt for one moment even to prevent a hurt that might be permanent. Charmian, if she were to be happy, must be treated by a man with comradeship but considered in secrecy as a child, and in this manner cherished.

The hostilities between her and Sholto ceased as suddenly as they had begun, halted by a silent mutual agreement.

'We must go,' Charmian said, 'it's late, and Claud's looking tired. You will see Mother tomorrow, won't you?'

I said I would.

'Don't you find life in general very wearing these days?' Sholto asked me. It was a covert apology for his behaviour during the evening. 'Everything seems so damned exhausting and stagnant. I don't think we get the right food.'

I suggested that he was looking none too well.

'I'm not,' he said eagerly, 'I'm sure I'm not. Have to take a course of Vitamin B, I think.' He took Charmian by her small and lemon-shaped elbow. 'Come on, darling. See you soon, Claud. Come round whenever you like.'

As they went out together he knocked down a pile of books from the edge of a shelf and snapped at his wife when she tried to help him gather them up.

When they had gone I decided that, if it killed me, I would find Charmian grounds for divorce.

On the following afternoon, as I had promised, I went to see Helena. The door was opened by Ella, who had been her maid at Pont Street. She spoke as if there were death in the house, softly, and with the familiarity bred less by contempt than by anxiety. 'I'm so glad you've come! I can't do anything with her and she won't try to help herself.'

'What's the matter with her actually?'

'If only one knew!' Ella exclaimed, with an air of irritation that she speedily turned to one of frustrated devotion. 'She's just low. She's been low for days.'

I knocked at Helena's door. A strong, fierce voice told me to enter. Turning the handle, I looked in upon a scene set for a third act. Propped up high against the headboard of a very tidy bed was Helena, wearing a brand-new dressing-gown of purple silk. Her hair, unbound, was spread over the pillow like snow trails on a white wall. On the cabinet at her right was a vase of great white rounded chrysanthemums, and at her left hand, lying upon the coverlet, was a small, strange kitten. On the bed-table, swung out across her knees, were three medicine bottles, a bottle of Australian wine, two pill-boxes, a spectacle-case, and a large handkerchief handsomely bordered with Brussels lace.

Helena, save for an unusual puffiness beneath her eyes, looked healthy enough. When she saw me she said nothing; she simply glared reproach that I had not visited her before. I sat down on the edge of the bed, admired her dressing-gown, and asked her where she had got the coupons.

'Ella didn't want hers,' she replied automatically. She pointed to the kitten, which seized upon the pointing finger and began to fight it in an ecstasy of savage purrs. 'Martha died,' said Helena, and burst into tears.

Martha was the old cat. We had all been fond of her, but I did not think her death would in itself have been sufficient to drive Helena to a sick-bed.

'She got run over.'

'Poor old Martha,' I said.

'I made Ella go out and buy me this one from the Pet Shop. I only had him yesterday.'

'What's his name?'

'Lance,' said Helena. 'Give me my handkerchief.' She sopped up her wet cheeks.

'Lance, Lance, Lance,' I called to the kitten, wheedled it to me, and gave it a towsling all over Helena's feet.

'When you've finished amusing yourself with the cat,' she said, 'perhaps you'll inquire about me.'

I put the kitten down to scamper over the carpet and terrify itself into a succession of fat tails. 'Charmian told me about you yesterday. You know I'd have been before, if I'd had the least idea anything was wrong. I've been driving busy. What is the matter, anyway?'

Helena twisted over on to her side and slid down lower in the bed. She blinked her eyes as if repressing new tears and for a moment would not reply to me. Then she said, 'I don't know. General depression. Weakness. My heart's been funny.'

'Have you seen Stillyer?'

'That old fool. No. He'd hurry me into my grave – as he hurried Daniel,' she added, with preposterous unfairness.

'I'll send my man along, then, He's young and bright. You'd like him.'

'If you do I'll have Ella turn him away. I don't want a doctor. I only want to be left in peace and have someone show a little sympathy.' Her easy tears flowed again, dripping off her waxy cheek on to the pillow.

'I'm sympathetic,' I said. 'Come on, tell me. Have you got a pain, or what?'

She shook her head.

'What can we all do to help? Everyone wants to help. Even Boiled Owl.'

'He came here last night,' Helena murmured, forgetting grief, 'and sat right on my feet and tried to lecture me. Charmian looked as if she could have murdered him. Don't you think she's looking thin?'

'Never mind Charmian. What about you? How long are you going to stay here?'

'For ever, probably,' Helena replied firmly. 'I couldn't face the thought of getting up.'

'Well, I shall send McMorrough along, and God help you if you refuse to see him.'

She sat up. 'No, don't. Please, Claud, don't!'

Her anxiety was so real that for a moment I had a horrible fear that she might indeed be ill, and concealing the cause of that illness from me. 'I must, if you go on like this. You can't just lie around and cry.'

I watched her carefully, saw the thoughts flashing behind her fine black eyes like birds through a clouded mirror.

'I'd be all right,' she said at last, 'if I weren't so lonely.'

'Why need you be lonely? You know plenty of people. Hasn't Naomi been in?'

'Oh, people,' said Helena contemptuously. She was thinking of one person.

'Even a doctor would be company.'

'I tell you I won't have a doctor!'

'Charmian said you had palpitation and pains round your heart.'

'Indigestion,' Helena retorted, straightening her back and looking hardy. She was taking a new line with me. Lance ran up my trouser leg and hung there like a bat to a barn door. I picked him off, played with him, and gave him to Helena, who clutched him, despite his struggles, to her breast. 'Puss loves me,' she murmured, 'Puss loves his mother. Don't you, Madman? Aren't you Mother's comfort?' She tossed him to the end of the bed and asked me for a cigarette.

'Come on,' I said, 'tell me.' I took her hand and held it. Helena started to laugh, her eyes brilliant through the glass of recent tears. 'That's better,' I told her.

'Doan'ee be saaft,' she said in some hybrid stage accent, and brought her fist down on my knee. 'I'm all right. I suppose it's the strain of the war – I told you I was frightened all through the blitz, though I don't suppose you believed me – war-strain, and Dan's death. I'm not so young as I was. You leave me alone and I'll get well again.'

After that she would discuss no affairs but my own and Charmian's until I was on the point of leaving. She began cautiously, 'It's funny how you worry when you're lying in bed. All sorts of silly little things.'

I sensed that this was significant. 'What's worrying you, then?'

'Oh, just some stupid thing about Johnny Field. I gave him a little gold seal of Dan's that he took a fancy to, and I can't help wondering if he's still got it.'

'Why should you care whether he's got it or not?'

'Only because I've found another, and I think they're a pair.'

'Well?' I prompted her.

'He might as well have the two. One's not much use without the other.'

'You don't owe him anything?'

'No, the little brute,' said Helena, with great indignation. 'All the same – I hate things being *odd*. They get on my mind.'

I guessed the end to which this conversation was leading.

'Send it him, then.'

'But how can I, when I don't know whether they really match?' She took the plunge. 'Claud. Do ring up and tell him to drop in and see me. He can bring the seal with him. You can tell him I'm ill.'

'I shan't do anything of the kind,' I told her.

She looked at me. 'I think you might. It isn't much to ask.'

'You were well shot of him. I'm not going to help you get him back.'

She said angrily, 'There's no question of "getting him back". I simply want to ask him a question and have a chat with him. One has to be civilized! Would you expect me to cut him in the street?'

'You needn't meet him in the street.'

'I might.'

'Well, then, you can give him a pleasant bow.'

She lay down again and seemed to sleep. A cream-coloured tear forced its way through her lids and rolled compactly as a pearl down the side of her nose. 'You're getting so hard these days, Claud. There are times when I feel I don't know you. When I feel you're a stranger.'

I said nothing.

She looked at me very quickly to see how I was taking this new appeal, then closed her eyes again. 'It's so little to ask, when you know how much it would mean to me. He's such a *boy*. I couldn't bear to feel he was going through life with a grudge against me.'

'Why should he have anything of the sort?'

'I was sharp with him. I should have been able to do things better, to see things from his point of view. We understood each other, Johnny and I. I know Dilys is driving him mad; I feel it in my bones.'

'If I find Field up here again,' I said, 'I'll put him out myself.'

'This,' said Helena, with real grandeur, 'is *my* home.'

I got up, dislodging the kitten from a sleeping sprawl half on the bed and half on my thigh. 'If you're not feeling any better by tomorrow I shall send McMorrough. I'll look in to see how you are.'

Helena let me go without a word and then, when I was in the hall, summoned me back.

'If you won't phone Johnny I'll make Ella do it.'

228

I had nothing to say to this, and left her.

The next day and the next, Helena was still defiantly in bed, and she convinced me that it was no use whatsoever me sending my doctor along. 'You can stay away,' she told me, 'if you don't want to help me. In fact, I'd rather you didn't come just at present. It can't be very amusing for you listening to the ramblings of a sick old woman.'

There are few people more infuriating than those who dramatize themselves in a ridiculous role, know perfectly well that you will be unable to accept it seriously, and yet take umbrage because you refuse to play the absurd scene with them; so I took Helena at her word, and said I would not visit her again until she or Ella got in touch with me. She did not get in touch, however, so after four days had gone by I was prompted by curiosity to ask Charmian for news.

'Oh yes,' she said, when I telephoned, 'I've seen her. And him. ... Yes, together. It's quite a story. Evan's out with Norman tonight, so if you like to take me to dinner I'll tell you all about it.'

I named a restaurant in Greek Street, and we met there within the hour.

It seemed that Charmian, calling unexpectedly upon her mother the previous evening, had found a picnic in progress in Helena's bedroom. Helena was reigning in bed, serving cold fowl, tongue, and salad from a tray to Field upon her right hand, and Naomi upon her left. 'They might have been posing for a great big historical painting,' Charmian remarked, reminiscently smiling. I suggested Saint Francis feeding the birds, but she said it had not been in the least like that. 'They were all looking meek and happy and rather embarrassed. I gathered neither Field nor Naomi had had the least idea they were going to meet each other there.'

'How was Helena to you?' I asked her.

Charmian ate a piece of bread very slowly before replying, and wrinkled her brows as if it were an effort to be exact. 'She bluffed it out, really. She said wasn't it nice to see Johnny again, and didn't I think he looked well? She'd telephoned him over some little business matter, and directly he'd heard she was ill he had insisted upon coming to see her. She looked so damned handsome,' Charmian added, 'and so full of joy.'

She repeated the words quietly, emphatically, as if she understood them. 'Full of joy.'

'And Naomi?'

'Looking puzzled. I'd never met her before, you know. I thought she was very pretty in a breezy way and very keen on no-nonsense. Rather the same type as your Meg.'

This was true, though I had not realized it. 'Do you think she'd be better for Field than Meg was for me?' The memory of my own marriage was never a pleasant one; it had been so exhausting, so gradual a failure.

'Oh, yes,' Charmian replied surely, 'she could draw Field along behind her on a hurdle. He'd be quite contented on it, too, if they put a nice cushion under him first. Your trouble was that you *would* struggle.'

'Why, do you think I shouldn't have?'

She gave me her little maternal look, anxious and touching. 'No. I think you should have struggled earlier.'

'Perhaps.' I reverted to the first subject of our conversation. 'And how was Field?'

She paused. 'I should like to be fair, because I never liked him as well as you did, really. Last night he seemed to me just a little ... oh, I don't know. Nasty.'

'How?'

She explained that despite his politeness, his eagerness to please, his displayed concern, she fancied that he was trying in some way to punish Helena. He had talked much of the shop and of Mrs Olney, how quick she was to take advantage of a new idea, how industrious, how generous of heart. 'Naomi didn't like it much either,' said Charmian. 'She's in love with him, quite obviously, and I think he is with her, but he was too keen on getting his own back on Mother to notice how he was irritating his young woman. You know, I think Mother really did get him on the raw that night.'

I was indignant at this.

'Oh yes, oh yes! I know how much to blame he was. But I don't believe he ever saw himself as guilty. I should think he'd always taken comfort wherever it was offered, and couldn't see any wrong in doing it.'

'This isn't the first time you've stood up for him. Why? He doesn't fascinate you, surely?'

She disclaimed this suggestion with a grimace. 'Good God, no. But I often think I understand how he feels better than you do. You see, I, in my way' – she spoke with quaint, mock-tragical deliberation – 'am a weak character. And so I know how it feels to be on the weak side.'

On impulse I said, 'Don't be, when it's a matter of your whole life. You were rough enough on me for struggling too late.'

She looked at me blankly – 'I wasn't being specific about anything' – and took out her powder-compact. 'Do you like my hair?' She had made a central parting from her brow to the nape of her neck, and had drawn up the hair in a plaited tiara over the crown of her head. She had the royal and help-less look of a princess awakened at three in the morning to be told she is now a reigning monarch. 'It's all right from the front. Not the back.'

'What's wrong with the back!' She strained for an angle of reflection between the wall-mirror and the glass in her hand.

I told her it was like a horse's hindquarters.

'Damn you,' she said, 'now you've made me miserable.' She began to laugh, because she was amused, outraged, un-happy, and I found it hard to make her stop.

'It isn't such a funny joke as all that,' I insisted. 'Be quiet, will you? People are staring.'

'It's not your joke,' she gasped, 'it's not that at all. I was thinking of Mother being ill in the grand manner. The flowers, the cat, Ella back again. She really was upset, too, she was really horribly miserable. And it was all to get Field back. For nothing else! All to get Field back, every bit of it. Oh, I don't know what we're going to do, do you?'

I thought of Helena and her desperate clowning, Mrs Olney with her lovely hungry face and grotesque fat legs, the bright, no-nonsense Naomi who, in any given situation, would know exactly what to do.

'We can't interfere,' I said, 'it's gone past all that. We can do nothing now but let things take their course.'

Chapter Two

'I CAME to you,' said Field, 'because it was you who felt worst about me, and I hoped I could make you feel a bit better. Not that there's any reason why you should feel better but anyway ... Well, as I said, one does hope.'

It was a bright Saturday morning, the autumn air fresh-scented as spring. My landlady had left the front door open to air the house, and through it had come Field, brushed and spruced, flushed with the excitement of moral courage. He found my room easily enough, knocked once, walked in as if he were already late for an appointment, and made his speech. On my table he put a bank envelope with five one-pound notes in it.

'It's some of the back keep I owe Helena. Make her take it, please, and tell her the rest will follow as soon as humanly possible.'

He leaned back against the wall, his gaze flashing about the room. I told him to sit down, but he shook his head.

'Why don't you give it her yourself?' I asked.

'Because she'd try to refuse it. I don't want to go through all that. Besides, she mightn't remember to tell you I'd paid it, and I want you to know.'

'All right.' I put the money in my pocket.

'I've got a job,' said Field. He was bursting to talk. Raking in his pockets he brought out a handful of loose cigarettes. 'Mind if I smoke? Will you –?'

'I won't take yours.' I lit one of my own cigarettes and pushed a chair across to him. He sat on it.

'I've got a job,' he repeated, 'my aunt found it for me. She said she would, and she never does let people down.'

'What is it?'

'I'm an M.P.'s secretary,' Field answered proudly, 'five quid a week and more later, maybe, with luck, if I'm any good. He's got plenty of money.'

'Who is he?'

He mentioned the name of a young Conservative member, one of the 'Tory Progressives', holding a safe seat in the South of England. 'He's not a bad fellow,' Field added, 'though I hate his politics like hell. Not that he knows it. He's better than some of them, I suppose. And he's on the up-and-up, and if there's anywhere up for him to go, I go up with him. It's pretty terrific, really.'

He seemed to have lost his first embarrassment, talking to me now as if we were on terms of most charming amiability. This capacity to ignore the uncomfortable was a perfectly genuine thing with Field; with him, the desire that the uncomfortable should not exist was equivalent to obliterating it. In some respects he was acutely sensitive. While an unpleasant scene was actually taking place he suffered atrociously, but once it was over he would wipe it from his memory – or if not that, could so gloss it over that it no longer appeared formidable.

'It's pretty hard work,' he went on, 'but it's interesting. Dilys isn't pleased, naturally, because I won't be able to give much time to the shop, except at week-ends. Still, as I tell her, the thing's under way now and I can still manage the business side. She's got a rotten head for figures.' He laughed. The fact that the five pounds were in my pocket and out of sight seemed to have destroyed for him all recollection of the original reason for his visit.

He reached for an ashtray. 'I mustn't drop ash in your nice room. Helena says I can make any floor look like the bottom of a parrot's cage, but I think she exaggerates. She insists that ash does not kill moths.' He leaned across my table. 'What are you reading?' He looked at the book, mentioned the name of a French novelist. 'I like him, always have. I wish he hadn't been a collaborator, or a near one, or whatever it was, though of course it was only logical. Still, I don't know. I always felt he had his tongue in his cheek about his terrific hero and those girls. Now I suppose we must assume he hadn't.' He flicked through the pages, stopping here and there to read, top lip clipped over the lower, eyes shining with the concentration of the accomplished book-taster.

'What had the girls to do with collaborating?' I asked, interested despite myself.

'Oh, *amour, amour*, all lovely, all dirty, no morals, take 'em or leave 'em – it all adds up,' he said rapidly, his attention less upon my query than on the book itself. 'So long as you can enjoy that sort of thing you won't notice whether Nazis are around or not. They wouldn't disturb you, anyway. Love makes people harmless.' He muttered through a paragraph, laughed, repeated it more slowly. Then, regretful, he closed the book, sat up straight and looked at me. 'You don't want me sticking around.'

'I'll give your packet to Helena.'

'She looks better, don't you think?' Field inquired timidly. Helena was up again, energetic and blithe.

I agreed, but made it clear that I did not wish to talk of her. Instead, I asked him about Naomi Reed.

'I don't see her as much as I'd like to,' he said confidentially. 'She's living in a sort of boarding-house where there's no real public room for having a talk in, and Dilys doesn't like her coming up to my attic. She says Milsey – that's my landlord – is very sticky about things like that. Silly, isn't it? Naomi came once, but Dilys got in a tear and told me Milsey would never let me keep the room if it happened again. Not that he ever said anything to me himself.' He gave me a long, hard look. 'Of course, it may be just a complex of Dilys's.' He had no doubt, and meant me to have none, that this was the case. 'In any event, it makes things damned awkward. Helena's let me see Naomi at her place once or twice.'

He got up, walked to the window and flicked the ash from his cigarette into the street.

'Right on a bright pink hat,' he said reflectively. He turned and looked at me. His eyes were mournful, entreating friendliness. Life was hard for everybody. Was there any need to make it worse by harking back to old muddles and quarrels? 'I do love Helena, you know. I told you that before, and you didn't believe it. I admire her enormously. She doesn't seem angry with me any more, but I'm still fed up with myself.'

I told him I was not going to discuss Helena and wanted to hear no more of the whole business. If I had my way, I said, he'd stay away from her for good; but even as I said it I remembered how much her happiness lay in him.

'Yes,' he said patiently, when I was silent again, 'I know all that, but you see, I have to explain things to you. I'm compelled to. It's the only way I can feel better.'

I didn't care, I replied, what he felt, not did I see why I should put up with endless explanations simply because it eased him to make them.

'All right,' said Field, 'all right.' He left me without another word.

When I saw Helena that night, I gave her the money he had repaid. She opened the packet as if it were a jewel-box, her fingers delicate, her face colouring with pleasure. 'There!' she cried, 'I told you! I told you he was all right.' She smoothed out the notes, folded them neatly. 'Fancy wasting his salary on me,' she murmured, 'when he knows I don't really need it. It was silly of him, wasn't it?' She looked at me dreamily.

'It was a debt. The least he could do was to pay it.'

'Lots of people wouldn't have,' said Helena, as if this were a credit to Field. She put the money in her bag, folded the bank envelope in four and placed this, like a holy relic, in the enamel snuff-box that stood on the desk. She was still in her trance. 'Never mind, I can always help him if he needs it later on.'

She began to chatter about Field's new job, showed me a press-cutting about his M.P., asked me whether I wouldn't like to dine at the flat on the following night, when he and Naomi were expected, and when I refused told me with assurance that I couldn't keep up that sort of attitude for ever. 'We're civilized people,' she said, 'we're beyond the Law of the Jungle. ... Don't you laugh, Claud, don't you dare laugh. I'm serious.'

'So am I. I'm not meeting Field here. He shouldn't be here at all.'

'We are told,' she said with self-conscious simplicity, 'to forgive people seventy times seven.' She struggled for sincerity. Her lashes fell; she clasped her hands, awaiting persecution. Her glasses slid to the end of her nose and dropped off. With a swift movement she caught them. 'Allezoop!' She began to laugh. 'No, seriously, it's only right to be kind to him. He hasn't anyone but that aunt of his, and she's as sour as a crab-apple. Be generous, won't you?'

I replied that I had been. I had spoken with Field for fifteen minutes and had not kicked him downstairs.

'Very well,' she said, 'if you feel like that, stay away. I can do without you.'

I asked her how she was. 'How am I?' She had forgotten her illness. Memory returning slackened her body, pinched her nose. 'Oh, stronger, I think. On the whole.'

I could see she was feeling splendid, joy reborn running through her like a current of electricity, and that to play the convalescent was the greatest possible strain upon her powers. She was, I knew, full of hope. She had lured Field back for an hour, an afternoon, an evening. She was full of hope that before long he would return to her for ever.

That night I went to see Jane Crossman and her husband, who had just moved into a flat near Victoria Station, and on my way home met Finucane. He was returning late from work. 'First really late night for six months,' he told me. 'Come and have a drink at my place, will you?' He was living in furnished rooms in Ebury Street. His home was in Ireland.

He gave me some gin and showed me his collection of art books. 'Expensive hobby, these days. Never mind, it's a harmless one. Better than drink and women, not that I don't like *them,* but they both seem under proof these days. Ha ha!'

He was the only person I have ever known who really said 'Ha ha!' convulsively, in two distinct syllables.

Turning the pages of a book of Leonardo drawings he looked lovingly at the head of a girl, sly-eyed, secretly smiling, the hair clustering like grape-hyacinth about her ears. 'You don't find them like that these days. Where have they all gone to? Aren't they bred any more?'

There flashed into my mind the memory of Mrs Sholto remarking that an eighteenth-century miniature bore a strong resemblance to Field; the observation had had no point save to introduce a certain subject.

'She's a bit like Sholto,' I said.

His mind was too distracted by the girl and by the gin to remember what he should and should not say to me. 'Like old Bunny? I can't see it. The nose, perhaps.'

'How is he, these days?'

'He's back in civvy street. I never come across him.'

'I expect he's a good miss,' I said.

Finucane laughed. 'Oh, he was harmless. Slow, you know.

236

He always had a softish time, because no one who wanted work done quickly ever gave it him. It doesn't pay to be efficient. ... I like that blonde, don't you? I knew a woman a bit like her. Her name was Katie.'

'Wasn't Katie the name of Sholto's girl? The one he used to see at Richmond?' This was the wildest shot and I had no hope of it.

Finucane turned a page and began to pore over some mechanical drawings. 'Look at the old devil! He made it look so bloody easy. You can imagine old Leonardo just dashing it down before he went out to lunch. ... Richmond? It wasn't Richmond, surely. Chiswick.'

'That's right. Katie someone, at Chiswick.'

'Not Katie. Ann.'

'Oh yes,' I said, 'Ann.'

He glanced at me sharply. 'No news to you then. I'd forgotten you and he were related.'

'No news. ... Related? Oh, that. I hardly ever see him, anyway.' Before Finucane could begin to worry I said dogmatically that there was no modern English painting worth a penn'orth of dog's meat, and we lost Sholto in the ensuing argument. It was so lively an argument that he walked the best part of the way home with me, insisting that my judgement was bigoted and that the next great period of painting would be an English one.

'Chauvinism,' I said.

'And why should I be chauvinistic about the English, tell me that?' he retorted, blood boiling. We liked each other, and were friends.

For days I wondered how I should use my new knowledge. Sholto had a girl at Chiswick whose name was Ann. Could I find out more, without recourse to the dingy business of inquiry agents, or was the information I had sufficient to work with? If I put it into Charmian's possession she could probably do the rest herself, and with a better heart than I should have. Yet I did not attempt to see her, and could take no decision as to what it would be best for me to do.

At the end of a fortnight I made up my mind to see Charmian at once. I was just about to telephone and ask her to meet me when Connie, my landlady, came in to say that a Mrs

Olney was downstairs. Connie was a brawny, black-haired woman of forty-five or so, who still wore the gipsy styles made fashionable round about 1912 by Augustus John. For twenty years she had kept rooming-houses in one part or the other of Chelsea.

'Did you ever see *Mary Rose*?' I asked her. 'I'm the Island that Likes to be Visited. Anyway, I'm the one that gets visited. I never seem to get any peace.'

She smiled doubtfully. 'I'm afraid your visitor's rather upset. I do hope you're going to be nice to her.'

My spirits, which had drooped at the very news of Mrs Olney's coming, sank even lower. 'I'll try to be.'

'Be of good heart,' said Connie, 'because *she* isn't.' She turned to go.

'Wait a moment. I'll pay the rent while you're here.'

'Now listen, any time'll do. Don't keep her waiting, poor soul.'

'Do her good.' I counted out the money.

'Callous,' said Connie. She was quite incurious, would never wish to know who my visitor was, what I was to her, and what the visit could be about. Her interest was stimulated instantly by any new personality, but once a familiarity of even five minutes had been established with it, that interest passed to something or to somebody else. She scribbled a receipt, urged me again to be sympathetic, and went out.

Mrs Olney came to stand like Clytemnestra in the doorway, one hand upon the doorpost, the other hanging limp at her side as if it had just done murder and was ready to be lopped by the hangman. She looked at me without speaking, her face narrowed by the shadow of a great black hat. Her eyes were red, squeezed small and dull with crying. The powder was thick upon her stained cheeks and she had rouged in her mouth with a magenta lipstick. Because she was horribly unhappy she needed the comfort of admiration; even in her distress she was waiting for some sign of it.

I made a formal remark of greeting and of surprise at seeing her, asked her to come in.

She burst into violent tears. Blindly she groped her way to a chair, sat down, and put her head in her hands. I shut the door. At the sound of its closing she looked sharply round, tried to speak, but could not. I watched her as she tired herself with grief. She cried without shame, without consciousness of me, even jerked herself nearer to the table so that she might lean her arms upon it and weep at ease. All I could see of her was the top of her head, the round bow of her forehead from which the hat had been pushed back. She was as lost in her arms as a drowned woman floating face downwards in the sea, and I dared not touch her. At first she cried noisily, swallowing the mucus of tears, rasping for breath. After a while there was no sound in the room but the ticking of Connie's tin clock, which she had lent me when I broke the mainspring of my own.

I found myself forgetting Mrs Olney, was startled when at last she spoke.

'What you must think of me. In front of you, of all people.'

I lit a cigarette for her. She was trembling too much to light it herself.

'I made up my mind I'd be calm,' she said feverishly, 'all the way along I was saying to myself, "Now you mustn't get upset, men always hate it when you get upset," but the moment I saw you I couldn't control myself. You must have thought I was mad. "This terrible woman," you must be thinking, "I wish she'd go away."'

I tried to comfort her, told her to take her time, not to talk till she felt like it.

'I can't just sit here,' she said. She rose suddenly and clumsily, knocking herself against the table. She rubbed her knee, gazing at me with the lost, reproachful air of a child who cannot tell what to blame for its hurt. Then, gathering up her bag, she made for the door. 'I oughtn't to have come here, I know that. You must be loathing me. You must be praying I'll go.'

'I'm curious now,' I answered, 'I want to hear the rest of it.'

She stood irresolute for a moment. Then she sat down again, folding her hands in her lap. 'I came to you because there was nobody else. After all, you're Johnny's best friend.'

I let this go.

'He's gone back to Helena,' she burst out, 'he went this morning. They've been hatching it between them.'

The news that Helena had got her own way so soon came as a surprise to me. I tried to speak, but she checked me with a violent shake of her head.

'We had a quarrel. We need not have had it – he made it. He must have been lying awake all night thinking how he was going to make it – I know him well enough. It was all arranged. I said some little thing and he jumped down my throat, and it began from there. He was so cruel – you can't imagine how cruel he can be, men never know other men – I expect you thought he was always gentle and kind.' She gave a great gasp, raised her head and shut her eyes fast. 'Give me just a moment. I'll control myself.'

I gave her a moment. She sat like a medium in a trance, only her lips moving. Then, very slightly, her lashes lifted and a gleam showed through. She was conscious of me, praying that her grief should drive me, in some unimaginable manner, to help her. Her head returned to its normal position. Her eyes, wide open, were magnified by tears. 'I was in love with him. I suppose you think that's disgusting. I suppose you'll laugh at me, tell everyone what a fool I am.'

'No, I won't. But I'm sorry about it.'

'You're young,' said Mrs Olney remotely, 'you think love's something for the young only. You think women are finished at forty. Let me tell you, that's the tragedy – love hasn't any age limit.' The phrase seemed to give her a flicker of mournful happiness. She amended it. 'Love has no age limit. Love can live on in a . . . middle-aged body.'

She stiffened, and glared at me. 'Censure me if you like! I loved Johnny. I do love him. I always will.' Rising, she began to prowl about the room, steps slow, gaze searching the floor as if she had dropped some minute article of value. 'You don't know how gentle he could be when he liked, how considerate. He used to pretend I looked after him, but actually he looked after me. He used to notice if I looked tired, or if I had a head-ache. "Don't you think you ought to rest?" he'd say, or, "Let me do that, you've done enough today." He was so old for his age really, and I'm young for mine. At least' – she added defensively, with a quick, shamed glance – 'I feel young. He never knew I loved him, don't you think that. I wouldn't have had him know for anything. He used to think of me just as an elder friend, or an elder sister, even. If he had known he'd have been horrified. Just as you're horrified.' She whipped round on me, the hat flapping with her. 'Aren't you horrified?'

'No,' I replied, 'but I wish you'd tell me what you want me to do about it.'

She said very quietly, 'You're his friend. You could persuade him.'

'To do what?'

'To come back.'

'What about his job?'

She flamed into temper. 'That damned job! It's the cause of all the trouble. Directly he got a salary he felt he was independent of me. It's too much for him, anyway, in his state of health. If you're his friend you ought to be able to see that. You don't want him killing himself.'

'So you think Field should give his job up?'

'Oh no, no,' she cried impatiently, 'I suppose not. I suppose that's too much to ask. But he could come back to his room, couldn't he, and then he could still interest himself in the shop? Helena's bad for him. She wraps him in cotton wool. She doesn't let him lead his own life.'

This was so contradictory that I could not keep from checking her.

'Do you?'

'Do I?' she said blankly, anger draining out of her and leaving her pallid.

'Do you let him lead his own life? You seemed to resent his salary making him independent of you.'

'Don't cross-examine me! All I meant was that I wanted to look after him. Not Helena's kind of looking-after – just care, and watchfulness, and seeing after his health.'

I said nothing.

She watched my lips. 'Well?'

'There's nothing I can do,' I said.

With startling quickness she dodged behind a chair and leaned over the back of it, confronting me. 'Oh, isn't there?' She had forgotten to be beautiful in grief, to appeal, to enlist me upon her side. Disappointment raged in her like a poison, distorting and destroying. 'Oh, isn't there? You can tell that stepmother of yours what a filthy old vampire she is, what a

241

common, sneaking old beast she is, tell her she's enough to make anyone split their sides laughing with her Lady Archer airs one minute and fishfag tomfoolery the next! That's what you can tell her, and you can tell her as well that I know what she's after, that a child could see through her —'

I told her to be quiet.

She rocked to and fro over the chair-back as if in an agony of pain. Her eyes were full of terror, but she could not stop the words spurting from her mouth. I watched her in disgust and in pity, knowing she would not reveal herself in this horrible manner except through the propulsion of great misery. She would detest me from now on, be unable to hear a name that even resembled mine or look at a person in the least degree like me without a spasm of humiliation and self-contempt. At eight years old I had been caught by a friend of my father's in some act of petty childish dirtiness. He had looked at me but had made no comment either then or later; yet from that time onwards I could never bear to be in the same room with him. I would go to great lengths to avoid him now. It is impossible for me to believe that he could look at me without remembering, twenty-eight years later, that one thing.

So, because I realized that I should become an object of horror in Mrs Olney's memory, I told her she must go.

She fell silent. Straightening, she looked at her handbag that lay on the table. I gave it to her. 'Thank you.' Hanging above the fireplace was a small mirror. She crossed the room to it, peered at herself intently, and adjusted her hat with a hand that vibrated like a violinist's on the strings. She turned and again thanked me.

Knowing I should never see her again, I wished I could find something to say that would ease the future for her. She was stripped and lost, all enterprise in dust with all pretences. I should forget, quickly enough, the ugly spirit of her attack upon Helena and remember only the sound and shape of the words. They had been words spoken in madness, chosen at random from a hotchpotch of associations gathered throughout a lifetime and they would be regretted bitterly. So far as I was concerned Helena would never hear them, and no words spoken by an enemy could affect my own idea of her.

'I'm sorry it all happened,' I said.

'*You're* sorry,' she shot at me, squaring her mouth, and was gone.

On my next slack afternoon I called to see Helena, knowing Field would be at work. The flat was full of him again, his mark on everything. A book of exercises was open on the piano, and on the lid was an ashtray still with his stubs in it. The novel he had been reading lay in a corner of the settee, the place marked with a match-stick. Through the open door of the bedroom I could see the familiar clutter that Helena had not yet cleared away. Hanging on the end of the bed was a handsome-looking dressing-gown of some light blue stuff, that I had not seen before.

'Rubberneck,' said Helena, coming out of the kitchen with a tea-tray.

'What a mess you're in! What do you pay Ella for?'

'It's Ella's day off,' she replied. 'She demands whole days now, instead of halves, and I daren't say anything. I tell you, these women have us where they want us, and they glory in it.'

She seemed, I thought, ten years younger, satisfaction shining in her like light in a tower. She had the fulfilled look of a young girl upon her honeymoon, something at once charming and smug. She had dressed herself and painted her face with great care; but delicately. I had known Helena buy clothes designed exclusively for theatrical matrons, paint her mouth like Grimaldi's, and permit the hairdresser to rinse her hair with some horrible stuff that made it look like violets of wrought iron. All this, however, had gone. She dressed simply, as if all competition were over, or the world were in a revolutionary epoch. Helena was at peace. She could now permit herself to grow old.

'Oh yes,' she said, as if I had spoken, 'that's his dressing-gown. Poor Dilys gave it to him, the stupid woman. It was her husband's. She bought it for his birthday the week before he died, and of course he never wore it, so she kept it wrapped up for years in tissue paper. Then she got sentimental and gave it to Johnny. He thinks it's all rather gruesome, but that doesn't stop him wearing the thing.'

When we were sitting over tea she gave me a sly, confidential smile. 'I'll tell you something.'

'What?'

'Do you know, I believe poor old Dilys really was in love with Johnny, He'd no idea of it, of course, but one woman knows another. How furious she must have been when he left her!' Helena visualized this scene of parting and began to laugh.

'Don't do that. If you are right about her, it must have been damned painful.'

'She's no right to make such a fool of herself at her time of life,' said Helena cruelly.

I was angry with her then. However ridiculous to a stranger eye may be the disparity between lovers, the agony of loss is no less sharp to the forsaken. Love is always funny to people who are not in love; it seems funny to them because they are jealous, and because if they did not laugh they would hate. Yet it is a hundred times more funny to those who repress love in themselves, to those who, out of some unrealized shame or sense of decency, dare not admit to it. All the world detests a lover, because he has escaped.

I did not reply, and she let the subject drop. Instead, she spoke of Field as if she longed to transfigure him in my eyes. He was so kind, so considerate. He teased her – she loved being teased – he made her laugh. He was clever, hard-working: the M.P. thought the world of him. He was so nice to Naomi, too, treating her in the charming, thoughtful way a young man would have treated a girl half a century ago. They were friends, real friends. She was good for him. Helena was delighted with the friendship, yes, absolutely delighted.

'But of course I have to watch my step with him,' she said luxuriously; 'he has a tremendous sense of dignity. . . . Would you have thought that? He has. You remember how upset he used to get when I made fun of him? I didn't realize then what sort of man he was. I know better now,' she concluded submissively.

To me, all this was sad and dishonouring. For the sake of Archer, his position and his money, she had deliberately dulled her own richness; now, for the sake of a young man who wanted nothing better than to curl himself up like a cat by the most comfortable hearth, with the biggest cods' heads in the kitchen, she had accepted this dulling process once more. Love, unrecognized as such, had sandpapered the sharp edge of her reason, blurred her capacity for self-recognition. If she ever laughed at herself again it would only be on account of some surface absurdity that a stranger could not fail to see, and never because she had suddenly realized and analysed some grotesque motive of her own heart.

Because I could not bear her to talk any more about Field, I told her I had at last some definite news of Sholto's late nights. She was scarcely interested. 'You'd better tell Charmian. She'll know what to do, and then she can get rid of the brute.'

She sighed deeply. Rising from her chair as if she could now afford to move slowly, to ape no longer the whipping strength of a young woman, she went to the piano, put on her glasses and began to pick out, with one finger, the study for black notes which Field had been practising that morning. 'I'm so happy, Claud,' she said, half-chanting to her own uncertain music, 'you can't think how happy I am. I don't even want to cross my fingers as I say it. I feel at peace with the world. With luck it won't blow itself up in my lifetime, and even if it does I shall have had a good run for my money. Never be afraid of old age. In old age one doesn't worry. Things still happen to you, but only little things. You don't have to make them happen any more.' She botched a note, put it right again. Forsaking the study, which she found too difficult, she vamped a three-four accompaniment with her left hand – *one* two-three, *one* two-three – '"O I love the dear silver that shines in your hair, And a brow that's all furrowed and wrinkled with care . . ."' She broke off. 'That's just how I feel. Quiet. Peaceful. No worrying.' She began again: '"O I love the dear fingers so toilworn for me . . .!"'

Comedy crept in. 'O-o-o-oh!' sang Helena, upon a howl, 'God bless you and keep you, Major C.P.' She gave me a broad smile of pride and delight. 'I can still make a joke,' she said.

She would not let me go until a quarter to six when, she told me, Field would be in at any moment. 'You might as well stay and meet him,' she urged, 'you can't keep up this silly business for ever.'

'Oh yes I can,' I said.

I thought about her all that evening, and was afraid. I had

learned to fear the uncommon sense of happiness that comes suddenly, bringing with it a certainty of fair weather. Helena was certain, I knew: certain, and wrong. It could not last for her. Yet, all the same, my one impulse was to stay away, to mind my own business. When we take upon ourselves the charge of another person, seeing him through crisis upon crisis, we often grow tired just before the final catastrophe is at hand. We have done enough. We have worked overtime. We needn't reproach ourselves, as our conscience is clear. We have a tremendous desire to fail our friend just at the moment when we are most needed, most trusted, to step aside and let the devil take him.

Helena, I thought, must meet her own tragedy in her own fashion. I was due for leave: I might go away for a week or so, could probably pull enough strings to get myself over to Paris.

But then, there was Charmian. I had to see that business through.

The brief vision of the great H of Notre Dame, the blue bowl of twilight and fireworks lying below Montmartre, the glittering black horn of the Champs Elysées on a rainy night, faded like some youthful dream of grandeur. Later on, perhaps. And I began to explain to myself why it would be better later on, why I should enjoy it so much more in a year's time, why it would be a thoroughly bad thing for me to go to Paris just now. Within ten minutes I had succeeded in shrivelling my own desires to silliness and shame.

Chapter Three

NEXT day was a Saturday, the first in October, and very mild. I telephoned Charmian, asking her if she could get away from Sholto and spend the afternoon with me. 'Why?' she asked warily. 'I want to talk to you.' 'What about?' 'I'll tell you when I see you.' She argued for a few minutes, then told me she would come. Evan would be out anyway; he was to watch football somewhere or other. 'Shall I come to you?' I suggested that we should walk in the gardens of the Royal Hospital. I felt that the very discipline of being in a public place was going to help her. 'How very dismal,' said Charmian. Not a bit of it, I told her, it was a nice day and both of us could do with some fresh air. 'I'll meet you by the memorial at half-past two.'

I was there before her. It was a melancholy afternoon, still and soft, a quality of saffron in the colour of the sky. The few leaves on the trees were damp and brown, and the old soldiers sitting along the walk seemed as frail as they. Some little boys were kicking a ball about the damp grass. A few mothers trailed perambulators along the slow hours to tea-time, and an elderly, short-haired woman in a flat hat called hoarsely, like a frantic Bo Peep, after a dozen scattered dogs. The barracks clock struck the half hour and a tug hooted on the river. Two nuns who had been walking slowly began to hasten, skimming across the earth like half-open black umbrellas held by invisible hands.

Though I dreaded the talk with Charmian, I was certain that I brought her release. I expected that at first she would feel nothing but the anger of humiliation and disgust; but that when this had passed, she would see the future and be glad.

She was coming towards me now, leisurely, as if reluctant; she raised her hand and smiled. Her bright green dress took the light of the gardens to itself, dulling the sky. It was a new dress, too bright, and it made her look sallow. Coming up to me she said I had queer ideas of meeting-places, that it was too chilly to walk about, that she had a hole in her heel. We sat down and she showed me the farthing of pink skin set in the stocking, asking if it hadn't already begun to blister.

She was full of small-talk. Stockings were terrible, and didn't wear. Some women went without them, but her legs always felt cold if she did so herself, and her feet were too tender to stand the rub of the shoe. Did I like her dress? When she was little she had had a doll dressed in just this shade of green (perhaps I remembered it?) and she had always longed to wear such a colour herself. Talking of dolls, what a misery it must be for mothers, especially poor mothers, to find presents for the children! It was all right with very small children, because they always liked clothes-pegs and cotton-reels better than any elaborate toy, but for the ones who were beginning to notice. . . .

'All right, Claud,' Charmian said abruptly, 'what's it all about?'

'Evan.'

'I thought so.' She looked away from me, sat rigid. 'I shouldn't, if I were you.'

'Shouldn't what?'

'Interfere.'

'Look here,' I said, 'I can't sit around, month in, month out, and watch you being miserable. Do you think I'm blind? It's been worrying me to death.'

'Then don't worry. It's not your business.' She turned to me, her face strained, young, and affectionate. 'I don't mean that as it sounds. I'm not being nasty. You do know I'm not?' She put her hand on my arm.

'I know. I don't mind you snapping my head off, if it helps at all. May I talk to you?'

'Let's walk,' she said, and rose. We went slowly down the long path towards the river that showed like steel through the iron screen of the trees. Charmian put her arm through mine. She was nearly as tall as I. Without looking directly at her I could see the double shadow of her features, the straight brow, the comma of eyelash, the delicately aquiline nose, the vulnerable lips, the round chin with its faint hint of a second curve; Helena's chin.

'You haven't got to go on living with Evan for the rest of your life,' I said.

'Haven't I?' She sounded disinterested.

'No. You can cut free whenever you want to, now.'

She stopped dead. No one was near us. Far away the little boys shouted and raced and one of them blew a whistle. The woman with the flat hat had chased her dogs together and was now a maypole in a maze of stretched leads.

'Now listen,' I said, 'and don't talk for a bit. Why you married Sholto God knows, but anyway it didn't work out. Do you think it hasn't turned my stomach to hear him snacking at you, to see you left alone night after night while he strolled in at all hours?'

As if she had not heard me she knelt on one knee, fumbled in her bag, tore a piece of paper from an envelope and stuffed it into the back of her shoe. Getting up, she walked a few steps and then said, 'It's no use. My heel hurts like sin. We'll have to sit down.' She limped across the grass to an iron bench. 'That's better.' She looked blankly at me. 'All right, Claud. Get on with it. I'm listening.'

'I know pretty well how you've been feeling. I felt like that about Meg, when I couldn't see how the devil it would all end. The moment I realized I didn't love her, was able to tell myself consciously that I didn't, I got into a panic. I could see the years stretching on and on in boredom and misery. And I knew that however miserable they were, I mustn't let her know it. I couldn't punish her for something that was my fault. She'd done nothing.'

'Poor Meg,' said Charmian, 'poor Meg. I couldn't stand her, I know, but I'm still sorry for her. As you say, none of it was her fault.'

'But your case is different.'

'In all ways different.' She smiled oddly. 'I wonder if you know what my case is?'

For a second all sympathy between us seemed to have run dry. My ears sharpened to all manner of sounds; a woman laughing from the embankment, a twig cracking overhead, a bus changing gear, a catherine-wheel of gulls mewing and screeching inland.

'All right,' I said, 'I'd better get it over. Sholto's late nights

249

at the office were bogus. He used to go and see some woman at Chiswick. I don't know who she is, except that her name's Ann, or anything about her, but it ought to be easy enough for you to find out.'

At first her face did not change. She might have been a wax model in a shop window, posed upon an ornamental bench to display a green dress. Then her eyelids drooped and two vertical wrinkles appeared at the corners of her mouth. She seemed to smile, but was not smiling. 'Oh, my dear Claud,' she said in a quaint, drawing-room fashion, 'her name is Ann Gaston. Is there anything else you'd like to know?'

'Then if *you* know, why the hell haven't you done anything about it?'

'What a fool you are!' She was clenching her fists in rage. 'Oh, what a fool you are! I've known about it for ages. Do you know how I knew? Because his dear friend used to tell me.'

'Tennant?' I could not understand her now, knew only that I had made a blunder for which she must be long in forgiving me.

'Yes, Tennant. He was always around, wasn't he? Did you think he was in love with me?'

'I didn't know what to think. No, I didn't think that.'

'Oh yes, you did,' said Charmian, working herself into a fever of anger and misery, 'you thought I wanted to divorce Evan so I could marry him. Mother thought so, too.'

'Nobody thought it,' I began, but she rushed on.

'You think you know about people, don't you? Well, you don't know about me and you don't know about Tennant. It was his idea to give Evan away to me. He did it by little hints. It made me ill to listen, but I couldn't resist it. I had to know. He always told me just enough one night to make me listen the next – it was his idea of fun. I *had* to listen to him, do you see? It was like being compelled to some horrible vice – the very thought of it makes you retch, but you can't resist it. You see, I love Evan. I love him, do you hear that? I've seen you and Mother trying to break up my marriage, seen you quietly making fun of him, trying to impress on me that I'm worth somebody *much* better –'

She mimicked some imaginary demon that chid her, nudged her, tormented her.

'You are worth better,' I said. 'Why do you love him, for God's sake? He's a fool, he's unfaithful to you and he's without the least charm of any kind.'

She fell into soft speaking, very reasonable, very bitter. 'Yes, it's so easy, isn't it? One has to be in love because of this, because of that. I tell you, there's no *reason* for one person to love another. Loving somebody's nothing to do with charm, or cleverness, or being good. I don't give a damn whether Evan's clever or not. He has charm for *me*, though I don't know what it is. And if he ran off with a hundred women I'd still sit around and wait for him.'

I was so appalled that I could not answer her. She began to cry, covering her eyes with her hands.

'Don't,' I begged her.

'You mean to be kind,' she said, 'so does Mother. If I were you I'd feel just the same. I'd hate the sight of Evan. But no one else in the world matters to me, only him.'

A misty rain had begun to fall, lying like silver dust on her round dark head and upon her shoulders. Now the gardens were empty. The clock struck three.

'What's going to happen?' I asked her.

'Nothing.'

'But things can't go on as they are.'

She stopped crying, took out her handkerchief and dried her eyes in a finicking manner. 'Oh yes, they can. And, of course, they will.'

I looked with horror into Charmian's future, the waiting, the enduring, the permanent humiliation, and I could not face the thought that Helena and myself, who loved her, would have no power to change it.

'The trouble with you is,' she said, half-smiling, 'that you're such an optimist. You really believe that if things are hopelessly bad, then they must improve. What nonsense it is! Things can be bad, and stay bad. And they can be endured. You think because a man has nothing to commend him – you think Evan hasn't, anyway,' she added quickly—'nobody could possibly be in love with him. Can't you see that we've all got to make the best of things as they are?'

There was a deadly logic about all this that scared me. 'One thing you can't put up with, and that's Ann.'

'Oh, Ann's finished,' said Charmian hideously, 'according to darling Norman. There'll be somebody else soon enough, but at present Evan is quite innocent.' She stood up. 'I don't know how I'm going to get home. What chance do you suppose there'd be of a taxi?'

'Charmian, listen. What about Tennant? Why did he tell you all this?'

'You don't understand. He didn't tell me a thing. It was like those "find the clue to the criminal" plays on the wireless. He threw out little clues and I had to piece them together. I got quite good at it. Thank God Evan's sick of him. I don't know why he's sick of him, but they don't see each other these days.'

'But why did he tell you? . . . Why did he hint, if you want it all cut and dried?'

Charmian looked thoughtful; the effort of trying to comprehend seemed to ease her a little. 'God knows,' she said at last. 'Motiveless malice.'

'I don't believe in it. Was he jealous of Evan? Was he in love with you?'

'He may have been. But I think he was one of those people who simply like to have some beastly secret and can't resist telling it where it will do the most harm. School-girls do that, some of them. There's something school-girlish about Tennant, in a funny way. He's not happy; I don't think he likes happiness. He's always failed at things. He studied to be a doctor, but kept failing his exams. He may have been jealous of Evan.'

'Not because of Evan's success, surely?'

'Oh, Evan's been successful in one thing,' Charmian said proudly, 'he's loved.'

In the face of this I could only admire her, prepare to accept the truth she forced upon me: that things could be bad and remain bad, and that the only solace was pride in endurance.

She started towards the gates, moving painfully. I put my arm around her. 'That help?'

She leaned on me. 'Better. Claud, there's one thing more.'

'What is it?' The gentleness between us now was something for which I had hardly hoped. It was by this alone that I should be able to sustain her; by this, and by acquiescence in whatever she should desire, even if it were her own defeat.

'There's not much you don't know about me now, and there's not much I can't say to you. Evan is a failure; I admit it. He'll never do a useful job of work – he can't concentrate, and so he can't learn. That's why I had to keep Dan's money.'

We stood in the shelter of the embankment trees, watching for a taxi.

'If Evan can live an easy life, have a decent home, dress well, entertain and look prosperous, he'll keep his self-respect. The awful thing for him would be to have to clerk, or sell cars, because he *needed* the money. Oh, he'll go out to work all right – he'll get a job of some sort that'll take him out in the morning and send him back at six. But it won't matter if he loses it. That's the important thing. . . . Claud, there's a free one!'

I stopped a cab and we got in.

'Have I got to admire Evan for all that?' I asked her, as gently as I could. 'Because it's hard.'

'No,' she replied, leaning back on the cushions, her eyes closed, 'no. You haven't got to. I don't admire him myself. But you see, he can't help it. It's no fault of his that he is . . . as he is.'

'I'd give my eyes if you hadn't married him.'

'I'd give mine if I'd never met him. Then I shouldn't have fallen in love with him. Obviously.' She gave a faint smile. 'But I do love him, and so you see there's no help.'

She came back to my rooms and sat there for a while, not saying very much. The realization that for her sake I must accept something I knew to be wretched and hopeless seemed to shake the foundations of my entire thought. The mainspring of our strength to live is our belief in a solution. Right must triumph over wrong. The dockleaf must grow somewhere near the nettle. Jack must have Jill, nought must go ill, the man must have his mare again and all must be well. And the Patience cards must come out.

But supposing there's a fallacy somewhere in all this? If there is, the handrail to which we cling above the humming abyss gives a crack, and the platform tilts.

'Now what is it?' Charmian asked me. 'Don't look so miserable. It's my misery, after all. And my joy as well – you just remember that.'

'I was thinking that there must be a solution somewhere. If not –'

She smiled at me. 'Of course there's bound to be an adjustment. And that's as much as most people can expect in their lives.'

'You shouldn't have found that out, not at twenty-three.'

'Oh, don't slop,' she said impatiently, 'don't be prosy. I hate that. Do you know what comforts me? When I remember that I'm not important.'

'You are to Helena, Even to me, now and then.'

'Oh, yes, yes. I didn't mean that. I'm incredibly important to myself. But not to the whole world. Even if my marriage is a mess, it won't make any difference to the world as a whole. I often think,' said Charmian pathetically, 'of the universe, with all the stars.'

I clung to the one word that had held a promise: adjustment; and I believed that the words 'adjustment' and 'solution' might in time become synonymous.

There was nothing more to be said, no comfort in drivellings about the smallness of man and the greatness of the stars. The facts were that Charmian had made a wretched marriage from which she could have freed herself; but that she loved her husband and was prepared on that account to face a life which at best might be made tolerable. And because my care was for Charmian, I must accept her decision, be brotherly towards Sholto and forever conquer my impulse to break his neck. Which three things could, of course, be achieved. And because they could be, they must.

When I told all this to Helena she said, in the voice of someone who rolls up sleeves for battle, 'I'll talk to her.'

I tried to persuade her that it would do no good.

'I could kill that fish-eyed devil! Do you really mean you're going to condone his . . . his . . .' She could not complete the sentence.

'If Charmian insists on condoning it, where are we? Anyway, as she says, he's innocent at present. And next time he isn't innocent, she'll take good care that I don't find it out.'

For a while Helena mourned for her daughter in silence; but she had news of her own, good news, and could not keep from telling it. 'Johnny's got a rise in salary!'

'Very nice,' I said, 'that's splendid.' I looked at my watch and told her I must go. 'He'll be in any minute, and I'm not going to see him.'

'Oh no, he won't. He's going to the House tonight and he won't be back till late. Naomi's coming in to keep me company. You don't mind Naomi, do you?' She urged me to stop for dinner. It would be nice for the girl if I did, for she (Helena) was poor company for the young these days, garrulous like all old women, she insisted, in fact a shocking old bore. 'You and Naomi can talk about the things that interest you. She's nice and pretty and bright. You two ought to get on well.'

'I'm not nice and pretty and bright. Why should we?'

'The attraction of opposites!' Helena cried triumphantly, giving me a great slap on the shoulder. She had, I knew, a fine plan for the future. I was to fall in love with Naomi Reed, marry her, and so leave Field perfectly free to be petted and chided by Helena for the rest of her life. The trouble with Helena's plans, however, was that she began to work towards their achievement without a moment's consideration of those whom they might affect. Naomi came, and directly the meal was over Helena told her in the liveliest possible fashion, not caring whether or not the announcement was plausible, that she had a headache and must lie down. 'You talk to Claud. Cheer him up. He works too hard.'

In a silence made rather awkward by Naomi's embarrassment, she put her hand to her forehead, sighed, beamed, and left the room.

'At last I have you in my power,' I said to Naomi.

She laughed.

'Helena wants to throw us together, I'm afraid.'

'Perhaps she really has got a headache,' she suggested without conviction.

'Perhaps she really has. What's this about Field getting a rise?'

She brightened, and was reassured. 'Oh, did she tell you? Yes, another pound. It'll make such a difference to him. You know, some people can't realize the tremendous gulf between five pounds and six.' I thought of Helena, who had never realized the difference between five and twenty-five thousand. 'It's the difference between skimping and being able to stretch,' Naomi told me earnestly, leaning forward in her chair as if she

255

were telling a dream to a psychiatrist. 'Reaver must think something of him, don't you agree? It isn't as if Johnny's been with him any time.'

'I imagine he's good at that kind of job.'

'It's a more *suitable* job for him. All that nonsense at the shop. . . . I used to hate that. It was all such a fake. It made him look so stupid.' She was really angry, full of hate. 'You can't think how glad I am he's out of it!'

'Mrs Olney isn't.'

'Mrs Olney! . . . I'm well brought up. If I weren't, I'd tell you what I think of her.' The energy of confidence lowered Naomi's social pretensions and made her twice as attractive. 'Do you know, she used to pretend Johnny's landlord objected to me coming to Johnny's room? It was absolute rubbish. It was simply because *she* didn't want me there.'

I said, 'Naomi, are you the sort of woman who likes looking after people? Is that going to be good enough?'

She looked at me sharply for a second. Then, without any pretence that she had failed to understand she replied, Yes; it was going to be good enough.

I pitied her, and admired her. She was one of those people, kind, unsubtle, firm as rocks, who realize early that their function is to support the weak. It is not a happy destiny, and they know it; but they are determined to accept it without any futile struggle. Were Naomi to search for some lover who would make her his charge, take decisions for her, give either a yes or a no to her questions, she would be deceived by the first weakling who could thrust out his chin in obstinacy. She was aware of that, knew where her demon would drive her; and so, she went without being driven. She could have been an excellent nurse, school teacher, or missionary to the heathen. Instead, she would be a faithful and tireless nurse to John Field. As she grew older, so her lips would become less soft, her smile less conciliatory; her stride would grow longer, the movement of her hands more deliberate; but she would never cease to believe that she was happy.

She sat quietly at my side, love giving to her face a great peacefulness. Everything was decided, her future lay clear. After a moment or so she asked me about my book, when it was to appear, who was the publisher, what did I mean to write next.

She was a talented listener, knowing just when to ask a question that would flatter vanity, and when to make a leading comment. She was charming to see, and she wore her good qualities like a necklace of pearls. I would not have married her for the entire contents of the National Gallery and the French rooms of the Tate.

Helena came back, entering the room with a sort of arch little hop, as if she expected us to rise hand in hand to greet her and ask her blessing.

'I've got to be going,' I said. 'How's the headache?'

'A little better,' she answered, seeing that nothing had happened and being extremely disappointed. 'It will pass soon.'

'I'm going too, Lady Archer, if you don't mind,' Naomi said, 'I've had a whole run of late nights.'

'Won't you wait for Johnny?'

'I don't think I will. The House may be sitting late.'

'It would be wonderful if he was in Parliament himself some day,' Helena sighed, seeing him walking between his sponsors towards the Speaker's Chair, his eyes shining with the inspiration of Pitt the Younger. 'You never know.' She speeded Naomi with some enthusiasm. 'Claud will set you on your way. Now don't keep her up, Claud, she's looking fagged.'

She offered her cheek. Naomi bent and kissed it. 'Bless you, my dear,' Helena said. She reminded me of the wolf in grandmother's bed.

I walked round to World's End with Naomi and put her on a bus. She called after me, 'Thank you for everything,' and I knew she had determined to have me forever on her side, to hold me in reserve for any times of difficulty through which she might have to steer John Field. I was equally determined to stand in no relationship whatsoever to either of them.

A few days later I took Helena to lunch in town. She had been shopping in Kensington, and when she met me displayed a bag full of brightly-coloured articles for which she had no real use, a belt worked with shells, a scarf printed over with the names of Paris streets, a nylon sponge-bag, a pair of plastic earrings shaped like starfish, a carnation made of red felt, a bottle of magenta nail-varnish, a clothes-hanger painted with green and yellow stripes and a blue woollen hood with matching gloves.

I

'You wouldn't believe how much I've spent.'

'I believe it.'

'All trifles, too; but I did want something to amuse me. It's just like old times, really, counting my pennies and seeing just how far they'll stretch. I never wanted to buy things nearly so much when I was rich.'

'You aren't going to look very nice in that hood.'

'Don't be a fool,' said Helena, 'it's not for me. It's for Naomi. The poor little thing's got to take her holiday next week, and I thought she'd like something new to wear. Miss Norrish couldn't spare her during the summer.'

'Where's she going?'

'Penzance – with Miss Norrish, as a matter of fact. Doesn't sound much of a change to me. Still, it ought to be warmer there than most places. She'll be away for three weeks – won't our Johnny be lost without her? Not that it will be a bad thing. She's rather bossy with him, I think, doesn't let him decide things for himself. It's good for Johnny to have to decide,' Helena added, with the air of a devoted Spartan mother who will not, for his own good, pick up her baby when he tumbles down.

Several times during the meal she referred to Naomi's holiday. She was delighted by the thought that once more she would have Field to herself.

Happiness gave her much of her old radiance. She made little jokes to the waiter and was rewarded with a dish of olives, produced stealthily, with a wary glance, out of nowhere. Everything seemed charming to her, the white half-curtains at the window, the pink table-lamps, the scallop-shells that served as ashtrays. She pointed out to me the most commonplace things as though they were *objets de vertu*, insisting that I should join her in praise.

'Now that's a nice hat!' she exclaimed, pointing to a stout woman upon whose head was a small round cap adorned with a propeller of yellow feathers. 'I bet she paid something for that.'

I told her it was an awful hat.

'I always said you had no taste,' Helena murmured, still gazing. 'Nine or ten pounds, I'm sure of it. If not more.' She was suddenly irritable. 'I'd like something like that, something striking, but of course I can't afford it any more.' Her bag of pretty junk toppled over, and the waiter scrambled to pick up the spilled scarves, bottles, earrings. 'If only Daniel hadn't been silly about that one silly thing, he'd have left me the lot.'

'What silly thing?'

Helena looked embarrassed. 'Oh, nothing worth talking about.'

'There was some specific reason why he left you short?'

She shrugged. 'I suppose it was that. Anyhow, I've always thought it must have been.'

'Tell me,' I said.

'That doctor he had before Stillyer – do you remember him? Whitelaw. No, you wouldn't. You never met him.' She took on girlishness. 'Daniel thought I liked him.'

'Did you?'

'Of course not.' She looked at me indignantly, yet hoping I would not altogether believe her disclaimer. 'I think perhaps Whitelaw did grow rather fond of me. We understood each other. It was at Christmas. I gave him a kiss, just for fun – there *was* mistletoe,' she assured me anxiously, 'and Daniel walked in and was stupid about it. It was ridiculous, when you come to think about it, because Whitelaw was over seventy.'

'Good God,' I said, fascinated. I wanted to laugh, yet felt this was no laughing matter. This stately Christmas flirtation between an elderly woman and an old doctor had cost Helena some thousands of pounds.

'So now you know,' she repeated, 'and you can stop staring.'

Yes, now I knew.

Chapter Four

Helena had only one week of Field's company, for at the end of it she telephoned to tell me, with forced brightness, that he had gone away on holiday. He had felt suddenly tired, she said, good for nothing, and had seemed to pine for a smell of the sea. So he was going to spend a week in Truro with an old friend of his mother's, and then perhaps go on to Penzance for a few days. 'It will be company for Naomi,' Helena said firmly, 'and a change for him.' She rubbed salt into her wounds. 'No fun for him looking at an old woman all the time.'

I asked how his M.P. was able to spare him.

'Oh, he's going off on one of these missions to somewhere. Johnny will be at a loose end.'

'And who's going to pay for it?'

'The Government, of course,' Helena replied, wilfully misunderstanding.

'I don't mean for the mission. For Field's holiday.'

'I expect he's saved up,' Helena said. She added too quickly, 'Anyway, it's his business. I dare say there were ways and means.'

'Your means.'

She told me sharply not to be stupid; but when I went to see her confessed that she had lent Field some more money. When I tried to protest she stopped me, saying simply, 'Probably you're right. But doing things for Johnny is all the happiness I have now. It may seem silly to you, but it's important to me. And does it really matter?'

Because she was lonely, because she suffered from a jealousy which, though admitted not even to herself, was as torturing as a girl's, I did my best to keep her amused. We lunched together, went to the theatre and cinema, had Bill Swain, Clemency, and the Crossmans to spend an evening with us, even went one night, at Helena's request, to a dance-hall in Charing Cross Road where she sat absorbed for over two hours, commenting upon the dresses of the women, comparing the dancing of today with that of her own. 'We had some spring in us,' she said, 'these people either caper or slither.' She remembered how she had once danced in a pink dress adorned with bows of black velvet. 'You may not believe it now, Claud, but I looked really handsome. I never needed rouge then. I could waltz longer than any of the other girls and never get tired.' She nodded contemptuously at the slow fox-trot in progress. 'That lot are tired before they begin.'

Yet the tiredness of her own body was, these days, beginning to defeat her. Her mind struggled to be rid of its mastery, to force nerve and muscle to keep pace with mental energy. It infuriated her to find, at ten o'clock, that her eyelids were heavy, her legs aching, the treacherous body longing for the anaesthetic of sheet and blanket. She fought it: she didn't want to go home just yet, she was still fresh, it was a beautiful night, a night for walking just as far as Hyde Park Corner. No need for a taxi. Piccadilly was full of lights and people, and she wanted to walk down it. She had never lost the excitement of seeing streets lit up again.

'If you're not tired,' I said, 'I am. Walk by yourself, if you like – I'm taking a bus.'

For form's sake she argued a little; but I could tell that she was relieved almost to tears by the thought that she would not have to drag herself any further. Her pride was saved: I had faltered, not she. 'No buses, though,' she insisted, 'I shall treat you to a taxi. I may be poor, but I can still afford small luxuries.'

She made me come back to her flat for a while. Just as I was about to leave she spoke of a thing which, she said, had been for a long time upon her mind. 'It's about my Will.'

I asked her if she were going to die.

'I hope not,' she answered, not amused, 'not yet awhile, anyhow; but one has to make arrangements. All there is goes to you, Claud.'

I did not know how to answer her. When some person we love suggests, however obliquely, with however great a delicacy and affection, that we might in any way gain by their death, we are tormented with anger at them for expecting us to be pleased, and by shame and anger at ourselves because, for an infinitesimal part of a second, we have made a profit and loss account.

'What about Charmian?' I said at last.

'She won't need it. She's got Dan's money. . . . Oh, no,' she continued with a great assumption of cheerfulness, 'you'll have whatever there is.'

'Why are you worrying yourself about all this just now?'

'I want you to know, so you won't think I might have other ideas.'

I told her I had not considered the matter at all. 'Do you honestly believe I've been sitting around licking my chops about it?'

She gave me a gentle buffet. 'You might have been. You're capable of most things. The point is . . . I've decided that I shan't be leaving anything to Johnny.'

It had never occurred to me that she might. Now I saw that this was a matter to which she must have given great thought. I told her that her money was her own, and that she should dispose of it as she wished. 'If you want him to have it, then leave it to him. You know quite well that I'm never likely to be really hard up.'

She shook her head. 'It wouldn't be fair.' We were standing together in the hall. Helena sat down on one of the hard chairs, as if she were suddenly exhausted. 'I've made up my mind to that. You see, I know what's real and what isn't, for all you think I'm not fit to manage my own affairs. I'm very fond of Johnny, as you know. Oh, he's not such a fine fellow – I realize that; but he means a great deal to me.' She pondered. 'Perhaps it's because he's not so fine. I'm not sure.' She gazed up at me, her eyes full of tears. She looked tremulous and old, unequal to the task she had so courageously set herself; which was to recognize those things which were reasonable, and which were not. 'I feel I couldn't bear to be without him now. You know him in a way, but not the side he shows to me. We have so many jokes together, and we think the same about so many things.'

She stopped speaking, and I thought she would break down.

'You stop upsetting yourself,' I said. 'You don't want to start worrying about Wills at this time of night.'

She went on as if I had not spoken. 'But I do realize that

whatever he is to me, and however important he seems, he isn't important in the way you and Charm are. There was Dicky, and Belgium and all that, and seeing you through that business with Meg, and then Cecil. . . . Johnny's just new. I've nothing to remember about him. Years ago he wouldn't have mattered, and that's what I understand. He only *seems* to matter now' – she smiled waterily, deprecating her own foolishness – 'but it feels real to me.'

She was silent for a long while seeking, I think, for some words with which to dispel the warmth of sentiment she could not have helped but generate. When two people are as intimate as Helena and myself, a display of sentiment is always repellent; repellent, perhaps, because the expression of love is so greatly desired and so ruinous if achieved. She said at last, 'Anyhow, I owe you something for the time I gave you when you were a boy. Not that you didn't deserve it. I'd do the same again.'

'Go to bed,' I said, 'you're losing your looks.'

'Ah,' she retorted, shooting up all energy from her seat, 'but at least *I* have some to lose.'

She never mentioned her Will to me again.

One evening, nearly a fortnight later, I went to the flat and found her in overalls, repainting the woodwork of Field's room. Ella, who was just leaving, whispered to me that she had tried to stop it, but Heaven help you once Lady Archer had made her mind up.

Helena was at the skirting board when I went in, head tied up in a scarf, sleeves rolled to the elbows. She had spread newspapers to catch the drips of paint and was in a rage because they would not stay in position. She was an untidy worker. There were smears of pale blue on her forearm and on her cheek, and some of the paint from the door had smudged over on to the wall.

'Here,' she said when she saw me, 'you try and stop those papers shifting, will you? Just make yourself useful.'

'Why are you doing all this? It's much too much for you.'

She told me Field would be back in three days' time and that she was making things nice for him. 'It's the first time I've ever done any decorating,' she said proudly, 'except when I whitewashed the scullery at the Dyver. You wouldn't remember that.'

I told her to get up and let me finish the job for her.

Helena protested that I mustn't soil my clothes, that I didn't know the technique (she had listened to a wireless talk on how to paint a room), that she was doing perfectly well by herself. Leaving her to these objections, I found an old pair of khaki shorts and a sweater belonging to Field, went to the bathroom and changed into them. When I came back I put Helena in a chair and set to work. She watched me luxuriously, all the while complaining that she could do it better.

I had finished within an hour.

'Will it dry by Thursday?' she asked me anxiously.

'God knows.'

'I do hope it will. Don't you think it looks better? So much more bright. You don't think he'll say it's too pretty-pretty?'

'If he says anything of the sort I hope you'll wring his neck,' I retorted.

But Field might have been a son returning from five years of war. She showed me a quilt she had had cleaned and relined for him, a new table-lamp, elephant book-ends which she had found among some lumber of Daniel's. She would not take off her overall or wash herself; it gave her pleasure to appear as a servant for Field's sake, to feel herself in his employment. The scarf that concealed her hair and showed only a triangle of brow made her seem like some old tribal queen, fierce-eyed, inexhaustibly resourceful; though she thought humbly of herself there was little humility in her looks, and I wondered how often Field had been afraid of her.

'I must have a biscuit before I have a drink,' she said. 'When you're full of paint-fumes you must never drink before you've eaten, otherwise you may be sick.' She sat by the fire, legs stretched out along the settee, Lance upon her lap. The kitten, fascinated by the blue smear along her arm, tried to claw it off. 'Ah, you little horror!' she cried, tweaking the cat's tail. Lance twisted round, gave her a small warning bite and leaped off her lap to hunt shadows. Helena ate biscuits steadily, now and then asking me to reassure her that the paint in Field's room was not too girlish a colour. 'I do want him to like it. Psychologists say it's very important what sort of room you live in. You can go quite mad by living in dark crimson.'

I went to wash and to change back again into my own

clothes. I was returning through the hall when I heard a rattle at the letter-box and saw the corner of an envelope projecting through it. I opened the door to Helena's next-door neighbour, an elderly woman recently returned to London from the country.

'I'm so sorry,' she said, withdrawing the letter and handing it to me, 'I couldn't make it go through. It kept sticking.'

The envelope was addressed to Helena, and the postmark was Penzance. The writing was tiny and elaborate, almost monkish, the capital letters florally curled, the figures – house and district number – flowing into the script.

'I didn't get home till late or I'd have found this before. It was stuck behind one of my own letters. If you'd please apologize to Lady Archer from me . . .?'

I thanked her, and carried it to Helena.

She turned the envelope over, smiling anticipation. 'It's from Johnny.' She opened it, and began to read.

Her smile did not fade immediately; it narrowed and became rigid. She seemed to be holding her breath. Her gaze rapidly criss-crossed the page. She looked up at me, the smile still there, but her eyes quite blank. Then, turning over, she read the second sheet; read it once more and then threw the letter to me.

My dear Helena,

Bless you, but I think my news may be a shock. Naomi says it can only be a nice shock, as it was you who made it so easy for us to be together, and I do hope she's right. There are two of us to be fond of you and grateful to you now, so maybe she is. We were married in Penzance this morning.

I looked quickly across at Helena. She had taken Lance to her breast and was smoothing his fur rhythmically. Her face was turned away.

We decided to do it the day I got down here, only I never said anything to you as it seemed the sort of decision that couldn't be carried into effect – a sort of pipe-dream. Then we both got a fit of wanting-to-be-helped and talked it over with Aunt Norrish who, angels guard her, gave us a tremendous shock by sitting right down and organizing the whole thing. She reckoned that now I was getting six pounds a week instead of five, we ought to be able to manage; because Naomi gets seven, and collectively we'd be quite well off. I did say feebly that I'd rather wait till *I* got seven, but Aunt Norrish told me not to be sentimental.

It was all quite extraordinary. One minute there seemed to be no hope and the next it was all settled. The next terrific thing was when she said we could have one of her flats, for a year, anyway. She's got a bit of property, but it was blitzed, and they only repaired the first house a fortnight ago. She's scared stiff at having it requisitioned, and Naomi said that's why she was so keen to marry us off and instal us in it, but I think that's taking a dim view. Aunt Norrish wants to live in it herself when she retires (it's out at Richmond and too far from her office now), but that won't be for a long time.

Helena was lying with head thrown back, every muscle of her face tightened against tears. There was no sound in the room save the kitten's loud purring.

I mustn't write much more now, but get to the *clou* of the whole thing quickly. We were married by special licence, for which Aunt Norrish paid!!! Honestly, Helena, I don't know whether I'm on my head or my heels, but it feels like my head.

Are you pleased? Claud will be, because he feels I pross on you, and fag you about, and generally make a nuisance of myself, which of course I do, and always have done. Naomi and I will both make nuisances of ourselves now and again, I hope, if you'll have us.

Here the script grew cramped and minute, as if the writer had been in a great hurry to conclude but did not want his reader to guess it.

One important thing. I owe you for my holiday and lots else. I promise it shall be paid. I wish I could repay all the tremendous things you've done for me – there's no one like you – but I could never do that without being as good as you are, which I'm not.

I won't be coming back to the flat, of course, because Nao and I will stay at Aunt Norrish's establishment till we can get the flat ready, but we'll both come to see you at the earliest poss. mom. – that is, if you write and say you want us to.

Do be pleased, Helena. God bless.

                                    Gratefully and affectionately,
                                              Johnny.

The kitten yawned, stretched itself up Helena's breast, and went to sleep.

I could not speak. Silence stood in the room like a pillar of dusk. Helena turned on her side and lay with her back to me.

I tried to re-read Field's letter, but could not. The fear in it, the shame, the bluffing, the desire to salve conscience, made me at first unable to see how much he was in the right. Pity for Helena made me fix my chief hatred upon Field's efficient and determined aunt, a woman who could not have failed to realize what she did.

By all simple standards, Field was free to marry any girl he liked when he liked; Helena had no claims of love upon him, only of gratitude. She was an old woman, he a young man. It was true that she had tried to keep him by her, to stunt him by her love and her service, and it was equally true that he could have had no growth without breaking free of her.

Nevertheless, he was perceptive. He had realized the nature of her affection for him, realized it better than she; and he had known also that in it there was no ugliness. Therefore he owed her pity. And he had dealt with her pitilessly.

I was glad that he had married Naomi Reed, had passed to her firm, automatic mothering, and I was glad myself to be free of him. The evil lay in this one thing: that he had not gone to Helena and told her what he meant to do. Instead, he had worked subtly, slyly, on a scheme he must long have planned, had invented the story of his need for a holiday, and had borrowed money from Helena in order to destroy her. I did not believe in the suddenness of Miss Norrish's decision, was not even sure that I believed in the special licence. What was sly in Field was sly also in Naomi Reed, and because of it they had committed the unpardonable sin: they had made a fool of a friend. When Helena had forgiven everything else, this would remain unforgiven. It was the worst thing: and the only thing that could medicine her pride. Now she could no longer love Field utterly, but must have always the saving grace of contempt.

'What can I do to help?' I said at last.

She moved her head slowly from side to side. 'Nothing. What is there to do? Only don't, for God's sake, tell me it's all a good thing.'

'Of course I won't. All I can say is that time passes, and things lose their edge.'

'The little sneak,' said Helena, 'the little sneak.' She shielded her face. On her forearm the streak of paint was like the scar of an old burn. 'And that beastly little girl, and that scheming old woman.' She used the petty adjectives of belittlement, drawing from them both comfort and self-disgust. She mimicked Field's voice. 'You're too terrifically kind, Helena. I know you'll be most terrifically pleased.'

'There was no reason why they shouldn't marry,' I reminded her, partly from the nudge of conscience and partly because I felt it would ease her to be angry with me.

'No reason,' she said quietly, not angry at all; after a pause she added, 'but it was the way they did it.' She brought her arm down, baring her dulled and tearless face. 'If they'd told me first I could have made myself happy about it. *And that is true.*'

I knew that it was true. She would have pretended happiness until it had become a fact, would have given Field, out of her love, the thing he most desired: release not only from that love, but also from the obligation of gratitude.

She sat up, the sleeping kitten dropping from her breast like a fed leech. 'Is it raining?' A few drops glittered on the pitch darkness of the window and the curtains stirred in a draught. 'I didn't see it start. You'll be drenched going home.'

'I'm not going home yet awhile.'

'Oh, go!' she said. 'You'd better.'

'I don't want to leave you all upset, like this.'

She made a gesture of not caring whether I stayed or went. I watched her as she sat there, the lamplight shining on the smeared overall and upon the tribal head-dress. She was quite motionless, as if the worst of her sorrow lay ahead and she would make no move to meet it. Time was suspended where Helena sat. 'You see,' she said patiently, 'nothing will ever happen to me again.' The thought of blankness appalled her. The tears broke from her eyes.

She was facing the one-way street with nothing at the end of it, the street without sky, without doors, and for a moment she felt she could not bear to be engulfed by it. The members of her body, combining against her hard will, had at last defeated her. Nothing would ever happen because she could take no steps to meet it; or, if it came to her, she could not keep pace with it.

'The smell of that paint's awful,' she murmured, 'it makes me feel sick, doesn't it you?'

And, indeed, it pervaded the whole flat, forcing memory of its colour and the way it had risen like a tent upon the hairs of the brush. Forever, blue would be Field's colour. Helena would never again be able to see a certain shade of it without remembering humiliation and loss, and her own ridiculous image. There was nothing I could do to help her, no words in which I could tell her that all love (if it really is love, and not self-adoration) is honourable, and no cause for shame.

She got up, took off her overall and unwound the long strip of silk from her dulled and flattened hair. 'Serves me right. I ought to have known. . . . Go on home, Claud, I'm being silly. Youth to youth the wide world over, as it goes. I ought to be glad, and I will be glad, I expect, when I've had time to think. But the method, the *method* . . .' She swung round. Anger possessed her, enlarging the pupils of her eyes, swelling the cords of her neck. 'He is a swine! However bad and silly I may be, I could never have done a thing like that! He's a damned little swine, and I hope he gives her a hell's life. I hope he goes on running away and running back, I hope he keeps her watching for him from the window, and then I hope she grips him by the neck so that he *can't* wriggle, and that will be his hell.' She held out her hands to me with a curious gesture; the fists clenched, as if she wanted help but could not bring herself to ask for it, and would repel it were it offered. Then she let them fall. When she spoke her voice was calm, exhausted. 'Don't take any notice of me. You know what I'm like. I shall feel better tomorrow.'

Always she believed that tomorrow would bring relief.

She insisted that I should go, that if I stayed she would only make a greater fool of herself. She fetched me my greatcoat and cap and then, after I had said good night, begged me to wait a moment and went into her bedroom. She came out again carrying in the palm of her hand a pretentious signet ring that had belonged to Daniel. It was set with an agate and a diamond.

'Here,' she said, 'this is no good to me. I almost forgot. I've been meaning to give it you for some time.' She dropped it into my pocket.

I took it out again.

'I couldn't wear this.'

'Don't wear it then,' she insisted feverishly, 'sell it, and buy one of your rotten old pictures.'

She took my hand, clenched it over the ring, and forced it back into my coat. 'I want you to have it. It's always lying around, and I'm sick of the sight of it. Take it, and don't argue.'

I thanked her, understanding. For a moment it seemed as if she were struggling to make some joke by which she could remind me of her lost self; but then the energy died out of her face, and she only said, 'Good night. Come in tomorrow, if you're not too busy.'

I had thought that she would refuse to see Field and his wife, but she did not. On the evening after their return she asked them formally to dinner, inviting the Leipers also. I gathered that the meal passed off all right and that Helena considered it the end. Naomi helped her to pack up Field's few belongings.

A few days later I dined with Charmian, Sholto, and old Mrs Sholto. I went in determination that all should be well. I was committed to endure Sholto decently for the rest of my life, and I fancied I had so subdued his mother that no trouble was likely to arise from her. I was wrong. Mrs Sholto was one of those women who accept finality half a dozen times a week, yet are always able to begin again upon just that course to which they have agreed to put a stop.

At first, all was agreeable. Since the afternoon in the gardens of the Royal Hospital, Charmian seemed to have gathered new resolution. The sluttishness, prompted by disappointment and damage to self-esteem, had disappeared. Tonight she wore a new dress of very dark red silk, and her hair was carefully and beautifully combed from the broad central ray. She seemed to repose in her husband a most charming confidence, looking to him for approval whenever she made a small joke, or ventured an opinion. Her method was that of the teacher who chooses for monitor the worst, grubbiest, and most eccentric boy in the class, hoping that trust and responsibility will reform him.

In Sholto's manner there was little change, though tonight he showed no sign of irritability. He teased her a good deal, but with pleasant humour, and seemed anxious that his mother and I should admire her. He was, undoubtedly, in one of his 'innocent' phases. His broad, handsome face had a look of holiday content; the moment was sufficient, and he was enjoying it.

During the early part of dinner the old lady was rather silent. When she addressed Charmian it was with an air of affectionate approval; once or twice, during the course of some mild political argument, she pretended to support her against Sholto. It was not until coffee had been brought that the atmosphere began to thicken. Mrs Sholto had been expressing optimism at the prospect of English social life re-establishing itself at the point where war had brought it into chaos.

Sholto contradicted her. 'Mother,' he said, 'this is a wicked world. Only Claud and I can see it in all its horror. People like you and me are dogwards-bound. After us, the deluge.'

'I shall survive,' I said.

'Oh, people who write books always can. But the poor *rentier*'s finished.'

'The poor *rentier* will go down fighting,' Charmian said diffidently, as if unhopeful that any opinion of hers would be taken seriously, 'or egg us into one last scrap, in which we'll probably all be blown up.'

'Scrap with whom?' Mrs Sholto smiled at her own use of the colloquialism. She glanced round the table as if around the concourse of England. 'Is there anyone in this or any other country who really *wants* a war?'

'Nobody wants it,' I said, 'but a lot of people are going the right way to get one.'

'Hang together or hang separately,' Sholto nodded, 'that's

the stuff. But there are some countries it may be hard to hang with.'

'Now which?' Mrs Sholto demanded roguishly.

Sholto whistled the 'Volga Boatman' and raised an eyebrow.

'Oh no,' said Charmian heatedly, 'we're not going to have that. We should have learned something by now.'

'Quite right,' the old lady approved her, 'quite right. We've all got to trust one another, whatever we may feel about things. The future's with you young ones. It's your business to keep watch, so we must listen to you respectfully.'

'Just leave it to Charmian,' Sholto agreed. He glanced slyly at me as if I would join in the joke against her.

I said they might go further and fare worse, at which the old lady gave a humorous jerk of her brows, Sholto a sharp glance, and the subject was dropped. I thought of Charmian spending the years in their company and was depressed.

'I met Susan Leiper in Harrod's this morning,' Mrs Sholto told me, 'with her little girl. Such a nicely-behaved little soul she is, but she still has that odd look in her eyes. They never *will* tell you just what's wrong, will they?'

'I think it's rather a private grief,' Charmian said, in the gentle, rather elderly manner that occasionally made her enemies.

'I don't think anyone means to intrude upon it, my dear,' Mrs Sholto replied, with a fondling and dangerous look, 'but surely it's legitimate to speculate, just between ourselves?'

'The Leiper child goes round and round the trick-cyclists from one year's end to the other,' Sholto said, 'yet I've never really seen her with straws in her hair.'

Mrs Sholto was still gazing reflectively at Charmian. 'How pretty that dress is! You ought always to wear that dark red.'

'Thank you,' Charmian replied freshly. She acknowledged a compliment as if it were a surprise to her, and welcome.

'Dark red, yes. Very nice indeed, don't you think so, Claud?'

I agreed.

'By the way, Susan tells me Lady Archer has lost her young knight.'

'He's just got married,' I said.

I saw Sholto give a wary glance at Charmian, who relaxed rather self-consciously and looked at nothing. I had told both of them about Field, and they had listened without comment.

'Only to be expected.' Mrs Sholto smiled, and shook the smile slowly from side to side. 'But she must feel it. I know. She was so devoted. Tell me, Claud,' she said, punishing Charmian, 'what is her young rival like? Is she pretty?'

I saw her face fixed in inquiry, saw Sholto's abrupt movement, Charmian's bright flush. I said as quietly as I could, not knowing what I might precipitate, 'Mrs Sholto, I spoke to you once before about suggestions you made concerning my stepmother.' This was too like business-English. She noticed it, and her lips twitched. 'They're insulting to her and to Charmian. Will you please apologize?'

There was a long, fantastic silence. Mrs Sholto simply laid down her fork, folded her hands and looked at me in a lively, quizzical fashion. I think all four of us in the room were waiting for the other to speak.

Then Mrs Sholto thought of a reply, and she opened her lips to make it; but before she could speak Charmian said sharply, 'If you don't apologize, *belle-mère*, I shan't be able to ask you here any more or to come to you.'

Mrs Sholto turned on her. 'I think that would be unfair to Evan, don't you?' She said to me, 'I've made no suggestions to which anyone could take exception, Claud. Lady Archer's attachment to young Field was very noticeable, and I think I made less suggestions than most people.'

Sholto rose and walked over to the fireplace. Then, with the courage of heat at the back of his legs, he spoke to his mother. 'I'm sorry. I'm with Claud and Charmian about this. I've had nothing but kindness from Lady Archer, and I think all this gossip's a damned bad show. What's more, I shall tell the Leipers as much next time they start it.'

His mother looked at Charmian and me. She was apparently untroubled, thoughtful, in control of herself; but she did not know what her left hand was doing. It was closed, and the thumb was beating a tattoo against the first finger. A real little personality of a hand, at its own devices.

She said, 'Very well. In a democracy one accepts the majority opinion, isn't that so? I'm not conscious that I've ever done Lady Archer any harm, but since you all think I have, I'll apologize gladly. To her through you, Claud – to Charmian, and' – she looked directly at Sholto – 'to her son-in-law. Now are you all satisfied?'

We were all satisfied and all, I think, illogically ashamed. The drawback about any apology is that it implants a sense of guilt in the recipient.

A lesser woman than Mrs Sholto, after this incident, would quietly and early have taken her leave. She did not. She began at once to talk of coupons, rationing, and the rudeness of butchers, and would have outstayed me had I not firmly resolved that she should not.

When she had gone I thanked Sholto, not saying for what.

He understood. 'I do try to be fair,' he said, not pompously, but as a statement of genuine and conscientious effort, 'and I did realize you were in the right of it. Mother's no longer young, you know, and she does get rather a lot of fun out of scandal. I suppose there's not much else for her. All the same, you only did what you had to.' He gave me a swift look of fear and appeal. 'Don't hold it against her.'

I promised I would not.

'One can't feud in small families,' he added anxiously.

When Charmian saw me to the door she kissed me. 'Absolutely wonderful,' she whispered.

'I'm afraid I've made things bloody for you in the future.'

'Never mind that. I've got Evan on my side.'

I believed she had, and was comforted. For the first time it seemed to me possible that she and Sholto had not chosen each other altogether lightly, and that her future might not be solely a matter for patience, toleration, and the achievement of public civility.

Chapter Five

I REMEMBER being visited, as a boy, by a friend from a foreign city that I too had lived in and loved. When he sailed for home I saw him off at the docks, and shall never forget the desolation that took me as the water broadened between the ship and the side of England. My friend was going to new pleasure and discovery, to perpetual change and delight, while I was left behind as upon the face of a clock that had stopped. At sixteen it is easy to believe there is nothing new under the sun; sixteen is the age for realizing the meaning of dust and ashes. The boat drew the sun away with her, leaving me in the midday twilight and the cold.

The sense of being 'left behind' may never again arise from any one specific thing; but I believe it comes inevitably with the understanding that one has grown old. For years we cling to the belief that we are young for our age, that young men and women appreciate us far more than our contemporaries do. Our minds are strong, and our legs also. We are still learning, we can still change. And then, suddenly, we realize that the marchers are passing us by, and we are taken by pure panic. Soon we shall be alone upon the interminable road, seeing in the distance only the jolting, merging backs of those that continue on.

Helena had enjoyed her life. At best it had been a tremendous performance, all staircases and revolving stages, with herself as heroine; at worst, it had been interesting. Now, the last important thing had happened to her, and there would be nothing more. Only the necessity for eating and drinking, suggesting and agreeing, sleeping and dying. Had she lived less vigorously, had she looked upon the world with an eye less ravenous, she could have accepted the normal decline without anguish – might, indeed, scarcely have realized that it was taking place. But she hated age, because for her it had no compensations.

Now that Field had left her she fell prey to an awful restlessness. The sight of a young woman seemed to anger her; the young were so fortunate! When they loved and lost, they had the heavenly consolation of being able to shout their heads off about it and cry themselves sick in public. About their love, their loss, there was nothing fundamentally ridiculous. But Helena, having never admitted, even in her thoughts, that her love for Field had been more than a nepotic devotion, was unable to permit herself even the comfort of an acknowledged grief.

She made her claims upon me, now, not as a friend, but as an employer of labour. I must go with her here and there, sit with her night after night, say only what she wished me to say. Helena must go to First Nights, and I must escort her. I must bring my friends to her, and take her to visit them. She raged insatiably through the first weeks of desolation, garrulous, unsmiling, detesting the spectacle of happiness but driven to seek it. She passed in a day from the wildest extravagance to the most ludicrous economy. On one occasion she paid eight pounds for a bottle of perfume, and that same evening began to cut up an old sheet because, she said, she could not afford to buy new handkerchiefs.

She was divorced completely now from the life that had been Daniel's. She would no longer have Stillyer for her doctor, but choose a seven-and-six-a-visit-man recommended by Ella. When Sue Leiper telephoned and asked her to dine, Helena was so brusque in her refusal that the invitation was never repeated. She told Lady Esch bluntly that she could not accept hospitality she was no longer able to return. The Cayleys, who had gone to live in America, wrote to her twice, but she would not answer their letters.

'I don't want them, Claud, not any of them. All that's over and done with. They always thought Dan had married beneath him, and now they know it. Thank God I'm free of them!'

One evening, baffled by some query concerning income tax, she asked me to look into her affairs. She had recently taken them out of the hands of Daniel's solicitor, saying that she wasn't going to pay six and eight, or half a guinea or whatever it was, a letter, when she could handle her business herself.

Fighting my way through a mass of muddled papers (she

had torn the headings off many to light cigarettes) I discovered that Helena was considerably poorer than she should have been, and that her capital was much depreciated. When I questioned her she hedged at first, but afterwards admitted that she had sold a sizeable block of shares.

'What did you do with the money?'

'I put some of it into Dilys's shop.'

'How much?'

She hesitated. Then she said defiantly, 'Two thousand.'

I was aghast. 'Were you mad?'

'I thought it would be worth while.' She gave me a look of bulldog obstinacy.

'What the devil did *she* do with it?'

'Well,' Helena replied, 'she had the place done up. And then, there were Dennis's school fees.'

'What had you to do with his school fees?'

'Don't bully me! It was only common sense. If she'd all that worry on her mind – all that debt – you couldn't have expected her to keep her mind on her work. I thought of it as an investment.'

We stared at each other. After a while a faint smile tightened at the corner of her mouth, and her gaze fell. She was trying not to laugh.

'Helena!'

She did laugh then, relievedly, rather tearfully, waving her arms at me like the flappers of a seal. 'Oh, all right, all right! Don't even you make mistakes?'

'Not that kind.'

'Well, you can't expect me to have second sight,' she murmured, enjoying the inward spectacle of her own absurdity, 'for all I knew the shop was going to make huge profits and I could have kept my carriage-and-pair. It's the luck of the game,' she added, with some splendour.

I asked her what she had done with the rest of the proceeds from the sale of her stock. It appeared that she had bought from Mrs Olney some shares in a mining company.

'What shares?'

She named them. To forestall further inquiry on my part she admitted that they had not paid a dividend for fifteen years, but that she believed they were about to rocket.

When I demanded why on earth they should do anything of the sort she answered. 'They were bought for Dilys by her father quite thirty years ago, and he always begged her to hang on to them because he said they'd make her a rich woman some day. She only sold them to me because she was desperate, and even then she made it a favour.'

I felt guilty. I should have watched Helena more closely.

'What did Cayley have to say?'

Cayley had been Daniel's broker.

'It wasn't his business to say anything. Anyway, he didn't know. I made him sell out my stock, and that was all he had to do with it.'

'Wasn't he worried?'

'I didn't ask him,' she told me, re-enacting, for my benefit, the cold look she had given the broker. Then she put her hands to her forehead and rocked herself gently to and fro. 'I know I've been a fool, you don't have to tell me. But it looked all right at the time.'

I was out of the army now, all the day upon my hands. On the morning following this talk with Helena I went to Notting Hill Gate to see Mrs Olney's shop. It was empty, the display window yellowed with grime and weather, the first-floor windows uncurtained. Only the 'Dilys' sign was left, swinging beneath a letting-board on which it was stated that excellent shop premises could be viewed upon application to a Knightsbridge firm.

I reported this to Helena who said, surprisingly, 'Poor old Dilly-dally, as she used to call herself, I hope she has better luck next time. It can't be much of a life, failing at one thing after another.'

'She didn't fail with the shop. Thanks to you, she must have got out of it with a nice profit.'

'Can you honestly see Dilys making a profit?' said Helena, with an air superior and kindly. She fell into silence. Later, she made me come with her to stand upon the pavement and stare into the empty shop. The sight of it seemed to give her some profound satisfaction, some easing of the spirit, and I had difficulty in drawing her away.

From that day forward her energy began to flag. She would sit for hours in the flat, long-faced and complaining; it was as if, for the first time in her life, she had noticed the petty mechanics of living. She complained of the rations, the quality of clothes, the queues, the poorness of the street lighting. She railed with the tender bitterness of a Mrs Sholto at the rudeness of public employees, and went to the lengths of writing a four-page letter to the railway company insisting that they should remove the graffiti from compartment walls.

At first I found this amusing and rather pathetic. After a while I became irritated, conscious of a longing to be free of Helena that was like a longing for the sea, or the sight of a foreign land. I had sustained her long enough, taken her through the worst weeks of her despair, accompanied her on her hagridden journeys in search of a pleasure that could no longer bear relation to her own desires. I had sat with her through the long evenings when depression kept her silent and unmoving, had fought with myself against the voices which told me it was high time she pulled herself together, that she was a selfish old woman, that this brooding over a young man was a repulsive thing from which her own shame should be sufficient to save her, and that I was exposing a weakness in myself by allowing her to batten upon my patience. I longed for her to talk to me, that these voices might fall silent. So long as her tongue was still, theirs were clamorous. I wanted her to make just one remark of splendour or high nonsense so that I might again see her in the colour of her great days. I said to myself, Helena in the Grand Place on a shopping-day, striding between the stalls like the lord of a province, her hair rough gold in the sun, her black eyes sharp for a bargain, her tongue ready with a salutation or a cheerful insult: but no image came. I could see only the Helena in the chair by the fireside, the old woman looking in hatred upon a future without importance.

One day a letter came from Field. A cheque for twenty-five pounds was enclosed in it. Helena looked at it, held it to the light as if afraid it might be a forgery, smiled at it with a great pride and tenderness and then gave it, with the letter, to me. Field had been adroit.

My dear Helena,
   This isn't all I owe you, but will you accept it on account?

Don't dare to tear it up or send it back, or you'll spoil things for me. It's the money you lent me for my holiday. The rent, the food, the laundry, etc., etc., all of that I hope to repay you later on. (So many weeks at three pounds p.w. plus so many – endless – extras.) I know what you'll say; you'll write and tell me I don't owe you a thing. But I do, and now that Nao and I are doing well I can put myself in the clear financially.

And then, when all the money business is over and done with, I can tell you just how terrific you are without you thinking (as you might well think) that I'm doing it with a view to future kindnesses. No, I don't believe you would think it. You're too generous in every way. All the same, I really have behaved badly . . .

This last sentence was crossed out in such a fashion that the words could still be read without difficulty.

I could say a lot more, but I can't put it properly. Naomi sends her love and says she does hope to see you again some day. Needless to say, I join her in all that. At present we are all tied up, working like fiends, staggering to bed exhausted every night – but things are bound to clear a bit eventually, and then perhaps you'll come and eat out with us (not eat in, because of rationing) and see our flat.

Do give me news of Claud and Charmian. I'll write and let you know when things ease up and we'll make a date. That is, if you still want to make dates with me.

Nao's always talking about you; you made a huge impression on her, which isn't surprising. 'All is dross that is not Helena.' How many times have you been told that?

Not much news. My M.P. is an ass, but I can't help liking him. Aunt Norrish has been sent to Germany to help pull the place together, which no doubt she'll do all by herself, given three weeks and an aide-de-camp. I saw Dilys in the Tube the other day. She was with her son and a fat man. She didn't see me.

Au revoir – really?

Affectionately,
Ever yours,
John Field.

I noticed how cleverly he had given Helena the impression he wished to see her, while at the same time indicating that no meeting was likely; how he had coupled all his own compliments with Naomi's; how much thought he must have given to the formal choice of signature, with its suggestion of finality.

These things Helena would see for herself, when she had studied the letter in solitude; but at the moment the first designed impression filled her face with light. She told me over and over again how right she had been about Field, and how wrongly I had judged him. Again she referred to his 'vein of iron,' his essential core of honesty. Yet for all this, I had an idea that if ever they should meet again she would be able, unsuspecting, to punish him. To be loved, no matter by whom, is a matter for pride. One may be bored to repugnance by the lover, yet feel a shock of indignation and loss if the love is withdrawn. Helena would love Field till she died, but in a different fashion. Whether she knew it or not, she was really regarding him now in a 'correct' light; as a child to be cherished and pleasured, his faults discounted, his small virtues magnified into qualities of man's worth. And this is not the love that flatters.

'"All is dross that is not Helena,"' she murmured. 'Where does that come from ? You ought to know.'

I told her, and she sat down to search for the passage in the *Oxford Book of Quotations*.

'You know,' she said, sitting up straightly, her eyes glittering, 'I have had a lot of literary compliments in my time. Dicky was always thinking of them. It's not because I was ever a beauty, but I suppose I was big, and knew how to carry myself. That's the thing about French women – they carry themselves well. Daniel once said I walked as though I was brought up to carry a vase on my head. Don't you think I walk well, Claud,' she pestered, 'for an old one?' She waited for a protest at this self-description. 'I've never let myself go. Johnny used to admire that, how I never sagged or went to pieces. I *was* a damned good-looking girl, you know. I can say that now, can't I? Now it's no longer true. I had a wasp-waist. Anyway, I did for a bit until I couldn't stick it any longer. Thank God your father liked women to be natural, not to say fat –

though I wouldn't let myself get fat to please him. We used to play a silly game that he was the Grand Turk and I was the beautiful slave of the harem. I remember once how I plaited my hair with pearls and he said what Johnny said, about all was dross that wasn't me. Isn't Johnny acute, guessing someone else might have said it?'

Embarrassed by the thought of my father as the Grand Turk I told her I must go, but for half an hour longer she kept me by her, while she rehearsed old compliments, remembered old glories, in memory strung pearls through her dyed and fantastic hair.

Alone that night I struggled with the violent impulse to escape from her. I remembered now all manner of things I had forgotten, and they seemed, to a midnight logic, to excuse my enmity towards her now. I remembered how badly, because she loved my father, she had once used me; as a boy I had been an intrusion upon her days of pleasure. I would talk to her while she was enjoying the guilty richness of a daydream and so destroy it for her. I would be resentful if she and my father made an open display of their affection. The passionate woman can be an evil mother; surely my hatred for Helena had never really died, but had only germinated in its long darkness? It seemed to me that her present mind-sickness was her own fault, that she could rid herself of it if she chose, but for the sake of plaguing me would not make the effort.

And still, below all these thoughts, all this ugliness, the affection that was sane and healthy fought to break through. An incredulous voice which I could hear, but to which I could not force myself to pay attention, cried to me incessantly, This is *Helena*. You are destroying *Helena*. I lay down to sleep in the hope that when I awoke in the morning I should hear no other voice but this. Yet my first thought upon waking was that I must go abroad, anywhere, out of England.

It was a thick grey day. The fog caught and looped upon the spires and chimneys and a drizzle greased the pavements. I breakfasted by electric light, telling myself it would not be long before half the population of the British Isles had emigrated in search of a bearable climate. That morning I found in the appointments column of *The Times* notice of a vacant lectureship on the History of Art at a university in Central

India. I wrote an application and went straight out to post it. The action soothed me and, though I felt it a vain one, did something to restore my sense of balance. I had no degrees and no qualifications, save my half-dozen published works; but I thought Crandell might speak for me. I called in upon him at his office, the first time I had seen him since Nina's death.

'Filthy day,' he said, trying to smudge the mist and grime from the window-pane with the palm of his hand, 'makes you feel sick as a dog. What a bloody country! Years and years without a summer to speak of, and then this sort of thing.' He looked grey and irritable, a man dedicated to perpetual guilt. 'What do you want me to do? Give you a boost if these people do happen to fancy you?'

I said I thought it unlikely that they should.

'Oh, I don't know, I don't know. India's in such a mess I don't suppose there's a rush to go and live there.'

'Get some fine weather, anyhow.'

'Months of muggy rain. You can have it. Why do you want to go? I might dig something up for you here.'

This was the kind of offer he would never have made had I angled for it. I replied that I wanted a change of scene.

'Oh, God, so do I, so do I. Only I can't make up my mind to engineer one. Do you feel you can't take any decisions these days?'

We encouraged each other in misery for half an hour, went out for a drink together and parted. Just as he left me he said, with a hideous writhe of conscious bad taste, 'The more I think of Nina the more I respect her judgement. Perhaps she had the right idea.'

The stimulus of talking with, and despising, somebody who had sunk to a level of depression a degree lower than my own, cheered me greatly. I looked down in contempt upon Crandell and upon all the defeated, and when the sun broke suddenly through the fogs in a cluster of orange lights felt it had done the proper thing.

In Piccadilly I met Jane Crossman, her hair scooped up like the waves of the sea and crowned with a ribboned hat that was like a sailing-ship. She walked with a new and splendid stride, Hellenic, bearing the new sunlight upon her beautiful head.

283

'Well, now!' she cried in the penetrating voice peculiar to some women assured of the present and the future, who converse as loudly in a bus as in their own drawing-rooms, 'Just as I was going to ring you! I was going to do it today. News!' Her bright blue eyes widened and flashed. 'Erica's home.'

This was Jane's cousin, the girl who had gone to South Africa.

'It was bizarre, absolutely and completely. One hears of such things, but they don't happen to people one knows.' Jane saw me in detail as if I had swelled into close-up. 'No uniform? Civvy-street?'

'Yes, I'm out at last.'

'Oh, pity, pity, pity,' she murmured rapidly, little-girlishly, staring me up and down, 'you don't look half so nice. . . . About Erica. You know she went out to get married? She got engaged to him just before the war and came back to see her mamma for a fond farewell. Then war broke out, and Erica was trapped. For six long years,' Jane continued in narrative fashion, her finger pointed at my chest, 'for six long years she pined for him and wrote him letters every other day.'

We were obstructing passers-by. I edged her into the passage by the ruins of St James's Church, and she talked on.

'Every other damned day.' Eyebrows and the finger shot up. 'Believe you me, or believe you me not. It was beauty, beauty all the way. She was the good girl who sat at home night after night, till she had that little fling with you. Now *do* you think,' the voice fell to a bass whisper, the azure ribbons nodded upon the miniature galleon fastened by elastic to the tide of furious gold, 'now *do* you think that could have had anything to do with it?'

'Anyway,' she spoke normally again, 'she went out to Jo'burg, took one look at him and turned tail. It may have been more than one look – she stuck him for a week, I believe – but at all events, she used her influence and caught the first plane to the States. Now she's back here again.' She spread her hands proudly as upon a display of rabbits and Union Jacks. 'What do you say? Do you want to see her, or are there those' -- she mimicked the accent to which we refer ironically as 're-fined' – 'with pri-ah *cleems*?'

'Look, Jane,' I said, 'don't match-make.'

284

'Oh, but I'd love to! I want to see you all cosy with bairns tumbling all over the carpet. You do want to see her? Shall I ask you both to dinner?'

I replied that I should like it, but that she was not to be arch either in word or deed. I told her how beautiful she looked, and listened while she depreciated her husband to me in terms of utter fondness. There is a type of woman who cannot bear to praise her husband to another man, even if she loves the husband devotedly and would not leave him for the riches of the world. This incapacity arises partly from a genuine desire not to hurt, and partly because she wants the pleasure of feeling available coupled with the security of being nothing of the kind.

'Well,' she said at last, 'you haven't quite forgotten me? Still some auld lang syne about?' She looked warily around her as if we were in an empty room surrounded by keyholes, then jerked forward and kissed my cheek. 'There! Now I'm compromised.' She looked at her watch. 'I must go; I'm meeting Edgar for lunch. You'll come and see us if I telephone? We're both longing to have you around again. I know Edgar is.' She waved her hand and made off, the blue ribbons flickering away like kingfishers through the crowds.

I considered Erica, found I could hardly remember her face; and yet the thought of her return gave me a feeling of lightness and freedom. There was still a life outside the circle of Helena's need, still a reason for staying in England. Erica in herself did not seem important, but as a symbol of possible joy she gave me a new hope.

I met her again, took her to dinner and a theatre, danced with her and sent her flowers; but we did not fall in love. Jane was disappointed. 'What *do* you want? I think Erica's lovely.' She smiled at me secretly as if to say, I am your tragedy; don't think I don't know that.

'I think she's lovely too,' I replied, 'and we get on very well. We're having a fine time, so don't you interfere.'

Meanwhile, I had left Helena much alone.

Then, one morning, I had a letter asking me to appear before a selection board for the appointment in India. There were three applicants. I was accepted, and was asked to be ready to sail at the beginning of January.

I was utterly surprised and unnerved. I had applied for the post on an impulse of boredom and irritation; I had not expected my application to be successful. The thought of this new and strange life, the journey, the unfamiliar work, the laborious business of acquiring an entirely new circle of acquaintances, made me feel like the mayor of a borough who is suddenly called upon to open the new swimming-bath by jumping into it. It appeared necessary, but impossible.

That night I went to see Helena, who greeted me with the accusation that I had become a stranger whose looks she had almost forgotten.

She was kneeling in her bedroom, tidying out a chest of drawers, and the coloured litter was hopelessly spread about her.

I showed her the letter from the university. At first she seemed to read it with no great show of interest, simply saying that she could not make out the signature, and that she thought people should make an effort to write plainly. Then she read it through again, her lips moving soundlessly over the words. She looked up at me.

'You never told me anything about this.'

'I forgot to. I only applied for the thing more or less as a joke. I didn't expect anything to come of it.'

Methodically she rolled up gloves, stockings, and ribbons, put handkerchiefs and trinkets back into the drawers, then went to sit on the edge of the bed.

'So you'll be going in January? That doesn't give you much time.' She looked away from me towards the table, on which stood the oiled and gleaming portrait of Daniel. 'I wonder how you'll stand the climate?' She rose. 'Would you like some tea? We haven't had our tea for quite a time, have we?' She rose, not looking at me, and went out of the room.

It was then that I saw all things clearly, knew that I should be leaving Helena not only in space but in time. It was upon her now, the desolation of the docks and the water that widens between the ship and the shore. There was a future for me but none for Helena, only the turning back to the road without escape, where it is still and quiet and nothing will ever happen, nothing at all, save that happening which is the end. And she was prepared for it to be like this; she had accepted. She believed it right that the old should relinquish their claim to comfort by the young, relinquish the demand that the young should, at least, solace them with vicarious joys. I was perfectly within my rights to leave her; she had made this acknowledgement by the steadying of her voice, the assumption of interest in the details of defeat, the casual averting of her face.

I was perfectly within my rights; and I knew now, loving Helena in the full return of memory and of gratitude, that I had no rights worth a twopenny damn. If we take from a person in their richness, it is our duty to pay them in their poverty. It may not be nice for us. It may stunt us, clip our wings; but there the matter lies. As Charmian had hinted, I had wanted everything to be cut and dried, had believed there must be a solution to every problem, that the detective must always discover the murderer, that the curtain must always fall upon a tidied stage. In fact, this is not so, and we shall save ourselves a great deal of disappointment by realizing it. There was no way of righting Charmian's marriage, and indeed, she did not wish it righted. There was no means by which I could stay with Helena, and yet maintain my own freedom. I had simply to make the best of things.

She called me to the front room, where she sat above the tea-tray, pouring tea with the majesty of the Archer days, her hair tidied, a string of pink beads, worn in my honour, about her neck. She looked brightly up at me. The misery lay far back in her eyes.

'So you're going to be a professor and a sahib, are you? You'll have to write me hundred-page letters telling me all about it. Mind you do.'

'The trouble with you,' I said, sitting down and taking the cup she handed me, 'is that you go rushing off before anyone has the chance to finish what they're saying. I showed you the offer of the job. You didn't give me time to tell you I wasn't taking it.'

Her breathing stopped. Her piled hair caught from the lamps a light that was the colour of tea-roses. We were together in the mirror as wax figures behind glass, caught for ever in a moment of history. Then she relaxed, took a mouthful of tea and swore because it was too hot, gave me a casual glance and said, 'You'd be a fool not to.'

'Well, there it is. I don't want to leave England just as it's getting interesting.'

'God knows what you find interesting about it,' said Helena. 'Well –' She paused, trembling a little, not wishing me to observe her closely. 'Well, in that case . . .'

She began to plan for the spring.

THE END